WHITESPACE

Season Two

SEAN PLATT
DAVID WRIGHT

STERLING & STONE

WHITESPACE

Previously...

Here's a quick re-cap for those wanting to catch up before starting *Season Two*. If you've not yet read *Season One*, you should probably do that first, rather than have the mystery spoiled.

IN THE NOT TOO DISTANT *future...*
Hamilton Island, Washington

HAMILTON ISLAND IS the perfect bedroom community off the coast of Washington. It's home to Conway Industries, one of the most powerful biotech companies on the planet, led by transhumanist icon, Blake Conway, who longs to help humans achieve better lives through technology and medicine.

In addition to running Conway Industries, the Conway family also runs Conway Medical Center, a state-of-the-art hospital which employs many island residents, and provides free health care to all on the island.

Conway Industries also supplements the local police force, led by Chief Kevin Brady, with a private police force called

Paladin, (much to Brady's chagrin, as he can't compete with the staff or money behind the private force). Paladin has a huge staff and closed circuit-cameras all over the island, and have managed to help quell crime on the island (which had been on the rise prior to Paladin's formation).

All is quiet and peaceful on Hamilton Island, on the surface anyway.

THE SHOOTINGS

High school English teacher Roger Heller walked into his classroom one morning looking disoriented and crazed before opening his briefcase, taking out a gun, and shooting six people, including five of his students, before turning the gun on himself.

The sixth victim of the massacre was an accidental victim, a teacher in the next classroom named Sarah Hughes.

JON CONWAY

In the aftermath of the shooting, black sheep of the Conway family, Jon Conway, a 30-year-old Hollywood star, returned to Hamilton Island for the funeral of Sarah Hughes, his one and only true love whom he hasn't seen in a decade.

At Sarah's funeral, he wound up meeting Sarah's 9-year-old daughter, Emma, and Sarah's twin sister, Cassidy, who still resents Jon for what he did to her sister. Jon, caught up in Hollywood excess, cheated on Sarah, who decided that she didn't want to see him ever again. Heartbroken, and feeling guilty, Jon ceded and granted her wish, and stayed out of her life for the past decade.

After Sarah's funeral, Jon found out that Emma was, in fact, his daughter.

Turns out that his brother, Warren Conway, coerced Sarah into keeping the pregnancy secret in order to spare Cassidy from doing jail time for her repeated drug offenses. The Conways, in turn, put Cassidy up in a posh treatment center to get clean and get her life in order.

Jon, incensed, got into a heated fight with Warren, who told Jon that it wasn't his decision to interfere, but rather their father's, and it was an attempt to spare him a life with a woman Blake felt was beneath Jon.

Jon wanted to confront Blake, but his father has been out of town since before the shooting.

CASSIDY HUGHES

Cassidy Hughes is Sarah's 30-year old twin sister, and a drug addict, mostly pills, who has made a shit ton of bad life choices and has grown jaded and bitter.

To make matters worse, she feels like she could have saved Sarah if she'd only spoken up.

She'd had a dream about Sarah being killed, and wanted to warn her sister, as there had been a few times in their lives where she'd had almost psychic like dreams. And this dream felt like one of those. However, those dreams had also come when she'd been using, and Sarah knew it. And at the time, anyway, Cassidy was clean. She didn't want Sarah thinking she *was* using again.

So Cassidy kept her dream to herself.

And now, she's forced into a position of caring for both her aging drunk mother, Vivian, and Sarah's daughter, Emma. She's not prepared for this, and began to crack, succumbing to her inner addict's lure, by taking painkillers again.

Despite her dislike for the Conways, she wound up falling for Jon. In a way, it seems as if being together helps them get over Sarah's death. When Jon found out that Emma was, in fact, his daughter, Cassidy admitted as much.

While she feels like she'd make a horrible mother, she also feels an obligation to take care of her niece, who she is incredibly close to. Plus, she hates the idea of Emma becoming a Conway, as she loathes Warren and Blake both.

She and Jon danced around the issue of what's coming next regarding Emma's custody, with Jon assuring her that he's not looking to upset things.

One night, at Vivian's, where Cassidy and Emma are staying some nights, Cassidy has what she thinks to be a dream of the TV clicking on and off, and someone speaking through static, saying something to her — "Eleven" over and over.

Then she heard Emma scream.

She tried to run to Emma's room, but suddenly there was bright light and a loud popping sound. And then she blacked out.

When she woke in the morning, Emma was gone.

MILO ANDERSON

Milo Anderson is a 17-year-old junior who was a witness to Roger's massacre of his students and watched the girl he loved, Jessica, and one of his closest friends, Manny, get shot. Jessica died instantly while Manny was rushed to the hospital and wound up in a coma.

Milo's best friend is the killer's son, Alex Heller, whom he blamed for Roger Heller's rampage. Milo soon met someone on a message board claiming to know about the shooting, a kid named "Cody." The kid turned out not to be a kid at all, but a man, who claimed to have information, and who also warned Milo to be careful. After Manny died in the hospital, Cody claimed that "they" got to him, whoever *they* is.

Meanwhile, Milo's bitchy stepmother, Bea, who he also calls OtherMom, started acting weird. He caught her staring, almost trancelike, at the TV, not even realizing he was there. Another time, he saw her loading cold cuts from the fridge into her purse without even realizing what she was doing.

One day as Bea drove Milo home from school, she started getting that vacant look again, as the radio went all static. Suddenly, she slammed her foot down on the gas pedal and crashed into the front of Jordy's supermarket, nearly killing them both.

Milo woke to find his father, Conway Industries employee Stephen Anderson, by his bedside, worried about him, happy that his son is still alive. It's been forever since his father had shown any love to Milo, always busy with work. So Milo is touched.

When Stephen Anderson left Milo's room, he received a phone call from one of his superiors indicating that Stephen knew what they would do to Bea, but did not expect Milo to be involved. When his superior asked if Milo knew anything, Stephen lied, not telling them what Milo remembered of Bea's weird behavior. The person then warned Stephen to make sure Milo stays dumb or else they'll activate a chip they put in him.

Stephen was shocked and incensed that they put a chip in his son. He also knew that they could now use that to keep him and his family in line.

With Bea relegated to a mental facility, Milo was sent home to heal. One night he headed out to a survivor's meeting at the school, where he was approached by Cody, who is in fact, a 30-something-year-old man named Don Bellows who lost his entire family one night. They just vanished without a trace while he slept. In fact, there are more than 15 people missing on the island in recent years, and several more who have killed themselves.

He suspects something sinister is happening on Hamilton Island and wants Milo's help in getting to the bottom of things.

ALEX HELLER

Alex Heller is the 17-year-old son of Roger Heller, left to pick up the pieces after his father shot his classmates. Fortunately, his girlfriend, Katie, is there to help him through the difficult time.

And a tough time it is. Soon after the murders, one of the parents, Bruce Henderson, of the slain Teddy Henderson, showed up on Alex's doorstep with a bat, ready to attack.

A Paladin officer appeared out of the blue and stopped the attack. Bruce was then taken into custody as Alex's mom, Liz came home, scared and angry.

However, that wasn't the end of violent acts on the family. On Alex's return to school, he decided he couldn't take the whispers and dirty looks, and wanted to leave early. He told Katie to meet him near the racquetball courts.

While waiting, he was confronted by Jake Brewster and Ray Wilson, friends of another slain student, Eddie Tarroza. Jake and Ray had bullied Alex when he was younger. This time, however, they were out for blood.

Jake then came at Alex with a knife. Somehow, he managed to wrangle free and slammed Jake's head into one of the walls, where he fell into a lifeless slump.

As Alex stared in horror, certain he'd killed Jake, Ray attacked him from behind and wound up on top of him, punching him repeatedly. And then Katie showed up, picked Ray up and threw him, quite impossibly, at least 10 feet, to Alex's shock.

They took off into the woods, scared and not sure what to do, with Alex now certain he was a murderer just like his father. There was no way he could ever have a normal life now.

They took harbor in a cave during a storm, where Alex and Katie made love for the first time. They then fell asleep together. When Alex woke, he was in darkness, surrounded by whispers, and was unable to move. And Katie was gone.

. . .

LIZ HELLER

Liz is the wife of Roger Heller and mother to Alex and her 6-month-old daughter, Aubrey. She is a former teacher, taking time off for maternity leave. But following the murders, she realized she has no future in Hamilton Island, let alone at the school where her husband killed students.

Liz soon found herself waking up at 1:11 a.m., night after night, hearing weird noises on the baby monitor in Aubrey's room. Eventually, she heard Roger's voice, whispering to the child.

She ran into Aubrey's room to see her baby awake, saying, "da-da." But there was no sign of Roger actually having been there. Still, she couldn't shake the feeling that somehow, Roger is trying to contact her.

Meanwhile, people in town are looking at her with suspicious stares. One night, while in Roger's home office, she stumbled upon two things he'd hidden — a flash drive and a list. It was a list with the names of the students he'd shot. The only difference between the list and the actual dead was that Manny's name wasn't on the list, but Alex's girlfriend, Katie's, was.

Since the authorities had taken away hers and Roger's computers during the investigation following the shootings, she went to the public library to use their computers to see what was on the flash drive. On the way there, she had an overwhelming feeling like she was being watched, and was nervous as hell as what she'd find on the flash drive.

Most of the files on the flash drive were encrypted, all save for one, which showed Roger walking through the caves, presumably on the north end of the island, eager to show the camera something. While Liz watched, she saw that a Paladin officer had come into the library and was headed toward her.

Just as the officer was about to reach her, Liz saw what Roger had wanted to show the camera — several dead people in a pile.

Shocked, but trying to keep a straight face with the officer coming toward her, Liz pulled the flash drive out and palmed it. When the officer reached her, he asked her to come outside.

She went, scared that he'd somehow known what she was holding. But that wasn't why he was there. Instead, he showed her that while she was in the library, someone had spray-painted her car with the word, "Murderer!"

She realizes that it's only a matter of time before someone tries to hurt her or her family.

Following Alex's attack at school, Police Chief Kevin Brady showed up at her house to tell her what happened and that Alex is now wanted for questioning for his role in the attack, which left Jake in a coma. He asked if she had any idea where Alex might have run away to.

BROCK HOUSER

Jon called his Private Investigator friend, Brock Houser, to come and help search for Emma. After a false lead which led to Houser getting arrested for roughing up a pedophile who'd been taking pictures of Emma, along with other children at the church playground, Brock found Emma in the woods during a freak storm, naked and crying for her mother.

Emma was brought to the hospital where it was revealed that other than a loss of memories of what had happened since she vanished, she was unharmed.

Brock soon got a call from another person with a missing child — Liz Heller.

Houser went to Liz's house to meet her. However, while Houser was there, Alex came home, saying he'd fallen asleep with Katie in a cave. When he woke, Katie was gone. However, Alex got a hold of Katie on the phone, and everything seemed OK.

As Houser was about to leave, Liz told him about the flash drive she'd found, but was unable to read, and asked if he could look into it. She was scared, thought something weird was going on, and perhaps her husband knew what it was.

Houser agreed to look into the matter.

Houser headed back to his hotel room. Before he could decrypt the flash drive, a smoke grenade rolled into his room, and he soon found himself, and the flash drive, on the run from Paladin officers.

Houser fled in his car and managed to outrun Paladin for a while. Soon, he was found by the officers with the aid of some kind of robotic bird thing. Houser managed to escape and drive away, but lost control of his vehicle along a steep ravine and crashed.

When he woke, he couldn't remember anything from the past few hours and was missing his right leg. It was then replaced with a state-of-the-art robotic leg, courtesy of Conway Industries.

Little did Houser know that Conway Industries also did something else to him…

LIZ HELLER (CONTINUED…)

Following Alex's return, Chief Brady explained that the boys who Alex fought with are not pressing charges, and they're now doing well. She was surprised and relieved, hoping that things might just return to normal.

Liz, having trouble sleeping, heard Roger's voice again on the baby monitor. She ran into the room, and this time saw him, holding his daughter, but he was flickering like a TV image in static.

He told her he had to come back "to finish."

He then put a gun to his baby's head. She begged him not to kill Aubrey while he screamed that she was conspiring against him. He was talking like a lunatic, and then snapped and shot his daughter.

Liz woke, terrified at the dream, unsure what it meant, but relieved that her baby was still alive.

SARAH HUGHES

During a flashback, we learned that Sarah had briefly gone missing 20 years ago during a game of chase in the woods when she was 10-years-old.

She was found soon after, so the memory is mostly forgotten.

However, Vivian said something to Cassidy about Sarah and the "people in the sky," which left Cassidy wondering if the old lady was confused, and why she couldn't remember Sarah having vanished.

In the season finale, Sarah Hughes woke, following her death during Roger Heller's massacre, and found herself in what she thinks to be a hospital room.

When she got up to look outside the window, she saw that she was no longer on Hamilton Island. She's in space, with Earth floating beneath her.

AND NOW, **WhiteSpace: Season Two...**

Episode 7

Prologue - William (Billy) Conway

Hamilton Island, Washington
  1861

Billy watched from the bluff as his father pointed down at the sea. "Do you see it?"

He stared in wide-eyed awe as the gray whale breached the sea's surface, seeming to almost stand in the water, kissing the endless blue sky before crashing down hard into the ocean, leaving only its memory and a white, foamy splash. Water erupted in a geyser around its giant, disappearing body.

Billy kept staring, leaning out toward the ocean, barely able to hold his joy. "Oh, wow, Father! I wish Jonny had come with us!"

"It's okay." Father put a hand on Billy's shoulder, then squeezed gently into his flesh with an affectionate thumb. "Your brother will see it another time."

"You could take him up here, and I could stay and watch the farm," Billy offered.

"Thank you, son, but Jonny will see the whale soon enough. Maybe when Uncle Martin visits."

"Why won't you let me watch Ma and Sis?"

"You're not old enough. You know that."

"But Jonny's only thirteen. That's just four years older than me. What can he do that I can't?"

"He's a good shot, for one."

"But I thought we didn't need to worry about the Indians." Billy continued to stare at the sea, waiting for the whale to surface again.

"Come on." Father ignored Billy's argument and pulled him away from the show. "We'd best get home before supper."

Billy followed Father as they headed back toward the plains, wanting to argue but thinking better of it. Even knowing he must always respect his elders — especially Father — Billy couldn't manage more than two dozen steps before pushing his luck. "I thought you said the Indians here were the nice kind."

His father looked down. "I never said they were *nice*. I said they tolerate our presence. There's a big difference between nice and tolerant, and it's always better to be safe than sorry."

"But you told Ma the island was safe. I heard you, Father."

"I didn't want to worry her. We've bought a lot of land here, Billy. We're the first white settlers, and our crops are doing well. Things are great. Have no doubt, son, this is the right decision for our family. This island is ours. But between us men, we must always be cautious. Which is why your brother is home while we're out hunting duck."

Billy looked down at the leather sack, swinging lightly in his hands, slightly heavy with the pair of birds that would soon be their supper. He fell silent as they crested a ridge, leaving the bluffs at their back and stepping foot on the plains, which led back to their farmhouse.

He walked with his eyes down, staring at the rolling waves of long grass swaying faster, back and forth, like they always did when the sky grew gray and angry, as it started to do just a few minutes after they had filled their sack with the second duck. The island's weather was always changing, mostly to rain.

They walked in silence, picking up the pace, neither wanting to get caught in the brewing storm.

Something stopped Father.

He quit walking, suddenly enough to send a chill through Billy's body. Father stood statue-still a few feet in front of Billy, eyes to the sky and a rigid arm out lengthwise beside him as if telling the boy not to pass. Then he swallowed, loud enough for Billy to hear, even above the breeze.

Billy's gaze moved from the grass to his father to the clouds, expecting to see them thick and gray, swirling like they did before dropping buckets of water down to the ground. Instead, Billy saw something that took him a second to understand — a spiral of thick, dark smoke, standing out even within the churning clouds above.

It was coming from the direction of their home.

Father grabbed his rifle from its sling and broke into a run, charging toward the farm.

Billy dropped the ducks and, as fast as he could, darted after Father until they saw the smoke's source — their farmhouse, and the land around it, on fire!

Father screamed, but Billy couldn't. He feared the worst as they continued to race home but was unprepared to find the nightmare true — the bodies of his brother and mother, sprawled in the dirt with their heads cut off.

No! Mama, Jonny!

Billy stared, trying to reconcile his vision with reality, not wanting to accept the truth before him.

No, this can't be.

Father sputtered, then groaned, and finally yelled, "Oh, God!" Then he turned to Billy, eyes wide, holding a terror Billy had never seen inside them before. "Run! Head to the caves!"

"No!" Billy cried out, furiously shaking his head.

"Go, Billy! *Now*, before they see us!"

Before who sees us? Billy looked around but saw no Indians.

Father stared at Billy, mouth gaping wide but saying nothing.

"Father?"

Why isn't he answering?

"Father?" Billy repeated, his voice in a girl's pitch.

He fell forward, an arrow in the back of his skull.

Billy screamed.

Another arrow flew by, thunking into the ground beside him. Billy couldn't see who fired the shot and might not have been able to, even without the thick smoke watering his eyes.

His entire life, Father had always said, "Root your heels to the dirt and raise your fists for a fight." But now Father was gone, along with Ma and Jonny, and his final words were a contradiction to his frequent teachings.

Billy made an about-face and followed Father's command. He fled the farmhouse and headed toward the forest and the caves within it, hoping the Indians' arrows wouldn't strike him down before he reached the woods.

He ran as fast as he could, pumping his feet and darting through the grass as the sky opened up and rain poured down, soaking him in an instant. He dared to look back once and confirmed there were two Indians, on horseback, chasing him. Perhaps there were more he could not see, but he didn't dare stop to look.

There was no time.

There was no way on Earth he could outrun Indians, let alone those on horseback, yet he had no choice but to try or die. He wanted to cry out to God for taking his family, for being so damned cruel, for not giving him a chance in hell of getting away — but he had no time for tears. Not if he wanted to live.

One of the Indians screamed something behind him, and it sounded so close, he could imagine an arrow wouldn't be too far behind. He forced his legs to work harder, run faster. His heart pumped just as fast, making him thankful for the many vegetables his mother fed him, saying, "They'll make you strong, like your brother and Daddy."

But they were both dead.

He needed to be stronger than they were. Faster.

The thick, dark tree line was just fifty yards away when he saw and heard an arrow sail by him. He also heard the thunder galloping hooved.

Should he zig and zag as he ran, to keep himself from being an easy target? Doing so would only slow him down. He kept soaring forward, pushing his legs straight toward his target.

Billy slipped. As he hit the cold wet grass, he heard one of the horses charge past him. The ground rumbled beneath him.

Oh, no!

Billy leapt to his feet, surrounded on either side by two Indians on horseback.

One was thin, young like him, holding a bow, aimed at Billy. The other was older, his muscular face concealed beneath paint. His dark eyes bored straight into Billy as if judging his fate.

The Indian said something Billy didn't understand. He wasn't even sure if the man was speaking to him or the younger Indian. His heart pounded against his chest.

Then the older man reached down and retrieved a large blade from a pouch on the horse. He held the blade up, ready to strike …

The sky blazed with lightning. Thunder boomed loud enough to rock the earth.

Both horses whinnied and reared, while their riders tried to hold on.

Run!

Billy seized the moment and sprinted, faster than he'd ever

run in his life, straight for the woods. It was the longest fifty yards Billy had ever run, and he was certain he'd be cut down the moment the Indians managed to get their horses under control.

He didn't dare look back.

An arrow flew past, striking a tree in front of him.

Oh, God.

Billy remembered Jonny saying Indians never missed their targets. But this Indian had missed Billy three times. He was certain his luck would not hold for a fourth miss.

He reached the woods and kept running, eager to find the caves his father had showed him a few months before. Would the Indians also know of the caves? If they'd been on the island longer, surely they would, but he had no other options. Even if they knew of some of the caves, they might not know all of them. And perhaps the tunnels inside them were vast and varied enough to give Billy a chance.

Hopefully, he wouldn't get lost himself.

Father had said run to the caves. So run, Billy did.

Lightning crashed again above, followed by more thunder, even louder than before. Perhaps God *was* helping him escape, even though He saw fit to allow his family to die.

Don't think about them now. Just run.

It had been months since he'd been to the caves with Father. Months since he'd been in the woods at all. A week after they last went exploring, Father had gone hunting alone. He looked different when he returned like he'd seen something that scared him, even though he wouldn't admit it. He did, however, forbid the family from going back into the woods. Father said they were too dangerous, and something "wasn't right."

Since that day, Billy had been plagued by nightmares about what evil monsters might be lurking in the woods, and the caves, in particular. His imagination was vivid, too vivid, at times. Still, Billy ran, knowing he would gladly trade whatever imaginary monsters waited in the caves for the true horror of the Indians giving chase behind him.

He hadn't heard the Indians or seen any arrows since first breaking the tree line. He hoped he'd lost them but didn't dare stop running. Not yet. Not until he found the caves.

Billy's chest grew colder and tighter as he fought to catch his breath. He tore past a thousand trees until he found the open mouth of a dark cave looming a hundred feet before him.

Was it really such a good idea to go inside?

He heard no Indians and knew he couldn't hide in a cave forever. Eventually, he had to find his way out of the forest and onto somewhere. *But where do I go? Who is left on the island to help me?* His family was alone, save for the natives. Father was friendly with a few of the island's Indians — maybe Billy could reach out to them for help getting to the other island or the mainland. But he couldn't be sure whom to trust after the Indian attack on his family.

Why were they killed? What did Father do to them?

Billy couldn't afford to give his questions much thought — not until he survived the night. At the sound of hooves in the distance, far more than two horses, Billy looked into the cave's mouth.

It was his only hope.

He paused at the dark entrance. Something inside him — maybe everything — whispered there was no going back.

As soon as he stepped inside, he felt as if he walked into another world. It was quiet, save for the gentle rain outside, which entered the cave, along with light, through openings above. The silence, had a weight of its own that felt heavy, pushing in on Billy from all sides. The cold air chilled him to his core. He stepped deeper into the cave, trying to get as far from the opening as possible, and looked around. Was this one of the caves he'd been to before? The cave was too dark and the rock walls too similar for him to be certain.

As he crept along the path, he heard a buzzing, loud and fuzzy, twisting his thoughts in a knot. Just beyond the sound, he thought he could hear voices whispering, *calling his name.*

"Hello?" Billy whispered, afraid to speak loud enough for the Indians to hear. He swallowed hard and stepped deeper into the black, then kept stepping forward until the darkness swallowed him whole.

He inched forward with painfully slow steps as if trying to pull a plow across frozen ground. When he and Father explored the caves before, they both carried torches. Now Billy had nothing, not even the benefit of knowing if he'd been in this cave before. His world was only darkness — and all the terror darkness held inside it.

He wanted to turn back. The scant sunlight bleeding into the entrance was gone. And the openings above were farther and fewer between. He couldn't be sure the way forward wouldn't lead him into a space too tight to get out of.

A low whistle lit the wind, coming from the tunnel ahead. And with it his name, again.

Billlllly.

He moved forward, marking the path in his mind, in case he needed to go back. But it was hard to remember each turn, especially in the dark. Getting lost inside the caves meant a death as certain as facing Indians outside. Yet he continued walking deeper into the cave until a cool gust of wind wafted from somewhere ahead, brushing by him so quickly, it nearly knocked him down.

Billy stayed frozen, pressed against the wall until he finally found the courage to creep forward, a few feet at a time, running the tip of his foot in a cautious semicircle in front of him.

His heart lurched when his foot found no ground.

If he had been walking, rather than slowly inching forward, he would have certainly fallen into the dark chasm, either dying instantly or lying at the bottom of a ditch with a broken limb and languishing for days until finally death claimed him. Either way, there his bones would have remained.

He took two steps back, then the ground beneath him crumbled and gave out, pitching him forward into the abyss. As he plummeted, his arms flailed, desperate to grab hold of anything.

Billy's hands found nothing.

The fall felt like a slowly-spinning forever until he finally landed hard on his back in something wet, knocking the breath from his body. Billy screamed, unable to help it, paying no mind to the threat of Indians finding him.

His entire body was wracked by pain as he tried to turn. He could only move his neck, craning but unable to see anything in the darkness. Had he broken anything? It felt like he'd broken everything. He tried getting up, but his body refused to do anything but lay there.

Oh, God, please don't let me be stuck here!

Could he die from pain alone? If not, starvation would certainly kill him.

His head swam as he tried to keep from passing out. Though he couldn't breathe and could barely think, something in Billy's memory reminded he had once heard Doc Dermish say people passed out from pain on account their brain lacking sufficient blood and oxygen. Dizzy, cold, and trying to hold onto his scant vision, Billy managed to sit, though his limbs refused to help him stand. His right leg felt like someone had stabbed him — or shot him with an arrow. He ran his hands down the length of his leg toward his knee, then felt what he could not see — bone jutting from his flesh, like Jack popping out from his box.

Billy screamed again.

I'm going to die.

There it was — the thought he could no longer question, truth as clear as island sunlight on its sunniest day. Billy had awakened that morning alive and happy, excited to hunt with Father, eager to see the whale. Now, he would probably close his eyes and never wake again. At least, he hoped it would be that easy. If he had to die, he wanted it to come in a hurry. Not slow and full of torture like it already was. Billy wanted to die like a man, then join his family in heaven — not lie at the bottom of a cave, with a bone popping out of his knee, sobbing pitifully.

He listened for any sign of the whispering he'd heard before but was met with only silence.

"Hello?" He yelled as loud as he could manage, not even caring if the Indians found him. At least they would put him out of his misery.

He heard the whispering again. First, his name, and then other things he couldn't understand. The voices sounded close, yet far away.

"Hello?" he called again, trying his best not to cry.

And then something odd happened. The cold he'd felt in his bones began to recede. He felt a sudden, comforting warmth like a blanket pulled to his chin in winter. It started in his head right beside all the tangled thoughts, then began seeping into every part of his body.

The whispering seemed to grow louder.

Warmth intensified on his leg, almost as hot as fire. He reached down, expecting to find the bone sticking through again, but instead, his fingers found flesh, smooth and unbroken.

What?

Impossible!

He felt suddenly whole. The pain had been erased from his body.

How?

The whispering grew louder as if it were coming from nearby. Still, he saw only darkness.

"Hello?" Billy called out again, certain someone was down there with him.

And then came the light — softly, at first, a dot of soft blue glowing above, at the top of his fall. The shelf was high, higher even than Billy imagined.

He should have broken his neck and not just his leg.

The tiny dot of blue bloomed larger on its descent, swelling in size until it was about as big as a basket hovering in front of his face, still soft blue and perfectly sphere. Until it wasn't.

Billy leapt to his feet, feeling suddenly stronger than Father, gasping as the glowing orb took human form before him.

"Billlllly," it said.

Chapter 1 - Warren Conway

Hamilton Island, Washington
The Conway Industries Boardroom
Monday
One month after the shooting

WARREN STARED at the head of the table, where Father *should* have been sitting. It was already ten past nine, and his dad had yet to show. Hadn't even extended Warren the courtesy of calling in to say he was running late. Warren told himself nothing was wrong, Father was simply being his arrogant self, putting his needs first and thinking nothing else mattered. But that was hard to buy — Blake Conway was *never* late for an inner circle meeting. The four others in the room, not board members, but still the most trusted quartet in the Conways' employ, avoided eye contact with Warren, likely embarrassed for him.

If nothing was wrong, then Blake's absence, or tardiness as it were, was no doubt intentional.

This is what happens when you disappoint Father.

He's trying to undermine me. To make me feel like a child, impotent, in front of the others.

And it was working.

Warren could feel Carl Kaiser, the recently promoted Paladin chief, looking his ways, so he turned to look him in the eyes — both the human pupil and the second robotic one, designed and manufactured by Conway Industries and years ahead of anything else available. As intimidating as Kaiser's eyes were — both of them — Warren held his stare until the chief looked elsewhere.

The boardroom, situated in a spacious room on the posh tenth floor of Conway Industries, was where Warren normally felt most energized, motivated, and comfortable in his skin. Even more than his house, it was where Warren felt truly at home, thriving in his environment as the company's CEO. Yet, the room now held none of its typical solace, smudged in black by a creeping uncertainty. A growing gloom thickened the air, and Warren was certain he wasn't alone in his concern, wondering if and when Blake would arrive. This was the first meeting since the school shooting a month before. The first time he, or any of them, would be hearing Blake's response. Everyone had to be wondering the same thing.

Would Blake shutter Project Raven?

Or worse, would the government decide the project was too risky to proceed and cripple Warren's biggest contribution to Conway Industries? Project Raven was *his* project. Warren had to beg Father to let him branch off from their nanotechnology in the health services sector and apply their findings toward military use. He'd said, "Just give me time to prove its value."

But following the shooting — at the hands of one of Project Raven's test subjects, no less — Warren knew his father's limited patience was likely to vanish. Conway Industries was in the business of saving people and advancing humanity, not taking lives. This type of disaster was just the sort of thing that could invite unwanted speculation into the company's covert testing. It was just the sort of thing that could endanger Blake's pet project, the covert Phoenix.

Warren looked again at the door, Father's private entrance. On the other side of it was the hallway leading to his office, a place even Warren wasn't permitted to enter. Father's office was his "thinking place," not to be "soiled" by others' thoughts.

Everyone else in the room stole glances at Father's door, as well. They likely wondered the same thing as Warren — *is Blake even in there?*

Suddenly, the door clicked then hissed open. The imposing man stepped into the boardroom, dressed in his signature black suit and shirt, with a thin red tie. His eyes narrowed on Warren — not the eyes of a pleased man.

Shit.

"Good morning," Blake said, his greeting making the rounds to the rest of the inner-circle.

"Good morning," they all replied, though their voices indicated there was little was *good* about this particular morning.

Blake usually carried a tablet that stored necessary documents, files, and clips — anything he might need for a meeting — and would circle the room once before sitting. This morning, he sat immediately, sinking into his tall seat at the head of the table. And he carried nothing. His hands were empty and folded in front of him as he leaned on the table.

Every eye turned to him as they first shifted in their seats, then sat at full attention.

"So," Blake said, "who the hell wants to tell me why Roger Heller decided to open fire on a classroom of innocent kids from Phoenix Project? Is this what you're doing with Project Raven, Mr. Conway? Using it to target rival projects?"

The inner-circle turned to Warren, who had been preparing his answer for the past three days.

"Well, sir, we don't really know why Mr. Heller opened

fire. But we can say it had nothing to do with our project. He had not been moved to Phase Six. I assume you saw the flash drive we recovered from Detective Houser?"

"Yes."

"And you saw Mr. Heller was assembling some sort of conspiracy theory package?"

"Yes. And I would like to know how *that* happened, too. How much did he know? How did he know it? And also, who was he working with?"

"We're still looking into it," Warren said.

"That is not the answer I was hoping to hear, Mr. Conway. You've had a month to work this. I expect better."

"I'm sorry." Warren tried to keep his voice strong in the face of his father's rage. Father only called him Mr. Conway when curbing his temper. "But right now, that's the only answer we have."

Blake turned to Kaiser. "Is it possible we have a leak?"

"No, sir. Our Watchers keep close tabs on everyone in the program, and Watchers are themselves monitored by our computers. Everyone involved has their every movement — at home, work, and away — tracked and catalogued. We've reviewed our archives to the minute and would know if there had been a breach. My thought is that somehow Heller began piecing things together on his own. As you can see from many of these documents, he was wildly off base on several things. Frankly, sir, his files look like the ravings of a lunatic. I can't even be sure he knew anything about the Project Phoenix, specifically, other than who was in it."

"So," Blake said, "he just snapped?"

Warren interjected, "Like I said, it's too early to tell what happened, but this has nothing to do with Raven."

"The whole idea of Project Raven is to control people, correct?" Blake said. "What am I to make of the program when one of its subjects shoots up a classroom? It would seem your project is a bit of a failure if you can't even keep people from going on a massacre."

"No, sir. Raven is not a failure. This was an anomaly. You don't shut down a project this large based on a single mishap. That would be … disastrous."

Blake sighed. "I don't have to tell you the folks at DARPA aren't happy. They're getting cold feet, threatening to pull the plug if we can't deliver what we promised to the DOD. I need to know we're still on timeline. Failure to deliver what we committed to calls *all* of our work into question, Mr. Conway. I will *not* allow your program to jeopardize Project Phoenix."

"No, sir, it won't," Warren said. Father had been wanting to close the project for a while and was actively seeking a reason. This heat was as good an excuse as any the senior Conway could have asked for. "We've come too far. Just give us another month to activate the next phase."

Blake closed his eyes, leaned back, and appeared to summon some inner restraint to keep himself from ripping into Warren and shredding him to nothing in front of the circle. "One month, but you clean your mess. Otherwise, your little experiment is shuttered."

The way he said "experiment" made it seem like some childish project of no importance. No, it wasn't lifesaving or even life-altering, but it stood to make Conway Industries trillions of dollars and could singlehandedly change the face of war. Perhaps even prevent the world from slipping closer to nuclear annihilation.

"What do you mean, clean up my mess?" Warren asked, purposely putting his father on the spot to clarify his directive.

"Mrs. Heller saw the flash drive, correct? As did Mr. Houser?"

"We don't know that either of them saw the contents. And even if they did, what are they going to do? We have it. And we have Houser under control. Do you want us to get Mrs. Heller and her son under control as well?"

"First, if Roger Heller is an example of Raven's effectiveness, I'd be careful suggesting you have *anyone* in control. Second, Mrs. Heller is leaving the island soon. We have no time for the slow approach."

Warren swallowed the knot in his throat. "So, what do you want done with the Heller family?"

Blake was clearly exasperated by the question. "I'm sure you and Kaiser will think of something."

"Yes, sir." Warren felt like a neutered dog.

He wasn't sure and didn't dare look up, but he swore he felt Kaiser smiling.

Chapter 2 - Jon Conway

"Come in, come in!" Jon extended his hand in a broad sweep to show off the house as Cassidy and Emma stepped inside.

Cassidy stepped over the threshold. "Thank you for watching her tonight."

"Thanks for letting me." He smiled.

This was the first night he would be watching his daughter solo. While the girls had both stayed in his hotel rooms a few times, Emma had never stayed with Jon alone while Cassidy was at work.

"Wow, it's beautiful!" Emma squealed, sprinting past Jon toward the stairs, which she immediately ran up and down three times in each direction.

"Nice digs." Cassidy raised her eyebrows then met Jon's lips with a kiss. "How did you manage to rent such a nice place so quickly?"

"I didn't rent it. I bought it."

"What? You *bought* a house here? I thought you were going to stay at one of your family's many palaces."

"I really don't care to talk to my family right now, let alone ask them for favors," Jon said.

"Ah, okay. Say no more."

He turned to the stairs and a delighted Emma. "Wanna see your room?"

"My room? I have a room?"

"Well, for when you stay over," Jon said, hoping Cassidy didn't think he was trying to take the girl from her and Vivian. They had all agreed to take things slowly and do what was in Emma's best interest. Even Vivian was playing ball. Emma, along with Sarah's house, were now in Cassidy's custody, according to her sister's will. But Cassidy was so far unable to move into Sarah's house, thinking it too confusing for Emma.

Emma stayed at Vivian's most nights since. Cassidy stayed on the nights she thought Grams might be hitting the sauce a bit too hard. Sometimes they stayed in Cassidy's tiny apartment. Other times, they stayed with Jon in his hotel. For now, Emma was a girl with no home and many.

At least now Jon could provide some permanence in a room that was only hers.

He said, "First door on the right at the top of the stairs. The door's open!"

Emma ran the rest of the way upstairs to check out her room. When she returned, jumping up and down like a rabbit and still squealing like Christmas morning, Jon could feel Cassidy's evil eye all over him.

Shit, I knew I went too far. She's gonna think I'm trying to woo Emma away with shiny, fancy stuff.

"Aunt Cass, I have my own TV! Wanna see it?"

"Wow!" Cassidy glared at Jon before returning Emma's smile with one of her own, matching in size but nowhere near as sincere, then following her niece up the stairs.

Jon followed closely behind. "It's not that big a deal."

But it *was* a big deal, and Jon could see it in Emma's delighted eyes and the already rosier tint to her skin. The TV was ridiculous, with the international satellite and a concierge installed, recessed into the wall like the rest of the home's sets. But beyond the TV, Jon hadn't spent much, at least not on actual things. He did, however, hand a blank check to the interior decorator who helped him put it all together.

The bedroom was designed for Emma, with plenty of space where she could be comfortably alone or spend time with family and friends, whatever she wanted. The room was overflowing with blankets, rugs, curtains, and pillows — in every shade of purple and pink. The walls were painted a soft blush — an almost rosy sand — highlighting the pink accents that peppered the room. The walls were bare, except for the single *Adventure Time* poster with Fiona and Cake, her two favorite characters. He imagined Sarah had introduced her to the show as she had loved it when they were teenagers.

Beyond all the comfort and simple decoration, Jon had future-proofed the space by giving Emma plenty of storage to grow into her room over time. Large, funky containers were stuffed into the corners, and neat shelves lined two of the walls. While he didn't fill Emma's closets with new clothes like he wanted to, there was plenty of closet space to thicken with time, and a single pair of pajamas spread on the oversized canopy bed.

If Emma were to have friends over, they would never be forced to sit on the floor, with a half dozen beanbag chairs in various sizes sprinkling the ivory carpet, along with a comfortable desk chair — tucked neatly beneath Emma's new long white desk — and the reading chair beneath the giant oval picture window, staring out at the white waves lapping the island. As in every place Jon stayed, the lighting was as close to perfect as he could get. To him, lighting was the most important and often overlooked. He hated cheap lighting and figured Cassidy couldn't possibly know how much that cost, so it was a safe place to overspend. The room felt immediately warm and cozy and would hopefully keep Emma's nightmares away.

Cassidy stewed beside him, growing angrier by the moment, even though every molecule inside Jon swore that she shouldn't. He set a gentle hand at the small of her back, and to his relief, she didn't shrug him off.

Jon was about to remind Cassidy that the girl was his daughter, softly and without using those words, and explain that Emma would never see her mother again, and likely cry herself to sleep many nights. She deserved another place to find solace. But he said nothing as he heard Houser's door open at the other end of the hall.

Houser stepped into the room, "Hey, we having a party?"

Emma spun toward the door, yelled, "Houser!" then ran across the soft carpet toward him, her arms parted as if Houser was her long-lost best friend.

"Hey, kid." He limped toward her. "Hey, Cass, how's it going?"

She hugged him, "It's going okay. I didn't know you were staying here, too."

"Yeah, Hollywood can't stand not having me around."

Emma looked up and laughed. "I like when you call him that."

Jon rolled his eyes.

"I hope he's not making you work too hard." Cassidy looked down at Houser's artificial right leg, which began just below the knee stump. The same spot Emma was staring at, looking as though she was trying to draw a picture with her mind.

The leg was a prototype prosthetic from Conway Industries, a dark, alloy blade attached to a fully functional robotic foot, all controlled by a tiny chip in Houser's head. He looked half-cyborg and all badass.

"How's the leg working out?" Cassidy asked.

"I'm finally getting used to it. I should be able to go back to work, and get out of Jon's hair, in another couple of weeks." He lifted his right leg and showed off the robotic foot, spreading the mechanical "toes" of which there were four, along with one in the back.

"Weird." Emma giggled. Immediately, she turned red-faced and met Houser's eyes. "Oh, I'm sorry. I didn't mean to …"

"It's okay." Houser gave her a big smile. "It *is* pretty weird."

Cassidy kneeled beside Emma. "I need to run a few errands before work. Is it cool if I leave now?"

"Yeah, I'm good," she said, her eyes still on Houser's false leg.

"Well, I can't compete with Mr. Roboto here." Cassidy winked at Houser then hugged Emma goodbye.

"I'll walk you out," Jon said.

AS THEY STEPPED OUTSIDE, Jon reached for Cassidy's hand. "Listen, I didn't mean to go overboard. I just, well, I didn't want to get too little."

"She doesn't need all that stuff, Jon. It's like a goddamned Neverland Ranch in there. How are we supposed to compete with that? She'll never want to come home."

"I'm sorry. But it's not a competition, and I don't like that word. I swear, Cass, I only want to give her a space to call her own. It's not like I filled it with games and toys, I just gave her a place to grow. I'm not trying to steal her away. You know that, don't you?"

Cassidy looked down, so he lowered his head to enter her line of vision. "You know that, right?"

"Yeah, I know," she said, almost reluctantly. "But seriously, even if there aren't games and toys, that's too much shit. Six fucking beanbag chairs and a giant 3-D spot in the wall? Really, Jon? Emma doesn't need all that. No child does. All kids need is your love, and to know that you're there for them."

Jon knew Cass was speaking from personal experience.

He opened his arms and pulled her into a hug. "If there's something you think I should send back, then I'll agree. Just give me a list, and I'll do it tomorrow when she goes back home. I can even tell her there's something wrong with the optics so we can't get TV reception in her room. She can watch with me in the front."

"Oh, sure, make *me* look like the bad guy."

"I'll say it's me that I overspent on my credit card or something."

"Yeah, right." Cassidy laughed, but just barely.

"Listen." He pulled back to meet her gaze again and took both her hands. "You know you can stay here, too?"

"You mean stay the night?"

"No, I mean, move in."

Cassidy looked away. "Oh, I don't know about that."

"Why not?" He felt like a rejected freshman.

"I don't know. It's just so much, and too fast. I mean, we don't even know what *this* is between us, do we? Besides, I keep thinking maybe we should move into Sarah's house. She might be more comfortable there, even if I'm not."

"Well, you have a place here — both of you. As for us, I'm trying not to think about definitions for what any of this is. I'm taking things a day at a time and following my heart, maybe for the first time ever. All I know is when I'm with you, and when I'm with Emma, things feel right. That's enough for me." Jon squeezed her hands tighter. "You all feel more like family to me than Blake or Warren, that's for sure."

"Paparazzi would feel more like family than them," Cassidy said, smiling to sweeten her words.

"I'm not saying it has to be forever."

Cassidy looked at Jon, an odd expression on her face.

Was that the worst thing he could've said? He wasn't sure if she'd interpreted forever to mean them or the living situation. And if he tried to explain the living situation, it might seem like he'd really meant *them*.

She sighed, then pulled her hands from his and started to pace. "I don't think it's right for us to set specific expectations for Emma if we don't know what the future holds. If you invite her to stay with you, then decide on a whim you're bored and want to go running back to Hollywood, it's going to crush her."

Did she mean Emma, or herself? Or maybe he was being arrogant, thinking everything was about him. "I'm not *running* anywhere, especially to Hollywood. Emma is my daughter. That makes her my number one priority. Okay, Cassidy?"

"Okay." She still wouldn't meet his gaze, turning back to look at her car instead. "I need to get going. I'll be closing tonight, and I don't want to wake you all, so I'll see you in the morning."

"Okay," Jon said, then kissed her on the mouth.

Half the time when they kissed, he could feel all of Cassidy. The other half of the time, she seemed barely there. As they parted, Jon felt sad that it was the one and not the other.

EMMA WAS all smiles as she sat beside Houser at the kitchen table, across from Jon's empty seat. He stood at the kitchen bar, pulling white cartons from a large brown bag.

"That smells SO good," Emma said, clapping. "What are we having?"

"Cantonese," Jon said.

"Is that like Chinese? It smells like Chinese. And it looks like it." She pointed to the cartons Jon lined along the bar.

"Yes." He scooped a small pile of honey garlic spareribs onto a plate for her. "Cantonese is a lot like Chinese. Actually, Cantonese *is* Chinese, just more specific."

"What's the difference?" Emma scrunched her nose with

interest as Houser petted her head. He looked near drooling — easy to do with the smells pluming out from the cartons.

"Chinese food, like the kind you get at Panda Express or places like that ..." Jon paused and looked over at Emma. "Have you ever eaten at Panda Express?"

"Twice." She nodded. "In Seattle."

"Well, that's not *real* Chinese. A lot of those dishes you couldn't even really get in China unless you went to a restaurant intended for tourists. Cantonese is the real deal, a way to order Chinese food without getting Chinese-American. It's mild, with fresher ingredients. Places like Panda use cornstarch to make their sauces, Cantonese uses natural flavors, so the finished dish is still delicious, but without being too greasy. Try it, you'll love it."

Jon carried Emma's plate — piled high with a buffet's worth of choices — from the bar to the table and set it in front of her.

Emma eyed her mountain of food, then started with the salt and pepper prawns, stabbing one of the deep-fried shells, then tearing into the orange-tinted shrimp. She held it in her mouth and smiled.

"So?" Jon raised his eyebrows.

She chewed, swallowed, then said, "It's crunchy and a little spicy. Definitely better than Panda."

"I should hope so." Jon smiled, then went to serve Houser.

"Would you hurry, Hollywood? I'm starving. And no shrimp for me, thanks." He turned to Emma. "You know shrimps are just roaches of the sea, don't you?"

Emma laughed. "Aunt Cassidy says that."

"I knew I liked her." Then he started back in on Jon. "So, are you ever planning to cook a meal in this big fancy kitchen, or is everything you eat gonna come from a bag?"

"Ask me after I've tried every place on the island."

"You mean every place that delivers."

Jon smiled and tried not to feel like an asshole. "They all

deliver, if you pay enough." He handed Houser a plate, filled with everything but shrimp, then went back to grab his own, which he had loaded alongside Houser's. "I don't hear you complaining when Emma's not around."

"I'm not complaining now. Just asking."

Jon sat across from Houser and Emma. "I get the arguments about not eating out. I just don't buy them. It's expensive, you don't know what's in your food, it's easy to overeat, bad for the environment, blah, blah, blah. Well, expensive doesn't matter — not to sound like a jerk, but it's true. I'm very clear about what I ask for in my food, and I'm content that my family gives hundreds of millions of dollars to the environment. That gives me license to toss a few containers. Besides, I don't want to start cooking."

"Why not?" Houser and Emma said together.

"Because I know I'll love it and am sure I'll get obsessive. When I really like something, it's all I want to do. I'll want to take lessons and do nothing but cook. Right now, I'd rather be obsessive about spending time with you." He winked at Emma.

She blushed, then changed the subject. "*I'm* a really good cook."

"Oh?" Jon raised his eyebrows. "What's your best dish?"

"Tortilla Pizza," she said without wasting a second. "Definitely."

Jon and Houser both laughed. Then Jon asked, "How do you make that?"

"It's easy! All you do is get a pack of tortillas and make a pizza on top of it. I've made them with sausage and pepperoni, and all of the stuff you normally put on a pizza. Mom used to like weird stuff on hers."

Jon felt a sharp pang, though Emma seemed unaffected. "Like what?"

"Corn." She wrinkled her nose.

"Gross," Jon said, though he didn't really think it seemed

too gross at all, especially considering the pizza was made with tortilla.

Emma recited recipes for another four dishes and told a few stories about Sarah that hurt Jon more than he wanted. After that, they finished the meal, and Jon announced the other best thing about ordering out.

"No dishes!" He laughed and scooped the remains of their meal into a garbage bag, including the paper plates. With their trash disposed of, Jon asked Emma if she wanted to watch TV, whatever she wanted.

"In my room?" she squealed.

He shook his head. "Nope, sorry. The optic's not working yet. But you can watch whatever you want in the living room. The TV's name is Angelica. Just say, 'Hi, Angelica,' then let her know what you want to watch. She'll find it for you."

"Thanks, Jon!" Emma hugged him hard, then ran into the living room. He felt another pang, this one from wondering when — if ever — she would start calling him Dad. He would never make her call him *Father* like his dad had made him until he was old enough to decide he didn't want to.

"Want a drink?" Jon asked Houser.

"Of course."

They sat at his kitchen bar, Houser kicking back a Heineken while Jon poured himself a glass of merlot.

"You remember anything else about the accident?" Jon asked.

"No, shit's still blank. Why?"

"I was talking with Liz Heller, and she said she gave you a flash drive. She wouldn't tell me what was on it, but it seemed like something that *really* bothered her." Jon paused for a second, choosing his words to not seem too melodramatic. "She seemed scared."

"I vaguely remember something, but only vaguely, like I know it was something important, but beyond that, I've got nothing. I've tried digging in my mind, but all I can say is it's a missing memory."

"Well, I gave her some cash to help her get out of town. She's going to California, a small place in Balboa. Great schools. Near your neck of the woods. Would you mind looking into the matter more, if she asks? I'd like to give her the offer, you know, so she has peace of mind. I'll pay you, of course."

"No problem," Houser said.

Emma ran into the room before Jon could say thanks, spinning around and speaking in a sickly sweet English accent, saying the same thing, over and over. "I am Angelica, what would you like to watch?"

Houser laughed. Jon couldn't stop smiling.

"Did you know I can watch *anything* I want?" Emma asked as if the TV wasn't Jon's. "Angelica will find it in seconds. I've tried like five things!"

"Already?" Jon asked.

"Yup! Now I'm going to go try more!" Emma raced away from the bar.

Jon stared at her bouncing hair as she ran back into the living room, loving her even more than he had five minutes before, hoping as he had for most of the minutes over the last few weeks that Cass would relax enough to let herself fall into the sweetness of their new family.

Chapter 3 - Alex Heller

Alex looked around his father's empty office, where the once abundant contents no longer spilled from every drawer and shelf. Instead, everything was reduced to a dozen cardboard boxes. He hadn't imagined packing his dad's stuff would be so hard. But for some reason, seeing the room empty only added weight to the realization — his father was gone.

Katie surprised him, her hands circling his waist and soft voice in his ear. "How's it going?"

"I'm all done. You?"

"Yeah, I just helped your mom finish the kitchen. She's putting Aubrey down for a nap."

"Thanks for helping us." Alex turned to meet her gaze. It was so hard to believe today was the last time he'd be looking into her eyes — in person, anyway — for at least a few months.

As if she were reading his thoughts, Katie said, "California isn't that far, Alex. I'll visit you on weekends, I promise. And then, before you know it, summer will be here and maybe mom will let me stay longer. After senior year, I can go to a university near you."

Alex nodded, even though everything in his heart was

saying things would never be the same between them. From everything he had ever read or heard, long-distance relationships always started strong, fueled by desire, love, and the constant of one wanting to be with the other. Yet, inevitably, flames flickered as the real world got in the way. The gulf between them would stretch, then fill with a layer of predestined ice, bred by distance and born to extinguish their fire.

"Let's not make promises," Alex said, finally broaching the subject and immediately regretting it.

"What do you mean?" Katie took a step back.

"I mean we shouldn't kid ourselves. Everything's changing. Let's not make plans so far in advance, especially when we don't even know what might happen tomorrow. A year from now may as well be ten."

"Is this about your dad?"

"I don't know." He shrugged as he tried to swallow the tears that had first started to threaten while he packed his father's life into cardboard.

Katie hugged him.

Alex collapsed into her embrace, his chin quivering as he fought the tears. He wanted to say so much, yet there was something in their bodies' tangle that required no words. Everything felt right with Katie — or as close to right as things could feel when everything else was obviously wrong.

He spoke, still holding her in a hug. It was easier to maintain his composure if she weren't looking at him. "It's just so hard to believe how quickly everything's changing. It feels like I'm in a nightmare and I *should* be waking up but just can't."

She squeezed him tighter. "It's going to be okay."

Another necessary lie.

The doorbell rang and startled them both. He thought of his mom putting Aubrey down for the nap, then ran to the door before their visitor rang again and derailed his sister's sleep for good. Alex swung the door open to find Milo standing on his porch, backpack slung over his left shoulder.

"Hey," Milo said. He wore a dark hoodie and blue jeans, and the dark circles under his red eyes betrayed his exhaustion. "I couldn't let you leave without saying goodbye."

"Come in." Alex widened the door's part. He'd been hoping Milo would visit and had even left a message on his voicemail. Though they'd made peace at his father's funeral, they had only spoken a few times since, and those conversations were on the phone, and decidedly awkward — like two former lovers trying to reconcile and pretend one of them hadn't betrayed the other.

Milo stepped inside and dropped his bag to the floor. "So," he said, clearly trying to rush through the discomfort, "have you checked out 'Bloody Mess' yet?"

"Bloody Mess" was a new serial on IC, an online network that seemed to be killing it with one awesome new show after the other. It was about a frat guy who woke with amnesia and found all of his brothers dead. Each week he had to put the pieces back together. Spoiler alert — Alex could tell the show was shit from the ten minutes he managed to sit through. But he didn't want to spoil Milo's enjoyment.

"No, I haven't seen it. It's been impossible for me to focus lately. I try, but my mind starts trailing as soon as I start watching anything. I haven't even really been reading." He shrugged. "Been playing a few games and moping. But other than that, not much else. Is it any good?"

Milo laughed. "Um, no. It's shit for the most part, maybe IC's first bad show. You can totally tell they're making crap up as they go. Everything is either sorta stupid or completely stupid." Milo smiled, bigger and more genuine than anything Alex had seen on his face since before Alex's father brought a loaded gun to school and showed everyone he knew how to use it.

"Our shit is *much* better." Milo went over to his backpack, unzipped it, pulled out a small card, then handed it to Alex.

"What's this?" Alex looked down at the card. It read,

Raconteur, MiloAlex1234.

"It's the app you need, and the password to use it."

"For what?" Alex kept staring at the card, trying to figure out what Milo was trying to say.

"To finish *The Atrium Divided!*"

Alex finally smiled back. "You still want to finish that?"

"Of course!" Milo held his grin. "I've already fleshed out a bunch of the scenes. Now it just needs some Alex magic. And Raconteur is this AWESOME writing software I found, collaborative shit, so we can write together. Just download it, enter that password, then we can work on it at the same time, or one after the other. It doesn't matter. You'll see once you log on."

That did sound awesome, and Alex wanted to know more about it, but before he could ask Milo anything else, his mom descended the stairs, wiping her brow as if exhausted. "She's finally down. Oh, hi, Milo!"

"Hi, Mrs. Heller." He sheepishly looked at his feet. "Just came to say goodbye to everyone."

"How about I make us all some lunch?"

"Oh, I dunno, I've gotta get back home soon and do —"

"Don't be ridiculous." Katie grabbed Milo by the hand and gave him a giant smile. Milo flinched as Katie touched him, but she didn't call attention to it.

Alex thought it weird, trading concerned looks with his mom.

His mom said, "Sit down, Milo. You're gonna eat with us. We'll have one last lunch together, just like old times."

"Just like old times," Alex repeated, his smile bittersweet, knowing things could never be like old times again. Not without his dad, anyway. But he *was* leaving the island, so they could at least *try* to put the past month behind them and play pretend one final time.

~

AFTER LUNCH, Alex and Katie sat on the porch beside Milo, reminiscing about the old days while steering clear of conversational land mines such as any mention of Jessica, Manny, or Alex's dad — the man responsible for both their deaths.

"Any word on Bea?" Alex asked.

"No, OtherMom's still in the loony bin." Milo scratched at his right arm. "Dad thinks she'll be there a while."

"Wow," Katie said. "I still can't believe she did that!"

Milo leaned forward. "There's something I've gotta tell you, Alex. Something I'm not sure you'll necessarily want to hear, but I can't *not* tell you."

"What is it?" Alex said, nervously.

"When I went to that Survivor's Meeting after your dad's funeral, one of the teachers, Mrs. Hawthorne, said she saw your dad in a trance, watching the snow on a TV set. She'd called to him a bunch of times before he finally came to, with no idea she'd been trying to get his attention. Weird thing is, that's the same thing that happened with Bea before she decided to drive through the front of Jordy's."

"What are you saying?"

Milo was scratching his right arm more intensely, and Alex wondered what type of rash he had under his long sleeves. "Well, it's not just your dad and Bea. Other people have been noticing weird shit like this with *their* families and friends — especially the people who go missing."

"So, what do you think is happening?" Alex asked, cautiously, like he was speaking to a crazy person. For all he knew, he might be.

"I know how it sounds," Milo said. "But remember that guy Cody I told you I was gonna meet? Well, I met him. And we've been talking on and off for the past few weeks. He's told me about some really weird shit happening on the island."

"Like what?" Katie asked. If she thought Milo was crazy, she was hiding it better than Alex.

Milo looked around. His eyes seized the street lamp as if

just noticing it for the first time. He shook his head, ever so slightly. "Not here."

"Huh?"

"It's not safe to talk here," he whispered, leaning closer and scratching his arm harder. "They've got cameras and microphones all over the island."

"All right, then," Alex said, weirded out. He looked down at Milo's arm, "You okay?"

"Huh?" Milo asked, his eyes still narrowed on the lamp.

"Your arm. You're scratching it like jock itch, dude."

Milo's gaze met Alex's. "You don't believe me, do you?"

"I don't know what to believe," Alex said. "I'm pretty sure there's something going on, sure, and I'd love to think that my dad really didn't mean to shoot up his classroom."

"No," Milo whispered, "I can guarantee you he didn't."

Alex felt a chill slither up and down his spine, like the sort he sometimes got when telling scary ghost and UFO stories with Milo in the middle of the night as they lay in his backyard, staring up at the sky.

Milo scratched harder, and finally, Alex grabbed his hand and lifted the sleeve.

"Oh, fuck!" Alex dropped Milo's hand immediately and stared at the dozens of red and pink open sores on his arm, severely irritated by his furious scratching. "What the hell?"

"It's these things," Milo whispered. "There are these things inside us. I can feel them moving around."

Alex lowered his voice, now unable to hide that he thought Milo had just gone full-on "Looney Tunes" and was about to follow Other Mom Bea right into the bin. "What the hell are you talking about?"

"I'll tell you later," Milo said. "I've gotta go home."

"Wait," Katie called out as Milo hopped off the porch stoop, jumped on his bicycle, and sped off down the street.

Alex stared at Katie. "What the hell is wrong with him?"

Chapter 4 - Cassidy Hughes

The jukebox was rocking, drinks were flowing, people were laughing, and ten different sports programs were on the TVs throughout the bar. The place crackled with energy, and it felt great to be back at The Shipwreck, doing her thing behind the bar.

Cassidy had been serving for two weeks, though the first week was anything but normal, with a constant stream of apologies and well-meaning sympathies over the loss of her sister.

Now, things were finally making a return to the usual.

She felt at home behind the bar, schmoozing, flirting, and earning her tips. Cassidy was good at her gig, and crap job that it was, working Shipwrecked allowed her to get lost in a familiar routine while navigating the new and unfamiliar life she was forced to look in the eye when not working, playing Mom to Emma and girlfriend — if that's what you'd call it — to Jon Conway. It was almost surreal as if she'd opened her eyes into Sarah's life instead of her own. Cassidy thought she could ride things out, that she didn't need to know what would happen next. But once Jon asked her to move in with them, everything suddenly became very ... *real*. The bar was a comfort, perhaps a narcotic, listening to her fellow bartender Lewis' idiot come-ons, joking around with her regulars, like Chris, Ray, and Sammi Jo. She didn't even mind the drunks like Bruce Henderson, who often got kicked out of the bar after starting stupid arguments over darts or pool.

It was chaotic but comfortably familiar.

"Whatcha smilin' about?" Lewis poured a bucket of ice into the storage bin.

"Nothing," she said, still smiling.

"You were checking out my ass, weren't you?"

"Yeah, busted." Cassidy laughed as Lewis went back to the kitchen for more ice. As he walked off, she found herself, ironically enough, checking out his ass.

Lewis was tall, well-built, and had pretty boy looks with blond hair and blue eyes, but he was also a big mouth. He'd slept with one of the waitresses, Roxanne, a couple years back. That shit had spread faster than herpes in a whorehouse. Any thoughts Cassidy had of hooking up with him died the day she heard him mouthing off about Roxanne "moaning like the Loch Ness Monster." It was bad enough that everyone on Hamilton Island knew everyone's business. It was worse when you worked with people you slept with, and everyone knew.

Lewis was also a dealer, though she'd never bought from him, specifically because he was friends with the owner Tom and didn't want to risk her job for the sake of convenient drugs. Cassidy figured Tom was probably even a client of Lewis', but she didn't want to take any chances. Shipwrecked was a shit job in a shit place, but the money was decent on most nights, definitely better than an uneducated addict could expect to make if she were to just pick up and leave.

"I need two Amstels," said the newest waitress, Tiff, a twenty-three-year-old blonde with a nose ring and several tattoos. This was the first time Cassidy had worked with the girl, but she was pleased to see Tiff hustled from table to table like a seasoned pro.

Cassidy slid the ice-cold bottles onto the counter and met the girl's gaze.

"Sorry to hear about your sister."

And just like that, Cassidy's mood went sour. She said nothing to Tiff, just turned on her heel to see if Old Man Willy at the end of the bar needed a refill.

She's not even from around here. Didn't even know Sarah. Why the fuck does she have to bring that shit up?

Over the next hour or so, Cassidy could tell that Tiff was trying to see why she had grown so suddenly cold. Cassidy knew she was being prickly, and the girl didn't deserve to get shit for being nice, but at the same time, she couldn't help how she felt. Ever since Tiff mentioned her sister, Cassidy's groove had gone missing. She was making mistakes on orders, couldn't concentrate, and even dropped a full glass mug. Fortunately, the glass bounced off the rubber mat beneath her instead of shattering, but still, she never dropped shit.

Tiff had thrown her off, and every time she saw the girl, Cassidy grew increasingly annoyed — and more anxious.

Once business started to wither, she went to the restroom just to avoid having to talk with the waitress, who was floating around the bar, obviously looking for a chance to talk with her.

As Cassidy sat in the stall, pissing, she looked down and realized her hands were shaking. The dull bass from the bar's music thrummed through the thin walls as if attempting to match its time with the beat of her racing heart.

It had been three weeks since Cassidy had taken a pill. Three long weeks.

She thought the worst was behind her, but fuck, how she wanted a pill right now.

Just one, to take the edge off.

She had two "just in case" pills in a folded piece of paper in her pocket. She'd been carrying the same two pills for twenty-one days, proud to have resisted the near-constant urge through each and every one.

You ought to reward yourself, the Addict cooed, waving its baton as it always did at the start of its familiar symphony of reasoning.

You already proved you're not addicted, right? Addicts don't go three weeks without using. You're good. Just one, to take the edge off.

No.

Cassidy left the stall. At the sink, she peered into the mirror, prepared to greet her ghostly reflection. Except the reflection wasn't hers — it was Sarah's, staring back, open-mouthed, as if shocked to be in her sister's body.

She shrieked, then blinked her eyes and rubbed them hard. Then she took a cautious look in the mirror and found her own reflection staring back.

A chill hummed under her skin, and her hands shook even more. She turned on the faucet, the busted one that blasted water so fast and hard that it always beat against the porcelain and splashed onto the floor. Cassidy didn't care. She took handfuls into her cupped palms, splashed her face, then ran her sopping digits through her hair.

I don't need them. I don't need them.

The door to the bathroom burst open.

Tiff stood in the threshold, staring. "Are you okay?"

"Yeah, why?" Cassidy snuck a peek in the mirror to see what about her had alarmed Tiff. Was it her shaking hands? Her bug eyes? Her wet hair and running eyeliner?

Shit, I'm a fucking mess.

Tiff moved closer as if she were about to tell Cassidy a secret. "Did I say something to piss you off out there?" Her face was kind, eyes wide and honest.

Cassidy felt a swell of guilt, and to her surprise, the sting of approaching tears. "I'm sorry." The first of them burst from her eyes. Suddenly, more than anything in the world,

Cassidy had to flee the bar. "Can you tell Lewis I don't feel well? I need to go."

"Um ... yeah. I ..."

Cassidy didn't wait for Tiff to continue. She fled the bathroom, tore the apron from her body, went to the time clock in the back, punched out, then half-sprinted out of the bar and into the cool night air, never once looking back as Lewis called, "Cassidy!" loudly behind her.

People were on the streets — they were always on the streets in the tourist district — looking at her as she passed by, sobbing. She went from fast to faster, eager to escape their curious or maybe even judging eyes, hurrying until she finally fell into a full sprint.

Cassidy kept running and crying until she found herself alone in a narrow alley behind two rows of shops. She stopped, stared up at the full moon, then lost her scream to the night.

She swallowed hard, reached inside her pocket — the left pocket with her cell, rather than the right with the pills — and dialed her Narcotics Anonymous sponsor, Roberta.

"Hello?" the woman said, obviously sleepy.

"I'm sorry to wake you." Another swell of guilt filled her. Roberta was a forty-year-old working single mother of two. It wasn't right to call her so late. She had her own shit to deal with. But that's what sponsors were for, and Cassidy had no one else. It wasn't like she was about to call Jon and admit to *still* being an addict. Her addiction had cost Jon and Sarah a shot at love and changed Sarah's life. No way her sister would still be on Hamilton if not for Cassidy fucking up.

Sarah would still be alive.

"It's okay, sweetie. What's wrong?" The click of a lamp and the rustling of covers came through the receiver.

"I really, *really* want to use."

"It's all right. I'm here for you. Do you want to come over? I can make some coffee or something?"

"No, no, that's okay. I just needed to hear your voice." Cassidy took a deep breath. "Also, I have to tell you I relapsed about a month ago. A few times." She thought about saying it was around the time Sarah died but didn't want to use her sister's death as an excuse — even if it was an excuse Roberta would understand.

Roberta's supportive voice was unflinching. "It's okay. The important thing is you're calling me now. Calling me instead of using. Let's talk."

"Thank you." Then she sat with her back to the alley brick, listening to Roberta and knowing the worst of her habits were like bulbs beneath a winter ground, waiting for spring and a blue sky to burst into bloom and control her. Roberta wanted her to go to another meeting, tomorrow if possible. Cassidy apologized for having missed the past few and admitted to avoiding the meetings because of her guilt.

It felt good to get it out, to have someone hear her confessions.

Cassidy tried not to shake as she listened to her sponsor. She held the phone in one hand while the other stayed in her pocket, fondling the pair of tiny dots that promised to make everything better.

Just one Cassidy. You can do it right now while talking to Roberta, then never do it again. She'll never have to know.

Just one will make everything better.

Chapter 5 - Bruce Henderson

Missing & Survivor's Group Meeting
  Hamilton K-12
   Thursday night

BRUCE HENDERSON SAT in the back of the auditorium, feeling the anger increasingly swell inside him as the people continued to speak about the school shootings as if *God* had somehow allowed tragedy to happen as if it was God's will and not the act of that fucking lunatic Roger Heller.

Missy Chissolm, a cafeteria worker who hadn't even lost any children, was on the stage crying about the "senseless tragedy" and a need for the community to "come together."

Bruce shook his head, sighing audibly enough for a woman two rows in front of him, Mary Stafford, who was at the meeting because of her missing daughter, to turn back and give him the old glare eyes. At least he thought that's what was doing. It was difficult to tell in the dark. The stage was the only part of the auditorium lit, showing the five people sitting in chairs, each taking their turn at the microphone like it was open mic night at the Tragedy Club.

The urge to call bullshit on the meeting rolled like a tide inside him, but he looked down at his tightly-clenched hands and resisted exposing it for the waste it was. This was his second one, and they were *supposed* to help grieving parents. They were *supposed* to offer solace.

All they were doing was fueling his anger.

But he couldn't take it any longer. He stood, fists clenched, and erupted, "Why aren't any of you complaining about Roger Heller?"

Connie Fawcett, the woman who'd started the missing children's survivor group years ago, went to the microphone. "Sir, if you'd like to come up and talk, please wait your turn."

"Talk? All you people do is fucking talk!" Bruce yelled, thinking maybe he shouldn't have emptied so many glasses before the meeting, but fuck, it was too late to turn back now. "Meanwhile nobody's *doing* anything. You got Heller's kid still going here, ya' know? Did you all hear what he did to Jake Brewster and Ray Wilson? He nearly killed them, left that Brewster kid in a fucking coma! Am I the only one who thinks maybe the lunatic nut didn't fall too far from the crazy tree?"

"What is there to do, Mr. Henderson?" Connie asked. "We're all here to support one another. That's all we're here to do. The police and school handled the other situation."

"You all just wanna sit here and wait for another tragedy, go ahead, but I'm done listening to you all fucking whine about this shit."

Jerry Barlow, the sixty-year-old school maintenance worker, sitting three rows up from him, stood and looked at him. "Please, Bruce."

"Please, what?" Bruce shouted as he moved down his aisle and up three rows to meet Jerry face-to-face. "Please what, Jerry?" he repeated, standing inches from Jerry, close enough for the maintenance man to smell his soured breath.

"Jesus, Bruce, you're drunk!"

The righteous tone of Jerry's voice dug into Bruce's skin

like a cat's claws into carpet. Before Bruce could give thought to action, he swung hard and slammed his fist into Jerry's jaw.

The maintenance man fell to the ground, throwing his hands over his face. "Please, Bruce, I don't want to fight."

But Bruce did. He'd been wanting someone to hit for a month, someone he could beat to a pulp. Someone to pay for what happened to Teddy.

Then he felt the entire room full of people staring at him. People he'd known all his life. People who were looking at him with an even mix of pity and fear.

He looked down at Jerry and felt a twinge of guilt for decking a man twenty years older than himself. He shook his head, then turned around, making eye contact with each person who stared at him. Part of him wanted to apologize, the rest wanted to finish saying what had to be said.

"You all act like God allowed this shit to happen to our kids. And I ain't talkin' about missing kids and crap. I'm talking about the shootings. They ain't got nothin' to do with God. Roger Heller pulled the trigger. Roger Heller, a man you all trusted, shot these poor kids without even thinking. You all deserve this shit to happen again if you don't wake the fuck up and do something about it now."

With the words finally out of his mouth, Bruce turned and stormed from the auditorium. He strode across the parking lot, climbed in his truck, slammed his thumb on the button to turn the ignition, then tore into the street, headed home.

Halfway there, Bruce decided he wasn't ready to walk through the door, especially so drunk. Linda would still be awake. She'd smell his breath and give him more shit than he was currently willing to take. He was a bit tipsy, but not so drunk he couldn't drive. He headed to Shipwrecked, then went inside, determined to get good and wasted.

~

"FINE. FUCK YOU, TOO," Bruce said as Lewis, the bartender, escorted him out of the bar and into the parking lot.

"I called you a cab."

"No, I'll walk." Bruce waved the bartender away.

Once he saw Lewis go inside, Bruce made his way to his truck, hopped in, then fumbled under the seat for his emergency bottle of Smirnoff. He found nothing.

"Mother fucker." He leaned over and fished for the bottle from among the cigarette wrappers and empty McDonald's bags littering the floor of the truck, finally finding it not under a bag, but under the passenger seat. He twisted the cap, took a massive swig, then replaced the cap and started the car, catching a glance in the mirror and realizing just how sloshed he actually was.

Bruce thought of Teddy, and burst into sobbing, heaving tears.

He flashed back to when Teddy was just six years old, back when he looked up to his Daddy so much. Back before he was the strict asshole bad guy he'd turned into after catching Teddy with his first blunt. Bruce remembered his son making him an elaborate drawing of the two of them together, fishing. While Teddy had drawn stuff all the time for Mommy, this was the first drawing he'd ever made for his dad.

"That is so beautiful, son," he said, hugging his boy.

Bruce caught his reflection in the mirror and shook his head in disgust — at both the situation and with himself.

I punched Jerry Barlow. Jesus Christ.

He thought of his son looking down from Heaven, ashamed at what he'd become. Bruce didn't picture Teddy as he was when he died, a seventeen-year-old young man. He pictured him as the six-year-old boy who had once admired him more than anything else in the world. Who had looked up to Daddy like he had an S on his chest and a big, red cape billowing behind him.

Bruce turned on the radio to kill some time before driving home.

He found a sports show on satellite that he liked to listen to whenever he had a chance. He leaned back in the seat and closed his eyes. The hosts, two guys, Rod and Rick, were making fun of the Seahawks — *again* — and their rookie wide receiver who got busted sending photos of his junk to a wrong number, which just happened to belong to his pastor.

Bruce laughed. "What a moron."

The radio signal started to crackle with a strange warble, as if stuck between stations.

Fucking signal is always bullshit around here.

Bruce put the truck into drive and tapped on the gas, inching it through the lot and aiming his tires toward a better signal. It was funny how a few feet could mean all the difference in the world between crystal clear and utter crap.

When Rod's voice came back loud and clear, Bruce put the truck into park and sat, engine still running, in case he had to move again.

Just as Rick was about to play an interview with the pastor, the warble was back. And with, it a static Bruce hadn't heard since the old days of regular AM radio.

He went to move the truck again, but his hand froze instead. Just like his body.

What the hell?

Bruce heard something in the static — another voice, like bleed from a different station. Something seemed oddly familiar about it, even though he couldn't make out who it was, what they were saying, or even if it was a man or woman. He perked his ears, trying to make sense of the words, until a single syllable rose in repeat over the static.

"Kill, kill, kill …"

What the hell? Is this some sorta joke? Some weird metal music or something?

The static grew louder, then a snippet of the sport's station broke through before the warble drowned it and the words returned.

"Kill, kill, kill, kill ..."

Kill? Kill who?

"Kill Alex Heller."

Chapter 6 - Liz Heller

Liz woke to the sound of Aubrey on the baby monitor, murmuring in her sleep. The clock read 12:01 a.m. She still had plenty of time to stay buried beneath the covers, but her mind immediately whirred into motion, contemplating the day's big move.

As much as she couldn't wait to leave Hamilton Island, it felt as if she were shutting the door on her past, a door which, for some reason, Liz was frightened to close. California was the new start her family desperately needed. Yet, part of her still felt like leaving the island meant leaving Roger behind.

Liz reached down to trace her fingers along her wedding ring, the ring she'd never removed except for a few times when washing dishes in the sink, afraid it would slip from her finger — a fear made all the more real since she'd lost her engagement ring nearly a decade before.

"Don't worry," Roger had said when she first lost it, "It'll turn up someday."

"But it's the ring you gave me," she said. "The ring has a story, one of our best. It's personal history, and I can't stand to think it might be gone forever."

Roger wasn't much of a jewelry guy. He didn't know a

diamond from a peridot, but he had seen this ring in a jeweler's window one day early in their dating, and to hear him tell the story, it had practically whispered his name as he passed. It was silver rather than gold, which Liz preferred, with two thin bands weaving together as one. The gem was an emerald, tiny and beautiful. Liz always thought emeralds were so much prettier than diamonds. Though they had never discussed it, Roger clearly agreed, drawn to the ring as he was. It was about two counties and a canyon outside his budget, but he saved for a year anyway. When he finally went back to buy the ring, it was gone. The jeweler had sold it to someone just two weeks before.

Roger was devastated.

He asked the shopkeeper if there was any way to get another ring of that kind, but the man said there wasn't. The manufacturer no longer made it. But he knew a custom jewelry maker who might be able to come close. It might cost more. Though Roger didn't have the money, he'd already spent a year saving to get what he did have, so he agreed, knowing he would find a way to pay for it someday. That someday came five months later.

Liz felt tears trickling down her cheeks as she remembered the night he proposed.

Roger wrote her the most beautiful love note, with a simple *Will you marry me?* like a kiss at the end, then slipped it into the book she'd been reading at the time — *The Princess Bride* — so it would fall out when she opened it, which it did, since he had written the note on stock that was slightly too thick for the book.

The Princess Bride was one of Liz's favorite books. She still had the hardcover originally bought by her father, and she read it at least once a year. The note was the most romantic thing anyone had ever done for Liz, and what it said was even more romantic than that. Of course, she said yes immediately, screamed it as she slipped the gorgeous ring on her finger. Roger ran into their bedroom, laughing and smiling.

And then she had somehow lost the ring, probably her life's most precious physical possession. Roger had practically torn the house apart to find it for her. But he finally gave up.

Liz had hoped to find it as they packed for the movers, but even though their house was inside out and sitting in cardboard, she had found it nowhere.

Now that they were leaving in the morning, she couldn't help but imagine the ring laying in some unseen corner, to be found by whoever owned the house next — someone ignorant of the ring's significance or the love it once symbolized.

As Liz thought of Aubrey and Alex, she knew their safety was far more important than any ring. They *couldn't* stay on the island. She knew that the minute she saw the video on the flash drive, then had it confirmed when their car was vandalized outside the library with the word "murderer."

Ironically, it was because of the flash drive that they were even able to leave the island.

Brock Houser, the investigator she asked to look at the drive, had lost it in a horrible car accident. Odd as it was, he didn't even remember her hiring him. When she hadn't heard from him, she reached out to his employer, Jon Conway, telling him what happened and why she was afraid. Jon felt so bad about everything, he offered to pay for them to resettle elsewhere, somewhere safe. People could say what they wanted about the Conways, but Jon had bought her a tiny place in a small beachside community called Balboa Island — not *really* an island — even after she insisted he didn't.

At first, Liz couldn't imagine taking the money and refused it outright. But Jon Conway was nothing if not persistent. So she'd finally said yes, she'd take the money — as a loan which she promised to repay.

"Take your time, Mrs. Heller. You've been through a lot. You worry about your family first."

She thanked him, let him buy the house, with her name on the deed, then dared to dream that they might truly be able to start over somewhere else, where their world would be safe and the schools were excellent.

But now, in the still of the night, Liz wondered if she'd taken blood money. If Jon was merely acting as an agent for his family and trying to get her out of town. She'd been on to something, the same something she was becoming increasingly convinced got Roger killed — or perhaps made him snap.

Regardless of the evidence and accusations, she would never believe her husband capable of shooting a schoolroom full of his students. No, something else was happening. Something which no doubt led back to the Conways. They were behind everything that happened on the island, so it only made sense they knew *something* about Roger's death, or maybe even had a hand in it.

Her stomach turned at the thought that she *had* taken blood money to walk away from the truth of what had driven her Roger to madness, before getting answers that would clear his name — not just for the man who could no longer use it, but for her and Alex and Aubrey, the three who would hold it forever.

But just as she was certain of Roger's innocence, she also believed Jon Conway's sincerity in offering to help her.

Well, of course, I trust him. He's an actor!

No, nobody's that good of an actor. I saw it in his eyes. Besides, he left the island a long time ago. He only came back because of Sarah Hughes. I have to trust that some people are good — even some Conways.

Liz finally drifted to sleep …

… And woke to the sound of the baby monitor crackling to life.

"Da-da," Aubrey said, sounding wide awake.

Liz shot up to sitting in her bed, and immediately turned to the alarm clock. It read 1:11 a.m.

"Liz!" Roger's voice called out, loud, on the monitor.

Her heart fell into her gut.

Oh, God.

She jumped out of bed, racing from her bedroom, into the hall, and through Aubrey's door.

Roger stood beside their daughter's crib, or rather a ghostly image of him flickering in and out of her still gummy sight.

He looked up at her, eyes wide as he shouted, but his voice was crackling as if coming through some distant transmission. There were many sounds that were sort of like words coming out of his mouth, but not a single sound made any sense.

"What?" she asked.

Roger tried speaking again, but his voice was still lost in the static.

No, this can't be real.

She inched closer, remembering the horrible nightmare she had of him shooting Aubrey.

This is a dream. This is a dream. I have to wake up.

Liz stepped closer. Roger grew brighter as the air around her grew frigid.

She reached out and touched Roger's chest. His image rippled as if she were dipping her fingers into a still lake. He faded for a moment, then rippled back into view.

What the hell?

Roger looked her up and down. His eyes were wide and terrified. His mouth continued to scream something with no voice behind it, eyes still glazed with panic.

Then it suddenly came through, as if on delay. "Liz! Get the kids and get out! NOW!"

"What?" she cried, confused.

Aubrey cried out in the crib, looking at her Daddy like she wanted to be held.

"Get OUT!" he shouted again.

An explosion of noise erupted downstairs and thundered through the house.

"No!" Roger raised his hands as if pleading with God — or something — to stop whatever was about to happen.

"What's going on?" Liz ran to the window. The back of a pickup truck stuck out from the front of her house like a hitching thumb.

Her heart beat like a hammer on brick as Roger began to flicker and fade.

"Don't leave!" Liz yelled.

Two loud pops pounded through the house — gunshots from down the hall.

"Alex!" Liz darted out the door before she thought to grab Aubrey and run. As she stepped into the hall, she saw a shape approaching from Alex's room — a man standing with his back to her.

He turned slowly in the darkened hallway until he faced her.

Bruce Henderson, holding a gun.

He shot Alex!

Liz cried out, "No!"

Their gazes locked. Something inside his eyes wasn't right, not just angry, but *mad*. She didn't have time to figure out what that meant since they were also burning with a fury that had likely murdered her son. Liz ducked into Aubrey's bedroom, slammed the door shut, then locked it as fast as she could.

Bruce's footsteps thundered in the hall as he ran toward her.

Oh, God! Oh, God!

Aubrey screamed as Liz scooped her up, terrified, confused. She weighed her options as the monster pounded on the wood. It was only a matter of time before he shot his way in.

The light went on in the hall, then Bruce jiggled the door-knob hard. "Oh, Mrs. Heller ... I've got a package for you." His sing-songy voice sounded both drunk and crazy.

Liz had to save Aubrey. Had to save them both. She

needed to get out the window, jump down to the ground, run next door, and call the cops. Had to do something. Anything.

Liz hoped to God her boy wasn't dead like his father, that he was still clinging to life in his bedroom, and that she, or the police, could somehow save him.

Bruce has come for payback. To take Roger's son, just as Roger took his. But he's not done. He wants to kill us all.

"Open up!" Bruce banged on the door.

Liz went to the window and unfastened the latch. She tried pulling it open, but it was stuck, and hard to manage with one hand still holding her baby.

She had to set Aubrey down.

Shit!

Liz leaned over, laying Aubrey on the floor beneath the window. Her daughter's shrill scream grew louder.

"I know, I know, Baby. Just a minute." She yanked on the window, but it didn't budge. She pulled again, tugging harder until her fingers were white with pain and desperate for leverage.

"It's okay, baby. It's okay. Mamma's gonna get us out. Mamma's —"

The door burst open behind her, slamming into the wall like booming thunder. Light from the hallway flooded the room, then a shadow blocked it.

Liz turned around just as Bruce raised the gun and shot her. Twice.

The pain was immediate, in her chest and somewhere in her head, though she couldn't tell where, as the feeling spread like fire through her skull.

The last thing Liz saw as she hit the ground was her baby screaming — and Roger's shadow draping them both.

Epilogue

Alex pulled himself from the bed, his lower back on fire, with no sensation past his waist.

Paralyzed.

It was all he could do to stay conscious. All he *wanted* to do was close his eyes and drift off, but if he did that, he was certain he'd never wake. He was also certain his mother and sister would die. He had to save them.

Light poured through his half-open doorway. He could hear banging down the hall. Bruce was going after his mother and baby sister, trying to get into Aubrey's room.

No, no, no!

I have to stop Bruce. But how?

Alex pulled himself along the floor, crawling toward his door, one bloodied arm at a time, like a wounded soldier.

He made it to the hallway just in time to see Bruce rear back and kick the door. And then he was through it.

Gunshots.

Two of them.

No!

Alex wanted to scream, but his voice was trapped in his throat — or perhaps he'd lost the ability to speak.

He threw one arm in front of another, moving as fast as he could, his heart racing as he waited to hear another shot. His mother's voice grew silent, leaving only Aubrey's screams.

Mom's dead! No!

Please don't kill Aubrey. Please, please, please.

Alex pulled himself closer to Aubrey's room.

Ten feet … nine …

Every move a struggle that felt like it might be his last. He had no idea what he'd do once he reached the doorway. How could he possibly save Aubrey, or his mother, *if* she were still alive?

Eight feet … seven … six …

Alex heard the man laughing.

No, please!

Five feet … four …

Aubrey's screams grew louder.

Is he hurting her? Get your fucking hands off my sister!

Three feet … two … one …

Alex slid his body through the doorway and saw the back of his mother's head, blood in a spreading lake beneath her.

No!

Bruce hunched over, his gun pointed at Aubrey's chest. He sang, "Hush little baby, don't you cry … "

No! Don't! Alex wanted to scream, wanted to stand, wanted to throw himself in front of his sister, take the bullet. But both body and voice betrayed him.

She's too young. Don't!

Bruce's gun shook, a tremor that spread from his hand and through his body, as if he were in battle with himself.

He shoved the gun against Aubrey's head.

Her scream cut through Alex's heart. He had to get to her.

No!!

Bruce screamed, "Die, die, die!"

No!

Bruce stood, but instead of shooting down at Aubrey, he thrust the gun into his mouth and pulled the trigger.

Blood spattered the window behind him as his body fell in a thunk to the floor beside Alex's mother.

Aubrey screamed, then turned toward Alex.

He crawled to her. Her eyes, so big and afraid.

Six feet ... five ...

I'm coming, Aubrey. I'm coming, Baby Sister.

Four feet ... three ...

As he drew closer to his mother, he saw her wounds, her wide open eyes, and realized she was dead.

No!

Don't look at Mommy, don't look. I'm coming.

Two feet ... one ...

He pulled himself to his sister and reached out to caress her face, pulling himself as close to her as possible, hoping to shield her from seeing their mother.

It's going to be okay. I've got you now.

I've got you.

But Alex couldn't keep his eyes open any longer.

He surrendered to the darkness, his final thoughts in vain as Aubrey's screams carried out into the cruel, dark world, with no hope of reply.

Episode 8

Prologue – Sarah Hughes (Age 10)

Hamilton Island, Washington
  20 years ago

"I think we should go, Cass." Sarah tried not to sound whiney. "If we're late, Mom's not gonna let us out tomorrow."

"One more game," Cassidy said. "Don't be such a goodie-goodie."

"I'm *not* a goodie-goodie." Sarah huffed. If they didn't get home soon, there was no way they'd be able to play chase again tomorrow. Mama had said so three times.

Tommy and Eric laughed. Cassidy cringed, giving Sarah the same look she always gave when embarrassed of her. They were identical twins, but that rarely stopped Cassidy from making her feel like a stupid little sister.

She wished Cassidy wanted to play with her as much as she wanted to play with Cassidy. How much of her sister's embarrassment was because Cass had a crush on Jonny Conway and didn't want Sarah around to point out how differently she always acted around him?

Cassidy didn't wait for Sarah to agree. She just leaned

against the home base tree, set her forehead against her arm, closed her eyes, and started loudly counting.

"One ... Two ... You all better run!"

Sarah glared at her. Of course, Cass hadn't waited for her to agree. Why would she? Sarah always caved in to her sister's whims.

We better not get in trouble!

Sarah tore off into the woods, running as fast as she could. Like usual, she would wait until she heard Cassidy go after one of the boys, then sneak back and tag home. Or at least try. Sarah didn't care if she got caught and was "it," but it would be harder to get Cassidy home if she was supposed to be it next. Cassidy would make her feel like it was her *duty* to play another round.

Sarah found a spot where she had successfully hidden a few times before. It was a bit far from home base but felt safe — a thick cluster of trees she could easily circle around if she heard someone coming and put immediate distance between herself and whoever was it. No one had ever found this particular spot. It was probably her best one and definitely her favorite.

For the most part, Sarah figured the spot was probably too far off for most of the others to consider checking. Usually, she could hear enough of what was happening over by base to let her know when she should start creeping back toward home. This time, however, several minutes passed with nothing but silence.

The longer Sarah waited for someone to find her or to hear some sort of warning, the more she felt she made a mistake coming out so far. At least at the end of the game when they should have been getting ready to call it quits and go home. What if everyone but her reached home base safely? Then she'd be up against her sister. And while Sarah was faster than Cassidy, at least by a little, Cassidy was usually clever enough to find a way to catch her.

Suddenly she heard laughter, Jonny loudly guffawing.

"Good God, girl! You playing football?!"

"You're it!" Cassidy shouted, sounding proud to have caught Jonny.

The rest of the group added their laughter to the chorus. Relieved, Sarah went to join them, but suddenly, her legs were frozen. She couldn't move.

What the …?

Sarah tried moving her feet, arms, anything, but couldn't, as if her body had decided to ignore her. She was somehow paralyzed. Or *something*. Had she been bitten by a poisonous spider, or perhaps a snake, and somehow not felt it? She could have touched a poisonous plant. The forest was filled with poison oak, maybe it was filled with something worse.

Though Sarah couldn't move her limbs — her hand just sort of hovered midair, almost mocking her — she could still feel twilight's cool breeze as it brushed her body. And she could blink and turn her head ever so slightly.

Sarah opened her mouth, desperate to scream for the others, but it, too, betrayed her.

Oh, my God, I can't talk or move!

She heard her sister call out for her, loud then louder.

"Sarah? It's safe to come out. I got Jonny!"

I'm here, Cassidy, can you hear me?

There had been many times throughout the years when it seemed as if one of them *knew* what the other was thinking. Cassidy told Sarah, several times, about stuff she read online — twins with psychic powers, telepathy, precognition, and all sorts of other stuff she didn't quite understand. Those sorts of stories always sounded exciting but were hard for Sarah to buy since the books usually had titles like *Mysteries, Monsters, and Untold Secrets*.

Despite Cassidy's insistence, or perhaps fascination, Sarah never saw any evidence of special abilities between them. At least nothing beyond coincidence. But now, as she heard them call for her, she wished to God that Cassidy was right, and her twin sister *could* hear her thoughts.

I'm here, Cass! I can't move. Help!

Thunder erupted around her, louder than any she had ever heard before. If Sarah *had* been able to move, she would have likely leapt several feet in the air. If she could speak, she would have filled the night with her scream.

Lightning flickered above, preceding a second, even louder round of rolling thunder. It crashed like regular thunder, just louder, but the lightning was weird — not bright white streaks stretching across an angry sky, like usual. This lighting seemed like it was made from a series of pulsing flashes, striping the sky, on and off and on and off, almost with rhythm. Though her body was frozen, her heart pounded so hard, she couldn't tell if she was hearing the sky's thunder or her own soaring pulse.

Something creaked behind her, a long, rasping groan like a door opening wide in complaint.

Sarah wanted to turn, desperate to see what was back there, but still couldn't move. She realized, to her horror, that she couldn't even blink. It felt as if invisible fingers were widening her eyelids, forcing her to see whatever was about to happen.

Her eyes watered, desperate to undo the stretching. Her mind felt frantic as thunder and lightning intensified. And then, all at once, it stopped — draping the world into an immediate darkness and wrapping it in a wicked, eerie quiet.

The night was still, save for Sarah's shallow breath. She again tried to scream but couldn't.

Finally, she was able to close her eyes, and did, feeling relief, and tears, wash her stinging eyes.

Help me, PLEASE! Cass?

Sarah opened her eyes and tried to look around despite her still-limited movement. The forest was black, the moon obscured by clouds, or *something*. All was silent.

A branch snapped behind her, followed by more of that horrible noise.

Creeeeeeaaaaak ...

A sudden explosion of blinding white, so bright it was all she could see, bled from everywhere, and all at once.

Alongside the bright light came a horrible popping.

Then the light swallowed her.

Sarah opened her eyes. Naked and shivering, she lay on a hard surface with a row of bright lights above her. There were shadows she couldn't quite make out hovering over her body. They were doing *something* to her, but she couldn't distinguish what, or make out much of anything other than the cold metal table pressed hard against her butt and back.

She couldn't feel her arms or legs. There was a vague yet insistent pressure close to her torso — a sensation unlike anything she'd ever experienced before.

Sarah tried to move, to cover herself, but couldn't.

Help.

Cassidy!

Help me.

She closed her eyes then blinked them open, trying to make sense of the thick shadows that refused to unblur around her.

Who are these people? Are they doctors?

Sarah had the distinct feeling she was being operated on. Had fallen in the woods, maybe smashed her head on a rock? Could this be the danger Mama always warned them about when she ordered them home before dark?

Sarah cried, or thought she did. It was hard to tell for certain.

Please don't let me die.

Why can't I see them? Why can't I feel anything?

She couldn't hear them, either. There were sounds — mechanical, something like a dentist's drill or worse — coming from somewhere nearby, but they didn't quite sound like anything Sarah ever heard. Everything was muffled like she was underwater.

The mechanical sounds faded to a few final distant clicks, then there was a length of silence followed by a whirring. Sarah remembered watching giant yellow vehicles clear the forests to build Ulysses Cove. She could hear the saw blades spinning, much like the whirring above her, and pictured herself standing outside the fence with Cassidy, watching as trees crashed down into the dirt.

Oh, God, are they cutting me?

The whirring stopped, and the sudden silence was almost painful, slowly building pressure in her ears and head. Sarah longed to hear words, or anything that would reassure her that everything would be okay.

Sometimes while she and Cassidy did their homework, Mama would watch a show on Blu-Ray called *Dr. Surprising*. She said was "sort of soap opera and sort of not." The show had a lot of surgeries, and the doctors were *always* talking during the operations. Sometimes her mom talked to the TV along with the doctors, loudly announcing to the girls, who weren't even paying attention, whether she thought the patient on the table would survive through the episode.

The surgeons were *never* silent, though, always talking to one another about things both relevant to the surgery and mundane, like trimming strokes from their golf games.

Can you hear me? Anybody?

Still, Sarah heard nothing but silence. She listened for the sound of her own breathing but couldn't even hear that. Just the mounting pressure in her head, which had its own odd low and piercing scream. It was odd that silence could have a *sound* — a sound that hurt, no less.

One of the shadows moved closer, as if leaning over her

body. The shape slowly swam into focus. It was a surgeon! A woman wearing a soft, blue mask at the bottom of her blurry face. She shined a light into Sarah's eyes, causing her to blink.

When the light finally faded from her eyelids, Sarah saw a second shadow above her. This one looked different, blurrier. For a moment, Sarah wondered if she had double vision, or perhaps saw two people close together.

It was *so* hard to see.

The second shadow leaned closer, and when it did, Sarah felt a giant knot form and tighten in her throat.

The shadow wasn't a person — it was something impossible, a thing that should not be. And as it inched closer, Sarah finally got her mouth to work.

She used it to scream.

Chapter 1 - Milo Anderson

Milo stared at the caskets waiting to be lowered into the earth, down into their new and ugly forever, feeling the déjà vu of death on Hamilton Island.

The vicious cycle started when Roger Heller opened fire on five students, including Teddy Henderson. Now it had come full circle with Teddy's father Bruce claiming vengeance by killing Roger's son Alex along with his mother Liz.

Milo couldn't believe his best friend was dead. Just five days ago, he'd gone over to his house for a clumsy goodbye. As awkward as it might have been, it also felt right, almost comforting, like maybe they had a chance for a fresh start, an opportunity for a different beginning. Sure, things would never — could never — be like they were. That was impossible. But at least there was a chance for something more than the decay they had been left with since the school shooting.

He had left Alex's house that day feeling *almost* hopeful, if not for life on the island, then at least for his chance to maintain a true friendship with Alex. They made plans to finish their script for *The Atrium Divided* and promised to keep in touch after he and his family moved to California. Alex had even logged into their shared Raconteur account later that day. Now all those tomorrows, along with everything said and unsaid between them, well, it was all gone with no hope of ever coming back. The unwritten pages of their stories and lives were now nothing but blank scraps torn, tattered, and tossed into life's cruelest winds.

Milo wanted to cry, maybe sob. He felt like screaming or doing anything other than standing there frozen. Helpless. But he had to keep his cool, had to hold it together for Katie and her mom, who were standing beside him, one on either side, both barely able to keep their shit stitched together.

Milo turned to Katie and looked into her red eyes. She reached out, took his right hand, and squeezed it softly. He squeezed back, but harder. It was sweet, that show of support, but it nudged him closer to the edge and pushed him deeper into his despair.

Milo turned his attention from Katie to Pastor Avery, who was offering the congregation comfort through prayer as two men from either the church or cemetery, Alex didn't know which, lowered the matching caskets into the ground.

Katie and her mom had each eulogized Alex and Liz already, at the church service, then again at the cemetery. They were the only ones, save for the pastor and a few people at the church, who had spoken on their behalf. Milo wondered how many people refrained from speaking because they sympathized more with Bruce Heller, the murderer, than they did with his victims. How many people still held Roger Heller's actions against the entire family? And how many people, of the three hundred plus watching the casket dip down into the open dirt, were there to say good riddance more than goodbye?

Milo scanned the crowd, hating every person, one by one.

Hypocrites. Assholes, all of them.

He reserved the most hate for himself. Or rather, the old Milo, who had felt the same rage for Alex in the aftermath of what his father had done. Even if it hadn't lasted, Milo *had* hated Alex, which made him no different from many of the assholes at his service.

He felt most awful for not eulogizing his best friend when given not one, but two chances. He was a writer, for fuck's sake. He should have been able to say *something*. Milo had four pages of notes scribbled for the occasion, detailing how much he loved, yes loved, his best friend. How much the Hellers, even Roger, had made him feel like a member of their family. Part of a happy family — not the cold, dysfunctional thing that passed for family at his house.

The Hellers deserved so much more than this.

Milo thought of Aubrey, now a ward of the state. She had to be confused, scared, not knowing what happened to her mommy, daddy, and brother. Or worse, unable to forget seeing her flesh and blood butchered before her eyes. The poor girl wasn't even a year old and had already lost her entire family to slaughter.

Can her life ever be normal?

The thought was too much. Though Milo clenched his fists and curled his toes to keep it from happening, tears still slid from both eyes and down his cheeks.

Katie, who he couldn't even look at without risk of losing one hundred percent of his shit, must have noticed.

She pulled him into the hug he needed.

Milo shuddered inside Katie's embrace. "I should've said something," he cried into her hair.

"It's okay." She patted him softly on the back. "Alex knew how you felt. He always did."

Milo nodded, unable to choke another word through his mouth. Even if he could, what was left to say? Everything was shit. The whole entire fucking goddamn piss-soaked world.

As Katie held Milo, he caught sight of Jon Conway and his entourage, Cassidy Hughes, twin sister of Sarah Hughes, whom Milo had as a teacher the year before, and the big giant black dude with the weird robotic foot sticking out from the bottom of his black suit. The guy looked like he was waiting for life inside the panels of a graphic novel.

"What the hell is *he* doing here?" Milo muttered.

He hadn't noticed the Conway bunch at the church service, but then again, the room was so crowded, with too many people crammed into the pews, it would have been easy to miss him even if he had been there.

"Who?" Katie said.

"Jon Conway. What the fuck is he doing at Alex's memorial? He didn't know Alex or his mom. Unless there was something I didn't know." Milo turned to Katie. "Did Alex ever say anything? Do you know if Conway knew his mom or something?"

"I don't know." Katie shrugged. "Maybe a long time ago or something. Alex never said anything, but Hamilton's not that big. Everyone sorta knows everyone here, right?"

"Maybe. Just seems weird."

Milo fished inside his coat pocket and grabbed his cell. He promised Don he would get pictures of the service, and he suddenly felt like he had to get one of Jon. If Milo knew anyone who could tell him the *real* reason Jon Conway might be at his best friend's funeral, it was definitely the man who seemed congested with conspiracy.

Don had taught Milo to be suspicious of everything. "Gather as much information as you can," he'd instructed in one of the many documents from the flash drive he'd given Milo a few weeks before. "Take pics and video, record conversations whenever possible. Go to common places — parks, stores, the library. Watch people. Be discreet but observant. Never stop drawing connections. Look for patterns until you train yourself to see them whenever you open your eyes. The hidden rarely wishes to remain buried and often reveals itself to those willing to pay close attention."

Much, if not most, of the stuff Don had given to Milo seemed a bit *out there*. Tin-foil hat shit for sure — the musings of a man whose family had gone missing and who was desperate for a way to explain it, even if answers existed only through the thick haze of conspiracy. At first, Milo believed little to nothing the man had to say, but the more Milo did as he was told and started paying attention to the details, the more he began to see the many nagging matters his mind couldn't quite reconcile — the connections were there.

Things on Hamilton Island were definitely weird. Everyone knew that, and few would argue the reality, even if they kept it stashed in the back of their minds. Milo had always felt that, and he and Alex had discussed it often. Hamilton *was* different, and the people who lived on the island took a sort of pride in their weird culture. But Milo no longer saw Hamilton as simply weird.

He saw it as sinister.

Though Milo had yet to hear anything from Don about Alex's death, other than a passing whisper in the international aisle of the recently-remodeled Jordy's requesting that he please snap as many pictures of the funeral as he could manage without sticking out, Milo felt somehow certain his mysterious contact would find a connection to the Hellers' murder, one more menacing than Bruce Henderson's vengeance.

As Milo stood beside Katie, staring at Jon Conway and company, he couldn't help but think perhaps the actor might be at the beating heart of all that was weird — or sinister — on Hamilton. Maybe Conway was part of some weird Hollywood cult.

He tried but couldn't ignore the feeling of a hundred eyes on him, all probably wondering what and how much he knew. It was so hard to sift between truth and paranoia. And even if he was paranoid, that didn't mean he wasn't right.

Milo could be paranoid and in danger.

He constantly turned the possibilities in his mind, searching for some grain of insight that would make sense of everything. But every time Milo felt close to an answer, the truth slipped through fingers in his mind.

As he watched Jon Conway, Milo grew certain the man had the answers he sought. He just had to figure out how to get them.

Chapter 2 - Jon Conway

"Jon, you know that kid over there?" Houser nodded toward the scrawny teenager with a cell trying to discreetly snap photos, or maybe even shooting video in their direction.

The moment the kid saw Jon and Cassidy look toward him, he pointed his cell elsewhere.

"No." Then, after a slight pause, "Wait, yeah, I do. I think it's that kid from the news, the one whose mom plowed into the front of that grocery store."

"Milo Anderson," Cassidy said.

"You know him?" Houser asked.

"No, but I remember his name from the news. His dad works for Conway Industries."

"So does half the island, one way or another," Jon said. "What's he do, do you know?"

"Nope," Cassidy shrugged. "But I know it's pretty rude to be taking pictures of you at a fucking funeral."

"Probably rude to swear, too." Houser smiled and gently nudged Cassidy with his elbow. Then, like a dog hungry to get a fox in his mouth, Houser turned to Jon. "Want me to go get his phone?"

"No," Jon said. "I doubt he's selling it to some website.

And the last thing I want is to cause a scene at a funeral, especially when there's real paparazzi waiting outside the cemetery gates. If there's one thing those assholes love more than anything else, it's drizzling blood over your personal life. Remember last year and what happened to that actor from *The Darkness* movies? I guarantee, you take that kid's phone and someone *will* get it on video. That shit will be everywhere by dinner. 'Jon Conway's Giant Robot Goon Takes Kid's Phone.'"

"Good point, but I think I like the sound of 'Giant Robot Goon.'" Houser grinned.

Jon turned his attention to Pastor Avery, who had just finished a final prayer, concluding his thoughts on Liz, Alex, and the Family Heller.

"At this time, I'd like you all to remember Liz and Alex Heller not as the fallen victims of this horrible tragedy, but as they were in life — beacons of hope, always laughing and inviting smiles from friends and loved ones. Liz, like her son, was someone you could count on, and all of us here can take great comfort knowing that at this moment they are both enjoying the Good Lord's eternal solace as they step beyond the gates of Heaven."

The pastor cast his gaze across the crowd, looking from left to right and back again.

"Earth holds no sorrow that Heaven cannot heal. God will watch over our loved ones up in Heaven, just as he'll keep watch over little Aubrey Heller down here on Earth."

Pastor Avery paused, raising his hands to the air, then turned to an older woman standing to his far left, a small mountain of silver hair piled high on her head.

"I'd like to close with our own Glynis Mayhew on bagpipes performing 'Amazing Grace.'"

Jon lowered his head, listening to the bagpipes' wail. There was something about "Amazing Grace" that reached deep into his saddest parts. He thought of Sarah and how he would never see her again. He felt Cassidy's hand find his, then wrapped it into his palm and squeezed, pinching his eyelids and holding them tightly closed. He thought of Emma and wondered how much she must miss her mother. Though they had spoken of Sarah several times, it was always with caution. It seemed as if everyone was actively trying *not* to discuss her — as if mere mention of her mother's name would pick at Emma's scab and threaten to tear the wound into something too deep for any of them to mend.

Jon wondered, not for the first time, how much of his and Cassidy's blooming relationship was some odd attempt by both of them to connect with Sarah by proxy.

What am I doing?

What are we doing?

Is this all horribly wrong?

What is Emma thinking of this? That her father, the man who hadn't seen her mother in a decade, was now dating her twin sister?

Jon wondered, like he did many times each day, if Cassidy felt as guilty as he did, and if her guilt was a similar breed to his. Perhaps part of her hesitation to let them grow closer was rooted in some fear that she didn't want Emma, or him, to see her as an invader, trying to take Sarah's place.

But Jon didn't see it that way and never would. Nor did he see any reason to think Emma would, either. If anything, she seemed to be doing terrific, considering. At least for the moment, Emma seemed to *need* the makeshift family that was blossoming beneath her otherwise mostly-gray skies.

To Jon's surprise, he needed it, too.

He squeezed Cassidy's hand tighter, turning to face her as she slowly spun her head toward him. She smiled, her eyes glistening with unspilled tears.

Jon tried not to think of how often he looked at Cassidy, but in his head, thought *Sarah*.

∽

JON HELD the Toyota Blacklander door open for Emma, waited for her to climb inside, then petted her shoulder. He smiled before slamming the door shut behind her. Cassidy's door closed a second after Emma's, followed immediately by Houser's.

Jon opened his door just as his cell rang. He looked at the card in his palm. The screen read Blake Conway.

He had been waiting for more than a month to confront his father about Warren's accusations — that Blake was behind the plan to keep Jon from knowing he had fathered Sarah's child, that they used Cassidy's legal troubles as a bargaining chip, and that Blake had bought and paid Jon's way into Hollywood.

Blake had been on a business trip since a few days before the shootings, and Warren was evasive about when their father would return. It took all Jon's willpower not to call his father and have their face-to-face over the phone. But he wanted — no, *had* —to see the look in Blake's eyes up close when confronted.

Now that his father was finally calling, Jon's stomach churned.

He lifted the glass card to his ear, camera off, not wanting his father to have the edge of seeing him.

"Hello?"

"Jon?"

It wasn't Blake. It was Mrs. Rasmussen, calling from the house.

"Yes, Madge?"

"Hi, Mr. Conway ... Jon."

He could feel her smile.

"I imagine you still want to know when your father has returned from his trip?"

"Yes." Jon's heartbeat raced.

"Promise you won't tell on me?"

"Have I ever?"

90

"No, Jonny, you haven't." A slight pause, then, "He came back yesterday, but I wanted to wait a day to tell you, so he wouldn't suspect it was me letting you know. If you're going to speak with him, I suggest not waiting too long. Warren and Melinda will be in Seattle all day, so now would be a great time to stop by."

"Great," Jon said. "And thanks, Madge. I promise I won't tell."

"Scout's honor?" she teased.

"If I were a scout, or had any sense of honor, I'd say yes, but we both know better than that," he teased back. "You'll just have to take the word of a Hollywood scoundrel."

"Your word will always be good enough for me," Mrs. Rasmussen said. "Goodbye."

"Goodbye." Jon ended the call.

His stomach knotted with all the things he planned to say to his father. Then he turned to his passengers. "Ready?"

"Ready!" Emma cried from the back seat.

Houser and Cassidy said nothing, though Jon could feel them both wondering what the phone call was about and knowing they couldn't yet ask.

As they left the cemetery, Jon gazed at all the vultures with cameras waiting outside, trying to steal a peek through his blacked-out windows. He smiled as he considered hitting the gas pedal and running one or five of them down.

In the back seat, Emma, who didn't know better, was waving at the paparazzi, though they couldn't see her.

He smiled at her innocence, longing for a day he might feel less jaded.

Chapter 3 - Brock Houser

Houser wasn't sure why he had a hunch about Milo Anderson, but something seemed off about the kid. Sure, he'd been through a lot — he'd lost a friend, his stepmother had lead-footed it through the front of a grocery store, and seeing as how the island wasn't all that large, he'd probably lost another friend or two in the shootings a month back. *Maybe* the kid was *just* traumatized.

But Houser couldn't help but think there was more to the kid and his camera. He'd been an investigator long enough to know when a hunch needed a follow-up.

After parting with Jon and Cassidy, Houser decided to park his truck down the street from Milo's house, then sit and watch, doing research on his tablet.

Milo lived in Ulysses Cove, not exactly The Gardens, but a damned site nicer than anywhere Houser had ever lived. It was a gorgeous community — not that many acres of clearing with thick, swaying forest surrounding three sides. The average home in Ulysses was worth well north of four million dollars. More than a few nudged the bottom of five. What Houser liked about the neighborhood, at least sitting at the end of the block and looking down Milo's street, was that the houses were far from the copy-and-paste blueprints you saw in most luxury developments, where it seemed like one architect, and maybe her brother, had designed from a single deck with barely-shuffled cards.

Each house on Cavern Avenue was unique. Milo's was bought eight years earlier for just under three million, right before the last giant spike in housing prices. Not bad. Houser wasn't sure what Stephen Anderson did for Conway Industries — his report showed his occupation as "Senior Analyst" — but it was clearly something important. His second wife didn't work, even before the accident, and loved to spend. Houser dug up a statement on the Open Report Directory detailing a dispute opened by Bea after someone stole her cell from a Starbucks. The charges prior to her vanilla latte were an embarrassment of excess. The sort that made Houser's skin crawl. If anything, the person who stole her cell and used it to charge shit was *more responsible* in their spending than Bea.

Jon would spend a hundred grand to scratch an itch, but he wouldn't drop a dollar to try and make someone think he was better than he was. Wouldn't waste money trying to fill whatever emptiness he had inside him, either — that's what booze was for.

As Houser grew restless in the Blacklander Jon bought him to match his own while staying on the island — midnight blue to Jon's silver — and found nothing on his tablet no matter how deeply he dug into the digital dirt, he started adding weight to the thought that something seemed somehow *off* about the whole damned island.

Houser couldn't remember much before the accident, and that bothered him, more by the minute. According to Jon, who had spoken with Liz Heller, she had given him a flash drive — a flash drive with something that scared her. Now that flash drive was conveniently missing. He wondered if it had been on him during the accident, or if maybe it had been in his hotel room, after he apparently "crashed through the glass after drinking too much."

That doesn't sound like me. I crash into shit when I mean it.

He had to find out what happened to the flash drive. Had the police found it? Were Paladin's island "army" after it, and did they find it? Were they the ones who trashed his hotel room and broke the glass door?

Houser couldn't help but wonder if the flash drive, or its contents, had anything to do with Liz Heller's death.

Sure, Bruce Henderson went into the woman's house and killed both her and her son before turning his gun on himself, but it seemed too *convenient.* It sang in the right key, but in the same way those software singers at the top of the charts sounded a little too perfect. Even in the best of those songs, a listener could tell when the voice wasn't real.

Houser hated conspiracy theories. As a cop and private investigator, he'd consistently seen that things rarely rose to the level of complicated schemes. Most people, and organizations, were too stupid, and too ineffectual to design, let alone maintain, elaborate machinations. Most often, cases were solved by the simplest, most obvious of answers. A woman was found dead in her home — the husband or ex was guilty nine times out of ten. Elaborate mysteries were for online serials and Hollywood.

But something about the island, its missing people, the sudden eruptions of violence, its security force, and the cameras on every fucking street corner, all lent credence to any number of possible conspiracies. Houser loved solving a good mystery, almost more than anything else.

Did Henderson have something to do with whatever was on the missing flash drive? It was possible he had gone to Heller's house, not out of vengeance for his son's death, but for some other reason relating to the drive. Maybe he was what had Liz Heller so spooked.

As Houser turned the idea, searching for holes, it quickly grew leaky. According to the news, Henderson went to the house just after the shootings, and tried to attack Alex Heller with a bat. Clearly the man had snapped long before trading his bat for a gun. Perhaps it was as uncomplicated as his being upset about Roger Heller shooting his kid. Shit made sense.

He was also pints past sloshed at the time of the murders, with a blood-alcohol level of .21. And a habitual drunk. Alcohol plus anger plus loaded weapon usually equaled something awful — a simple equation that made more sense than any plots Houser might write inside his mind.

As he watched Milo's house, waiting for something, he started feeling stupid, like he was looking for a mystery that wasn't really there. It was just afternoon. For all he knew, the kid was sitting in his room playing a video game with no intention of leaving for the remainder of the day, and maybe the day after that. Houser was likely wasting time on a hunch whose probability dimmed by the minute.

Houser's web surfing turned up nothing useful on Stephen or Beatrice Anderson, other than her ridiculous spending, so he decided to do a bit of digging on Milo himself before calling it quits and driving from the cove. He turned his eyes to the tablet, swiped a finger across the glass, and started his search.

Houser looked up from the first page of potential results to check on the house, just as Milo's front door exploded open. The kid ran to the side yard, swung onto his bike, which was already leaning against the garage, then shot like a rocket from driveway to street.

Shit.

Houser tossed his tablet on the floor, gunned the Blacklander, and pulled out from the curb, hoping like hell he could trail the kid without being seen. That, of course, would depend on whether Milo kept to the main streets, or went off-road into any of the many thickets surrounding the area.

He followed the kid, keeping his distance and hoping Milo wouldn't turn around and see the slow-moving truck behind him. Fortunately for Houser, the kid kept his eyes in front. He was also hauling ass, so Houser was able to maintain a reasonable speed rather than going suspiciously slow. Still, he was going leisurely enough that a few impatient drivers decided to pass him. Mercifully, none honked.

Unfortunately for Houser, just as their road split in two, Milo chose a third direction, pedaling straight into the woods. The truck's GPS showed nothing but woods sprawling all the way to the island's northeastern coast. It didn't seem as if Milo was taking a shortcut to somewhere, but rather, the woods were his destination.

What the hell?

He pulled the Blacklander to a stop where Milo rode in. No natural bike path, just a wall of dirt and trees. He wondered if the kid figured out he was being followed, then made for the woods to disappear, maybe surface on the other side and ride without a shadow. He might be hiding in the shadows, waiting to see if Houser would follow.

Houser didn't care if he'd been made. If he was busted, so be it. He'd figure out what to say once the kid confronted him. Hell, he might even tell the truth. Sometimes, people were surprisingly forthcoming once you laid your cards face-up on the table. Sometimes, they were even willing to help.

He parked and got out, deciding to follow Milo on foot, hoping the kid wasn't going too fast to keep up with. He traded concrete for dirt, then stepped into the thick woods, moving cautiously along the uneven, leaf-littered ground, going slower than he wanted since he was afraid to make the slightest misstep and risk injuring his right knee. Despite his caution, his knee felt surprisingly stable, muscles and ligaments supporting his weight and working effortlessly with the prosthetic leg and foot as if he was born with it.

Houser scanned the forest, growing quickly dark as the noonday sun sought harbor behind the clouds and foliage thickened above. Three hundred yards ahead, he saw Milo, no longer riding, but walking alongside his bike. Houser followed, surprised by the stability he felt from both his right knee and leg. As Milo crossed a hill, Houser picked up his pace, not wanting to lose sight for too long and risk the kid disappearing completely.

He stopped at the top of the hill and looked down, catching sight of Milo, who had stopped moving.

Houser's heart leapt in his throat, certain Milo stopped and saw him. He ducked behind a tree, his right leg slipping and nearly surrendering under his shifting weight. He managed to right himself, but not without a twitch of pain hammering his right knee, maybe suggesting a sprain or tear to his MCL or ACL.

Shit.

Houser stopped, his back to the tree, and tested the weight on his leg to make sure his knee would support it. It did. He waited through another moment, then peeked out around the tree to see Milo still standing in his spot, seemingly oblivious to his tail.

Then Houser saw why.

Milo wasn't alone. He was standing with a disheveled looking guy, so rail-thin it was even obvious beneath his over-sized brown coat. He wore a dark blue cap with long, unkempt, blond hair sticking out from the sides and back. The guy looked like the crazy vagrants Houser sometimes ran into back when he was a cop — people who had fallen so far off the grid, they no longer even pretended to try fitting in.

Who the hell is this guy?

He lifted his cell and started taking pictures, thinking it fitting that the only reason he spotted Milo was because he saw the kid taking pictures of Jon.

The crazy looking man reached into his jacket and retrieved something too small for Houser to identify from so far away. Milo pocketed the item quickly, as if it were drugs or some other contraband.

Well, what the fuck do we have here?

Chapter 4 - Milo Anderson

Milo hated riding out to the woods to meet Don, but the man was paranoid about the closed-circuit cameras littering the island. Given all that had happened, Milo couldn't blame him. Don was particularly eager to see him today, following the Heller funeral. He said he had "something very important" to tell him.

When they met up, Don looked more frazzled than usual. He was wearing a large, brown coat, jeans, and a dark blue Mariners hat. His hair looked like he'd not washed it for days.

"I need you to do something," he said immediately, the second Milo stepped into the clearing.

"What?"

"I need you to get into Alex Heller's house."

"What?"

"Your friend, Alex Heller. Did he ever give you a key or anything?"

"No," Milo said. "Why do you need to get into his house?"

"I need you to find something. A flash drive."

Milo took a step back, confused. "What the hell are you talking about?"

Don looked around, as if he expected someone to be watching, or for a squad of cops or Paladin officers to rush them at any moment.

"Roger Heller said he had a flash drive for me to see, something that would blow my mind. A day before the shootings."

"Wait, you knew Alex's dad? Why didn't you tell me that before?"

"I didn't want you telling Alex. Now," he shrugged as if it wasn't a horrible thing to say, "it doesn't matter."

"Why not? You think Alex would've ratted me out?"

"I don't know what he would've done. I don't know him. I know you. I trust you."

"How did you know Roger?"

"I didn't know him in person. He found me on an online forum where I was posting stuff about missing people. He messaged me, saying he was onto something, but was vague. He kept trying to meet me, but I was suspicious, thinking maybe he was trying to flush me into the open, since people on the forum didn't know who I was. The night before he shot up the school, he reached out and told me about a flash drive he had. He wouldn't tell me how he got it, or what was on it, other than it 'would blow my mind.'"

"Shit." Milo was barely able to believe it. "Do you think it was legit? I mean, Mr. Heller did snap and shoot up his class. Maybe ..."

Don's expression soured into anger. "Even with all that's happened, you *still* think Roger Heller meant to shoot those poor kids?"

Milo felt awkward, as if voicing doubts would crush the man's spirits. He believed Don was onto something, and there were definitely weird things happening on Hamilton, with more probably brewing. But Milo wasn't sure if it was some complex conspiracy-like Don was suggesting in his vague emails and documents, or something else. Maybe something simpler.

Rather than try to articulate his doubts, he said what Don wanted to hear. "No, I don't think he *meant* to shoot the kids. And yes, something's definitely going on. I was just wondering if Roger would have really known anything worth knowing. I mean, he was a teacher. How would he even have come across anything?"

"Well, let's see, Milo." Don paced, and his voice rose in pitch, inching toward frantic. "Roger killed himself, and then Henderson shot his son and wife before killing himself. That doesn't seem a bit *convenient* to you? Like maybe he was onto something big that someone else didn't want out there?"

"You're right," Milo said, more to calm Don than truly agreeing.

"Good." Don swallowed then lowered his voice. "I need you to break into his house and see if you can find it. I would do it myself, but if people see me sniffing around the house, Paladin will be there in minutes. If they bust me, I'm dead, Milo. They'll realize I'm Cody, along with the other dozen aliases I use online."

"And if they bust me, you don't think *I'll* get in trouble?" Milo shot back. "If you think they, whoever *they* are, killed the Heller family, what's to stop them from killing me? I'm just one person, pretty easy to silence."

"If you get caught, you can make up something. Say you went to get a game you lent Alex or some shit, I don't know. You were friends, we weren't. You have an easy excuse to be in there that I never will. I wouldn't ask you otherwise. Here, I have something to help you break-in." Don reached into his coat and handed Milo a black pouch.

He looked inside. It was a thin black strip, about the size and shape of a stick of gum.

"It's a skeleton key I had made. It *should* open the door."

"And what if it doesn't?" Milo slipped the pouch into his pants pocket, wanting to get it out of sight immediately as if Don handed him a loaded gun.

"Then find a way in." Don's stone-cold stare pierced Milo and filled his body with chills.

Chapter 5 - Chief Kevin Brady

Chief Kevin Brady was nursing the thought of hitting Earl's for a hot lunch when his cell buzzed with a call that turned daydreams of Earl's "World Famous Chili" from a rumble in his tummy to a thick and sudden sour in his stomach.

It was Shaw Jackson, a former deputy who retired from the department to work as a tugboat operator. "Hey, Brady, I think you ought to get down to the marina."

"What is it?" The knife in his gut knew why Jackson was calling, and the tone in his voice twisted the blade. Jackson sounded scared, his voice near trembling with a current of sorrow running right through it. He sounded nothing like the jovial Paul Bunyan Brady once worked with.

"Is it ...?" Brady asked, not needing to finish the question. They both knew he meant Christina. If Jackson found her while out on his boat, it was bad news. Brady wanted to ask, wanted confirmation, but didn't dare speak his daughter's name. As long as he didn't know for certain, Brady could pretend his little girl was still alive — that she'd not been found the same way she always was in his nightmares.

"I don't know, but I wanted to call you first, so those Paladin fucks don't hear it on the radio and try calling dibs."

"Where are you?" Brady asked, wondering if those Paladin fucks could hear their conversation anyway.

"Down at slip seventeen, the usual spot. I have Jerry watching to make sure no one comes snooping."

"Okay," Brady said. "I'm on my way."

He was five minutes from the marina, but the ride felt like an hour, with every passing moment another nail in little Christina's coffin.

It had been nearly six months since his daughter went missing. She vanished one night while Brady was working late and his wife was sleeping. He'd come home and thought the front door was locked but couldn't be certain since he was so dead-ass tired. He pressed the button on his cell to open the door, barely paying attention. He had no idea whether the light was already green before he pushed his way through the doorway.

Brady had gone upstairs to kiss his children goodnight, but Christina was gone. He went into his son's room, to see if maybe they'd had a "sleepover" in there, like they sometimes did when he worked late. She wasn't there. When he went to his bedroom and saw Molly sleeping alone, he *knew* Christina was gone.

The search was exhaustive, as were all the searches for missing people on the island. This one more so. They'd gone to every house, brought in suspects for questioning, and even sent dive teams into the caves on the island's north end, where bodies would sometimes wind up after the currents swept them in like floating garbage.

The girl was gone, vanished like so many others over the years. Most of the missing were chalked up to runaways or suicides washed to sea, but not a five-year-old. Someone had taken her. It was the only explanation, and not a day went by that Brady didn't feel as if the girl's captor might still be on the island, watching him, enjoying the torment he managed to inflict on the chief.

Despite the odds, Brady believed he would find her, or at least refused to believe he wouldn't. Not a day passed when Brady didn't spend it harboring hope that Christina would be returned to his family alive.

You heard of cases on the news, some whack job kidnapping a kid and keeping her prisoner for years. Sometimes it was a pervert, but other times, it was some misguided soul desperate for a child they couldn't have. If someone had taken Christina, Brady hoped it was the latter scenario — unlikely as it might be — and that she might someday return, physically unharmed, back into the loving arms of her family.

Brady was a cop, who had seen enough shit to erode his ability to hope, but he loved Christina enough to stitch some make-piece version of hope together. If anything, though, hope had done more damage than good, decaying his marriage and ripping into his wife's sanity.

Hope was a cruel fucker.

And now, as Brady pulled into the marina, the part of him which had slowly resigned itself to his little girl being dead wanted to know for sure.

A tiny part of him — a part Brady hated — almost *wanted* the body to be hers, just to finally silence the cruel hope still shredding his family to pieces. If the body was Christina's, maybe they could find a way to finally shove the horror behind them and move on.

Or maybe it would be the final blow to push Molly over the edge.

Brady climbed from his cruiser and headed over to Jackson's tugboat, where the large man waited with a solemn look on his oversized face.

Brady cleared his throat. "Is it her?"

"I don't know. Come look."

Planks squeaked beneath Brady's feet as he followed Jackson onto the boat.

Jackson said, "I was pulling some asshole on a schooner

from near the caves — why the fuck he was trying to go in there, I don't know — when I spotted her, floating. I didn't say anything, waited until the asshole left, then went back, so me and Jerry are the only ones who know."

Jackson turned back to Brady.

Brady was silent. He followed Jackson into the cabin where he saw the lump wrapped in a gray wool blanket. Jackson bent to pull the blanket to the side. Hollow splashes slapping the tugboat's hull seemed to slow, sloshing the wooziness stewing the chief's gut. Brady imagined his daughter's dead eyes, if she still had any, staring back. He thought of Molly demanding that he take her to the morgue to identify their daughter.

Jackson pulled the blanket aside, revealing the nude girl's grayish remains. Her hair was dark, like Christina's, but the face was dusky, bruised, and cut in several places — signs of mutilation, not from sea life — which caused his heart to ache even more, no matter who the child was. The wounds, along with the slight bloating in the girl's flesh, made it too hard to tell for certain if it was Christina.

Brady bent for a closer look as Jackson stood up and moved to the side.

It looked, on first appearances, as if the girl had been dead anywhere from a few days to a couple of weeks. If it was Christina, someone had probably kept her prisoner all this time and only recently killed her. Another kid could have gone missing, but Brady tried thinking back on all the missing children and couldn't recall any so young. At least not recently, or who couldn't be attributed to a parent maybe running off with their child.

Brady would have to wait for the medical examiner on the mainland to check against Christina's dental records. He reached down and pulled the girl's rubbery blue lips aside, to make sure her teeth were there, and to see if they looked like Christina's.

When his daughter disappeared, she had yet to lose any of her baby teeth. It seemed the bloated body was filled with baby teeth, too. About the same age.

Brady looked at Jackson. "Can you bring me to the mainland? I need to get her body to the ME, and don't want to attract any attention."

"Sure thing," Jackson said.

Brady got on his radio and called the medical examiner's cell. "I'm bringing you a body, and I need this quiet until I get there, okay?"

"Of course."

"Can you meet me at the docks? I'd rather not call the local police."

Dirk Holstrum agreed, thankfully without a battery questions. Holstrum was familiar enough with Brady to know he wouldn't request a favor like that without a damned good reason.

Brady killed the call, looked at the dead child, feeling his life's void stretching wider, growing darker, and getting deeper.

The tugboat held no closure. There were no answers yet.

Nothing but more fucking hope.

Chapter 6 - Milo Anderson

Milo's heart thundered. He figured the key wouldn't work, and he'd have to break a window or something. And if he had to do that, he couldn't imagine going through with it, despite his promise to Don. There was something weird about breaking his best friend's window, even if his best friend was in the ground.

He pulled the black strip from the pouch, ready to press it to the box on the back door of Alex Heller's house. His body's every fiber knew wouldn't work. He wouldn't get in the door … but he would get busted. His dad would be so pissed, driving down to the boat slips and pulling him from jail. He swallowed, dug his nails into his arm for several furious scratches in each direction, then pressed the strip to the box.

To Milo's shock, the green light lit, the lock clicked, and the knob twisted. The door flew open, snapping the yellow police tape tightly strung across the threshold, proving that someone had breached the house. He wished he'd thought to bring gloves, but then again, he could always say that *of course* his prints were all over the place — he had practically grown up at the Hellers'.

He stepped inside the house and gasped. The dozens of

brown boxes piled in tiny mountains and peppered through the living room and kitchen, packed and ready to go, were now spilled into disarray, contents strewn across the house as if thieves had pillaged the place.

"What the hell?" He started sifting through their belongings.

Was someone else here looking for the flash drive, too?

Milo didn't want Don to be right, but what if he was? A chill ran through him as he looked for the flash drive. Finding something so small in a mountain of stuff seemed like it could take all day. And night. But there was no way in hell he could stay that long. Even if there *was* a flash drive, couldn't it have been found already?

Milo couldn't shake the thought that every second spent in the house was borrowed, and that somehow, the police or Paladin Security would grow that much closer to knowing he was inside. His heart pounded, expecting the front door to explode open at any moment.

He had to be quick and look for any items that might have been in Roger's office. Digging through the Hellers' life was an invasion of privacy. Milo hated to think he might find a vibrator or something else equally personal. While he might have thought it hot for Mrs. Heller to own a sex device at one time, that thrill faded with her murder.

After Milo searched through a good chunk of stuff that looked like it was from Roger's office, he decided to head upstairs to see if anything was left behind. He froze mid-stride, swallowing as he saw blood in the hallway — a crimson trail leading into Aubrey's room. He followed the trail and nearly vomited as he saw more blood caked into the carpet.

His stomach churned and legs wobbled. He had to slap his hand against the wall to steady himself.

Oh, my God, so much blood.

Why didn't the police clean it?

Seeing the blood, and so much of it, somehow sickened

Milo's already soured reality. It wasn't just blood from a wound, it was blood from a murder, and not just any murder, but the massacre of his best friend and his family. Maybe in a way, Mr. Heller had been murdered, too.

Can't think about that now.

So much blood — once inside his best friend and his best friend's mother — now stained the carpet before him. A surreal violation.

Milo wasn't sure if he was more scared or angry, but his clenched fists hovered by his side as he deeply inhaled and exhaled, chewing his lip as he narrowed his eyes at the room. He swallowed, then turned and stepped back into the hallway, quietly closing the door behind him.

He finished walking the hall and stepped into the master bedroom, where there was an even larger mess, maybe the biggest so far: boxes overturned, sheets torn from the bed, and a mattress ripped open, gutted like a fish from Schooner Bay.

Someone was definitely looking for something.

Sorrow seeped through Milo's anger as overwhelm threatened to send him from the room. He gathered his breath, then turned to leave. Something pulled his attention back to the chaos, then yanked it, drawing his eyes toward an old copy of *The Princess Bride.*

Pick it up, his inner voice said.

Milo crossed the room, remembering the sweet, but corny, engagement story he'd heard many times before from Alex, Mr. and Mrs. Heller, and even one time from Katie, as if he hadn't already heard it more times than he could count, straight from the tap.

There wasn't a flash drive in the book. That would have been too convenient. But there *was* a bookmark with something written on it, and in Roger's handwriting. Milo wiped the blur from his eyes, then stared down at the list of names. As he ran down the list, his heart fell into his gut with the sickening realization that the names belonged to the victims. Well, all of the bodies except Sarah Hughes, who had been struck by a stray bullet in the next classroom and was likely an accidental victim, and Jessica. Manny wasn't on the list, either.

It was Roger Heller's "To Kill" list.

All the others on the list, were dead. Except one name.

The book fell from Milo's fingers and onto the floor.

Katie.

He meant to kill Katie, maybe instead of Manny!

Milo swallowed, then tried to swallow again, but couldn't. He tried catching his breath for nearly half a minute before he started to suck air through his teeth, still staring at the scrap of paper in his trembling hand.

Milo wasn't exactly sure of the list's meaning, but it felt like a massive discovery that surely meant *something*. He *had* to get the list to Don.

Roger had definitely written the list. Milo had stared at the teacher's whiteboard through enough mornings to know Mr. Heller's handwriting. And if he *had* written the list, he no doubt intended to shoot his victims. The murders weren't random, and Milo could no longer pretend they had been. Roger Heller went to school that morning with the full intention of ending every life on his list.

But why?

And why is Katie on the list? Why hadn't he shot her as planned? Why did he instead shoot Jessica?

Milo heard the front door open downstairs, immediately followed by the sharp crackling of radios — the kind worn by both cops and Paladin officers.

Shit!

Milo looked around, wondering what the hell to do as he heard at least two men talking back and forth. There was no urgency in their tone, and they didn't seem to be there for him. They were laughing, but he couldn't hear what they were laughing about.

Why are they here?

Do they know I'm here?

Should I just stay put?

Do I try and get away?

Milo turned to the window. He could climb out and drop to the ground. A second story fall straight into the grass shouldn't hurt too much. He went to the window, chills through his body as he stepped across the blood-caked carpet, and pulled at the window. It wouldn't budge.

Fu-uck!

Footsteps echoed up the stairs. A man said, "Yeah, this is where it happened."

Shit, they're coming in here!

Milo's heart pounded faster. Cold copper coated his tongue as he looked around the room. His only option was racing to the closet and hoping like hell they wouldn't open it.

He dashed across the room, tore the door open, slipped inside, then closed it quietly behind him just as the two men entered the room.

"Yeah, this is where we found the girl. She was holding onto her dead brother's hand. Fucking heartbreaking."

"Shit," the second man said.

Milo couldn't tell if they were Hamilton or Paladin officers.

The list felt hot in his hand, like maybe it was what they were looking for. Unless they were also there for the flash drive. In either case, he couldn't let them find him in the closet clutching the list. It would look many kinds of bad, and Milo could easily imagine himself as a sudden suspect, a collaborator in the shootings. Weren't the police always hoping to find a second suspect they could charge in these sorts of cases?

He carefully slid it into his back pocket, praying he'd be able to safely flee the house and find Don.

"And this is where Henderson offed himself?"

"Yup."

"Fucking scumbag."

"Amen."

"What about over here?" one of the men said, walking toward the closet.

Oh, shit, they're going to open the door.

Please don't open the door, please don't …

Shattering glass, which sounded like it came from out in front of the house, grabbed their attention.

"Shit, what was that?"

Footsteps headed toward the window. "You see anything?"

"Our car is on fire!"

"What?"

The men ran from the room then thudded downstairs.

Milo had no idea what to do — stay and hope the men didn't return or seize the opportunity while they were distracted and get the hell out of Alex's house, hoping nobody else was waiting downstairs.

Milo went with Option B and ran as if his life depended on it. He raced over the blood, through the hall, then down the stairs, feet loudly clomping with every step, giving no regard to his volume, banking on the officers still being occupied out front.

Once downstairs, Milo raced toward the back door, every inch feeling like a mile, certain that each second would be the one where "Freeze!" was being screamed behind him.

Milo reached the back door, opened it, and ran straight into the same giant black dude who followed Jon Conway around like a pit bull. He fell to the ground, losing a yelp. Sprawled on his ass, he looked up.

Conway's friend reached down and held his hand out for Milo. "Come with me."

It wasn't a request.

Chapter 7 - Jon Conway

Jon zipped along the coastline, smiling, even though his destination was anywhere but happy. He couldn't believe he was driving a Blacklander of all things. Toyota's evolution of the Blacklander (no gas!), was by all accounts an awesome SUV and reminded him of his father's old Land Cruiser — the first vehicle Jon drove up and along the island's steepest hills.

He was willing to drive the Toyota to prove he didn't *need* a Porsche, but of course, he still missed flying down the coast in a car that burned gas without apology. He didn't *need* a 924 Spyder — though there was nothing in the world he'd rather drive. Hell, even a Boxter would do. Not that the two cars were the same, but their weight and diameter were similar, and like every other Porsche, the Boxter's action was perfectly weighted and ridiculously efficient. No wasted motion, not from hand to shifter or brake to throttle.

If he could bear Cassidy's sour look, he would have had one sent to the island. But he couldn't, and he was about as willing to drive a car from the Conway's family garage as he was to schedule a daily root canal — even though the old bathtub in the garage was technically his.

He figured he would rent something, but nearly every experience Jon had ever had with a rental car was bullshit. It was like he was cursed. He had tried it on many occasions, each time swearing it would be the last. Most recently with the Avalon, things were fine, but the time before that was awful. Jon was in Austin, meeting a friend at his lake house. He wanted an SUV and asked for "something like a Tahoe." Apparently, a PT Cruiser was "something like a Tahoe," though Jon thought the PT should have stopped rolling down the line a while back. His dissatisfaction with the selection quickly turned into a mild argument about the many short-comings of Happy Driver Rentals.

Jon wasn't expecting anyone to kiss his ass because he was Jon Conway, but the frustrated asshole stuck behind the counter seemed determined to nudge their mild disagree-ment into a full-blown fight *because* of his last name. In this particular case, Jon didn't want to argue, or fight, and defi-nitely didn't want to end up on a fucking LiveLyfe page with some bullshit caption about him being a spoiled rotten, silver-spooned celebrity, so he took the PT Cruiser. The second he climbed inside he noticed a bunch of bright orange shit stains smearing the back seat, several missing levers and knobs, a cabin that smelled like piss, ass, and vomit, and about a foot of weather-stripping missing from the door.

Once Jon realized he'd be staying on the island a while, buying was a no-brainer. Still, mostly because of Cassidy, he tried first with a rental, standing in line for half an hour, before leaving pissed. He went back to his hotel and ordered a pair of Blacklanders, one for him and another for Houser. He would have gladly ordered one for Cassidy, but there was no mystery about how that would go over.

Both SUVs were waiting at Jon's hotel before the sun sank in the sky.

He chose the Blacklander because it gave him something

to drive that was a neater fit with the new life he was easing into more by the day.

Cassidy tried making Jon feel bad for dropping so much cash on a set of new SUVs just because he could, but what the hell was money for if not spending? That was *her* problem, not his. She could enjoy a life with him as much as she wanted and pluck all the ripe fruit hanging from his tree. It was too bad she had such an aversion to wealth, as if its very nature corrupted everything. Cass was wrong — Jon had tasted the fruit, and it was delicious.

Emma, on the other hand, was too young to be affected and thoroughly enjoyed everything Jon was permitted to give her. He had a hard time not loving her for this, even more than he already did.

Driving Emma around the island was now one of his favorite things. It helped him see his first home as if for the first time. Jon didn't realize it, until Emma was sitting in the back of the Blacklander while the two of them zipped from one side of the island to the other a few days earlier, but he had never been alone with a child in a car. He didn't count time spent with Leslie Wyoming — a surprisingly gifted tween who starred in *Glass Houses* with him and Jessie Riley — since that car went nowhere and was surrounded by cameras.

Being in a car with a kid was awkward at first, not knowing what he should say to someone he barely knew and who was so much younger than him. Cassidy had always been the buffer between them. Without her, Jon was left to navigate conversation on his own.

Eventually, after a few of the lamest jokes to ever leave his mouth, conversation flowed, like river to ocean. Once Emma started talking, she found it hard to stop.

Jon loved driving with her. It gave him a chance to see the world, as well as the island, through her innocent eyes. What he saw was beautiful and made him think that perhaps he'd allowed himself to grow too jaded. His filter had kept him from enjoying things for what they were.

It wasn't just the world she saw differently. She also saw *him* differently than anyone else. Sure, Emma had seemed impressed with his stardom when they first met, a bit, but now she treated him like something else entirely — family. And the *good kind* of family, not the version warped by the Conways.

In some ways, Jon wished he could adopt Emma's manner of dealing with people — honestly, without worrying about their hidden agendas, without worrying about saying the wrong things, without worrying about his comments being taken out of context or twisted by the media.

As he drove to The Gardens and was about to face off with his father, once and for all, Jon decided it was time to do just that — tell his father exactly what he was thinking. There were few things he hated more than arguing with him, but he was certainly looking forward to this one.

It was time.

He deserved answers.

And he was going to get them.

What his father had apparently ordered Warren to do all those years ago — coercing Sarah into keeping Jon's child a secret — was beyond wrong. He had been robbed of what was rightfully his — the chance to decide what was best for *his* life. Sarah might not have been his Happily Ever After, but he deserved the right to see how their tale played out. And Jon deserved to know, and have a relationship with, his daughter.

It was bullshit — bullshit he had been wanting to correct for the last several weeks, ever since Warren spit the truth in his face. Yet, no matter how many times Jon tried calling, he didn't reach him. He'd tried his dad's personal line, his private inbox. He'd even tried going through Hillary, who still worked for Blake all these years later, even though "she still messed up his schedule, and it was still a goddamned question of his sanity why he kept her on payroll."

Jon smiled at his father's almost blind loyalty.

Hillary, like everyone else, was either evasive or in the dark about Blake's whereabouts. Until Mrs. Rasmussen called to tell Jon his father was home, he'd been unable to get in touch. The more time passed, the angrier Jon grew. It was crap, his father avoiding him like he had been. And odd. Blake Conway was many, many things, depending on who was reporting the story, but Jon couldn't imagine even his father's fiercest critics calling the man a coward. For his father to be so completely MIA, and after the worst tragedy on island record, didn't strike Jon as odd so much as oddly conspiratorial.

He would have bet both balls that Warren was somehow behind his father's distance. His brother was an asshole, and stupidly jealous for no reason at all. Always had been, ever since they were kids. He was twelve years older than Jon — just old enough to suffer from regular outbreaks of envy, as if Jon had personally ruined his life. Of course, Jon could understand a bit of it — Warren blamed him, and perhaps rightfully so — for their mother's death during Jon's birth. But it wasn't as if Jon chose to be born. Just because he never had the chance to know his real mother didn't mean he didn't miss her. Not having a mother left a permanent void in him, but that didn't mean he went around making other people's lives miserable because of it.

But it wasn't just their mother who created a gulf between Warren and Jon. Some of it was also their father.

No matter how tightly Warren clutched the reigns of Conway Industries, claiming family fortune and legacy for himself, he remained almost vigilantly jealous of Jon, as though he held a spot in their father's heart that Warren could never worm his way into, no matter how many science fairs or government contracts he won.

Jon might have felt some sympathy for Warren's situation — even if it mirrored his own so many times, that feeling of being second in his father's eyes — if Warren hadn't allowed envy to turn him into such a dick.

Jealousy, so far as Jon saw it, was the weakest of all emotions. A competent, self-confident person wasn't jealous, since jealousy was a symptom of neurotic insecurity. As the CEO for one of the largest companies in the world, Warren shouldn't have been capable of such spite, yet Jon saw more insecurity and pettiness in Warren than he had in the past ten years he'd spent in Hollywood — the vainest place on Earth.

Warren imagined himself similar to Blake and saw Jon as the black sheep who didn't belong. But that was absurd. Jon knew both the public and private versions of his father well. Neither were like either of his sons.

Blake Conway wasn't just a successful father with a long shadow, though. He was an icon, currently number seven on the *Forbes* list of billionaires, up from #number ninety-eight just three years before. His trajectory was unparalleled, and many people from Wall Street to Silicon Valley figured he'd be in the top five by decade's end, if not sooner. Blake Conway was so admired a figure, he wasn't just quoted in business circles, his quotes also lit the walls of LiveLyfe accounts all over the world. He was one of the few billionaires who was a household name, even among people who had never read a business article in their lives. His vision of an evolved humanity was slowly becoming the zeitgeist of the moment.

The man had lived a colorful life, and whenever someone put a mic in front of him, he'd tell equally vibrant stories.

One of the favorites was from when he was just seven years old. His father loaded him into the back of his truck, drove him down from The Gardens to the beach, dropped him off at the boardwalk — right in between a pair of empty boat slips —told him he was responsible for finding his way back home, then then drove off.

This wasn't his father's idea of punishment. No, Billy

Conway just thought it was important to teach his son a bit of self-reliance.

It took Blake most of the day to find his way back to The Gardens, but he did.

When he reached the top, stumbling through the gates and practically collapsing through the front door, Blake didn't stop to say hello to his father. He went into the kitchen, pulled two cookies from the jar, said, "Because I earned them," then marched upstairs to his room and slept for twelve hours straight. To this day, Blake didn't remember exactly how he managed to find his way home, but he remembered the taste of the cookies, and had never tasted one better since.

Few people in the world — and Jon knew none personally — were able to stand up to Blake Conway and win. Jon knew several studio heads, and even some agents, who seemed to practically live at the peak of Mount Olympus, decreeing orders with everyone tripping all over themselves to obey, but he had never come close to meeting his father's verbal equal. The man was a master of words and an elegant manipulator, always able to spin the tables toward his side of any argument while moving strings as if he had a puppeteer above him.

Jon drove through the gate's entrance, and after a quick greeting to Carl, parked the Blacklander in front of the Conway estate.

No sign of Warren, or his asshole Bentley.

Jon went to the front door and readied himself to knock, but Mrs. Rasmussen opened it wide before he could.

"Well, good evening, Mr. Conway," she said.

"Well, hello to you, Madge." He felt instantly better, ignoring her formal greeting and smiling at the only woman he'd known as long as himself. "I take it he's still here?"

"Hasn't budged." She turned and nodded down the immediate hallway. "He went into his office about fifteen minutes ago. Just remember, you promised you wouldn't rat me out. You're only here because you thought he might be."

Jon sighed. "Really? After all this time?" He shook his head. "I'm so disappointed."

"Well, I'm sure you'll get over it." She smiled. "In the meantime, I'd like to fall asleep tonight knowing I'll still have a job when I wake up. Your father's always been kind to me, but you know how he feels about loyalty. And those willing to break it. Things aren't always a happy game of Monopoly when you Conways are together, you know. I'm sure you don't need a reminder of how you left the last time you were here."

Jon looked at his feet, remembering how slobbering drunk he was, when he had come over to rip the skin from Warren's face, then left feeling gutted — the night he first had sex with Cassidy.

"I'm sorry about that," Jon said. "I'm sure that wasn't fun to watch." He smiled. "But you know that's mostly Warren's fault for being such an ass."

"It's never fun to watch the people you love hurting, Mr. Conway. Certainly not you."

She patted Jon on the shoulder, then stepped to the side, opened the door all the way, and gestured down the hall as if Jon needed a prompt to find Blake's office.

He nodded, said thanks, then approached his father's most private place in the world.

Jon knocked, softly at first, then harder. Minutes passed with no one at the door. He knocked harder, and louder. After another two minutes of silence, Jon grew just agitated enough to pull his foot back and launch it hard into the bottom of the door.

The door — alloy, not wood like the rest of the house — hurt his foot. He yanked it back, wincing, then hopped on one heel, trying to throttle his pain.

What the fuck, Father?

There was no use asking Mrs. Rasmussen for a key. She didn't have one. Blake's office was the one place in the estate she never straightened or had the cleaning crew do it for her.

No one entered Blake's office but him, and no one ever had. Even as boys, their father's office was the one place in all the grounds that was one hundred percent off-limits.

"Father!" Jon yelled, his frustration growing into anger at being ignored.

He heard a sound, then turned to see Mrs. Rasmussen standing behind him.

"Trouble?"

Jon turned to her. "Are you *sure* he's here?"

"Positive. He couldn't have left. No one came down the hallway. I've been keeping an eye out for you and would have seen him leave if he had. The door definitely hasn't opened."

"No way he could've snuck out?" Jon asked, as though she might be senile.

Mrs. Rasmussen shook her head no, then set her hand on Jon's arm and spoke in a nervous whisper. "Maybe he wants to be alone?"

"Bullshit," Jon said. "Father!"

He turned to Mrs. Rasmussen. "Would you mind leaving? I'd like to take care of this myself."

Mrs. Rasmussen swallowed, smiled, then turned and walked down the hallway toward the foyer. Jon could feel how much she hated what he was about to do, but they both knew there was no way of stopping him.

He *would* figure out the security code.

Jon started punching every combination he could think of into the keypad which displayed a full set of both numbers and letters, but nothing worked. Every attempt either preceded or followed a sharp punch or kick to the door, along with a bellow as Jon hollered for his father.

Finally, on a whim, he found four letters that worked.

EMMA.

Jon's daughter.

When did he start caring about the granddaughter he was trying to hide?

The alloy door to his father's office whooshed open.

Jon stepped inside. He wasn't sure exactly what he expected, but what he saw wasn't it. He imagined that his father's office would be large, with many monitors and bleeding-edge technology. Instead, the room was tiny. Almost a closet. A single glass monitor ran the length of the wall, installed above a long desk. Blake's tablet was on the desk along with his cell. His father was nowhere.

He never leaves his phone.

Suddenly, Jon felt like he wasn't alone, like his father was nearby, maybe even watching. A chill ran through him as he looked around, heart racing.

Jon spotted a single photo sticking out from beneath his father's tablet, then pulled it loose. He stared at the photo, confused. It looked like Emma's most recent school photo.

What the hell?

Epilogue

Sarah woke to the doctor with blond hair holding a small paper cup filled with pills. "Take these."

"I don't want to." Her voice was gravelly, her head full of fuzz. She tried thinking about how long it had been since she had woken from the dead.

A week? Two weeks? It was hard to tell.

The doctors kept coming into the room and handing her pills. Sometimes they gave her capsules which they said were like food. Other times, water. They said the medicine was for healing her insides, but all they did, so far as Sarah could tell, was make her sleep, for what seemed like longer each time.

"I can give you an injection if you prefer." The offer was made without a trace of malice or threat in his voice.

"Where am I?"

"You know I can't tell you that."

"Yeah, yeah." She'd seen three doctors at her count, two men and one woman, and they all played the same silence game, no matter the variety of her questions or order asked.

Each time Sarah heard some variant of, "Sorry, I can't tell you that."

"Please," she begged. "Tell me *something*."

The doctor shook his head. "I'm sorry, I can't."

Sarah lost it.

"You've gotta be kidding me!" she screamed. "Why are you doing this? Why even save me? Why take care of me if you're going to keep me locked up? My family must be worried sick! Please, let me talk to them."

Her words were garbled in sobs. The doctor's face, an emotionless mask thus far, started to crack. Sarah was certain she saw a look of concern furrow his brow. She breathed slowly, trying to regain her composure, feeling if she could find the right approach or appeal, the doctor might help her.

"Please," she said, meeting his gaze. "Just tell me *something*."

The doctor, whose name Sarah didn't know, even though she had asked more times than she could count, looked at her with eyes so sad they almost seemed anguished.

"I'm sorry, I can't. But I promise I'll find someone who can give you some answers, okay?"

His eyes were so kind, she nodded. "Thank you."

Still smiling he returned her nod. "But first, you have to take the pills." He handed her a glass of cold water to wash them down, then left the room.

Sarah immediately felt exhausted. Whatever they'd given her was even stronger than last time. She closed her eyes and saw nothing but black.

SARAH WOKE to a man's voice.

"Ah, you're awake." He sounded pleasant and … *familiar*.

She slowly opened her eyes, hardly able to believe what she saw — Blake Conway sitting in the chair beside her.

"Hello, Sarah."

Episode 9

Prologue - Warren Conway (Age 12)

Something was wrong.

Warren's father, Blake Conway, *never* paced.

Yet, here he was, polishing linoleum with his loafers, walking from one end of the New York City hospital room to the other, thousands of miles from home. No longer on vacation, he now pounded the floor in frenzied circles, wrapping his way around the small room, looping from bed to window and back, his face odd, if not haunted.

No, Warren realized, it wasn't *odd* or even *haunted*. Blake Conway wore an expression his son had never seen him wear before.

Blake Conway looked terrified.

"Will you *please* stop pacing?" Warren's mom, Kate, looked up at her husband with pleading eyes. "You're not making this any easier."

Father stopped at the foot of her bed and set his hand on the metal railing. "The anesthesiologist should be here by now, damn it. This is inexcusable." He managed to keep the snarl from his face, though it was still there in his voice. "This would *never* have happened if we had stayed home."

"Don't make a scene, Blake." Mother's quiet glance

ordered her husband to seal his lips and forego drama. Warren rarely saw his father back down from a fight and only did so at Mother's request. The man who seemed to tower over the rest of the world was never worried about *making scenes*. If things weren't his way, there was hell to pay. He was *the* Blake Conway. In New York, he was a visiting king. On Hamilton Island, Warren's father was almost God.

"Seriously," Warren's mom said, her eyes now a deeper shade of pleading, "not now."

"Okay, honey." Father left the foot of Mother's bed and returned to the top, stroking her long, soft hair before leaning down to leave a gentle kiss on her sweat-beaded forehead. "I just can't stand to see you in pain."

"It's okay," Mother said. "I'll be fine. Nothing I haven't done before."

Mother was the only person who could tame Father's fire, the only person who could ever tell him no. Blake collapsed into the short chair beside her long bed, temporarily soothed through the moment's tempest, though Warren knew that wouldn't last long.

Father was still anxious, desperate to storm the hospital hallway outside until he found someone to stare in the eye and find out what in the hell was happening.

Warren wanted Father to storm the hall, too.

This was the first time he had seen his father show fear, but it was also the first time Warren had ever seen his mother in significant pain. He was only a kid, but if Warren had his father's size, or wore his rather sizable crown, he would have been running down the hall already, screaming for someone to help his mother.

Mother's gaze met his. She smiled. "It's okay, baby."

"Okay." Warren looked away because it hurt too much to see her like that. He shifted his attention to the science magazine in his lap.

The glossy pages held several articles of interest — something about the reality of time travel, and one on how science might be able to one day cheaply map a person's DNA so anything that could possibly be wrong with a person could be discovered and, when possible, repaired.

Try as he might, Warren couldn't manage his focus for more than a few paragraphs before his eyes would flit up from the sentence, abandoning words at their period to grab another rare, unguarded glimpse of Blake Conway, proving his Father was mortal like everyone else, showing true fear in the face of something he couldn't control — the birth of his second son.

Warren turned from his mother's anemic smile and stared at the door.

Why isn't someone coming?

They better not let anything happen to my baby brother or Mom.

Come on, Father, get up. Go say something to someone.

But Father stayed sitting, holding Mother's hand and displaying more patience than Warren had ever seen from him before. Warren tried telling himself, as he had all morning, that if Mother wasn't worried, there was no reason for him to be. She had delivered a child before and would know if there was reason for rattled nerves. She didn't seem especially anxious, though Father was practically out of his skin. Mother said she wasn't really nervous, just in pain, and only because no one had yet come to put the needle in her back.

She's done this before, relax. Everything will be fine.

In a couple of days, we'll all be back home, and I'll have a brand new baby brother.

Warren loved being an only child, yet there was a part of him that had always wondered what it would be like to have a sibling, someone to play and grow with. Of course, he was already twelve, so his brother would be too young to share much in common, but still, Warren was excited. It was hard to see Mother's brimming excitement and not absorb her enthusiasm.

With Father always working, things had grown too still in their house, too serious. Quiet like a haunting. Something had slowly but constantly changed in Father over the past few years. While there was a time when he seemed to love spending time with Warren, doing normal things like any other father and son, their time together had started to change.

Father was treating Warren more like an adult, expecting more from him — especially at school and in his many science classes, two of which he took at the high school campus. It was as if overnight, as far as his father was concerned, he had stopped being a kid and was expected to be an adult, even though he wasn't yet ready. Whenever Warren tried to act like a kid — have fun, joke around, or do the sorts of things that once made Father smile and laugh — he would scold his son, telling him to "grow up" and "act his age," even though Warren thought he was.

A few months back, he had gone to his mom, and actually cried — something he could never do in front of Father — and complained about the way things were between him and his dad.

Mother said, "Don't worry, Warren. Your father loves you very much. He's just so involved with work that it's hard for him to let go when he's home. Things will change once your brother is born, you'll see."

She added, "I promise," with a giant smile, then fell uncharacteristically silent.

But he didn't need more. She had given him a peg on which to hang his hopes. Once his baby brother Jonny was born, he would have his old father back.

Warren's attention was savagely ripped from his magazine with a sudden, aching urgency in Father's voice.

"Honey, are you okay?" he cried out.

Warren dropped the magazine into his lap. It fell in a glossy accordion to the floor as he leapt up toward his mother.

She sat bolt upright in bed, arms stabbing out in front of her as she violently inhaled, gasping for breath.

"What's happening?" Warren shrieked as his mother's gaze met his, her face turning a mottled shade of blue.

Father jammed his thumb repeatedly on the bedside button, then tore into the hall, running and screaming, "Help! Please help me! Somebody help my wife!"

Doctors and nurses poured into the hallway then flooded the small room. A stern doctor, with thick eyebrows and a strong but weathered jaw, turned to Father and ordered the king from his room.

"What's happening?" Warren screamed, fear coursing in an unrelenting current through his body.

"I don't know," Father said, surprising Warren with his surrender, fleeing the room and holding his son tight as he held the door with his gaze.

They peered through the window together, though neither could see anything past the huddle of scurrying doctors and nurses.

Warren sat beside Father for nearly an hour, anxiously waiting for any word that might tell them what was happening. For the first twenty-five minutes, Blake made one phone call after another, searching through his contacts, frustrated by how long it took to find each number, keeping each call less than a minute long until finally getting one of the nation's top surgeons, Dr. Westing, to agree he'd fly to New York from Houston immediately.

Will immediately be soon enough? Even if he got a flight right away, we're still talking hours and car travel on top of that.

What if … No, don't think that.

Warren tried reading more of his magazine but could hardly get a few paragraphs before the words were a blur, swallowed by the hundreds of horrible what-ifs that wouldn't stop shuffling through his mind.

What if the baby dies?

What if Mom dies?

He thought a dozen variations of the same, awful terror, each with new and equally horrible scenes, spilling like liquid from the darkest corners of Warren's worry as he pictured a world without Mother, or a life without his new baby brother. Warren knew his father well enough to feel certain that any worst-case scenario promised to twist him into a very bitter man.

And Warren would no doubt become invisible.

At 12:09 a.m., a tall man in soft, blue scrubs stepped through the swinging double doors, holding a surprisingly large and silent baby, wrapped tight in a blue blanket.

Warren's heart swelled at the sight of his little brother. He felt suddenly safe. Joy flooded his body because he knew everything would be okay.

Then he saw the doctor's eyes and knew with a deeper certainty that it wouldn't be.

He swallowed, seeing the cursed truth in his pupils. Father stood beside him, squeezing his shoulder hard as he looked at the doctor holding the newest Conway. Warren looked up and, like in the hospital room, saw the terror and fear on his father's face.

Both Conways could see the reality, the horror of what the doctor was about to tell them.

He handed Blake his new son, the awful *what-if* turned to fact still silent on his lips. But Warren still knew.

"I'm sorry," the doctor said, "Mrs. Conway didn't make it."

Chapter 1 - Sarah Hughes

Sarah stared at Blake Conway, more confused than ever. There he was, the richest man on Hamilton Island, and one of the richest in the world, thick silver hair, bronzed skin, and perfectly tailored dark suit with his trademark red tie all making him look as if he had stepped out from an idling Bentley to take the seat beside her.

Sarah hadn't seen the eldest Conway in a decade, at least not counting his frequent TV and online appearances. Despite their both living on Hamilton, Sarah rarely ran into him. Even when she dated Jon, Blake Conway was out of town and off the island more often than not. In the decade since her first love went off to Hollywood, his father had gone from local legend to a near-mythic global figure, the sort the world hadn't seen since Steve Jobs. Seeing him sitting beside her bed was surreal.

Why is he here?

Sarah tried to sit but did it too fast and sent an ice pick to her brain. She rubbed her head, blinking her eyes as the pain started to subside. "What are you doing here?" Words came out cracked from her dry throat. "Where are we?"

"You're okay." He smiled. "That's what's most important. My people were able to save you."

"What people?" She looked around. Her room looked like any other hospital room in Conway Medical, but Sarah distinctly remembered looking past the curtains and seeing Earth floating in the endless black nothing outside her window. Unless she had gone completely insane, they were in space. "And where are we?"

"We're on a space station," Blake explained, as calmly as if he were announcing the weather.

"What space station?"

"I have a lab in space, at least that's the best way to put it. A safe place where my best scientists can do things we're unable to do on Earth. Cutting edge, state-of-the-art, experimental stuff, Sarah. The stuff that truly matters, and without all the bureaucratic red tape and regulations that can tie our hands and keep us from getting important things done."

"Like bringing people back to life?" Sarah swallowed, nursing the impossible in her mind. "I was dead, wasn't I?"

"What do you remember?" Blake asked his face a blanket of curiosity and wonder. "Bright lights or anything like that?"

"I don't remember much, it's all fuzzy now. Where is my daughter?"

Blake gave her what had to be his friendliest smile. "Emma is fine. She's with your sister and mother."

"Oh, God," Sarah said. "They must be worried sick. Do they know I'm alive? I have to talk to them."

"I'm afraid that's not possible," Blake said. The unfortunate truth soured his smile.

"What do you mean? I have to tell them I'm okay and I'll be home soon."

Sarah saw something in Blake's eyes — behind his crestfallen face — which sent a chill through her body.

No, Sarah suddenly knew, she wouldn't be going home soon. Maybe never again.

"You can't go back, Sarah," Blake filled her fear with truth. "Not for a long time."

"What?" Even unsurprised, air fled her lungs as she forced her breath into a rhythm steady enough to continue. "Why not?"

"Your family believes you're dead. And the world believes you're dead. A victim of a random school shooting. That means it must stay that way … for now."

Blake's warmth turned to vapor, and his eyes darkened into something so cold and callous, Sarah could hardly meet them. She swallowed, searching for the right words, but too many scrambled thoughts turned every word wrong and nudged her toward the edge of a breakdown.

"Why can't I go home? I'm alive!" Sarah was near hysterics. "My family needs me! I have to see Emma."

Blake shifted in his seat, then leaned forward.

"I feel for you, Sarah, I truly do. But before you can go home, there are things we need from you."

She definitely didn't like how *that* sounded at all. "What?"

"What if I told you the weaknesses plaguing humanity were nearing extinction? That cancer, disease, disabilities, deformities, birth defects, dimmed intelligence — all could be forever eliminated? What if aging and death could be paused or stopped, and in some cases, completely reversed? Wouldn't you agree that such impossible-sounding gifts would be what's best for our world?"

It was a question with only one right answer. Yet, Sarah had no idea how to respond. Of course, she was supposed to say *yes*, but Blake Conway was clearly selling something.

Does he really expect a serious answer?

"What does curing cancer have to do with me being up here?"

"Everything." Blake gave her the same smile Sarah had been seeing in interviews forever. "You're part of something remarkable, Sarah. You and your sister, both. You're both a

137

part of the next phase of human evolution. And I'm not talking small steps. I'm talking a series of thousand-year leaps!"

The light was back in Blake's eyes as he stood.

"Now that you're here with us for the foreseeable future, we will no longer be forced to pull you from your life in the middle of the night."

"What the hell are you talking about?" Sarah tucked her knees under her chin, then wrapped her arms around them and balled her fists.

"You have no memories of the tests, do you?" Blake's lips cracked into a wry smile. "Even now, up here?"

"What tests?" Sarah felt as if she were asked to solve a madman's riddle — a madman who had her locked in some secret space lab.

"We've been taking you for a long time now, Sarah, along with others who share similar traits. People we've engineered from birth to be better, more pliable, more receptive to humanity's next phase. Humans require a slight push, a nudge here and there, to fulfill our destiny without being forced to wait through the eons it would take to naturally reach the next rung in our evolution. *That* is where you come in."

"What do you mean, 'engineered from birth?'"

"Let's just say you're not among the first generation of subjects we've been working on."

"Wait? You did something to my mom?"

"You say 'did something' as if it's a negative rather than a positive, Sarah. We only fix what's broken. We've improved everything and continue to do so. We make people better than they could ever be on their own."

Blake's smile grew wider. Proud, in fact.

He asked, "Did you know there's a genetic flaw in your code which makes it impossible for you to conceive? This is true for both you and your sister. Or was, until we fixed you.

Now you have a nice, normal, healthy, intelligent child, don't you?"

Emma!

"Did you do something to my child?"

"As I said, Sarah, I'm only here to help."

"You fucker!" Sarah lashed out and swung her balled fists at Blake, slamming him repeatedly in the side of his head before he had a chance to recognize or defend her attack.

The door swooshed open, and two men in all white raced inside to yank her away from Blake. She screamed, kicked, and squirmed, trying to break free from the bed and race out the door.

You can't escape a space station.

How you going to get back? You going to fly?

You'll never see Earth again.

One of the men in white pulled out a small glass card and swiped his thumb across it.

Sarah fell limp, then frozen.

What did you do to me?!

She screamed inside. Wanted to fight, claw, bite. Was desperate to attack them for their violations. But Sarah could do nothing outside allowing the men to set her back into bed, like a doll dropped on a pillow.

"Are you okay, sir?" one of the men asked Blake as he stood, touching an already bruised swath of skin just under his left eye.

"Yes, I'm fine, thank you." Blake smiled at the doctor. "Please leave us."

The men left, and Blake looked down at Sarah, still smiling — a calm smile, as if she'd not just attacked him — like he was trying to put her at ease. He reached out to stroke her hair. She could feel him, just barely.

"You are family, Sarah. You gave birth to my grandchild, Emma. I swear to your safety, I will never, ever hurt you. I gave life to your daughter and returned yours when it was senselessly taken. Down there with your daughter, you would be dead. Up here, you are helping us all to build a better tomorrow. We are doing something that, as I hope you will soon see, is for the greater good. The future isn't about you or me, it's about what's next. It's about what is possible for your child, and her children's children. We are so fortunate to be alive right now, in this time, at the start of a new era. Future historians will discuss what we're doing right now for thousands of years. It *is* that big, Sarah. And the best part is, you and I are here to share the story, and neither of us is going anywhere. We can say we watched the dawn of mankind's greatest step, and that we helped him to take it. All I'm asking for is your patience. You will see Emma again, someday. Just not now."

As Sarah saw the light in Blake's eyes, gleaming behind a glint of certain delusion, she almost wished the bullet that had taken her life had done its goddamned job.

Chapter 2 - Milo Anderson

Milo stared at the giant black man he'd seen with Jon Conway and Ms. Hughes' sister at the funeral. His gaze traveled from his giant barrel of a chest to the robotic leg, then back up to his face.

His first instinct was to run but to where? Running toward the officers in the front yard wasn't an option, but how was he supposed to trust the mystery man offering help? But he didn't have a choice — his bike lay in the grass just past the giant. It would be impossible to get on it and ride away if the man wanted to stop him.

Milo's heart pounded as he considered his quickly slimming list of possible escapes. He felt as if he were standing on a bridge as dozens of rabid dogs raced toward him. Did he take his chance and fight the dogs, or jump, hoping to survive the fall into icy waters below?

He looked into the stranger's eyes, and saw something there, a quiet confidence Milo felt he might be able — *should* be able — to trust.

He had to jump and hope for the best.

"Okay," Milo said. "Where are we going?"

The giant man pointed south. "We'll cut through these backyards. I'm parked just down the street."

Milo followed him through a cluster of well-groomed backyards. He occasionally glanced up at windows, certain he'd see someone looking down at them wondering why the hell Paul Bunyan and some kid were stomping their grass.

"Don't look in the windows," the man said calmly. "Act like you're supposed to be here. Just keep walking, nice and easy. Look suspicious, and they'll call the cops."

"Okay." Milo followed the man's lead as he kept moving — his back straight and head upright, staring ahead with a confidence he only pretended to have.

Just keep walking.

As they stepped into the third yard from the Hellers', a dog started barking from inside the house.

"Keep walking."

Milo did, certain the back door of the house would burst open at any moment, sending a dog flying out from inside to attack them.

"Just over here," the man said, turning as he walked between two houses on his way toward the street.

Milo followed him to a dark blue SUV with tinted windows.

"Thanks." Milo looked back toward Alex's house. The Paladin car was still on fire, and the pair of officers were trying to douse it. "I'll find my way from here."

"Get in the truck," the man ordered.

"No, I'm good." Milo backed away from the vehicle, ready to sprint down the street if he had to. If he had to, he could outrun a one-legged guy without much difficulty.

"I'm a private investigator. My name is Brock Houser. You can call me Houser." The man flashed an ID card and badge, though Milo wasn't willing to step close enough to check it out, even if he could tell a forgery from the real thing. "I saw you at the funeral, taking pictures, and think you and I might be onto the same thing. I'd like to talk, compare notes, see if maybe we can help each other."

"Help each other what?"

"Find answers to what's happening here. We have shootings, missing people, plus God knows what else going down on the island. I'm guessing maybe you're thinking something's fishy about the Heller shootings, right?"

Milo nodded. "How do I know I can trust you?"

"Who are you going to trust? Them?" Houser nodded toward the Paladin officers, then turned back to Milo. "Good luck with that. Let me know how it turns out."

Houser opened his truck and got inside, as if seconds from driving off.

"Wait!" Milo called. "We can talk."

He rolled down the passenger window. "Okay. But not here. Too many cameras. Get in, and I'll take you home. We can talk on the way."

"How do I know you won't try something?"

"Try something?" Houser laughed. "Dude, I'm not going to *try* anything. I just want to talk. Here, take my gun. Will that make you feel better?"

Houser pulled a pistol from inside his black duster and laid it on the front passenger seat. "Go ahead and take it. All yours, bro."

Milo opened the door and grabbed the gun. The reality of the weapon felt much lighter in his hands than he would have expected. He held it up and looked down the sight at the woods in the distance, smiling without meaning to.

"Don't go waving it around, kid!"

Milo looked up to see if the Paladin officers had noticed him. They were only just getting the car fire under control and had yet to look in his direction. But they would be soon, searching for the person who started the blaze.

Milo got inside the truck. "Okay, let's talk." He closed the door, then Houser pulled his SUV from the curb.

As the PI drove, Milo surprised himself by opening up and spilling everything, starting with Roger Heller opening fire on the classroom, and ending with Don asking him to retrieve Heller's flash drive. He left out Don's name, calling him, "Mr. X," since he wasn't yet sure he could trust Houser, and didn't want to surrender anything that might draw Don into trouble. Milo was almost shocked by his candid eruption, and realized he'd been waiting for someone — someone other than Don, who *did* seem sorta batshit crazy — to confide in. Houser seemed trustworthy, even if he was working with a Conway.

After Milo finished speaking, he looked at Houser, waiting to see how he'd react.

Houser looked him up and down, then turned back to the road. "Wow, that's some crazy shit."

"Tell me about it." Milo started scratching at his right arm, then forced himself to stop, afraid he would invite unwanted attention to the scratches and scars blooming in angry red beneath his sleeves. He had left his incessant and impossible-to-relieve itch out of his story — the feeling that there was something inside him, the near-constant obsessive scratching and picking at his arms. If Milo told Houser about that part of the story, the man might think *him* as batshit as Don. Right now, Milo wanted, maybe even needed, someone to talk to — someone to help him make sense of the chaos.

Houser asked, "You said you were looking for a flash drive, right? Did you find it?"

"No, Paladin came inside the house before I could find it, but I did find something else."

"Yeah?" Houser turned to Milo. "What's that?"

"Can you keep driving?" Milo asked as they swung onto his street, approaching his house.

"Sure thing." Houser lowered his foot on the pedal.

"A list of names," Milo continued, feeling slightly odd for discussing the list with Houser before Don. "The list had all the students Roger Heller shot."

"Oh?"

Milo couldn't quite tell what was inside Houser's *oh?* though there was definitely something. He swallowed, choking out his next words. "Yeah, but there was a name on the list that Roger didn't shoot — Katie, who was also Alex's girlfriend."

"So you're saying Roger Heller planned to kill those kids, it wasn't random, and he intended to kill his son's girlfriend, but didn't?"

"I can't think of anything else it *could* mean."

"Was the teacher on the list? Sarah Hughes?"

"No, just students he shot. Except my friend Manny's name wasn't on it, and he got killed, anyway. And Katie's name was on it but didn't."

Houser stared straight ahead as if trying to process the new information. "You have any idea what was on this flash drive you were sent to find?"

"No, sir." The itchiness crawled like spiders along his arms was nearly too unbearable to ignore. He wanted to hide inside his house and scratch. "I need to get home now. My dad will be wondering where I am soon."

"Yeah, that's cool." Houser made a right and headed back toward Milo's. "Thanks for talking to me. I'm going to give you my card. If you think of anything else, I want you to call me, okay?"

"I don't know," Milo said. "Mr. X told me I shouldn't talk about any of this on the phones. He said they listen to us. Said they use the city's cameras to monitor us, too."

"Who is *they*?" Houser turned to Milo. "Paladin?"

"Mr. X definitely thinks they're part of it, though he's been super vague about pretty much everything. I'm not sure if that's because he doesn't know, or if ..." Milo didn't finish saying what he was thinking, which was that maybe Don was a few kernels short of a cob.

Houser filled in the blanks. "Or if he's crazy?"

"Yeah." Guilt washed through him for lending breath to the thought. His arm was too hot to ignore. Milo finally surrendered, raking his fingernails over his shirt, gently, casually, so as not to draw attention.

Oh, that feels sooo good.

Milo resisted the urge to scratch harder, but it was nearly impossible.

As they pulled into his driveway, Houser said, "I'd like to talk to this Mr. X."

"Oh, I don't know if he'll talk to you."

"Then you have to convince him," Houser said. "I think you guys are definitely onto something big here, and I don't think it's safe for you to go it alone. You need someone on your side."

"There's no way he'd trust you. You're working for Jon Conway, and, well, I'm pretty sure he thinks the Conways are behind all of this, especially since they control Paladin."

"Your Mr. X may be right, and I wouldn't be surprised a bit if he was, but Jon Conway is *not* like the rest of them. He's one of the good ones." Houser smiled wide and slapped the seat behind Milo. "You must already suspect that, kid, otherwise you wouldn't be talking to me. You *can* trust Jon. Your Mr. X has nothing to worry about with either of us."

"I don't know." Milo dug his nails harder into his arms and raked deeper while still trying to stay inconspicuous. He was far from it.

Houser looked down at Milo's scratching, though if he noticed, which he must have, the PI said nothing.

Maybe he was looking at his gun — still sitting in Milo's tightly-clenched right hand — and wondering how much longer he would hold it. The gun now felt awkward in his grip. He didn't think he could shoot Houser, even if the man *did* suddenly try to hurt him, but he clutched the gun just the same.

"What if you asked him to meet you and I just showed up?" Houser said.

Milo shook his head. "He would freak the fuck out, for sure."

"Okay, I won't push things. Just tell him about me, about our conversation, and that I want to help. Can you do that?" Houser slipped the card into Milo's hand. "Keep the card. If anything happens, or if someone starts following you, or if you see or feel anything weird at all, I want you to call me. Any time, day or night."

"What if someone's listening?"

Houser reached behind his seat and withdrew a medium-sized black leather zipper bag from the back. Milo tried seeing what was inside it, but the man moved too fast, retrieving whatever he needed before quickly zipping the bag.

He handed Milo a small, black phone. It looked ancient, mostly glass, though edged in hard plastic like the one Milo's dad kept in a box of memorabilia, and thick, nearly the width of his pinky.

"Keep this on you. It has my number inside it. Any calls you make, or texts and videos sent, are all encrypted. My phone's the only one that can decrypt them, and vice versa with anything I send you. So you never have to worry. Even if Paladin intercepts your call, they won't be able to crack the encryption."

Milo took the cell, staring at it as he turned it in his left hand.

"It holds its charge for weeks, too, so you can leave it on. I set it to vibrate, so nobody will hear it ring if I call. Okay?"

"Yeah." Milo took the cell and felt the tiniest bit like he was in one of his favorite comics, *Dark Agents of the Damned*.

He opened the truck door, then handed the gun back to Houser, thrilled to be rid of it. "Thanks for saving my ass back there."

"Anytime," Houser said with a smile Milo couldn't help but like. "See you around."

Milo got out of the truck, eager to get behind a closed door where he could finally dig into his arm, probably with a fork.

Chapter 3 - Jon Conway

Jon stood on the balcony, enjoying the cool evening breeze as twilight wrapped the sky in a blooming violet. He stared into his palm, waiting for his agent Marty to reappear on the cell. As he waited, Jon looked into the well-lit living room on the other side of the glass doors, watching as Cassidy and Emma snuggled beneath a big, red blanket on the largest section of the couch, Cassidy reading one of her niece's books aloud.

They were so comfortable together, close-knit, like the family they were, and had been for nearly a decade before Jon made it back to the island. Standing outside in a tangle of shadows, he felt like an intruder, eavesdropping on a life that didn't belong to him — a family that wasn't really his.

While Jon had grown closer to both Cassidy and Emma, closer than he'd felt to anyone since Sarah, there were still too many rough edges to catalogue. The three of them were absent the shared history which allowed one to *simply be* with others. Though it was no one's fault and simply the way things were, Jon felt more like a guest, or a distant relative, than truly part of Emma's family.

Standing outside in the dark, watching Emma's genuine glee with her aunt, he wondered if being a father — or any of the stuff that went along with it — would ever feel natural rather than forced. Would Emma ever feel as close to him as she seemed with Cassidy? Perhaps most of all, would Cassidy ever open herself to him, or would she always harbor their distance, with Sarah's ghost haunting the good which hung between them?

Marty's sudden voice snapped his attention back to the glass. "Okay, I'm back, Jonny. So, what am I telling the Maris Brothers?"

"I don't know." He shook his head even though he was draped in shadows and Marty couldn't see him well. "If they can't wait to shoot, then I guess you'll have to tell them to find someone else. I can't give them an answer more definitive than that."

"You have to, Jonny, at least if you want this. And you better fucking want this! *Black Nova* isn't a franchise. It's *the* franchise right now. Five fucking pictures, minimum. And I'd bet my commission they split the last movie into three goddamn pics. This is the Big One, Jonny. Bigger than *Darkness Everlasting, and* it's not coming from a shit book. The critics *want* to love you. *Black Nova* and the Maris Brothers will make it easy."

Jon shivered with want, then shrugged off the part of him that was hungry to make *Black Nova*. He had wanted to make the flick ever since he read the books, then wanted it more than anything when he heard it was the Maris Brothers' next project. Even begged Marty to get him a sit down, which Jon had never done before. Still, as much as he wanted it, he longed to be a good father more.

"The *only* reason you're getting this offer right now is because Cooper Ford is a fucking idiot. Plow hookers and snort blow all you want, but if you do them both at once and get caught, you can't be surprised when the studio gets ice on their feet."

Marty paused, waiting for Jon to say something — anything — then finally pleaded through the silence.

"This is a golden opportunity, Jonny, and I really, *really* think you should take it. I know you don't *need* the paycheck, but if you care about your career, then this is your best possible move. You don't say no to *Black Nova*, or to the Maris Brothers, not unless you're content being the answer to a trivia question years from now. 'Hey, did you know who was up for the lead role in the *Black Nova* series after Cooper Ford got busted with two hookers and a quarter pound of coke?' I know you care about the 'Jon Conway legacy,' and I know indie stuff matters. If you want to preserve and nurture your name, man, this is it."

Marty's eyes were big and pleading. Jon was glad his were mostly shrouded in darkness.

"I need more time," he said. "This isn't something I can just sign off on without thinking it through. I'll have to be in New Zealand on and off, mostly on, for the next three years, at least. You're asking me to pick up and leave everything behind. That's not easy, Marty. I have other people — other lives — to consider."

"Take the girl with you," Marty said. "There's plenty of cool shit for kids there. Plus, she can tell all her friends she got to live in New Zealand for three years while her daddy was shooting *Black Fucking Nova!* Come on, Jonny. This is the best thing you can do for her, trust me!"

"It's more involved than that," Jon said. If it were anyone other than Marty giving him parenting advice, he would've told them to go fuck themselves. Despite being an amazing agent, Marty was also a helluva dad, and even though the man loved his commissions like Houser loved onion rings, Jon knew he always had his client's best interests at heart.

"Listen, Jonny, I'm not saying this because I'll get a big fat payday if you sign this deal, though that's certainly a part of it, and I've already promised Sharon a week in Parrot Cay. I'm telling you to take *Black Nova* because I fucking love you, man, and know you've got some seriously awesome movies left inside you. You can be one of the best ever, but if you want to make the movies you *really* want to make, and not just because you're the billfold behind them, well, you *need* a blockbuster. *Black Nova* gets your next dozen direct distribution indies inked. Say no to this, then … well, I don't know what happens after that."

Jon closed his eyes, hating that the one blockbuster he wanted to do, and had fought for nearly a year to get, was only now coming into his life. Marty was right. This was a once-in-a-lifetime sort of opportunity. And the *Black Nova* series, directed by the Maris Brothers, was as close to a box-office guarantee as you could get. It would be damned good — a popcorn movie he *could* be proud of, one that would give him the credibility needed to not only get his pet projects made, but earn them the attention they deserved beyond his name.

"I'll think about it," Jon said.

"Okay, Jon, but you don't have long. I might be able to stall the brothers a bit, tell 'em you've got shit going on, and blah-blah, fucking blah," Marty said with an exaggerated sigh, "but they are waiting. When do you think you'll have an answer?"

Jon looked back through the long glass wall at Cassidy and Emma, thinking about how the girls might take the news and wondering if they would go with him if he took the deal.

Will I take Emma anyway if Cassidy says no?

"I don't know," Jon said. "Can you stall them until next Friday?"

"I think so," Marty said. "But if you make them wait that long and then say no, they're gonna be pissed, Jonny. And they'll have every right. Plus, you know as well as I do, if the brothers are pissed, the studio will be pissed, too."

"Yeah, yeah, I get it." Jon paused, then said, "Thanks for

everything, Marty. Sorry I can't give you a better answer right now. I promise I'll figure things out as soon as I can, then call you the second I do."

Jon tapped the glass, killed the call, then dropped the phone in his pocket.

Rather than going inside, he stood on the balcony, still staring at Emma and Cassidy who looked equally content as they sat in a snuggle. He wondered how they might respond to his opportunity. Emma would probably be excited by all of it, from a trip — or full relocation — to New Zealand to the shooting of a movie. But how long before the novelty thinned to burden? How long before Emma resented him for dragging her away from her home, friends, and family?

Shooting a movie, especially one where he was the lead with a ton of heavy effects, meant endless days on the set. Those long days would feel like forever, and mostly be spent in Emma's absence. Unless Cass came with them, there was no way he could take Emma without subjecting her to long periods of isolation, loneliness, and maybe even despair — a prisoner far from home.

As Jon watched Emma and Cassidy bundled together, he realized he wouldn't be able to bear their separation. It would hurt them, and him, far too much.

Jon considered calling Marty back immediately, telling him not to waste the Brothers' time. That way Jon could avoid pissing them — and the studio — off when he eventually turned them down. Marty would be upset, but he'd get over it.

Jon pulled out his cell, thought of Father and the unfinished business they had yet to settle, then dropped the phone back in his pocket.

He still had to confront Blake about his part in keeping Emma — and the truth — hidden. That conversation *could* go horribly wrong, and if it did, the fallout could be horrible not just for him, but for Cassidy and Emma as well. Perhaps the aftermath of their battle would see the girls *welcoming* any escape from the island.

Cassidy looked up and caught Jon's gaze through the glass. He wasn't sure how much of him she could see, since the inside was bright and the balcony opposite, but she smiled at him just as if he were standing three feet away. He opened the door and slipped inside, making his way toward his two favorite girls on the couch. Before he made it five steps, the cell buzzed in his pocket.

Jon looked at the screen. Blake Conway.

He swiped the glass as he turned back toward the balcony. "Hello?"

"Hello, son. I heard you stopped by looking for me?"

Jon kept his back to Cassidy and Emma but didn't step out onto the balcony. "Yes, I was hoping to see you." He wanted to ask why he had a photo of Emma in his office, and why her name was his password, but figured it better to wait until they had their conversation.

"I heard you're back in town, that you even bought a place. Are you planning to stay?"

"I don't know." Jon tried to determine whether his father wanted him on the island, not that his tone of voice revealed much. "I'm here for now."

"How would you like to come over for dinner tomorrow?" Blake asked. "I'd love to see you."

"Tomorrow?" Jon looked back at Cass and Emma, whom he'd promised he would take to The Walrus and the Carpenter, his favorite restaurant in Seattle. "No, sorry. Not tomorrow. I already have dinner plans in Seattle with Cassidy and Emma."

"Ah," Blake said. "Then change them. Bring them both. They are family, after all. I'll have Carmen cook whatever you'd like."

Jon looked at Cassidy, "How do you feel about going to dinner at my father's tomorrow?"

Jon might as well have asked Cassidy if she had any interest in eating from Shipwrecked's crusted restroom floor.

"Ooh." Emma's face lit up. "I wanna go! Please, Aunt Cassidy?"

Cassidy sighed.

Jon shrugged then spoke into the phone. "Yeah, we can do that."

"Great," Blake said. "Can't wait to see you."

"Me, too," Jon said, though his reasons weren't what Father would likely suspect. He slipped the cell back into his pocket, then sat on the sofa beside Emma, with Cassidy on her other side. "So, what are my two favorite girls up to?"

"Aunt Cassidy is reading *Unicorn Apocalypse*," Emma said. "Want to listen?"

"It isn't too scary, is it?"

"No." Emma laughed. "It's funny, and fun!"

"Okay, as long as it's not scary. I don't like scary stories, and end-of-the-world stuff is usually a bit grim." Jon winked at Cassidy.

"Oh, yeah, your dad is a big ole scaredy-cat," she teased.

"Really?" Emma asked, her eyes wide.

"Oh, yeah," Cassidy said. "He slept with a nightlight until he was like fifteen."

"No, I did *not*," Jon said with mock indignation. "I was *fourteen*, I'll have you know!"

Emma laughed, a deep, infectious giggle, the sort Jon loved to hear. Not only did his daughter's laugh make him feel as if he was her favorite toy, there was something inside her giggle, and perhaps the laughter of all children, that was as thick with merriment as it was with perspective.

Life was always worth living when there were children laughing inside it.

Emma was right the other day — I need to make a children's film.

Emma turned to Jon. "So, I'm going to meet my grandpa tomorrow?"

"Yes, ma'am," he said. "Are you excited?"

"Yeah," Emma nodded as her smile split wider. "What's he like?"

"He's a peach," Cassidy said, then seemed immediately sorry for her sarcasm. "I mean, he's nice. Lots of people really like him."

Emma stared at her aunt, suspiciously. "You don't like Grandpa Conway?"

Jon stared at Cassidy, wondering how she'd dig herself out from Emma's question, imagining the lie she was about to light on her tongue. But Cassidy sat in her silence for a handful of seconds, then shifted in her seat and spilled truth instead.

"No." She wrinkled her nose and shook her head. "I think your Grandpa Conway is a cold, callous asshole."

Emma's eyes went wide, and she turned to Jon, probably to see if he was mad. Jon burst into sudden and almost fitful laughter. "He's not *that* bad. My brother, though, Warren, well, he's a giant asshole."

Cassidy laughed with Jon, and Emma joined them.

"*But*," Cassidy said, "You'd better not tell him we said anything!"

Emma ran a finger over her lips in a zipping motion. "I won't say a word, I swear."

"Good," Jon said. "Because I'd like to have a nice dinner without any drama."

Cassidy started to snort in derision, but Jon shot her a look and stopped her.

"What about Grandma Conway?" Emma asked. "Will she be there?"

"No." Jon shook his head. "She's in heaven. I never knew my real mom. She died when I was born. My stepmom died when I was graduating high school."

"Wow." Emma put her hand on Jon's arm, displaying the

maternal instinct that was surely wired in her brain. "So, you never knew your mom?"

"Well, I knew my stepmom, who was a lot like my mom and who I even called mom. She was a very nice woman. But no, I never knew my real mom."

Emma looked down, clearly thinking of her own mother.

Cassidy swallowed, visibly uncomfortable, then turned to stare through the glass and out at the sea.

Emma said, "That must have been really sad for you, to never know her. At least I got to know mine. A bunch of people keep telling me they know how I feel, but you actually do, maybe even more than me."

How can she be so mature?

With a heavy note of confession in her voice, Emma said, "I actually feel guilty a lot of the time."

"Why?" Jon and Cassidy asked together.

"Because I feel like I should be missing Mommy more. I mean, I miss her, but Aunt Cassidy helps me miss her less, I guess, just like you do."

Emma turned to Cassidy and smiled, then Cassidy turned and smiled at Jon. Something about the moment made him feel cold, lost, and surprisingly guilty.

Was being with Cassidy really the best thing? Sure, he missed Sarah, Emma missed her mother, and it was easy enough to play house. But were they merely numbing their mutual hurt? Was only a matter of time until it bloomed into something worse? Even though the smart part of Jon knew he was doing the right thing, and that every intention was good, there was another — more insecure — part of him that wondered if he was wasting weeks and working toward months, filling Emma's life with some dream of a family that would never be.

Jon took his daughter's hands in his and smiled.

She smiled back, wide, like she always did when interested in what her new daddy was about to say.

"It's okay that you don't miss your mom as much as you think you should, Emma. There is no *wrong*. Aunt Cassidy and I are here to make you feel better *because* we're your family. Believe me, you don't *want* to feel alone. There is no right answer or one formula for dealing with grief. There is no reason — one plus one equals everything, and two minus one can sometimes mean nothing. Just know that no matter what, your aunt and I are here for you, and when the time comes when you *really* miss your mom, which it will, we'll both be here for you. Okay?"

A tear slid down Emma's cheek. "Okay." She fell fully into Jon's arms.

He stroked the back of her head, running his hands along her hair as Cassidy smiled from behind, her eyes red and misty with understanding.

The door opened behind them, then Houser entered the living room. He looked over at their tiny family, his mouth half-open as if he wanted to tell them all about his day. Then he shut it, seeing that he'd stepped into a family moment.

"Did you want to talk?" Jon asked.

"It'll wait." He held a brown bag from Red Rockets in front of him, the fast food inside it pocking the paper with blotted grease stains along the bottom. "Besides, I'm starving. I'm gonna go watch some TV and pig out. We'll talk later, or tomorrow."

Emma said, "Guess what, Houser? Tomorrow we're going to dinner at my grandpa's!"

"Really?" Houser said with a surprised smile. "That sounds like ... *fun?*"

"Wanna come?" she asked.

"Um," Houser said, meeting Jon's eyes, as if seeking the proper response.

Jon shook his head no, just enough for his friend to take note.

"No, honey." Houser shook his head. "Sorry, but I've got some major work to finish up tomorrow."

"Oh," Emma said. "You think they're assholes, too, don't you?"

They all burst into laughter as Jon pulled his daughter closer and into a tighter hug.

God, I love this girl.

Chapter 4 - Warren Conway

Warren and Melinda sat across from one another at the gigantic dining room table, eating in silence. Again.

Melinda was poking at her asparagus tips and filet with her fork, taking dainty bites as Warren tore through his steak and swallowed gulps from his goblet of wine.

"How was your day?" he asked, trying to thaw the room's unmistakable chill. He wasn't sure what imagined slight was nested inside Melinda's skin like a splinter tonight, nor did he have the patience for a fight. He was on edge and required the sort of relaxation that fit so neatly in a glass. He took another swallow.

"It was okay," she said. "And yours?"

"Fine," Warren lied, stabbing another nugget of steak. He tried to think of something to say, some way to elongate their exchange but was afraid that doing so might unspool whatever Melinda was holding so tight inside her. He watched as she ate. He examined the crow's feet at the corners of her eyes, the makeup that was just a bit too excessive, and her hair, which Amanda had cut too short the last time Melinda had gone into Divine. Her newest haircut, coming just two weeks after the last, made Melinda look severe, and had Warren wondering what happened to the gorgeous, young woman he'd married.

It wasn't that Melinda didn't do her absolute best to maintain appearances. She did. Yet, there was something else, something just under the surface, which seemed to erode her from the inside a bit more each day. Warren wondered how much of her missing soul stemmed from the many mind erasures he'd had the doctors at Conway Medical administer over the years — things seen, conclusions jumped to or drawn, family business he couldn't trust she'd be able to keep private, at least not after Melinda had aired a clothesline's worth of dirty laundry to a few friends after three glasses of pinot six years back. If you can't trust your wife, who can you trust?

The doctors swore they had perfected the technique so that they were *only* erasing memories, but Warren didn't buy it. Their procedure seemed to strip more from his wife than memories, wiping her personality like marker from a board, leaving behind little more than an icy woman who seemed more like a distant stranger than a warm, loving wife — a hysterical harpy who would bottle herself so tightly, that by the she time boiled, the eruptions left her weeping for hours.

Melinda's eyes drifted up from her plate. For a moment, Warren watched a shadow of her — the Melinda she used to be buried somewhere deep inside her emerald eyes. In that instant, he felt something he'd not felt in years. A longing to leave, go somewhere with her, and rekindle fires doused by apathy and neglect.

Bad years rested on both their shoulders.

Before the feeling nested into something more, Melinda opened her mouth. "I was at Silvie's today for lunch. She was an absolute horror."

Warren sighed.

"She kept the thermostat at sixty-eight the entire time I was there, and for no reason. I was freezing, and it was horrible. I asked her to turn it up three times. Three times, Warren.

And she refused each time. Once she even lied about it, said she'd turned it up to seventy-four like I asked, but my cell said the temperature was sixty-eight when I checked."

Melinda's green eyes flashed as she stabbed her filet mignon with her fork, then dropped it into her mouth. She chewed and swallowed. The meat was half-down her throat when she spoke. Warren could see it like a rat in a snake.

"You know, Silvie lies about *everything.* Stupid stuff, too. Her cell has a sumo."

"A sumo?" Warren looked up, because this was the part of the conversation where he had to at least pretend to care, or else suffer through an even longer stretch of insipid blather.

"Yes, a Sumo. It's an app that sends you constant alerts. To make you seem like you're busier than you are. Silvie does it to infuriate me."

Warren closed his eyes, holding his sigh.

"Infuriate you? Really?" He should have had more wine, or something stronger — strong enough to dull the edge on his tongue. No, she was an adult. He could be frank. "Why do you let such stupid shit bother you?"

Melinda blanched as if slapped. "You don't need to speak to me as if I'm a child."

Great, it was going to be another one of *those* nights.

"Yes, you're absolutely correct," Warren said, half smiling as he pushed his chair from the table. He dropped his cloth napkin on his plate, then marched from the dining room without bothering to look back. He had to get out of the house, go for a drive. Let Melinda stew.

Warren walked toward the garage, agitated as he wondered if Kaiser had picked up the package.

His hand moved to the panel to open the garage for his Bentley. The door whooshed open, and Father stepped through it, exhaling his final puff of cigar.

"Ah, Warren," Blake said. "Just who I wanted to see. Have a moment?"

"Yeah." Warren hoped he looked relaxed, not wanting Father to see how much he wanted to flee the house and his life.

"Come." .Blake touched the panel and closed the door, then walked to the bar where he poured himself a scotch and offered the same to Warren.

"No, I'm good," Warren waved him away. "I'm going out for a drive."

"Well, this won't take but a minute. I wanted to tell you first before you hear it at our next Inner-Circle. I'm dropping Raven in two weeks."

"What? I thought you were giving me a month to clean up, which I already did. Immediately. The second you asked. The Heller family is already gone."

"True," Blake said, "but it was a mess. A large one. And an embarrassment. The entire situation could have, and should have, been avoided. Besides not knowing *how* Roger Heller got the information he did, you *still* don't know *why* he targeted children in Phoenix, do you?" He swallowed his Glenfiddich then stepped closer to Warren, and repeated, "Do you?"

"Well, no. We're working on it, but these things take time." Warren fell a step back.

"We don't have that kind of time. If there's a leak on your team, Warren, we can't take a risk."

"But —"

"No more arguing. I've made up my mind. I won't let your little project put our evolutionary work — our *real work* — at risk."

"Little project? Since when is a trillion-dollar contract from DOD little, Father? I've poured a decade of my life into this, and you're just going to flush it away?"

Blake met Warren's eyes without a twinkle of sympathy. "Best you not forget our company mission, son. It is not, nor will it ever be, about creating perfect killing machines for

Earth's highest bidder. We're evolving our species into something that sees war as the insect play it is, to give mankind more meaning and value than any blood money you could ever hope to earn."

Warren's leg trembled. He wanted to look down and see if it was evident beneath his black slacks, to see if Father had noticed. But he couldn't call attention to his shivering fear, not with Father. Not when Blake Conway respected boldness above all else. Warren locked his ankles, leaned forward, took a step toward Father, and shoved an index finger into his trim chest. "No!"

Blake's eyes widened. "Excuse me?"

"I said no! I refuse to let you put an end to everything I've been working for. Not without a fight."

"You can fight me." Blake shrugged. "But you won't win. I own controlling interests in the company, best you not forget. No one in the Circle will back you, son. You can go out and holler your plea tonight, but you won't even get the crickets to answer." Father slammed his glass on the table and leaned in close. "And if I were you, I'd think very carefully about the next words that come from the mouth I gave you, *boy.*"

Warren shook his head, adrenaline raging through his body. He wanted to scream, to thunder, to rampage. He wanted to cry. But he had to control himself and calmly consider his next move. With his boldness failing, Warren decided to play for his father's few thin slivers of sympathy, hoping he cared enough for his plight to listen. A risky gamble, sure. That move, played wrong, would only weaken him further.

"Father, I'm begging. Think back to when we started this project. You were excited, watching our teams make one new breakthrough after another. It was our advances in neural science that helped Project Phoenix more than anything else. This isn't about creating killing machines. *Of course,* that's why DOD wants the tech, but this is about so much more — about creating everlasting peace through our military's power. The government can use this tech to control the enemy, heads of state, rogue nations. We can singlehandedly end war. Forever. Why can't you see we're working toward the same goal, with two separate projects of equal importance?"

Equal wasn't gone from his mouth a second before Warren knew he'd gone too far. Comparing their projects was clearly an insult.

"Equal importance?" Blake shouted, his face reddening as he inched closer to Warren, the scent of Nat Shermans fogging his body. "I allowed you to work on your project so you kept busy, out of my hair, and away from the *important work* my team was doing. Tell me, Warren, what happens during the next phase of our evolution? How can you expect to control a brain infinitely more advanced than your own?"

Blake waited as if expecting an answer, but cut off his son's reply before Warren opened his mouth.

"You haven't the slightest idea what you're doing, *boy*. You can barely contain your subjects, you couldn't prevent a mass shooting. You can barely manipulate primitive brains! *Everything* advanced is out of your reach. No, Warren, the time for coddling is over. Your project is dead. End of discussion."

Blake refilled his Glenfiddich with one hand and pointed toward the door with his other. Warren opened his mouth to protest, but Father's glare said he'd gone too far. He turned and sat, shifting attention to his tablet and shutting Warren out.

Warren stormed from the bar, then opened the garage door and climbed inside his Bentley. He gunned the engine and tore from The Gardens, trying his best not to cry.

His best wasn't good enough. As Warren looked at his red eyes in the rearview mirror, he hated himself for being so damned weak.

Chapter 5 - Sarah Hughes

Sarah opened her eyes to black sky.

The seas of stars were hard to see clearly through her swimming, swirling consciousness.

Everything seemed so ... familiar.

Déjà vu, but worse.

Doors were missing, so were walls. The floor was barely there. Just a thin dust beneath her feet, there to hold her steady and keep her from picturing herself floating up into the sky.

Time, space, and a million lights bled her of thought and bleached logic like cotton. Minus the déjà vu, Sarah might have gone crazy — frozen, and staring into stars and space wherever she looked. Odd as it was, the empty all around her, pressing her like petals between pages, seemed as familiar as a second sneeze.

Something is coming.

A ball of light shot through the sky, dragging a plume of lavender behind it. After shrinking to a speck, the light expanded then detonated into a billion pieces, raining sudden splendor in cascades at her feet.

No ...

The room shifted *like always* and the déjà vu sent Sarah's heart into a gallop. Her knees went liquid as space spun around her. Stars glowed brighter, spitting their brilliance until one brushed another, then spread toward the others like water through a paper towel, until all were touching and the room was bathed in nothing but white.

The walls returned, sand-colored and straight, surrounding Sarah like a fence. Her memory was broken. Time meant nothing.

Perception was bubbling mud. Everything a bog.

Part of Sarah felt like she had been wherever she was — *space?* — for days. Some of her was certain she had been there most of her life.

With déjà vu burning like alcohol in her throat, anything was impossible. She closed her eyes, squeezing them tight to force her memory, desperate to know what happened last time.

So many things had shifted, too many times.

Something stood at the edge of her memory. Barely there.

Last time, Sarah was somehow sure, the room had turned from empty space into living nightmare. After she screamed, someone entered the room to tell her all was okay.

"Hold on," he had said.

Sarah swallowed, waiting, *knowing* it was coming.

Then it did.

On the floor, about midway between Sarah and the fresh door that had appeared from nowhere, sat a small pile of gelatinous creatures — three total, with nine eyes between them, four closed. The three globs were stuck together, just enough to make it clear the goopy blob was truly a trio. Though there were three, it was difficult, probably impossible, to tell where one stopped and the other started. The oozing pustule at the top, constantly swelling until it reached the size of an infant, had its mouth open wide in what seemed like a yawn. A scream seemed certain to Sarah, but the creature was mute. The two blobs just below began blinking, opening their mouths wider and stretching their gelatinous mass into a writhing taffy of agony.

Her heart pounded, edging eruption as she forced herself into a half frantic, almost calm. As Sarah self-soothed, the blobs shifted faster. It might have been a minute, it could have been an hour. Then three blobs were gone, along with their extra eyes and taffy mouths. In their place chirped a trio of birds — loud and beautiful. Pure white, with stripes of bright green, all three birds stared up to the ceiling — now a perfect blue; cerulean but for the puffy clouds swirling like teased cotton.

The birds, each the size of a handbag, exploded into tufts of feathered anger as a giant beak — about the size of a bus — crashed down from the ceiling to greet the baby birds.

Sarah screamed.

Like the space around her, the birds disappeared.

Sarah closed her eyes and kept breathing.

It's not real, it's not real, it's not real …

Though she had no idea how many times something like this had already happened, Sarah somehow knew, or perhaps remembered, that each time it happened, someone always came in to ask her questions at the end.

They want to know what I see. But why?

Sarah saw clean, white walls and a long and maybe endless hallway, lined as far as her vision with row upon row of neatly hung pictures. The first showed Sarah, or perhaps Cassidy, wearing a blush-colored prom dress that neither had ever worn. The girl in the picture, twenty-five or so, with Sarah's freckled shoulder and Cassidy's scarred bracelets, had her arm linked through Jon's.

The second picture showed Emma sitting at Vivian's kitchen table, reaching for a ripe banana from a bowl of rotting fruit. Fruit flies colonized the bowl, gathering in armies above the festering. Mold, fuzzed with something black and horrible, sprouted out from a kiwi, swelling from the bowl's center to swallow the rest of the fruit.

Like all the pictures, from the first two then all the way down the long aisle, the frame's glass wore a thin sweater of dust. Sarah ran her digit across it, then stared at her stained fingertip, sticky with fresh blood.

She screamed, then stepped back and screamed again. Pictures fell to the floor, starting beside her then dropping one-by-one down the hallway, crashing and shattering along the liquid floor, taking pieces and turning them to space and stars as they went.

Soon, Sarah was floating as she shrieked, unable to stop. She grew louder and louder until the door exploded open and a tall doctor in a white coat rushed inside. She had seen him before, many times it seemed, though who knew how far an echo traveled.

The tall man was suddenly standing beside her, calm, setting a gentle hand on her shoulder. His free hand held a glass of water, half full.

"Thank you." Sarah took the glass and gulped.

"Wait," the doctor said, his smile warm as he handed her a tiny paper cup with three pills inside it.

Where did the pills come from?

"Take these," he said. "To kill the terrors."

Killing terrors sounded nice, exactly what Sarah needed. And the doctor was right, the pills seemed to murder her terrors in seconds.

Sarah sank into her chair and stared up at the ceiling, smiling at the burning orange from an overdue sunset.

She held her smile through a battery of questions, though she lost each inquiry as it went by. Sarah would answer, but then forget what had been asked once she was on to the next one.

The man was asking her about the blobs and seemed

surprised when she reported they had turned into giant baby birds.

The man asked something else and made Sarah forget what she was thinking.

She was *so, so tired.*

He said it was important for her to rest, then he smiled and left.

Walls and door disappeared.

The world turned to black space and white stars.

She thought of Blake Conway, then wondered why. For a hysterical moment, Sarah giggled uncontrollably, lost to the thought that one of the world's richest men was Emma's grandfather.

Her insides suddenly screamed with irrational thought.

My baby is dead!

Too painful to think, Sarah closed her eyes and fell slowly asleep, then opened them to nothing but black, and the seas of stars in between.

Everything seemed so … familiar.

Déjà vu but worse.

A ball of light shot through the sky, dragging a plume of lavender behind it. It erupted and rained all around her.

No …

The room started to shift, and Sarah felt weak. Walls returned, sand-colored and straight.

Suddenly in front of her, festering, was the most horrible thing Sarah had ever seen.

She screamed.

Chapter 6 - Cassidy Hughes

Cassidy was hoping to stay the night at Jon's, but a phone call from Vivian dragged her from cozy anticipation and into the crushing reality of dealing with her mother.

Vivian didn't even wait for Cassidy's face to fill the screen before she was barking into her side of the glass. "I need groceries, and my back is acting up again."

She didn't snap at her mom like she wanted to, or like Vivian probably expected, she simply left Emma with Jon for the night and figured she'd stay with her mom, miserable as that prospect might be. If the last thing she wanted was to leave the sofa and go to the grocery store, she sure as hell couldn't imagine having the will to drive back after dropping the bags at her mom's.

Of course, Cassidy could go to her own place — it wasn't far from her mother's — but the thought of hitting hay in her shithole apartment was too depressing, especially after drying her naked body at Jon's with what might have been the world's most perfect towel.

I don't want to be alone.

When alone, Cassidy's mind circled the pills.

She looked at the "GrocerEZ" app, glanced at Vivian's list, said her goodbyes and goodnights to Jon and Emma, then got in her car and headed toward Al's Fresh Meats and Produce.

Nineteen minutes later, she was wrapping her hand around a can of steel-cut oats. Cassidy dropped it in her cart as an icy chill slithered her body, starting at her shoulders and — inexplicably — whispering *Sarah* as it went.

The *Sarah* whisper fled her body and — like crickets chirping — surrounded her in sudden echo, first hissing by the dozens, and then the hundreds. Half sang *Sarah*, the other rang with *Cassidy*.

She screamed, and the canister of steel-cut oats slipped from her hand, crashing to the floor with a thud.

"Sorry." She twisted her head to search Al's empty aisles.

Cassidy gripped her cart and rolled it toward the back of the store, feeling a hundred eyes behind her, though she couldn't see a single one. As she rounded the corner, she saw Jason Monroe, a biology teacher Sarah had dated maybe three times.

Sarah never told Cassidy much about her dates, but on the rare occasions when she had them, Cassidy had always watched Emma instead of their mom since Sarah hated discussing her dates, and unlike Vivian, Cassidy cared enough not to ask.

She wheeled her cart up to Jason. Before he turned to face her, words that weren't quite hers escaped from her mouth.

"Hey, Jason, how are you doing? I was just wondering if you ever managed to get things settled with Tom?"

Jason turned to Cassidy, his eyes two pieces of the same puzzle and the corners of his mouth drooped in a frown. His right hand seemed to twitch, showing the same uncertain nerves as his left, which he thrust deep into his pocket.

Cassidy could understand his anxiety. She *shouldn't* know

anything about Tom. Yet, somehow, she did. She knew Tom had been trying hard to become "Mr. Monroe's" friend, and that Jason had been discouraging any sort of relationship at every chance since according to Jason — and Sarah agreed — "Teachers should be friendly with students, but never friends."

"Um," Jason swallowed, then finally found a friendly smile. "Sorry about that, Cassidy, for a second there you looked just like a ..."

He couldn't finish. She did it for him.

"Like a ghost?"

A too-long pause, then, "Yeah ... sorry."

"It's okay." Cassidy smiled, feeling out of her skin.

"I think of Sarah all the time. You were another reminder." He looked away for a second, blinked, then turned back to Cassidy. "How did you know about Tom? Did Sarah tell you that?" He laughed, slightly uncomfortable.

"Yeah, I guess," Cassidy said. "Strange the things you remember."

She smiled, and Jason smiled back.

"I guess it's because you're twins, right? Sarah probably told you everything, whether you wanted to know it or not." He blushed, then cleared his throat. "You can probably read each other's minds or something like that, huh?"

"Something like that." Cassidy's heart pounded.

Not read it, BE it.

She had to leave, had to flee Al's. Pay for her stuff, get Vivian her shit, then fall asleep so she could wake back up with everything sort of normal again.

After a quick goodbye to Jason — probably abrupt enough to make her seem like a bitch, especially since she was the one to initiate conversation — Cassidy dashed to another aisle. She grabbed the final item on her list — a jar of Classico with sausage, mushrooms, and tomatoes — then headed toward the front of the store.

Cassidy was fifteen feet from the checkout when she had to force herself not to scream. She was breathing heavy, panting as she held her terror at bay.

Piled on the linoleum, oozing halfway between her and the cash registers, were three hideous creatures, all bulbous and made of gray jelly, congealed together. Each had three eyes, setting one apart from the other. The one on top looked as though it was trying to scream, though no sound left its mouth.

Cassidy still wanted to cry out. The mess in front of her started to pulse in its thick skin of goo, sending her heart into a heavier beat. She knew whatever the blobs were, they weren't really there, so she tried to ease by them.

They turned into birds as she did.

Giant, ugly, horrible birds.

Like the ones from the forest.

Another memory she couldn't remember as her own. *What birds, in what forest?*

Cassidy shook her head, confused. She was either losing her marbles or having the worst acid flashback ever. The only thing was, she'd never done acid, so far as she knew.

Who knew what dealers laced her shit with?

As she approached the checkout, a giant beak crashed through the ceiling. Before it could feed its birds, Cassidy lost it. She started to scream, then wailed for endless minutes until a pair of full-grown men managed to calm her.

"Are you okay, Ms. Hughes?" asked Ronald Lansing, Al's son.

"I'm fine." Her breathing had calmed enough to lay claim.

She went to the checkout, ignoring the many eyes pinned to her back, piled groceries in her canvas bags, held her cell in front of the scanner to pay, then left Al's and practically crawled into her car behind the groceries.

Terror, confusion, and humiliation whirled within her.

Then came the Addict's voice. Cassidy tried to ignore all of it as she pressed the button to start her ignition then pulled out from the parking lot, pointing her old beast toward Vivian's.

She made it less than a mile before losing her will to the pills.

Chapter 7 - Warren Conway

Warren sat in his Bentley with the midnight-tinted windows, parked behind Father's hospital, waiting, his foot tapping anxiously on the floorboard.

Where is he?

He looked at the dash. Five after ten. It wasn't like Kaiser to be late with a delivery.

The black Paladin van approached. It pulled up beside him and killed its headlights. A black, driver's side window rolled down, then Carl Kaiser greeted Warren with a smile. His grin always looked so odd beneath his angry blue robotic eye.

"Sorry, I had to wait until Johnson could get to me."

"You got it?" Warren asked.

Kaiser patted the front pocket of his black shirt. "I'm here, aren't I?"

Warren killed the engine, stepped out of the car, then walked around to the passenger side of the Paladin van and waited for Kaiser to unlock it. The door clicked, then Warren climbed in, eager, but not wanting to seem too enthusiastic. It had been too long since his last fix.

He held out his hand. Kaiser pulled the inhaler from his pocket, shook it, then handed it over.

Warren grabbed the inhaler, shoved it in his mouth, and squeezed it from the bottom, feeling the drug's mist coat his throat. The nanonarcotic's effect was nearly immediate, coating Warren's tangled nerves, soothing his frayed edges into straight currents of wrangled chaos.

Everything felt suddenly sweet — a flat line to his anxiety.

He closed his eyes and leaned his head into the seat. "Thank you, Carl."

"Johnson is out of town next week, so I nabbed a few extra doses." Kaiser patted his pocket. "But you need to space these apart. I can't get more until he gets back, not without risk of it coming back to one of us."

"Thanks," Warren said, preferring to enjoy his present ride, rather than hashing out the particulars of his next one. He kept his head back, eyes closed, feeling euphoria flooding his senses. "Fuck, do I need this tonight!"

"Why, what's wrong?" Kaiser asked.

"Father. He's killing the Project. He gave me two weeks, then he's ending it."

"I knew he'd do this." Kaiser's voice was laced with *I told you so.*

"I thought he'd change his mind. He's a logical man, after all. What kind of logical man turns down a trillion-dollar contract with the DOD?"

Kaiser gave a commiserated sigh, then his concerned hands rubbed the tight spots of Warren's neck. "You have knots."

"You would, too, if you had my shitty day."

"Don't let them get you down." Kaiser slid his hand to Warren's belt, tugging it loose.

Warren smiled,but kept his eyes closed, his cock hard as Kaiser unzipped his pants and put it into his mouth.

Opiates flooded his blood as well-practiced oral flooded

his senses. A new euphoria flowed through his body. Warren's hands found Carl's head as he thrust harder into the man's mouth, quickly exploding with a dizzying orgasm.

He exhaled, then kissed Kaiser on the mouth. "Thank you. I needed that."

"Thank you." Carl rested his head on Warren's chest.

They sat for some time, alone in the shaded black of the Paladin van, safe from prying eyes and cameras, the only time Warren felt like he could be himself and not hide behind a persona or fulfill other people's expectations. Things with Carl were never romantic. They were pure, to the point — two lovers fulfilling carnal desires, with none of the trappings of Warren's marriage. None of the false "I love yous" or dead echoes from long since hollow feelings.

With Carl, things were simple. For that, Warren was grateful.

As they glowed through their shared moment, Warren wondered if Carl would want his turn in the van's back. Warren wasn't sure he had the energy, but he didn't want to disappoint Kaiser, especially before setting the next part of his plan into motion — the part which required Carl's loyalty and discretion.

As if reading his mind, Carl said, "Don't worry. You can return the favor next time. I know you're exhausted."

"Thanks," Warren stroked Kaiser's bald head, allowing himself to fully relax. He wished he could drift off here in the van, beside Carl, but they both had lives and stages to play on.

Warren tucked his cock back into his pants and zipped up as he noticed Carl's expression — like the man was waiting to tell him something but wasn't sure how or where to start. Carl's hesitance was uncharacteristic, which was annoying to Warren and threatened his buzz. "Say what you wanna say."

"I think it's time we consider … you know."

Yes, Warren *did* know. It was the phrase neither would say aloud, yet they need not say at all.

It's time we kill Blake.

"Oh, I don't know." Warren shook his head, acting as if he'd not carefully led Carl down this road throughout the past year. Yes, it was time. Long past it, perhaps. But Warren couldn't seem too eager. Carl had to think the idea was his. "I'm just not sure."

"Are you really going to let him kill the Project? You've put so much of your life into this, Warren. He has no right to come in and shut things down!" Carl's voice flared as he punched the steering wheel. "No right!"

Carl's sudden outburst reminded Warren just how animal he could be — how quickly he could turn to violence. This was a quality that both attracted Warren and made him nervous.

Warren played coy. "True as that may be, I don't know that … *that* … is the answer. I honestly don't think I can do it."

"You don't have to." Kaiser voiced his quiet promise.

"Oh?" Warren met his gaze. Somehow even the digital eye's blue glow seemed to convey the depth of Carl's conviction.

"I have the perfect plan."

Warren couldn't help his spreading smile. He could tell by Carl's expression — he was about to hear some outside-the-box thinking.

"Go on," Warren said, "tell me more."

Chapter 8 - Brock Houser

Brock Houser stood naked in a field of flowing wheat, hot sun kissing warm skin, reminding him of some distant memory — another time when he stood in such a field, staring at a storm as it rolled in from the horizon.

As if in reaction to the memory, the horizon's bright blue was suddenly blotted — as if God himself spilled ink from the sky so Houser could watch it spread and churn in a roiling mass of angry clouds.

The wind grew cold, then icy. The sun's lips went missing, leaving an empty tundra behind. Houser's skin split and cracked as it sizzled with a crackle along the length of his arm. The wind grew angry, then violent. Wheat thrashed rather than flowed, tangled in a thick nest of dark thistles, lashing Houser with thorns and lacerating his skin.

Houser spilled blood from his arm, just as God had spilled ink from the sky. He ran in a frenzy, surrounded on all sides by twisted vegetation.

Straight was crooked. Crooked, upside down.

The wind grew savage, lashing Houser and sending him from his knees to the ground until he was curled into a fetal ball, barely protecting his face and stomach from the thorns still thrashing like angry talons, ripping into his back until his own screaming was thick in his ears. The copper and ammonia scents of piss and blood curled up into his nose.

This is a dream.

Internal logic begged him to wake.

Somehow, from deep in the thick of his slumber, Houser realized he was dreaming. Once he did, his pain faded.

He looked up and saw that he was again standing amid peaceful fields of flowing wheat, though day had now bled into blackest night. A faint buzzing hummed beneath the wind where he stood. He was about to search for the sound but a mechanical whir coming from somewhere nearby distracted him. Houser looked down to see his skin missing, replaced by black chrome, joints connected by gears, pistons, pumps, and tubes pumping dark fluid instead of blood to keep him running.

Curiosity, and the knowledge that he was dreaming, sent Houser's stare to his arm. He wondered how so many parts could work so fluidly together, and if the dark liquid was fuel or blood.

Ahead, blue light illuminated the sky, as if someone had turned on several spotlights.

He began to move forward, marching to the sound of his whirring gears, utterly fascinated by his every motion, and the space between them. The change to his form didn't scare him, at least nothing like the static bleeding out from the distance.

The sound rose as he drew closer to the light.

Every part of him screamed.

Turn around!

Houser couldn't. He had to see the source of the light because he knew it held answers. It made sense in dream logic. If he were dreaming, Houser could ignore the rising fear telling him to turn.

He had to know what was behind both light and sound.

Wheat thickened as the light brightened, and he moved closer. The cool wind picked up, and for a moment, Houser feared the thorny vegetation's lashing return. Instead, wheat surrendered to a clearing — a wide, flattened circle hundreds of yards in diameter, charred to black. In that burnt ground stood hundreds, if not thousands, of monitors, their screens showing nothing but snow as speakers blasted with an angry, crackling static.

What the hell?

Beneath the thick, buzzing layers of static, Houser heard what sounded like muffled speech.

He moved closer to the monitors, trying to hear better, to decipher what the person was saying. It sounded like a man, but he couldn't be certain. It might have been two people speaking. Tough to say. The louder the static, the more he wished it silent so he could focus on the voices.

What are they saying?

The screens flickered in unison, and for a moment, Houser would've sworn they all cast him in his robotic form, standing among them.

What the ...?

～

HOUSER WOKE, back in the real world, to pounding downstairs.

He shot out of bed, grabbing his pistol from the night-stand as he reached out for his prosthetic leg.

"Who is it?" Jon called from the hallway.

The door burst open, followed by the sound of barking men. "On the ground!"

Jon screamed something incoherent. Emma shrieked.

Houser fumbled with his leg, heart pounding as he tried to

fasten it. He secured it and stood just as his bedroom door exploded open.

Three black-clad Paladin officers stormed inside.

A bald man with a blue, glowing eye stepped forward. A mean-looking scar matched his wicked grin.

"Brock Houser? You're under arrest."

Episode 10

Chapter 1 - Brock Houser

Houser wasn't about to be intimidated by some macho military wannabe like Carl Kaiser.

He sat in the wooden chair, hands cuffed behind him, trapped in the shiny new interrogation room at Paladin Headquarters — a space not too different from, though fancier than, "the box" where Houser questioned suspects back when he was a cop. While his interrogation room had been a dirty, old, claustrophobic cube worthy of its nickname, with a single, two-way mirrored wall, this box was large, almost spacious, with mirrors on all sides, save for the wall with the doorway. The gleaming, white floor and ceiling were almost painfully bright. In many ways, the room was a reflection of Paladin, an armed private police force overcompensating, and full of flash, excess, arrogance, and pride.

As private police forces became increasingly common in America — a natural wave in the aftermath of government budget cuts, growing larger by the year — these private armies attracted the kind of officers who would never have made it in "real" law enforcement. Every private rent-a-cop Houser ever met had chip on their shoulder, resented legitimate authority, and was eager to prove what a Billy Jack Bad Ass he — and sometimes she — was.

Like Carl Kaiser, circling Houser, clicking his boots loudly on the shiny, white floors, clearly enjoying the echo of his steps against the mirrored walls. Hell, the bastard even stole glances, vainly admiring himself in the mirrors and enjoying the moment too much for Houser's comfort.

Kaiser had come into the room five minutes earlier, introducing himself in his crisp, black uniform with flashy patches that made him look more like an over-decorated boy scout than the military badass he was obviously aspiring to. He had since spent most of the time circling Houser as if performing a show.

Was Kaiser was stalling before putting on his show? Giving the rest of the rent-a-cops time to grab their seats on the mirror's more comfortable side?

Fuck that noise.

Houser wasn't the star of anyone's freak show.

He smirked. "So, you gonna ask me something, or do you prefer to keep prancing, maybe do a Broadway number or something in your tap shoes?"

Kaiser turned his nose up at the bait.

Houser wanted to get under the asshole's skin, draw a reaction, take control of the interrogation early, but apparently the guy was more experienced than his promenade suggested.

Kaiser waited a full minute before turning his attention to Houser. The man's artificial eye intensified its blue glow.

Could he control the robotic eye's brightness and color? Maybe those things were tied to Kaiser's emotions and he had no control over them. Perhaps the flare was a sign that Houser was getting to him, after all.

Kaiser spoke, his voice calm. "So, tell me, Mr. Houser, why did you light one of our patrol cars on fire?"

Houser said nothing. Just because the asshole asked a question didn't mean he had to answer.

Let Kaiser stew in his shit for a bit.

Kaiser pressed a button on a black, digital band circling his left wrist. One of the mirrored walls, the one directly in front of Houser, then showed surveillance footage of Houser lighting a Molotov cocktail and tossing it into the Paladin truck. Houser thought he had parked far enough from the security camera and had approached the truck from the side of the house where he should've been out of view. The screen's display meant there must've been more cameras than he realized, hidden of course.

What the hell? They have thousands of obvious cameras. How many hidden ones are there? How many do they need? What the hell are they up to that they need to turn the island into a police state?

"That is you, isn't it? I don't think there are too many other giant, black guys with robotic legs hobbling around Hamilton," Kaiser said.

Houser met his eyes, "I want my lawyer."

"And I want answers. You give me answers, you can call your lawyer."

"No. Now, I do get your boner for police work, seeing how badly you probably want to be a real cop when you grow up. But you see, we have these little things called laws, and they *always* apply, even to you and your fake-ass army. I don't need to say shit to you or anyone else without my lawyer."

Houser smiled.

Kaiser didn't.

Instead, he clicked his wristband again. This time a video, from yet another camera, showed Houser and Milo getting into his SUV.

"Tell me, Mr. Houser, why were you with Milo Anderson?"

Houser ignored the question.

Kaiser continued circling Houser, exhaling a large, exaggerated sigh. "You see, Mr. Houser, I was hoping you and I would get along better than this. I mean, we're both law enforcement. Well, you *were*. And we're both augmented by the generous folks at Conway Industries, the very folks whose car you set on fire, I might add. I was hoping to find you more cooperative, again, considering how much we have in common."

"We ain't got shit in common." Houser sneered.

Kaiser wagged his finger, smiling like a cat inches from a canary, "You see, Mr. Houser, that's where you're wrong. We're a lot more alike than you might think."

Even though Houser figured the man was bluffing, Kaiser's words sent a chill down his spine. Kaiser was working him, trying to get under *his* skin. But Houser was way too experienced to let that happen.

Never let 'em see you sweat.

Houser held Kaiser's stare as if to prove nothing the man could say changed shit. He would call his lawyer and be out in an hour, two tops. His lawyer was good, one of the best. Joe Tannakin, or Joe Fucking Tannakin — J.F.T., as he preferred — would tear these clowns to pieces. First, he'd shine some light on all the weird shit spreading across Hamilton like herpes, then he'd dig up evidence of wrongdoing. By the end of the week, Paladin would be offering Houser a comfortable settlement to disappear.

Houser smiled, hoping to throw Kaiser off his game. Maybe he could get the man to hit him, add battery to the list of charges J.F.T. would hurl at Paladin. "Tell me, something. You hard right now? Seems to me you're getting off on your little display of so-called-power."

Houser imagined chuckles from the other side of the glass. Surely the other rent-a-cops hated this prick Kaiser, too.

He cackled a lunatic's artificial laugh, then slammed both hands on Houser's shoulders. The sudden blow hurt and surprised him, but Houser held the flinch from his face. He met Kaiser's gaze as the man dug his fingers deep into Houser's shoulders, pulling him closer as if on his way to a secret, or to perhaps prove his lunacy by biting Houser's nose.

He considered head-butting the fucker, right in his fake eye, but wanted Kaiser to make the first move, as it seemed he was near doing. Houser's attempts to get under his skin were nested and now seemed ready to hatch.

Kaiser leaned in and whispered, "You know, I wasn't lying when I said we're a lot alike."

Kaiser released Houser's shoulders, stood, then returned to circling Houser, boots clicking on the floor with every step. "You see, Mr. Houser, when Conway Industries saved you after your careless wreck, they didn't just fix your leg."

That drew Houser's attention, though he pretended it didn't. Kaiser promised the truth behind his smile.

"Conway Industries doesn't hand out top-of-the-line prosthetics for free, you know?" Glee painted the corners of his mouth. "I mean, there must be *something* in it for them. You and me were seen as *investments*. Investments which might or might not pay, but investments certainly worth making."

Kaiser paused, holding his mirrored stare on Houser as he rotated around him, obviously unwilling to say more until Houser showed that he did, in fact, want to hear every word Kaiser had to say.

Fuck, he's got me, and he knows it.

Houser bit. "What does that mean?"

"It means it isn't just your leg Conway Industries made better. They enhanced your brain, too. Right now, you have all these little nanobots running around inside your head, waiting for instructions from their master."

"Bullshit." But he was suddenly uncertain. And terrified.

Kaiser smiled, sinking into the moment. "Oh, Mr. Houser, how I love your naiveté. You really have no idea what's happening here, do you?"

Houser pulled at the cuffs binding his hands behind him,

wanting to break free and run. He didn't know what in the hell was happening, but he did know Kaiser wasn't lying. They *had* done something to him. Now all the weird shit on the island was starting to add up, even if he couldn't quite see the equation.

Conway Industries was using people. But why?

Kaiser reached into his pocket and pulled out a tiny, black square that looked like the smallest phone Houser had ever seen. Kaiser held it up for Houser — there was a small, digital screen on it with a blue circle. In that circle was the number 789. "This is you, Mr. Houser. Number 789. When I press this button, I can command the slave nanobots in you to do whatever I wish. Or more accurately, to have *you* do whatever I wish."

Houser stared at the circle, unwilling to believe his life had been reduced to a number, that he could possibly be a slave to these fuckers' plans. This had to be another fear tactic — another attempt to break him, to get him to talk and divulge whatever he knew.

"I want my lawyer!" Houser shouted loud enough for anyone watching on the other side of the mirrors to hear — maybe someone with the authority to yank Kaiser from the room.

Kaiser continued, ignoring Houser. He pressed the button on the device and spoke.

"What I want from you right now, Mr. Houser is for you to tell me everything. Every little thing you've done since arriving on the island."

Something shifted in Houser's brain. He could feel it, as if someone shoved him from the driver's seat and took his steering wheel away. He tried to resist the directive.

No, don't say shit!

Houser's body ignored his mind and did as instructed, telling Kaiser everything.

Chapter 2 - Chief Kevin Brady

Chief Kevin Brady sat at his office computer, tethering his mind to the mundane, avoiding thoughts of the body — which may or may not have been his daughter — fished from the sea.

Brady hadn't said a word to his wife, or anyone, since calling the medical examiner Holstrum to come in from Bennet County to pick her up and bring her back to his office for an autopsy.

His hopes were up, that was enough. He didn't dare raise Molly's, too. He didn't think she could handle the news. If their daughter was found dead, she would crumple like foil. If the body wasn't Christina's, she'd see her lifeline of hope renewed and somehow strengthened. *If it's not her, that must mean she's still alive.*

A few months ago, Molly swore up and down she'd seen Christina in a dream, saying she'd be home soon. Molly wanted to believe the dream, desperately, enough to go out and buy a dress for when her little girl returned.

She sprawled the pink-and-white dress out on Christina's bed, as if preparing for First Communion, then visited the girl's bedroom each morning, expecting to see Christina trying it on while smiling into the mirror. Brady couldn't bear to see Molly, standing over the dress, planting seeds beneath a dead sun. So, he took the dress and threw it away.

Molly lost it.

She screamed and cried and hit him, slamming her fists into his chest over and over before she got so wound up, she smacked him straight across the face. She delivered another dozen wallops to his chest as he stood rooted, until she finally collapsed into a mess against him, empty but for her sobbing.

Brady hugged her for two hours without stopping, wishing he could take away her pain. Hell, he would absorb it and endure it himself, if it meant she wouldn't have to be subject to prolonged agony.

But he couldn't.

Best he could do was keep her from getting too hopeful.

So whenever any leads on Christina came in, Brady held them close — waiting for them to pan out before daring to whisper a word. He alone would bear this latest discovery's hope.

So Brady waited for Holstrum to get back to him, burying himself in busywork and steering an occupied mind from his missing child.

Or at least, he tried to.

Mundane as the expense reports were, Brady's mind wandered and flashed to the corpse on Jackson's boat, playing the images in a loop.

Christina had been gone for more than six months, yet the body wasn't badly decomposed. In order for the body to be his daughter's, it meant the girl was recently killed and dumped at sea, or in the caves, or maybe she'd been killed months earlier, but wrapped in something, like carpet, and had somehow come free from the shroud, floated to the surface, well-preserved in the cold waters, then wound up in the caves.

There was also a third option —the vic wasn't his child.

And if it wasn't his child, whose was it? How did she die?

Hamilton Island was home to misfortune, especially lately with too many missing people. Fourteen total, three kids. Could this be number fifteen? Or the fourth missing child? Or might it be a missing child from somewhere else? The body was found on his island — and was, for the moment, another of his cases to close. Or to leave open for God knew how long, hoping for resolution.

That word again, hope.

He'd questioned the "asshole on the schooner," a man named Ron Ellison, enough to figure the guy didn't know anything about a dead child, let alone play a role in the girl's murder. Ellison was cousin to one of Brady's friends, Bob Westcott, and Westcott confirmed what Brady suspected — the man might be an asshole, but he wasn't a killer. Just another drunk, dumb dickface, on an island full of them, with too much time and the money to match.

At the moment, Brady had no other suspects. His only evidence was whatever DNA — if there was anyone else's in the girl's nails or inside her body, if raped — Holstrum found during his examination, all of which would be filed on the network.

But Brady was limited in his investigation until after he heard from Holstrum. Anything else, such as requesting surveillance feeds from Paladin, would alert them that he'd found a body. For now, just in case this was his girl, he didn't want them fucking this up. If the body *was* Christina's, he wanted to make sure the killer saw justice — and not the legal kind.

No, Brady would find and kill whoever was responsible.

But that meant keeping things quiet as long as he could. Brady sighed, sipping his coffee — gone from cold to icy to frigid in the hour he'd been sitting numb at his desk. He hit save on his computer and logged off. The expense reports would wait. He needed to get out of the office, interact with others before going stir crazy.

He said goodbye to Judy at the front desk. "I'm headed out for some coffee."

"Okay, Chief." Judy waved goodbye and returned her attention to Earl, an old man who stopped by the station every day to chat her up with island gossip. Brady wondered if that's how he would be when old, hanging around in public places, or worse, at the station — assuming it was still around and not completely taken over by Paladin — hoping to feel part of something he wasn't. With the way things were going with Molly, it was easy to picture himself as exactly that sort of lonely, old man.

Brady hopped in his car and was about to pull out of the parking lot, when his phone rang — Holstrum.

He braced himself, then said, "Brady."

"Hey, Kevin. I've got the dental."

As Holstrum spoke, Brady felt his breath catch, waiting.

"It's not Christina. I'm extracting DNA from the girl's molars. We'll enter her into the database, see what comes up. But we know enough to rule her out. It's not your daughter."

Brady allowed himself a breath and chased it with a sigh. "Thank you, Nick."

"We're making this an official, open case, though, so I'll need you to fill out a report and send it over, soon as you can."

"I'll get right on it. Thanks again for doing this, and for keeping it between us. I really didn't want Molly thinking … well, you know."

"Yeah, I know. No problem, Kevin. I'll call you when we get more info." Holstrum sounded like he was going to add something more — perhaps an "I'm sorry" since he knew — as much as it was good news that Christina might still be out there, it was also bad, because they had no answers, and were again left with nothing but hope.

Brady killed the call and stared at the screen. It was a minute before he felt the tears.

Chapter 3 - Milo Anderson

Milo threw on his black hoodie, about to head out the door, when his father came home.

"Dad, what are you doing home so early?" Milo asked, hoping not to highlight his anxiety. He was about to head out on his way to meet Don and Houser and didn't expect to find himself stumbling through a sudden explanation. His father almost never came home in the middle of the day.

Was something wrong?

Maybe with Bea?

"I came home to have lunch with you, is that okay?" Dad set his briefcase on the couch and pulled his son into a hug.

While Milo's father was making an effort to be present, and more open to Milo since Bea plowed into Jordy's, it still felt weird when they hugged. Almost fake, as if they were trying to overcompensate for years of neglect. It felt forced, too fast, like a historically-inattentive guy suddenly showering his girlfriend with chocolates out of the blue — weird and awkward.

Milo felt guilty for feeling that way when his dad was finally trying to be a good father, but feeling guilty didn't make him any more accepting of the sudden gesture.

He looked at the TV — 11:15 a.m. He still had a bit of time before he had to meet Don and Houser in Don's usual spot in the woods. But he had to leave the house soon. Don had asked him to show up early, so they could talk about Roboleg before Houser showed. He also said something about the psychological impact of staking their turf, to put Houser at a disadvantage, as if they were entering into negotiations or something. Milo figured Don would get there an hour earlier than Milo, just to scout the place and make sure there was no one waiting in ambush. If something weird happened, anything at all, Don warned, "I'm gone like the wind, and you'll never see me again."

Milo being late would definitely qualify as "weird" in Don's book, so Milo had to scarf down his lunch.

"Okay," Milo said. "We can eat, but I've gotta run. I'm meeting Katie."

"Katie? Isn't she in school? Or is she being homeschooled, too?"

"She gets out early for work-study, but her work didn't need her today, so she asked if I'd help with an assignment."

"Okay." Dad headed into the kitchen and started looking for something to make. "Speaking of assignments, did you do yours for the day?"

"Yes," Milo said, almost snapped. "I can print an e-mail from the online instructor if you don't believe me."

His father looked at him oddly.

Maybe he'd been too defensive and revealed that he was up to something.

Shit.

Then Dad smiled. "Relax, son. I didn't accuse you of anything. Just checking up. That's all."

"Sorry," Milo said, trying not to oversell his apology. In his nervousness, he scratched at his arm and accidentally lifted the sleeve.

His father's eyes widened. He reached out and yanked

Milo's sleeve the rest of the way up. "Good God, Milo, what's this?"

Milo stared down, almost in shame. Red blotches pocked the length of his right arm. His father lifted the opposite sleeve, gasping louder.

"I don't know," Milo said. "I think I have some sorta rash or something."

"Why didn't you tell me?" He pulled Milo's arms up for closer inspection. "Does it hurt?"

"No, not really. It's just super itchy. And I didn't want to worry you. I figured you have enough going on with Bea and this would go away. You know, like those rashes I used to get from the detergent before mom switched. I figured it was something like that."

"We've gotta get you to the doctor."

No! I can't go now.

If Milo missed the meeting and Don took off, he would never find out what was happening. Milo *had* to know, needed to know unlike anything else in his life, but couldn't act like he *couldn't* go to the doctors, or his dad would know he was up to something besides meeting Katie.

"I'm gonna call Dr. Benson." Dad reached into his pocket.

"No!" Milo shouted, not meaning to yell.

His father put his phone on the kitchen island. "What's going on, son?"

Shit. Shit.

Milo had to think of something quickly.

"It's about Katie," Milo set his foot on the lie without knowing where the path headed. "I'm kind of in love with her."

"What?" Dad asked, surprised, but decidedly less freaked out than he would be if Milo suddenly started spouting off about Don, Houser, the flash drive, the conspiracy, and how the Paladin officers nearly busted him breaking into Alex Heller's house.

"Yeah, it just sorta happened after the funeral. We'd been talking online, and we're sort of, I dunno, just helping each other through something rough," Milo lied. "She called today saying she really wanted to talk, and well, I don't know what she wants, but it felt important. So, maybe the doctor's visit can wait? I mean, I've been itchy for a few weeks now, what's another day?"

"Okay." He took another look at Milo's arms and winced. "I *guess* it can wait." Dad looked down at the loaf of bread, then back up from the counter to Milo. "You're not really hungry, are you?"

Milo smiled. "Um, not really. Kinda wanna get to Katie as soon as possible."

"Okay." He held out his hand to excuse Milo. "It's all right. We can do this another time. Maybe tomorrow, and I'll take you to the doctor's afterward."

"Sounds good." Milo spun around, eager to get outside and onto his bike. Before he hit the front door, he again thought of how hard his dad was trying, and then about how he'd just lied to his face, manipulating his father's love to flee the house.

He went back into the kitchen and hugged his dad. "Thanks, Dad. I appreciate you coming home. I swear, we'll do this tomorrow. And thanks for understanding."

His father hugged him, hard, like Milo had just come home from camp. It was surprising. Touching. Parting from the embrace, he swore tears were forming in the corners of his father's eyes.

As Milo raced out the front door, he almost wanted to come clean and tell his dad the truth about everything. But a bigger part wanted to reach Don and Houser as soon as possible. There were all sorts of things that could go wrong if Milo wasn't there as a buffer between the paranoid Don and Houser. It could get ugly.

Milo hopped on his bike and raced away as fast as he could pedal.

❧

MILO REACHED the meeting spot with five minutes to spare.

Don was standing behind a tree, looking even more frazzled than usual. His hair, beneath his Mariner's cap, was wild, and his eyes darted from branch to branch then tree to tree, as if a group of Paladin officers might spring forth at any moment.

"You're here," Don said. "I was worried something happened."

"I'm early. Man, what's got you so spooked? I said we can trust Houser."

"Dude got a friggin' robotic leg from Conway! Don't you think he might be a bit indebted?"

"I don't know. I know he got me out of the Heller house. He didn't have to do that. Man, why are we even talking about this again? I thought you already agreed to trust me on this?"

Don nodded. "Yes, trust. Trust, but verify!"

"So, you're here to *verify?*" Milo asked. "And what if I'm wrong, and this guy brings the entire Paladin army?"

"Then ..." Don patted his jacket.

It looked suspiciously puffier than usual, draped on the man's lank frame.

"Then, I blow them all up with me."

"What?" Milo took two steps back. "Are you saying you've got a ...?"

"Shh!" Don raised his index finger to his mouth, nodding.

"Holy shit, you *are* crazy!" Milo turned around. "I'm not sticking around for this."

"Don't leave!" Don shouted. "You're in this shit deep, same as me, Milo. If it goes south, you go, too."

"Dude, you're gonna blow yourself up? Over what? Even if Houser was bad, even if he brings Paladin with him, what does it solve to blow yourself up, and maybe a handful of them? You're still dead. They still win!"

Milo wasn't even sure who *they* were, and even less sure now that Don was about to go all suicide bomber that there was a *they*, at least not in the way Don thought. What if all the weirdness of the past few months could, in fact, be nothing more than coincidences, misinterpreted by a man gone mad over losing his family?

He started feeling sick to his stomach, wishing he'd stayed home with his father. Suddenly that final hug, squeezing so hard, seemed almost prophetic.

Milo felt like he was about to die.

Chapter 4 - Cassidy Hughes

Cassidy was curled on the couch, waiting for Jon to get off the phone so she could break the news — she wasn't going to dinner at his father's tonight.

Her anxiety about the dinner grew as the morning unfolded, worsened when she arrived at Jon's house that morning to find him freaking out after Paladin officers had come and arrested Houser during the night.

She wasn't sure how he could get through dinner with all the drama. The thought of sitting with the Conway family, the people who used her as a wedge between Jon and Sarah, made her sick to her stomach. She didn't think she could stand seeing Warren's smug face without telling him and his shrew harpy bitch cunt of a wife to go get stuffed with something veiny.

But as she listened to Jon, who sat at the bar speaking to Houser on the phone, she reconsidered her timing. She wasn't sure what was happening with Houser, and if it was bad, she didn't want to throw a log on the fire.

Cassidy looked at the clock — only a couple of hours before she had to pick up Emma from school. She had hoped for a chance to tell Jon before then. Otherwise, the news would be too last minute and would damper their date in the city, which Jon planned to follow the dinner.

He spent most of the morning on the phone, calling everyone from Chief Brady to his lawyer to his father. Judging from Jon's conversation with Houser, someone must've done something. It sounded like Houser had been let go.

"Okay, see you tonight," Jon said as he hung up.

"Well?" she asked. "How is he? Does he need a ride?"

"No . They dropped him off here, and he left."

"What? Why didn't he come inside?"

"I don't know," Jon said. "He said he had work to finish. He didn't say what, but he sounded hurried."

"So, why the hell did they storm in here?"

"I don't know. He said something about it all being a big mistake."

"A mistake? What the fuck?"

"I don't know. It all sounds weird. I'm sure he'll fill us in when he gets home."

"I think we should cancel tonight," Cassidy said. "My mom's still bitching about her back, and I'm not leaving Emma with her."

"No, that's not necessary. Houser said everything was fine. He's still planning to watch Emma."

"I dunno," Cassidy said. "I mean, you just had armed officers burst down your door. I don't think I like the idea of leaving her here."

"What? Are you worried about Houser?" Jon asked.

"No, not him. Just, I don't know, it feels like the house is less safe now."

"Don't be ridiculous," Jon said. "They wouldn't have let Houser go if something was wrong. Come on, it'll be fine. I'll talk to Father tonight and add Paladin to my litany of gripes."

"I don't know." Cassidy was looking forward to their romantic night at The Hillside and desperately needed the time away, even if she still felt awkward with her growing closeness to Jon. A night away from Hamilton, from Ship-wrecked, from her mom, and, as loathe as she was to think it, Emma, was just what she needed. Just what *they* needed — a night away from the island, far from Sarah's ghosts.

Jon sat beside Cassidy on the couch and pulled her closer. "Okay, I've got an idea, then."

She met his gaze. "What?"

"We bring Houser and Emma with us."

"With us? To a romantic hotel?"

"Not *with us*, with us. I mean I'll check them into a room, at the end of the hall or on another floor. That way Paladin couldn't come breaking down the door even if they wanted. They have zero jurisdiction off the island."

"I dunno," Cassidy said. "That's a bit weird, don't you think?"

"If it means you're less nervous, I don't care how weird it sounds."

"You think you can get a room this late?"

Jon smiled, "Come on. It's me, *The* Jon Conway, movie star!"

She smacked him playfully. "Ah, yes, I should've recognized you by your world-renowned humility."

"Oh, I'm the humblest man ever." Jon leaned closer and kissed her. It was weird how quickly Cassidy felt familiar with his kiss, how comfortable — like a longtime lover. With most men she'd dated, especially ones with such different kissing styles from her prior lovers, it took a while for new lips to feel like an old home.

Jon's hands moved up her shirt, then his fingers brushed her nipples. She shivered. The good kind. Cassidy loved the electricity in his touch. Loved how they felt so right together. Loved everything about him, actually.

I love ...

And there it was — a thought she'd dared not consider, dare not ask, bubbling up to the surface.

Do I love him?

She shook the thought from her mind, then from her body. It was best not to consider such things, not to think too far ahead, or plan anything like love. If life had taught her one thing, it was that God, fate, the universe, or whatever didn't care for your plans. All the better to keep from tempting destiny by living day to day, never counting on anyone or anything.

Jon reached down and slid his hand between her legs.

Cassidy was wet, and ready, but as she closed her eyes, she felt suddenly short of breath, anxious. She had to break the news now, even if it murdered their mood.

She pulled herself from Jon. "I don't want to go to dinner at your father's tonight."

"What?"

"I'm sorry. I should've said something sooner, but I don't want to go. I don't want to be there — I'm not ready to play nice with the Conways. You can take Emma, and I understand why you want to. She's curious about her grandpa — only has the one and didn't know it until now. But I don't want to be there, can't be there, especially knowing you're going to take your dad aside at some point and blast him for all that happened. That is soooo not something I want to do tonight."

She expected protest. Instead Jon smiled. "Okay. I understand. And sorry I didn't think to ask you if it would be a problem. Hell, I'm not even sure *I'm* ready to sit at the table with them! You are totally, absolutely, one hundred percent right."

Cassidy swallowed. Blinked. Stared.

Jon raised a finger. "Okay, now that you've given me a moment to think with something other than my pecker, I remember I need to make some calls — let people know Houser is out before Marty sends a squad of lawyers parachuting down on the island or something! We'll pick this up tonight?" Then he kissed her.

"Okay," Cassidy said.

Jon popped up from the cushions like a hyper child, then went back to the bar separating kitchen from living room.

"Hey, Marty. Yeah, he's out."

As Jon made his calls, Cassidy sat on the couch and watched him in his natural environment — wheeling and dealing, discussing important things with powerful people, like ordering à la carte from the menu. Just a couple of months back she was disgusted by Jon's seemingly-insincere smooth-talking. This wasn't the Jon she spent time with, the Jon she was falling so hard for. This was a player, through and through, not too different from his father or brother.

As Cass watched Jon laughing and smiling like a smug actor, she was surprised to find her rising anger. She tried to quell her swelling disgust and the nasty thoughts behind them. Her mind flew to her pocket, where an envelope waited, offering release, and an immediate end to her anxiety — happiness just a swallow away.

Chapter 5 - Milo Anderson

Milo stared at Don, pacing the forest on the lookout for Houser — or anyone else. Milo wondered if he'd be able to outrun a blast if the man triggered his bomb vest from just ten feet away.

Milo was quick, but how fast was an explosion? In movies, heroes ran and jumped just in time to clear the blast, with debris swirling like snow flurries in the background. But that seemed like bullshit to Milo. In reality, he figured the blast would spread farther, likely roasting anyone attempting to run. Ten feet didn't seem like nearly far enough if the man beside you was wearing a bomb vest.

He could tell Don he had to piss and would be right back. Surely, the man would grant him privacy. As he opened his mouth to tell Don, Houser closed it by appearing on the path.

"Hey, guys."

"Hands in the air!" Don shouted, aiming his gun at Houser.

Where the fuck did he get a gun? Well, I guess I shouldn't be surprised since he has a damned bomb vest!

"It's cool, it's cool." Houser raised both hands as he

stopped at the top of the hill. "I just wanna talk, man. You and me, we're on the same side."

"Yeah, and what side is that?" Don asked.

Milo looked at Don, wishing he'd stop sounding like a crazy fuck. Humans had such talent for escalation. A glare so easily led to a shout, a shout to a stick. Sticks to guns and guns to Kevlar. Bombs, missiles, worse. Whether it was the whole wide world, or man-to-man, *real* men were taught to never back down, leaving them forever at the edge of war, real or imagined. Houser would have to defend himself. Then, BOOM! Don would respond. Don was, without realizing it, pushing himself toward the fate he hoped to avoid.

"I'm just looking for the same thing you are," Houser said. "Truth."

That seemed to calm Don a bit. His rapid breathing slowed, and his finger seemed less itchy. Don's left hand was still inside his jacket, though, likely on the button which would detonate his vest.

"Can I come down the hill?" Houser asked. "I'll need my hands to balance myself, what with this leg and all."

"Yeah," Don said almost reluctantly, fixing his aim on Houser as the man slowly descended the incline, carefully navigating the dirt with both his human and robot feet.

Milo looked back and forth from Houser to Don, hoping like hell Don wouldn't get spooked. All Houser had to do was reach them, then Milo was confident the big man could charm Don into trusting him.

Houser was a private investigator, and a cop before that. He'd said he was plenty used to dealing with people on the edge and comfortable talking them down. Milo hoped that between Houser's skills and the fact that Don, crazy or not, was a decent guy in a bad spot, everyone would be leaving the forest alive.

Houser finally reached them and sent his hands back in

the air, palms facing Don. "Just so you know, I'm packing. Gun in my jacket holster, if you wanna get it."

Don looked at Houser and shook his head. "No, that's okay. Just keep your hands where I can see them."

"Yes, sir," he said. "My name is Brock Houser. I'm a private investigator out of California. And you are?"

"What? Milo didn't tell you my name?"

"He called you Mr. X, and unless you're a bald professor of mutants, I don't think that X stands for Xavier."

Good, a geeky X-Men reference. That should put Don at ease, maybe even earn a laugh. Comic geeks rarely work for the bad guys, do they?

Milo considered laughing, to chill everyone's nerves, but was afraid to make any sound which might spook Don's trigger finger.

Don didn't laugh, though he did seem slightly less scared shitless.

"Name's Don Bellows."

His honesty surprised Milo. Maybe Don was coming around, or figured he had nothing to lose. If Houser betrayed them, they were all dead, anyway.

"It's good to meet you, Mr. Bellows," Houser said. "Thank you for agreeing to meet me."

"What is it you wanna know?"

"Well, I was hoping we could pool our resources. I tell you what I know, you tell me what you know, specifically what you know about the flash drive, plus whatever you can tell me about Roger Heller."

"You first," Don said. "You talk first."

Houser told his story — how Liz Heller asked him to decrypt what was on the flash drive, but that he got into a car accident before he could. After that, his mind was fuzzy and the flash drive gone.

"You think it was an accident?" Don asked, not seeming to mock Houser for thinking so, but genuinely curious if Houser thought it might have been.

"I don't know. As a cop, I always believed the most obvious hunch was the right one. But shit here on the island defies obvious hunches. So, I'm not sure what to think. What do *you* think?"

"I think there's something going on with Conway Industries. I think they're somehow involved in Hamilton's missing people, with Roger Heller shooting his classroom before killing himself, and even with what happened to Milo and his stepmom. They're doing something to the people."

"And what do you think that something is?" Houser asked, still standing with his hands airborne.

"I don't know, exactly. But I've been gathering evidence. One night, Roger Heller reached out to me and said he had something he wanted me to see. It was on a flash drive, and he seemed eager to get it to me. Next thing I know, he shoots up the school, then kills himself. I think the flash drive is the missing piece. Tell me, Mr. Houser, when you got into the accident, where was it?"

Before Houser could answer, a blue arc of light lit the sky above, striking Don, who fell to the ground, flat on his face. The gun flew from his hand.

Milo braced for an impact, but there was no explosion. He looked around, trying to see what happened.

Was it lightning?

Milo looked back at Houser, now holding his gun and aiming it at Milo, "Don't move."

"What did you do?" Milo shouted, looking down at an unmoving Don.

Suddenly, Milo saw them — dozens of flying metal bird-like *things*, hovering in the air over Don's body. A blue arc of light crackled beneath one and sent light flying at Milo.

He fell to the forest floor in a heap.

Chapter 6 - Cassidy Hughes

Cassidy stopped by her mom's house after picking up a bottle of wine and some food from the store. Her mom hadn't asked for anything, but Cassidy knew if she didn't stop by with something, Vivian would call her in the middle of night, knowing she was out of town, just to guilt-trip her. Cassidy had wised up to her mother's ways years ago, and with her nerves already on edge from not knowing what the hell would happen with Jon during dinner, she didn't need Vivian to worry about.

She knocked on the door. "It's me, Ma, I brought some stuff."

"Well, come in, already. You have a key!" her mom barked from her nest, six feet from the TV.

Cassidy went to unlock the door, but noticed it was already unlocked.

"Mom, you left the door open again. How many times do I need to tell you to keep it locked?"

"I haven't even been out today!" Vivian shouted over whatever inane game show was polluting the screen.

Cassidy didn't bother arguing. It was pointless. Besides, anyone on the island who knew Vivian wasn't likely to fuck with her. She may be an old drunk with a bad back, but she was feisty as fuck. Anyone dumb enough to come into her house uninvited would surely regret it.

"Okay." Cassidy brought the bottle of wine into the living room. "Got you some Coppola."

"Oh, you sprang for the good stuff," she said. "Did your *boyfriend* give you some shopping money?"

Vivian spat "boyfriend," barely barring judgment from her voice and taking Cassidy by surprise.

"What? I thought you liked Jon."

"Like is a strong word. I'm getting used to him, let's say," Vivian slurred her words. "And Emma seems to like him."

Oh, great, she's already hitting the sauce, and she's Angry Drunk tonight!

"He's a nice guy," Cassidy said. "And he's been very nice to you, so drop the attitude."

"So why are you bringing me stuff? You came over with stuff yesterday."

"I'm going into the city with Jon and Emma. I'll be there tonight and tomorrow, so I wanted to make sure you were set."

"The city? Why?"

"We wanted to get out of town for a bit." She felt like a child having to explain herself.

I'm a grown woman, for Christ's sake.

Cassidy wanted to snap back at her mom, but it wasn't worth the argument. Vivian was likely looking for attention since Cass was about to go off and have a nice evening.

God forbid I do something fun.

She headed to the kitchen to put the groceries away. "Want me to make you something while I'm here?"

"Oh, I don't want to trouble you, *Sarah*."

Cassidy sighed, not sure if Vivian called her Sarah absent-mindedly as she was prone to doing these days, or if it was on purpose, to drive a knife in her psyche.

Just another little dig. Why the hell does she always have to snipe at me? I'm the only one left who will put up with her shit and take care of her. She ought to be nicer.

I've news for you, Viv. Sarah ain't here anymore. I am. So cut the shit.

There was a time Cassidy might have said all that to her mom, but that was when Sarah was still around. Back when it didn't matter if her mom was pissed, since Sarah was there to commiserate and usher her back to normal. Now, without anyone else, Cassidy didn't want to push back. Or allow Vivian to push her away completely. Vivian was too stubborn to ever apologize or admit she needed anyone, so if they fell into a huge battle, she might very well retreat into isolation. In isolated Vivian would be a dead Vivian before too long, without help. So Cassidy had to let things slide and not allow her mother to further sabotage their relationship.

Cassidy had given up on trying to prove Vivian wrong, or achieving the small victories once so important to her. The war was over, and Cassidy just wanted peace in her life.

"It's no trouble," Cassidy called back. "Would you like a grilled cheese and some soup?"

"Sounds good," she said. "You staying to eat with me?"

"Yeah." Cassidy pulled a pot from the bottom cupboard. She went to set it on the stove when she noticed the interior, crusted with gunk from the last time Vivian made something. She wondered if her mom forgot to run the dishwasher and simply put the pot away dirty, or if the dishwasher had just done a shit job cleaning that pot. Cassidy pulled out a few pans and noticed that they, too, were dirty. As were several cups and plates.

Jesus, Mom.

Cassidy wanted to say something but didn't want to embarrass her mother. She hated thinking her mom might be going senile, even though it seemed increasingly difficult to ignore. She thought about Silver Linings, the island's largest age-in-place retirement community, and wondered if she could convince her mom to sell the house if she could afford living there — where staff could help take care of things like this.

Cassidy pulled the dirty dishes from the cupboards and loaded the dishwasher. Vivian continued watching TV, off in her own world, oblivious to Cassidy.

∼

AS THEY SAT at the dining room table, Vivian nibbled her grilled cheese, slurped her soup, and went on about her day, covering several inane topics. Cassidy feigned just enough interest to keep her mother from getting offended.

Cassidy drifted through her thoughts, wondering how Jon was handling dinner at his father's and whether he had yet spoken to Blake.

Vivian rambled on and on, until suddenly — out of the blue — she said something to snap Cassidy to attention.

"You know, that boy will never love you, Sarah."

"Who won't love me?" she said, not bothering to correct her on her name.

"Jonny. He's like his daddy, all charm and good looks, but underneath it all, a snake. They're all snakes, believe it." Vivian filled her empty glass with more wine.

Cassidy couldn't let it go. "Why is it you hate the Conways so much, Mom? What in the hell did they ever do to you?"

"Not what they did to *me*," Vivian said. "What Blake did to your daddy."

"What do you mean what they did to Daddy? He skipped out when we were born, what does Blake Conway have to do with that?"

"Your father used to work with Blake. Well, before ..." Vivian trailed off, first into mumbles, then into silence.

"What, Mom?"

"Huh?" Vivian said as if snapped back from a catnap.

"You were saying Dad worked with Blake Conway before … before what?"

"Why don't you ask your boyfriend?"

Cassidy hated how Vivian kept calling Jon her *boyfriend*. "This is the first time I'm hearing that my father, a man I never knew, worked with Blake Conway. I'm pretty sure Jon would know nothing about it."

"Then ask his daddy. *He'll* know. Though I doubt he'll tell you." Vivian cackled before falling into a long fit of coughing.

Cassidy was annoyed at Vivian for her pettiness, and at herself for not having gone to dinner with Jon and Emma. "Just tell me, Mom."

"I don't want to talk about it anymore."

"Then why the hell did you bring it up?" Cassidy's voice rose to a whine. If Vivian was baiting her, Cassidy had been hooked into a fight.

"I'm sorry. And don't yell at me." Her mother launched into crocodile tears.

Great, more drama!

"Come on, Mom, I wasn't yelling at you. I'm just frustrated. Why can't you tell me something that happened more than thirty years ago?"

Vivian's tears were gone. Anger burned in her eyes. "Just fucking ask *him* if you wanna know!"

Cassidy stared at her mom, whose hands shook. She snarled at Cassidy as she reached for her wine. then downed it. Glass empty, she stood, snarled again, went into the living room, sank into her recliner, cranked the volume, and stared at her monitor as it lit back with color.

Cassidy sat at the kitchen table, stunned, mouth agape.

Vivian then shouted over the blaring TV, "That means goodnight, in case you can't take a hint!"

Cassidy fumed. She wanted to march into the living room and yell at her mom for being such a fucking bitch, and for ruining her night, thank you very much, but she wasn't about to fall further into her mom's trap. She wasn't going to give Vivian any more of what she craved.

Instead, she left the table, not bothering to put her bowl or plate in the sink, then walked out the front door, slamming it shut behind her. She was about to stomp off, but turned back, locked the door, then left.

~

CASSIDY DROVE BACK to Jon's house, pissed, confused, and wondering what Blake Conway had to do with her dad leaving them. If Vivian was telling the truth, and there was no reason to suspect she wasn't — her mom might be angry, drunk, and confused, but she never knowingly lied to Cassidy, so far as she knew — then Blake had done something to chase her father off forever. But what? And why? Did Blake Conway have some fetish with chasing dads from the Hughes family?

She pulled into Jon's garage wishing he was back from Blake's. But the garage was empty, which meant the house was, too. Just her and her pills.

Cassidy went in through the kitchen, passed the bar, then plopped on the couch, surfing channels, searching for something, anything, to distract her. But the Addict was back, whispering sweet nothings in her ear like a lover.

Come on, relax, Cassidy. You deserve it after dealing with your crazy bitch mom!

"No! Leave me alone."

Don't be mad. I'm only trying to help.

"I don't need you."

Why? Because you're all Suzy Twelve-Step? Who the fuck are you kidding, Cassidy? You think you're Sarah? Moving in with her man, mother to her child? Come on. Who the fuck are you fooling? You're only mad at your mom because she calls you on your bullshit.

She knows you're trying to replace Sarah.

"No, I'm not."

Come on, Cass. Just a pill or two. What harm is there in a pill or two? Nobody ever died from taking a couple of pills. Besides, it will make tonight so much better. You think Jon wants to be with you when you're stressed out? You do know that's when you're at your bitchiest, don't you?

"Stop it. Stop it. Stop it. I don't need you."

Even as she said it, and believed it, her hand reached into her pants pocket and pulled out the small envelope with her tiny pills. Six. She felt their shapes so close beneath the thick paper. She didn't need to take them. She just wanted to touch them, count them, make sure they're still there.

She opened the envelope, pulled two pills into her hand and stared. "I don't need you," she said to the pills as if they might answer.

Cassidy didn't know who she was lying to — the pills or herself.

She did need them.

She did want them.

Cassidy popped them into her mouth, grabbed a bottle of water, swallowed, then waited for the pills to deliver their sweet promise.

Chapter 7 - Jon Conway

"God, it's only four o'clock," Warren said from his side of the table. "We're eating dinner like old people."

Warren sat across from Jon. Emma sat beside her father, across from Melinda, who seemed to *almost* thaw in Emma's presence. Perhaps she was a different person around children. Jon remembered when Anastasia was born and how happy Melinda had been back then. But now that her daughter was away at school, and she was stuck with Warren and Blake all the time, she'd become a different person — not that Jon could blame her.

Family, at its worst — parasitic, and robbing you of joy one rotten word and act at a time.

Blake, as always, sat at the head of the table, to Jon and Emma's right.

"Thank you for doing this early," Jon said. "We're going into the city later."

"Oh, for what?" Melinda stabbed her salad then filled her mouth with fresh greens.

"Cassidy wanted to show me a few of the places that have sprung up since I left. She especially wants me to see The Hillside. She says I'll love it."

"Oh, The Hillside is *wonderful!*" Melinda agreed. "You've never stayed there?"

"No, never had a reason, though I've heard great things."

"Why isn't Cassidy with us?" Melinda hadn't been in the room when Jon told Blake and Warren that Cassidy had a few things to take care of, and that she'd love to come next time.

"She had more pressing things 'to take care of,'" Warren said, setting his disdain for Cassidy on display. "Good thing she'll get them tidied before Jon checks her into the five-star hotel. She's not stayed there herself yet, has she, Jon?"

Jon shot Warren a look, but otherwise didn't rise to the bait.

Don't trash her in front of her niece, bastard.

As if to squash his eldest's swagger, Blake said, "So, tell me, Emma, what keeps a smart girl like you interested?"

"Everything," Emma said, not missing a beat. "I love to write and draw and watch TV. I also like to play puzzle games and cook, and I really, really like to talk. I also like spending time with Aunt Cassidy and Jon and Houser. And sometimes Gram." Emma spit her four sentences so fast, they sounded almost like one. "OH! And sometimes I like to sit and think without doing anything else."

Blake laughed at the last part, amused by his granddaughter. "And what is it you like to think about most?"

"I don't know." Emma shrugged. "I guess I've been thinking a lot about my mom lately. Before she died, I used to think a lot about my best friend Rachel, though I don't really play with her that much anymore. I used to wonder who my dad was, but that was before I met Jon." Emma shrugged again. "Lately, I've been wondering if I'll always feel alone."

Jon said, "But you're not alone, Emma."

"Sometimes, I feel alone, even when I'm not."

Blake reached across the table, not quite touching Emma's hand. "May I tell you something?"

"Of course," Emma said. "You're my grandpa. You're supposed to tell me stuff."

He smiled. "Whether you like it or not, you'll be alone many times throughout your life. This is true for everyone, but especially so when you're a smart girl, as you clearly are. Loneliness is the burden of genius. Expect to spend much of your life in isolation, even when surrounded by friends, of which I'm sure you'll have many, and family, of which you've recently added some more." He winked. "I have both, yet I've been plenty lonely myself, I'd say more than most. I feel it deeply sometimes, Emma. Permanently, like a scar inside me. The trick isn't in learning not to be lonely, it's in learning to find the comfort inside yourself because you know *that's* the one thing in your world that once built can never disappear or be taken from you. Embrace your isolation and you can find comfort in anonymity, building rooms inside your brain that will forever lend you space to feel comfortably alone."

Blake didn't wait for Emma to respond, changing the subject, and the mood, instead. "How is your dinner?"

"Amazing." She smiled then shoved another forkful of cheesy pasta into her mouth.

Emma had been worried she would have to eat some sort of "grownup food," at dinner, something awful. She complained on their way to the Gardens. Though Emma had brave taste buds and was willing to try most everything Jon introduced her to, she was also nervous, and maybe intimidated, that the Conways would serve her something new and gross that she didn't care for, and that she would be embarrassed if she couldn't eat it.

Emma had nothing to worry about. While the grownups did have plenty of adult options spread on their table, from steak and lobster to eggplant and asparagus, Carmen prepared a casserole with mac and cheese for Emma, white not yellow, by far the fanciest mac and cheese Emma had ever had. His daughter squealed as the first forkful melted on her tongue, then repeated at least once every fourth bite.

~

CONVERSATION, as minutes, flew through dinner. Jon was shocked at how naturally banter passed from one Conway to the next, words making their way around the table like passed butter. How different would it have been if Cassidy had decided to join them? He imagined the conversation would have been crippled and anxious, littered with land mines.

Emma was happy, Blake engaged. Melinda was attentive and borderline talkative. Warren, oddly enough, didn't appear the least bit jealous to be sitting outside the spotlight, staying relatively quiet. Every now and then Jon would catch Warren looking at him oddly, like he was about to say something but chose not to. Or perhaps he was wondering why Jon had brought Emma to dinner.

As dishes were swept from the table, Blake suggested they take their dessert in the sitting room. A few minutes later Emma giggled as she was handed a single scoop of vanilla ice cream.

"What's so funny?" Blake asked.

"Nothing," She giggled again.

"It must be something," he said. "No one ever laughs at nothing, unless they're nervous, and you, darling, don't seem to be anything of the sort."

"I'm just laughing because I thought we'd have something fancy for dessert, but this is only ice cream."

"What did you expect?" Jon asked.

"I don't *knoooow* ..." Emma gave *know* three extra syllables, " ... something with a French name, like you would order."

"You mean like strawberry Savarin? That's not hard to say at all."

Emma laughed. "I don't know. You always order hard-to-say stuff. This is just ice cream, and it's vanilla."

"Well," Blake said, "that's because vanilla is the best. You can try and get fancier, most people do, but they need a lot of luck and expensive unnecessaries. Other flavors try to improve something that can be tweaked, not bettered. Homemade, *handmade* vanilla ice cream?" He laughed. "It's the best."

"What makes it better?" Emma stared down at her still unlicked and unbitten scoop.

"Well, everything, I suppose." Blake smiled. "When you make ice cream yourself, you can use the best ingredients and know exactly what those ingredients are. No guessing, which is important since you should always know what's in your body. You'll carry it around for as much of forever as you can manage to grab, after all. Store-bought ice cream can sit in my fridge for months. I won't touch it. A batch of Carmen's vanilla bean, well, that's gone along with that day's sun."

Emma looked up at her grandfather like he invented each word from his mouth. Her eyes were wide like her smile. She turned from Blake to her scoop, darted her tongue like a lizard at its hardened frost, smiled wider, then nibbled a bite and marred her perfect sphere.

"Oh, wow," she squealed then dove for another. "That's the best ice cream I've ever had!"

"Wait until summer," Warren said from behind. "It tastes even better then."

Despite the chill of his own ice cream, Jon was suddenly warm. He had expected to feel many things, bringing Emma over for dinner, but comfortable wasn't one of them. He was starting to second guess his showdown. Things were going too well, and there hadn't yet been a natural break in conversation which allowed him to get Blake alone. Perhaps the night would end on a happy note, after all. *The fight can wait.*

Jon, like everyone else, finished his ice cream in satisfied quiet, until Emma shattered their silence by saying something impossible.

"Mr. Billy!" she shouted as her gaze landed on his picture hanging about the sitting room fireplace. It was an old one, painted on canvas pulled from a photograph.

"Huh?" Jon said, turning to his daughter.

"That's Mr. Billy, isn't it?"

The adults passed glances and confusion.

Blake said, "That's my father, William Conway Jr."

"Yes, I know Mr. Billy. I remember him."

Melinda laughed, "But, Honey, he's been dead for more than fifty years."

"No, he's not," Emma said. "I met him."

"Where did you meet him?" Jon asked, slowly lowering his body until he was kneeling beside her.

"I don't know." Emma furrowed her brows. "But I remember meeting him."

Warren laughed, as if Emma were telling a joke. Jon looked to see if Blake was laughing, too.

He wasn't. He was staring at his granddaughter, seemingly as confused as Jon.

"She has an active imagination," Jon said, setting his hand on her shoulders.

"I'm not imagining!" Emma shot back defensively. "He talked to me. Told me to call him Mr. Billy."

"Really?" Warren smiled like the asshole he was. "And what else did he tell you?"

"I can't remember everything, but I remember being scared. He told me not to be. I told him I couldn't help it, and he said that sure I could, people could help everything they did, and that it was an easy way out to say I couldn't. That made me more upset, I think, since I sort of remember crying harder. Then he said that fear's the strongest emotion of all, and that I had to learn to control it. If I did, I could control everything else, too. Mr. Billy said fear leads to superstition, and superstition can make a man cruel. He said nothing will make me smarter than managing my emotions, and I must be smart, since my blood was the best."

Blood was the best?

Emma looked up, saw every eye on her, and continued.

"Mr. Billy told me about a time he was ice skating on a frozen lake when the ice was thin. He said he would have drowned if he hadn't crossed the lake as fast as he had, and I should always remember — if I'm ever skating over thin ice, real or otherwise, I'll find safety in my speed."

Jon felt chills through his body.

Warren leapt from his chair. "Is this some sort of joke?" Spittle flew from his bottom lip. "Did you tell her that story?"

"No," Jon said. "Hell, I barely remembered Father telling us that story, it's been so long."

Warren's tone grew sharp, his voice raised. "Why are you saying this, why are you lying?"

"I'm not lying!" she shouted back.

Blake stepped between them. "There are plenty of Billy Conway quotes floating around." He turned to Warren. "This isn't surprising. It's amazing how much children pick up, these days from everywhere, and how easily information's absorbed in their psyches."

Emma chewed her bottom lip.

Jon could tell she wanted to protest but didn't. He was confused, no clue how he should respond to her Mr. Billy story, so suddenly disarmed he didn't think he could possibly confront his father, even if he wanted to, which at the moment, he didn't at all.

It was late. The house, warm just moments before, had fallen under sudden frost — a rare pleasant Conway dinner had curdled. Jon couldn't stand Emma's face, her expression melted from happy and confident to clearly nervous. Like she felt stupid. Maybe scared. As if stuck on thin ice, too slow for crossing.

They traded more minutes of uncomfortable small talk, not many, then Jon set his hand on Emma's shoulder and said, a bit loud, "You ready to go, Honey? Aunt Cassidy is probably waiting, and we still have a long night ahead of us."

"Sure." Emma was clearly relieved.

They all left the sitting room in a huddle and headed toward the front door together. Blake's phone buzzed in the foyer a few feet from the door. He pulled out his cell, looked at the glass, silenced it with a swipe to the screen, and spoke one word to his caller, "Hold." Then he fell to his knee. "Emma, it was wonderful to meet you. I hope to see you again soon." Then he rose and disappeared, without waiting for a reply.

Melinda also retreated.

Warren walked Jon and Emma the rest of the way out. She climbed into the Blacklander's backseat, then Jon shut the door.

Before he turned around, Warren clenched his arm and spun him into more of his spittle. "That's some clever shit you pulled in there. Your daughter's quite the actress."

"What in the hell are you talking about?" Jon shrugged from Warren's grip, annoyed that his brother would have something negative to say about Emma.

"This. This little act you've got going. You think I don't know what you're up to?"

"Well, I'd love it if you told me," Jon said, his voice swelling louder than he wanted.

"Don't play stupid. I know this is some ploy to get your bastard child into Father's will!"

Jon stared, shocked by Warren's audacity. It was one thing to talk shit about Jon, or even Cassidy — she was an adult — but to trash a child?

To trash my daughter?

Jon swung, slamming Warren hard in the jaw and sending him to the cobblestones. Jon wanted to hit him again, hell, he wanted to kick him like a locked door. But aware he'd drawn

Emma's full attention — he could feel her staring through the Blacklander windows — Jon resisted the urge to kick Warren's ass. Instead, he leaned to meet Warren's red and angry eyes. His brother was clutching his jaw, not yet ready to stand. Jon said, in a low, steady growl, "If you ever talk about my daughter like that again, I will put you on the short-list for a prosthetic jaw. Are we clear?"

Warren said nothing, just glared up at his brother.

Jon kicked him in the crotch. "I asked you a question, asshole. Are we clear?"

"Yes," Warren gasped, red-faced and holding his nuts.

"Good." Jon tipped an imaginary hat at Melinda, who watched from one of the many windows, before he circled the Blacklander and climbed in. Heart pounding, knuckles throbbing, and adrenaline racing, Jon painted his face with a brush of calm before turning to Emma in the backseat.

Her smile beamed, and her eyes lit with a reflection of her daddy as hero. "Thank you!" She reached past the console and hugged Jon tight.

He wasn't sure why Emma was thanking him — had she had heard his threat or was it because Warren made her feel like shit earlier? Either way, Jon felt an odd sense of nobility in defending his daughter against his asshole brother. He softened into Emma's warm embrace and felt a deep bond echoing out from his violent act — a bond that swore Jon would do anything to anyone who dared try and hurt his little girl.

"Thank you, Daddy," she said.

Tears stung Jon's eyes as the love that had rooted inside him one month before for a daughter he'd never known, finally fully blossomed.

Chapter 8 - Cassidy Hughes

"You should've seen it!" Emma squealed after they got home from The Gardens. "Daddy punched Uncle Warren right in his face. Then he kicked him in the privates!"

"So, I guess dinner went well?" Cassidy grinned.

Jon laughed, "Oh, yeah, a typical Conway dinner. But no, before you ask, we didn't get to talk about you know what."

"What?" Emma asked.

"Nothing, nosey, go get your bags, we've gotta get going." Cassidy pinched the tip of Emma's nose.

As she ran upstairs, Emma saw Houser coming down. "Houser!" She wrapped her arms around him. "Are you okay?"

It was the first she'd seen him since he was escorted from the house in cuffs by Paladin officers.

"Yeah. Just a big mistake. Everything's fine. I'll tell you all about it later, okay?"

"Okay." She hugged him hard, then went to her room.

Houser came downstairs and filled Jon in with the story he'd already told Cassidy twenty minutes earlier when first getting home. He'd been taken in, a case of mistaken identity or some bullshit. It seemed more than anything, that they were trying to make him feel unwelcome, to maybe send a message, though he wasn't sure why, other than a case of professional jealousy.

"Ain't nothing I can't handle," he said with a laugh.

Jon asked, "You sure? I'll call my dad tomorrow and settle this shit. Get those bastards fired."

"It's all good," Houser said.

"And you're sure you're cool to watch Emma tonight at the hotel?"

"You ever known me to turn down a five-star hotel? I bet they have some damn tasty onion rings!" Houser smacked Jon's arm. "Enough about me. I wanna hear about this big ole fight at Rancho Conway!"

Jon told them what happened, and Cassidy laughed, more at ease with the pills in her blood. The smile came easy. "Good thing I wasn't there. I would've beat the shit out of him right in front of his daddy and his wife!"

"Now *that*, I'd pay to see!" Houser said. "You all better invite me to the next Conway dinner, especially if you're inviting Bruiser Hughes, here!"

THEY LEFT THE HOUSE, stopping at the car rental place, at Houser's insistence and despite Jon's objections. After making fun of Jon for ten minutes, Houser finally got him to agree it was silly to take their Blacklander on a ferry when they could rent a car in the Hamilton office, which wouldn't be crowded this time of night, and have a car waiting on the other side. They could leave the rental in Seattle and not worry about waiting forever to get on and off the ferry.

Houser was right, Jon was wrong. In a few minutes, they were all four on the ferry, heading to Seattle and staring up at the lights of The Hillside as Emma oohed and ahhed.

The Hillside Hotel wasn't on a hill, nor did it offer any hill or hill-related views. It did, however, boast a striking panorama of Seattle, and as one of Washington's newest hotels, The Hillside was also a state-of-the-art masterpiece — exactly the sort of place Jon loved to stay.

Though he'd not yet been there, he seemed especially happy to have Cassidy with him for his first time, which made her almost uncharacteristically giddy. Cassidy kept their conversation on the hotel, since that seemed better than listening to Jon discuss dinner drama, which she wasn't especially in the mood to hear.

The Hillside was urban chic, with miles of white like a blanket behind an occasional flash of fiery red, and a few other peppered colors spattering walls with vibrancy at random. As with most urban-themed hotels, The Hillside's architecture was mostly sharp lines and well-balanced geometric shapes. It reminded Cassidy a little of Promises Kept, though The Hillside blended old and new in a way that made the entire building feel like a work of art.

They checked in, then took the elevator to the twelfth floor together. Jon and Cassidy said goodbye to Houser and Emma at the end of the hallway before doubling back and heading toward their room, holding hands.

They stepped inside their suite to Jon's satisfaction and Cassidy's awe. The room was lit in a warm glow, washing through the ample space and gleaming on the freestanding copper tub, then falling matte against a gorgeous, opulent bed with tons of pillows and the plushest, whitest, softest-looking bedspread she'd ever seen. If heaven were a bed, this would be it.

Cassidy was in the mood before they opened the door, had been since the lobby. Yet, now, a few minutes later, even in a beautiful room perfect for lovemaking, she felt inexplicably nervous.

Her anxiety was back, dragged to the front of her mind by her Addict, then left to fester.

As much as she wanted Jon, her anxiety craved a pill more. "Sorry." She looked Jon in the eye as she grabbed her makeup bag from the small suitcase she'd packed, "I should have gone before the ferry. But I really, *really* have to pee now. I'll be back in a minute, then I'm yours."

Cassidy smiled awkwardly, hoping Jon couldn't tell that she was Jonesing for a pill.

"You'll be worth the wait," Jon said, a bit too Hollywood-smarmy for her liking, though again, it could have been her Addict bitching.

She crossed their oversized suite, stepped into the bathroom, smiled again at Jon as he turned his back, then closed the door behind her. As she sat on the toilet, she crossed her legs at the ankles and started rocking back and forth while staring at the giant porcelain tub. There was also a tub in the living room.

Who needs two fucking bathtubs?

Her Addict piped up. *Stop your bitching. Take a chill pill and enjoy the night, Cass. You deserve a happy night out.*

It had been forever since she'd had a romantic night out. Cassidy didn't want to ruin it with her mood and anxious craving for a pill. She was already off the wagon — what was another pill or two going to matter?

I can always quit tomorrow, right?

Right, quit tomorrow, Cass. Enjoy tonight, her Addict whispered.

There was no arguing with her Addict this time. She grabbed the bottle buried in the bottom of her makeup bag, deep inside a hidden slit. Then she popped the cap and shook two pills into her sweaty palm.

Cassidy slapped them past her lips, swallowed with her own spit, then slowly rocked harder, back and forth, while waiting for her anxiety to die.

She sat there, hating herself.

If Cassidy gave a shit about herself or anyone in her life, she wouldn't use; wouldn't manipulate, lie, steal, or decay every solid corner of her world until it was mush. Like every other addict she had ever known, Cassidy cared so little about herself that even while rocking on a gorgeous toilet in a beautiful bathroom with a billionaire boyfriend on the other side of the door, the only thing she truly wanted was to close her eyes and sleep a long time, then wake to find everything better — a happy life where she didn't need pills just to cope with the shit most people dealt with just fine. The shit that crippled her.

She just wanted a normal life ... *like Sarah's had been.*

All Jon wanted, as he told Cassidy each day, was for her to love herself. She swore she did, whenever he said it. Yet, if she truly loved herself, she wouldn't beat herself the way she did.

Rocking on the toilet while waiting for pills to numb her and put her under their spell, Cassidy decided her lies were too heavy to lift and that she was no longer willing to drag the burden behind her.

Enough with the lies.

Cassidy was sick of lying to everyone, but most of all she was sick of lying to herself.

It was in the self-deception where things grew gnarled past repair, where the rip tore so wide it couldn't be stitched. A person who was willing to lie to herself, as Cassidy had been for far too long, would eventually find herself falling through the thin fissures between truth and dishonesty, unable to distinguish one from the other. Confusion led to a loss of respect, first for herself, then the world around her.

After that, everything was empty.

If Cassidy expected a normal life, she had to take control of the one she was given. It wasn't going to come magically, or thanks to some pills.

She marched out of the bathroom and into the suite where Jon was now naked except for boxers, displaying a pin-up's body his month of island indulgence did little to dim.

Cassidy walked straight up to Jon, set her right hand up on his shoulder, and spun his body toward her.

"I'm a junkie," she said.

"What?" Jon's face lit with concern and confusion.

"I'm a junkie," Cassidy repeated, shoving the bottle into his hand. Then, before he could protest or give her a bullshit platitude, like maybe saying it wasn't her fault, or that she had done her best, Cassidy continued.

"I've never stopped using," she said without stopping herself. "At least, not really. The first night Emma went missing a month ago, I took some pills then. Got them from Craig, and I was scared shitless when Brady pulled me in for questioning. I figured he knew, then I thought you knew and I, well, I thought you wouldn't — couldn't — ever see me the way it looks like you might be seeing me now, and I'm just ruining everything like I always do, and I don't know what to say or do or feel, or anything, Jon," she sucked air through her teeth as if fighting sobs.

"I don't want to say I have a problem, Jon, but I do. I really do. I'm an addict. A stupid, worthless, pile-of-shit junkie. Some days I'm okay, and I think I've got it licked. But then another day comes, and the pills are all I can think about. It's like I can't be happy without them."

Cassidy cried harder.

"I can't sleep, unless you're in bed with me, and I'm always exhausted, wanting to close my eyes since at least then I can ignore the craving." She stared deep into Jon's patient gaze. "I don't know why I'm telling you this, except that I don't have any other answers and I'm scared of losing you, terrified of losing myself."

Jon said nothing. He looked at the bottle in his hands, popped the cap from the top — with a twist of his hand a flick of his thumb — then looked up at Cassidy. "How many did you take?"

"T ... t ... two," she managed through trembling lips.

Jon tapped two pills into his palm and slapped them past his lips, just as Cassidy had done just minutes before. "We all slip sometimes."

He then went into the bathroom and flushed the rest down the toilet. When he came back, he handed her the empty bottle. "All gone."

For the briefest of moments, she wanted to run into the bathroom and try to grab whatever pills might still be floating in the toilet. But no, she was stronger than that — especially with Jon at her side.

"I thought you were Mr. Clean and Sober, well, except for the alcohol and weed." She laughed hard through her sobbing.

"Yeah, well, we're all hypocrites sometimes," he said, his lips on her neck, then her ears, teeth nibbling her lobes as he pulled them gently into his mouth.

Cassidy moaned softly. Jon moaned slightly louder as he pushed her onto the soft mattress.

His hands were everywhere, in every spot she wanted, and all the places she imagined him pressing against her, when she wasn't thinking of Emma or the pills.

She was naked in seconds, but Jon kept himself from entering, instead covering Cassidy's skin in a thin carpet of kisses, taking his sweet time to prove he wasn't angry or disappointed or sad. They were blissed out in tandem, not just through the swirling euphoria of pills, but in their mutual hope and heartache and loss.

After she begged him, Jon entered her, taking his time and making the sweetest, most passionate love she'd ever had.

When finished, they lay together, bodies hot despite the room's cool climate, sprawled as one atop the plush comforter.

Cassidy had shared many encounters with more men than she could count, sometimes sober and often numb, but in all her life, Cassidy had never, ever experienced anything like what she just had with Jon Conway. It felt almost as if two had briefly become one in a shared moment of ecstasy.

Her heart beat faster than she wanted, faster than she understood. Something new was happening inside her, hatching like a baby from its shell and bringing something with it she didn't quite — or couldn't quite — understand. It wasn't just that Cassidy felt post-coital euphoria. Lately with Jon she had laid there just like this, wondering if she was falling in love. Now she knew it was true, enough to feel it trembling at her lips.

There was nothing scarier than saying "I love you" for the first time. Cassidy had said it more times than she'd meant it. Had said it more times than she'd heard it said back. It was terrifying each time, but never more than now. There was so much at risk, not just laying her feelings on the line and being willing to admit her *I love you*, but she was also wrestling with guilt and uncertainty — Sarah, Emma, *her*.

And what *was* "love," anyway?

It was what Cassidy had with Jon. It was being willing to let one person in more than any other, opening doors to each of her deepest, darkest, and ugliest secrets — the stuff she was willing to share with no one else, not even Sarah when she was here, somehow confident that in the end, no matter what she said, Jon wouldn't think less of her.

Love was complete and utter trust.

Cassidy wanted to tell Jon she loved him. She wanted him to know she loved how hard he tried, adored his arrogance and frailty. Admired his strength. And through all of that, she loved him like she didn't know she could.

Cassidy was sure she had not yet seen the best or worst of Jon Conway, but she had certainly seen the beginnings of both. And for her, that was enough.

"I love you, Jon."

He turned to Cassidy, draping his body on hers as he circled her right nipple with his fingers and brushed her left with his lips. "I love you too, Cassidy."

They lay together as Cassidy tried to untangle a truth she couldn't believe.

She was actually happy.

Chapter 9 - Emma Hughes

Emma had just brushed her teeth and was about to climb into bed when she looked over in the next room and saw Houser staring at the TV.

"Goodnight, Houser."

But Houser didn't answer.

He stared at the TV like there was something funny stuck to the screen.

She walked into the room, thinking he was messing with her like he sometimes did, until she noticed the monitor's picture was scrambled with many images at once. All were different and none made sense, especially moving so fast. Along with the messed-up picture, there was a loud crackle, like a hundred bowls of Rice Krispies.

"Hello? Earth to Houser, come in."

Emma smiled as she moved closer to tap Houser's shoulder, then stopped dead. A cold chill ran through her body as she found his glazed expression, eyes wide and fixed to the monitor. The TV's blue glow and scrambled images bathed his face in a ghostly hue. The mirrors in his eyes didn't match the blurred images on the screen. There was something else inside them — something horrible, impossible, and not anything Emma knew how to understand.

Houser wasn't moving. She couldn't tell if he was even breathing.

Is he dead with his eyes open?

Emma's heart felt like it was going to burst from her chest. She forced herself to reach out and touch Houser, anyway.

When her hand touched his, a spark shot from him through her as he turned on her, eyes still vacant, yet staring.

Then his hand flew to her face and stifled her scream.

Epilogue - Jon Conway

Jon was awake for several minutes before he opened his eyes, then spent another few staring out at the water and skyline before turning back to Cassidy and kissing her good morning, first on the lips, then on the cheek and back on the mouth and — because he was hard and she was still naked — on both of her nipples, along an imaginary line between them, and down toward her bellybutton.

Cassidy slowly moaned herself awake and parted her legs for him. He had his way, quietly, without any words, then finished and collapsed beside her, just as he had three times since opening their hotel room door the evening before, preceding an evening of euphoria and confession.

They lay in silence until Cassidy broke it with a yawn and a question. "Think we should check on Emma?"

"Definitely." Jon reached across the bed toward the hotel phone. He swiped a finger on the glass, then tapped #1214 and let it ring in Houser's room, nine times with no reply.

"Weird." He turned to Cassidy. "Probably went down to get coffee and breakfast. No matter how many times I tell him it's cool to order room service, Houser *never* believes me, especially in places like this. He's cool with me paying for the room, but not so much with the extras."

Cassidy said, "Some people like to pay their way, Popcorn. Can you try his cell?"

"Of course." Jon dropped from the bed, went to the bathroom, took a piss, then returned to the front room of the suite. He fished the cell from his pants, scrolled through his contacts, pressed a thumb to Houser's face, and waited through four rings that sent him straight to voicemail.

"Hey, it's Jon, call me," he said before hanging up. Then he looked at Cassidy. "No answer."

Cassidy wore worry all over her face. She looked far more frightened than she should have been, considering they were safe in a hotel and Emma was with Houser, the jolly black giant.

"Relax," Jon soothed. "I'm sure he's downstairs with Emma, getting food. Like I said, Houser doesn't like to order room service. It makes him uncomfortable. He probably pulled on some sweats and left his phone upstairs. He doesn't take it everywhere like I do. Besides," he grinned, "I'm sure he figured we wouldn't be disturbing him this early."

Cassidy's face was red and upset.

"It's okay," Jon said. "I'll go to his room and check on them. Cool?"

"Sure, cool," Cassidy said, "but I want to come with you." She pulled pink panties up over her ass, then jeans up over her underwear. She was on the way to the door as she tugged on her shirt and slipped into shoes.

They left their room together, then walked down the hall to the end where they said goodnight to Houser and Emma the night before. Jon knocked and waited, then waited more, through a long minute that would have felt endless enough without Cassidy tapping the carpet beside him and making it longer.

Jon knocked louder and waited through another minute of nothing. "They're probably downstairs having breakfast," he suggested for the third time. "Wanna check?"

"Yes." Cassidy nodded. She still seemed more worried than what Jon thought reasonable, but then again, Houser was like family to Jon, and she didn't know him nearly as well. He wondered if it was her addiction making her anxious. It was tough to break habits, especially when they were chemical, and Jon figured he'd have to put up with some of this for a while. But he *would* help her through it.

Cassidy said, "But I don't think we should both go. We could miss one another in the elevators, and I'd really like to stop feeling so edgy. How about I head downstairs and you stay here? I'll text you if I see them, and you text me if they come back. Sound good?"

Jon smiled, wanting to soothe her. "Sounds great." He pulled her into a hug and whispered in her ear. "There's nothing to worry about. Houser is the most responsible man I've ever met, which is why I trust him with my life. Besides, he's half robot now, and who's going to mess with a cyborg? Emma couldn't be in safer hands."

Cassidy laughed, but Jon could tell her laughter was there as obligation, not out of sincerity. She turned then walked toward the elevator, taking her nerves with her.

Jon wasn't alone outside Houser's door long before the same nerves he thought left with Cassidy made a nest in his own brain and body. A gnawing chewed through his gut, insistent that something was wrong, and that his logical mind wasn't being so logical.

When Jon's cell buzzed in his pocket it nearly rattled him out of his skin.

It was Cassidy.

"I can't find them anywhere," she said, voice in near panic. "I've looked everywhere and asked a bunch of people.

They'd be an easy pair to spot, right? But no one's seen a thing."

"It's okay, Cass, just relax." Jon's heart now raced.

You're just being nervous, Jonny. Chill.

"I'll call Houser again, then call you right back, okay?"

"Okay."

Jon heard her swallow before the call ended. He dialed Houser, then waited. By the third ring, Jon heard a faint echo of the ring — a beat behind the original — trilling from the other side of Houser's closed hotel room door.

He killed the call, dropped the phone in his pocket, and started pounding hard on the door.

"Houser? Houser!"

No answer.

Jon thought the majority of what he learned as an actor was bullshit. Sometimes, like now, he was grateful for a few of the seemingly-trivial things he had managed to pick up, like how to properly kick open a locked door. He could make a phone call and get someone to open the door, but something told him he wanted to get inside the room ASAP and see if there was something only he should see.

Jon examined the door — it looked like the inside frame was softwood with laminate on each side, meaning it probably had a chipped wood core that would require average force. He stood sideways a few feet from the door, his right leg facing the frame.

Being upset wouldn't help, only serving to dim the strength of his kick, and increase the odds of him hurting himself. Jon drew a deep breath, prepared to strike, then kicked at a spot just below the sensor panel, sending the thrust of his kick into the target.

The weakest part of a door was usually the frame, latch, or lock. This door was no different. Though his first kick did almost nothing, Jon's second caused the trim around the door to shatter then break, and finally swing open.

Jon ran into the room and gasped.

Emma's bed was still made, and her bags were on the floor beside Houser's. A lamp lay broken on the ground.

Oh, my God. She's gone.

Episode 11

Chapter 1 - Stephen Anderson

Stephen sat in the bunker's underground room, staring at the giant monitor that displayed everything the twenty-nine people he was responsible for monitoring saw, said, and heard, all at once in a constant, uninterrupted flow.

He was watching their live feeds, as he'd done nearly every day for the past six years.

Some squares were dark — people sleeping in late this morning. Others showed points of view from people driving, working, shopping, eating, talking to others, and some watching television. Observing the world through people's eyes while watching TV always felt especially odd to Stephen. The only thing that might make it weirder would be watching through the eyes of one of the other Watchers working for Conway Industries. Stephen had no idea how many other Watchers were in The Program. He knew only of the four sharing his shifts. But Stephen *did* know there was at least one other group of four Watchers on the island. He'd gathered that bit of intel after overhearing something from a superior.

But just how many Watchers there were, or people in the Program being watched, Stephen had no idea. So far as he knew, none of the Watchers was actually implanted with the chips that allowed for remote viewing of *their* feeds. But since the program was secret, and none of the participants knew they were being spied on, Stephen hedged on the safe side, always acting as if someone *might* be watching him.

Any of us can be spied on.

Stephen was forever careful in what he said, saw, and read, always cautious to never cross his bosses or give them cause for suspicion.

To most people, seeing and hearing everything the chips showed, from so many varying subjects' views, would be little more than a chaotic blur of confusing images and dissonant noise. But Stephen was one of the enhanced — through drugs and genetic modification — and his gift was an ability to process massive amounts of data at once.

His gift hadn't always been a gift, though. Once, it was a curse.

Stephen had developed autism as a child, but thanks to Conway Industries' experimental programs, he was able to live a normal life. No, not just normal. Conway made him *better*. They had turned an occasionally debilitating weakness into an asset. Stephen was now someone who could separate and filter information at an amazing rate, easily spotting anomalies, while still maintaining a normal life in all other ways, even if so much of that life was now a façade.

Stephen's job was to watch and nothing more. He kept an eye out for sudden awareness within the patients — awareness they were being spied on. There had been only three such instances in his half dozen years of watching, a trio of times when someone seemed to suddenly become aware that they were being watched, or at least sense that *something* was wrong.

The first was Patient 0191, a forty-one-year-old woman who began showing acute symptoms of paranoia, watching people a lot, and running from some at random. She'd even put towels and sheets over everything in her house with a reflective surface. She knew she was being watched but didn't know how or by whom. Since she wasn't an immediate threat, Stephen flagged her for an *adjustment* during her next trip to the doctor's. Sure enough, Patient 0191 was back online in a week or so, returning to Stephen's screen with no hiccups in her daily routines, going through life's motions as if nothing was amiss, and never was or would be.

Another of Steven's subjects, 0319, a thirty-nine-year-old man who worked at one of the dive bars in the tourist district, began speaking directly to his unseen observer.

"I know you're watching me," he said, staring into the mirror with squinted eyes. "What I don't understand is *why*."

Stephen ordered that Patient 0319 get picked up immediately, as the Program needed to find out what had gone wrong and what the man knew. They had to ensure he didn't go off telling people what he suspected. Stephen never learned what became of the man after he was picked up. He knew only that 0319 was no longer in the feed, his slot in the large monitor replaced precisely one shift later with fresh-streaming surveillance of a fifteen-year-old girl with long, black hair and a slight speech impediment.

Stephen wasn't sure what it was about the monitoring process that these few, isolated cases managed to sense. Surveillance was done discreetly with tiny chips and even tinier nanobots — so small they were virtually undetectable. Why a rare few were able to feel something amiss while most were completely unable was something Stephen wondered often. If the scientists at Conway Industries knew, and they probably did, they certainly weren't telling someone in Stephen Anderson's low-on-the-totem-pole position.

As he again wondered how some people could just *tell*, Stephen thought of Patient 0466, a fifty-one-year-old man named Sal.

While Stephen was never told the patients' names, he was usually able to figure them out quickly by watching them go through their daily routines. Enough people had called Patient

0466 "Sal" that Stephen was able to piece that much together on his own. For the most part, he let his attention drift when people signed their full names or did anything to identify themselves. Because, for the most part, Stephen didn't *want* to know the patients' real names, and didn't think Conway Industries wanted him to know, either. He never wanted to be that involved. His subjects were work, thinking of them as Patients Numbered so-and-so was always easier.

Rarely assigning names to faces also made it easier when Stephen ran into his patients in his off-hours, which despite spending most of his time at the Conway facilities, he still did, and more often than he'd like. Not remembering their names made it far less likely that he might accidentally greet one of them by name and make them suspicious. It was always unsettling, seeing someone in person after spying on them for so long. He often wondered if someone could somehow sense that he had seen them through the raw vulnerability of their most intimate moments. Every now and then Stephen would get caught staring, eyes wide and fixed. He'd have to quickly adjust everything from his body to face, act as if he hadn't been staring, bolting his attention to something else, so as not to seem like a weirdo.

But for some reason, Stephen had always thought of Sal by his name rather than his number.

Sal was a retiree, spending most of his days sailing, bird watching, and dating a steady procession of the island's single women, ranging in age from early forties to late fifties, depending on their amount of surgery. Sal never stayed with anyone longer than a few weeks. Twenty-two days was his record, at least since Stephen had been watching.

He wasn't sure if Sal was trying to *avoid* a long-term relationship or was merely incapable of *keeping* one. Stephen only had access to what the patients said, heard, and saw, not what they thought. And with Sal, it was tough to tell when women broke up with him, which they always did, if he was surprised and hurt or if he had so carefully orchestrated the splits that he managed to flee his union without looking like a jerk *and* making them feel like the guilty party. Either way, Sal always bounced back, which Stephen figured either meant he intended the breakup or was a man who refused to live with regrets.

Overall, Sal was one of Stephen's happier subjects. At least, that's the way it seemed, until one night six months ago when he started staring into the mirror and pursing his lips into whispers, just like Patient 0319. Difference lay in the escalation, which Sal did so quickly that he spilled his bottle of crazy to empty before Stephen had a chance to make the call and have him brought in.

"You think you can get away with spying on me?" Sal growled into the mirror, just three days after his first suspicious whisper. "I will *not* be spied on!"

Sal pulled a screwdriver from his right pocket — a screwdriver Stephen had unfortunately missed seeing in time — and jammed it through his right eye.

Stephen jumped back from the monitors, screaming through his shock, helpless as he stared at the screen, watching through Sal's one good eye as he stared into the mirror at the blood spurting onto the glass, gushing from his socket and running down his face into the white sink below.

Patient 0466's right eye was entirely gouged. As protocol prompted, Stephen reported the incident immediately to the Director of Control, told him what was happening and said that Sal was still standing in his bathroom, breathing heavily as he stared in the mirror, looking like he was seconds from stabbing himself in his one working eye.

For ten excruciating minutes, Stephen watched Sal scream into the mirror, cursing whoever was watching in silence, asking why they'd driven him to this and what they wanted from him.

It was awful, but Stephen had seen plenty of terrible

things during his time as a Watcher and would have likely forgotten the horror eventually, if not for what happened next.

Sal bellowed a final anguished cry, grabbed the screwdriver from the bathroom counter, roared, then stabbed his left eye and turned Stephen's screen to black.

All the darkness in the world could do nothing to hide the sounds of Sal's anguished screams, silenced three seconds later by a single gunshot.

When Sal's death was reported by the news three days later, it was said that he killed himself after writing a lengthy suicide note. Stephen knew there was no note. What he didn't know was whether Sal had actually killed himself, or if someone at Paladin acted at Conway Industries' behest and put the man down.

A chill shuddered through Stephen as he thought of Sal, then he turned his attention back to the present and the screen in front of him.

He watched as Patient 0514 sat in her kitchen, sipping coffee while reading the morning news on the table monitor. She bypassed the real news, heading straight to the latest celebrity gossip. Stephen yawned and decided he'd like some coffee, too.

He hit a button on his table's screen and waited for someone upstairs to respond.

"Yes, Mr. Anderson?" It was Felicia, one of the new girls, whose heart-shaped face lit his monitor. She smiled, and Stephen couldn't help but smile back. She was young, kind, and pretty, and her smile brightened an otherwise dull workday.

"Can you send down a coffee? Black, two sugars, please?"

"Yes, sir. Anything else?"

"No, that'll be all for now. Thank you."

"You're welcome." Her face disappeared from the screen, and he let out a small sigh.

Stephen tried thinking of a reason to call her again, if

only to see her face and talk to her for another few seconds, a small break from his mostly lonely job. So many lives, so little contact. The bosses, who monitored his movements via the cameras behind him, wouldn't take kindly to him diverting his attention from the feeds to sit and chat with a co-worker. At least not until his lunch break, when he would be relieved by Harrison, who worked remotely, from his house, covering Watchers as they took breaks or in the minutes between their shift changes.

A few long minutes later, a bell behind him pinged. He stood, went to the door, then stepped through it into the hallway where Felicia was standing. Her perfume reminded him of vanilla, and he wanted to inhale its scent deeply but resisted the urge.

"Here you go, sir." Her green eyes peeked out from behind auburn bangs.

"Thank you." Stephen tried to hide his swelling fascination. He allowed himself only a flicker of eye-contact.

In that moment — that one fleeting second where their gazes met — Stephen felt alive and energized. He wanted to get up, leave the bunker, and take a long drive up the coast with Felicia at his side, salty wind in their hair and warm Washington sun on their skin.

"Will there be anything else, sir?" she asked politely, interrupting Stephen's fantasy and highlighting his awkward pause as he stood there like a foolish schoolboy, lost in thought for far longer than the socially appropriate moment.

Oh, God, she must think I'm an idiot.

"No. Thank you, again." Then he turned and returned to his room, hot coffee in hand.

Stephen sat, sipping his slightly-too-hot coffee. He set it on his desk and pushed it a few feet away, thinking about Felicia and wondering why he had started allowing himself to think such silly thoughts. He didn't know the first thing about her, and yet here he was fantasizing about running off with her and living some sort of ridiculous happily ever after — all while Bea was still locked in the mental ward.

He turned his attention back to the feeds. If he allowed himself to wallow in could-have-beens or maybes, he would likely find himself lost down the same dark hole of despair where he had fallen so many times before. His bosses would order another psych evaluation and again question his fitness for the job. He couldn't allow that, couldn't put himself in a position where he might be fired.

Stephen knew too much, or at least enough, and was reasonably certain that if — *when* — the time came that Conway Industries no longer recognized his value, they wouldn't simply hand him a pink slip and escort him from the island. They would order him locked up somewhere. Or killed. Anything to avoid exposing the Program. The only way he could keep himself, and Milo, safe was to keep doing exactly what he was doing, day after endless day.

Stephen was watching the screen and falling into another lull when he noticed a new square light up — a thirtieth square on his board. The square was dark, save for yellow text at the top of the square which read, "Patient 0719."

He perked with unexpected excitement. It had been a while since he'd had a new patient's feed to view. He wondered who the patient was. Male or female? Young or old? What sort of life did they lead? Why were they chosen by Conway Industries?

Oh, the many mysteries of a brand new square!

Stephen zeroed in on the screen, still paying moderate attention to the other twenty-nine, though most of his focus, and new enthusiasm, was aimed at the freshest feed.

At first, the screen displayed nothing but darkness. Patient 0719, whoever it might be, was still sleeping.

"Wake up, wake up," a man's voice said to Patient 0719. The voice seemed familiar, though Stephen couldn't place it just yet.

The patient opened his eyes.

The room was bright, white, and the ugly face in front of the patient was one Stephen Anderson had never once been happy to see — Paladin Chief Carl Kaiser.

"Ah, you're awake, good, great, excellent," Kaiser said, looking down at the Patient. From the vantage point, it seemed as if 0719 was sitting in a chair.

The Patient groaned, his words in mumbles. He was either groggy or drugged, maybe both.

What the hell am I watching?

Kaiser disappeared from view, then returned a moment later holding a small hand-mirror. He held it to the Patient's face.

Stephen's heart leaped in his chest as he saw Milo's face in the mirror, his son's face bruised, eyes confused and frightened. Almost haunted. Milo was in a chair, hands cuffed to the chair's arms.

What the hell are they doing to him?

Kaiser set the mirror on the ground and leaned down, putting his face and its big blue electronic eye, in front of Milo's.

"Hey, there, Daddy. If you happen to be watching, your little Milo here has been a very, very naughty boy."

Chapter 2 - Jon Conway

Jon paced Houser's hotel room, trying, again, to reach his friend by phone.

Where the hell is he?

Cassidy sat at the suite's small dining room table, staring into space, her eyes red and hands running over one another in constant worry, likely craving pills to calm her.

This can't be happening again.

Emma went missing one month before, eventually returning but with zero explanation for her time away. Was she sleepwalking? Was she lost? Had she woken and sleepwalked her way out of the hotel this time? And why the hell was Houser now gone, too? The rental was also missing, which Jon chose to see as a positive sign. Houser was likely with Emma, which meant his daughter was probably safe.

Cassidy was less certain — afraid Houser had taken her niece. "He fucking took her!" she'd screamed earlier, repeatedly and with increasing hysteria, until Jon finally managed to calm her. A bit.

He tried talking sense into her, to assure Cassidy there was no way in hell Houser had kidnapped Emma. He had known the PI a long time and trusted him more than anyone in his life. No fucking way Houser would ever do something like that. There had to be a good reason, a logical explanation. But Cassidy wouldn't — or couldn't — hear him. She was terrified beyond reason or logic. Jon couldn't argue with her, though. It would only make things worse.

So, he did what was one of the hardest things for him to do — he exercised patience while waiting for any number of people to return his call,

He'd placed calls to the local police, his brother and father back on the island, Chief Brady, and even a couple of Paladin officers Warren put him in touch with. Nothing yet. Brady was trying to get GPS data on the rental, but for some reason was running into a roadblock with the rental affiliate on the island. The chief told Jon he wasn't sure if the company was stonewalling, so Jon put a call into his lawyer, to put pressure on the District Judge to issue an order for Brady.

All this shit took way too much time. Jon wanted to be out there, looking, but his logical side kept telling him to relax — his daughter and friend would surely be returning soon.

As the clock ticked, and morning grew older, Jon kept trying to think of something, anything, which might explain Emma and Houser's absence. He had run his mind through dozens of possible scenarios — everything from Houser taking the girl to the grocery store to get something she needed then getting somehow waylaid on the way back to Paladin officers returning to reclaim Houser and this time taking Emma with them.

Houser wouldn't take Emma to the store without letting them know. He wasn't that thoughtless. And nobody had seen Paladin guards storm the hotel, which seemed like something that would have been impossible to miss. Plus, Paladin had no jurisdiction away from Hamilton. Nothing made sense, and every discounted idea only added fuel to his anxious fire.

As Jon stood, waiting and hoping his phone would buzz with some new answer or thread so he wouldn't have to talk to

Cassidy again without knowing something more, Wan Yikuro, head of hotel security, opened their door, knocking only after he'd already opened it.

"Mr. Conway? Can you come with me?"

Jon's heart beat faster.

They found her? Please, God, tell me you found her!

Jon followed Yikuro from the room, with Cassidy a step behind him. For a moment, Yikuro looked like he was going to ask Cassidy to wait, but the fiery look burning hot in her eyes, with the same *don't you fucking dare* that she'd naturally worn since high school, managed to murder any such intentions.

Yikuro led them down the hallway toward the elevators. He walked without looking back, apologizing for the delay and explaining he had finally managed to find the security footage they had been looking for, but only after waiting through a temporary shutdown in the computer, which took a small forever to bring back online. He led them into the hotel basement, then into a large, dark room marked SECURITY.

The room was lined on three walls with giant, closed-circuit monitors, which showed at least forty different feeds per screen. In front of the monitors sat several wheeled chairs, enough for a staff of eight to keep watch on the hotel. A young, black man in a security uniform with the name "Anthony" on his badge nodded and pointed to a section of six squares on the screen he'd isolated inside a white box onscreen. "I found them, here."

He pressed play on the table's touch screen and spoke as he pointed. "Watch here. This is from the hallway outside Mr. Houser's room, just after midnight."

Jon watched, Cassidy beside him, her fingers digging hard into his arm, dreading what they were about to see. The hotel door opened and Houser walked out, carrying a large, rolled-up bedspread slung over his shoulders.

Emma had to be inside it.

"Oh, God!" Cassidy cried out, digging deep enough into

Jon's arm to draw blood, though he was too transfixed by the monitor to look down and check.

Houser walked the hall, stepped inside the elevator, and disappeared. Anthony turned to Jon, then pointed at another square in the box. "Here's the parking garage feed, three minutes later."

Houser was still carrying the bedspread. He went to the back of his rental car, popped open the trunk, laid the bulky comforter inside, closed the trunk, then climbed into his seat. Seconds later, he pulled out of the parking garage and was gone.

"Here's one more shot, him leaving the garage, south on 12th Street," Anthony said, playing the final bit of footage and maybe the last they might ever see of Houser.

Just like that, Houser was gone. And Emma with him.

Cassidy lost a cry as she finally let go of Jon's arm and collapsed into one of the chairs.

Yikuro's solemn eyes met Jon's. "Sorry, that's all we have. After that, you'd have to see if the city has some traffic camera or CCTV footage. Maybe trace the car from there. Or perhaps you can get the rental agency to track the car?"

"Yeah, we're trying that." Jon was about to say more but was interrupted by Cassidy's shrill and sudden scream.

"He took her! He fucking took her, Jon!" She stood and yelled in his face. "I thought you trusted him! What the fuck did he do with my baby?"

My baby? She's Sarah's child. And mine, not yours.

Jon wasn't about to argue semantics with Cassidy. He wasn't going to argue anything, because, really, what the hell could he say? The evidence, as bizarre as it seemed, pointed to Jon's most trusted friend in the world leaving The Hillside with Emma, wrapped like a pig in a blanket.

"I don't know," he said, not even sure he was answering Cassidy's question. He no longer remembered. The last five minutes, if not the entire morning, was a soupy stew in his mind. His head flooded with every awful story he'd ever heard of abducted children, the sort that rarely, if ever, ended in anything less than the worst sort of horror.

Jon grabbed Cassidy and pulled her to him, hugging her tight. "We're going to find her," he whispered, over and over, as if repetition would somehow turn his words true.

Chapter 3 - Chief Kevin Brady

Brady was at the Hamilton Island Car Rental Agency trying not to glare at the counter weasel, Paul Flakman. Brady knew if he had to look at the self-important customer service rep any longer, he wouldn't be able to hold back — he would deck the fucker in his face, then climb behind the desk to check the computer himself.

So Brady sat in the reception area, pretending to read through a magazine as he swiped the tablet desk in front of him, wondering why in the hell Paul was refusing to cooperate. Brady explained the circumstances, that they had a missing girl and a suspect with one of their rentals. No, the car had been checked out in the Seattle branch, but arrangements were made here at this location and Brady wasn't about to go off to Seattle when he could get the information here from this weasel's computer. He just wanted to know the location of the car while they still had a chance of finding the girl.

But Paul was apparently a legal scholar, inciting his rights and demanding a court order, even though he was an employee, not the agency's owner, leaving Brady with no idea why the jerk would go to such great lengths to be difficult.

Brady sat and waited for either the District Judge to issue a warrant, or to hear from the agency's owner, Frances Spaulding, currently vacationing in Utah. Paul had called Spaulding and left a message for the owner only after Brady practically begged him to. Brady had been nothing but pleasant to the smug fucker, and it was adding bile into his already acidic throat, having to hold the patience on his face like slowly drying paint.

Paul, who was working with a young blonde trainee, Suzy, kept glancing over at Brady.

He tried to ignore it, but finally, the chief looked up. "Is there a problem?"

"Well, I was just thinking that if there's a missing girl, maybe you should be out there instead of smearing our monitor."

Brady couldn't believe the bastard's goddamn balls. He stood, laughing as he approached the counter. "Excuse me? Are you trying to tell me how to do my job, *Paul?*"

Paul's eyes went saucer wide. Brady smiled at the asshole's clear realization that he had just pushed the police chief an inch or ten too far. Brady unholstered his gun and set it on the counter, then the badge from his shirt pocket, and set it beside his sidearm.

"Maybe *you'd* like to be Chief. Is that it, Paul?"

Paul shook his head, his Adam's apple bouncing.

"No?" Brady said, "Are you sure? I mean, you have such terrific ideas in that hard-working noggin of yours." Brady jammed his index finger hard into the side of Paul's head. Twice.

Paul stepped back and put his hand to his head. "Ow!"

"Aw, does that hurt, Paul?" Brady asked. "You better man up if you wanna be Chief O' Police!" He rounded the counter then thrust two fingers hard into the man's chest.

Paul took another step back, "Hey! You're not supposed to be back here!"

"Call the police." Brady smiled. "Oh, wait, you are the police now, Paul. So ... do something."

Paul's eyes went to Suzy, who looked down, as if ashamed for her co-worker. When they returned to Brady, they were wet, as if near tears.

"You want me to leave? Then why don't you get me the information I've been asking for since I got here? Now!"

Paul scrambled to the computer, punching the keyboard as Brady holstered his gun and returned his badge to its home.

"Okay," Paul said. "Um, I've got the car scheduled to return on the ferry this morning."

"To Hamilton?"

"Yes, sir," Paul said.

"And where is it now?"

"2747 Evergreen."

Brady wasn't certain, but the address sounded like it might be Jon Conway's new place.

"Thank you, *Paul.*" Brady burst through the rental agency's front door and hopped in his cruiser.

He grabbed his radio and called dispatch. "I want two deputies at 2747 Evergreen immediately. Suspect is Brock Houser, and he may have Emma Hughes. Go in dark and wait for me. And for Christ's sake, don't shoot the girl! If the suspect attempts to leave, detain him. I'm on my way. Make sure you use the secure channel."

The last thing Brady wanted was involvement from Paladin.

He texted Jon, letting him know Houser's rental was on the island, he was following up on the lead now, and would be in touch the second he had news.

Brady was about to pull out of the rental agency's parking lot and put on his light bar with the siren silenced, when his phone rang.

The screen said, "Private."

Brady, thinking it might be either the judge or the car agency's owner, picked it up.

It was a man, his voice disguised with a digital scrambler. "I found a dead girl."

"Where?" Brady asked, his heart racing.

"Washed up on the shore just under the pier. Better hurry."

"Why?" Brady asked, but the man hung up before giving an answer.

Brady flipped on his light bar and raced to the pier as fast as his cruiser would fly. In four minutes, he arrived to find a small crowd of people trying to peek down at the shore, held at bay by yellow police tape and a handful of Paladin officers.

What the hell? How did they get here so quick? Did the guy call them first?

Brady got out of his car, observing the scene — the pier had been completely cordoned off, and a group of fishermen and others were being questioned by another group of three Paladins. The crime scene had to be at least fifteen minutes old, maybe older. Whoever called Brady with "the tip" had sure taken their sweet ass time.

Why call Paladin first?

Brady was annoyed as he pushed his way past a dozen or so gawkers, craning their necks for an awkward view of the rocky shore. Paladin Officer Petigrew stood just outside the police tape, nodding at Brady as he made his way down the wooden steps along the steep incline to the shore.

Another trio of Paladin officers was on the sand, standing over the body.

A chill whistled through the chief as he caught a glimpse of another naked girl, fished from the sea just like the last.

As he moved to get a closer look, he somehow felt that it wasn't his daughter. He prayed it also wasn't Emma Hughes. The family had seen too much tragedy already with Sarah's death. He couldn't bear the thought of calling Jon or Cassidy with more horrible news.

As Brady moved closer, his heart froze. He stopped dead in the sand, feeling kicked in the gut.

"Oh, Jesus."

It *was* Emma — dead, eyes wide to the indifferent gray sky above.

Brady's cell rang. It was Jon.

Chapter 4 - Don Bellows

Don woke to the sound of boots clicking on a hard floor. He opened his eyes, still in the same bright, white room he'd been in since one day before, his hands still tied behind his back, still naked, shoulders and back still aching.

Once again, Paladin Chief Carl Kaiser stood before him, smiling like a power-mad tormentor.

"Are you ready to talk, yet, Mr. Bellows?" Kaiser's voice oozed with artificial warmth. He hadn't been quite so kind yesterday, as evidenced by the many bruises Don could feel running in ravines of dull pain along his ribs, chest, and back.

Yesterday, Don refused to say anything. From the moment he woke in custody, he repeated the same thing, over and over. "I know my rights, and I want a lawyer."

A day later, Don was singing the same song to Kaiser.

Don's tormentor held his smile. "Oh, come on, Don. You and I both know that's not how things *really* work in America. I read your little conspiracy blog, and all your rants about police-state this and new-world-order that. Or should I call you Cody Delfin, or Stan Trenton, or maybe Louisa Abernathy? So prolific. So many names and so many profiles and websites, Mr. Bellows."

Don wasn't surprised they'd been able to link him to his work. Hell, maybe they had long ago and were merely waiting for the right time to nab him up. Perhaps his anonymity had been an illusion, after all.

Kaiser continued. "Oh, yeah, I'm a *huge fan* of your work, even if you didn't get all the facts quite right. For one, we don't have the ability to read people's minds. At least, not yet. Oh, but don't worry, we are working on it." He chuckled. "And we don't poison drinking water to make people complacent. Such lengths would be entirely unnecessary. That's what the media and religion are for, Mr. Bellows. Didn't Paranoia 101 teach you anything?"

"So, what *did I* get right, then?" Don said, unable to resist Kaiser's conversational bait and feeling as if he had nothing to lose.

"Oh, you want to know, do you? *Now* you want to talk? Well, first, Mr. Bellows, I'd appreciate you telling *me* something useful, something *I'd* like to know."

"What?" Don asked.

"Two things, if I may be so greedy. First, what did Roger Heller tell you? And second, who else did you tell?"

Truth was, Don didn't think he had much. He had theories based on random scraps loosely pieced together, but not the damning proof he'd need to actually pursue Conway Industries or Paladin. Nothing concrete. He'd hoped Roger Heller's flash drive would be the smoking gun, but alas, that was gone, and with it, Don's hopes for nailing the bastards. As Don sat, bound to his seat, naked and helpless, he realized how weak his cards actually were. He probably didn't have enough information to trade with.

The house usually won, even when the gambler held solid cards. Don didn't stand a chance. The best he could hope for was a bluff that might draw something from Kaiser before he was forced to show all of his hand.

"I don't want to know what I got right," Don said. "And to

be honest, I don't care. Not anymore. I just want to know one thing. Then, and only then, will I tell you what you want to know."

Kaiser stared at Don for a long while, as if trying to weigh his approximate volume of shit. Maybe his electronic eye could somehow read heart rates or in some other way calculate whether Don was lying about how much he knew. If so, there was nothing Don could do but try to believe his own deception and perhaps broadcast an air of false confidence that might make Kaiser's test easier to pass.

Don tried thinking in those terms — how much he knew and how it would rock Conway Industries if revealed, hoping that if he thought it hard enough, he, and Kaiser, might believe it.

Kaiser smiled. "Well, those weren't the terms I offered, but never let it be said I'm not an accommodating man. Go ahead, Mr. Bellows, please, ask me your question."

Don swallowed, giving voice to the only thing that meant anything. "Where is my family?"

Kaiser leaned his head back, looked up at the ceiling, and cracked his neck right and left before returning his creepy gaze to Don. He smiled like an alligator.

"You're going to ask one question, and that's what you ask? You sure you wouldn't like to ask something else? I mean, come on, Mr. Bellows, I can tell you anything else you want to know. Anything at all about Conway Industries, Paladin, and all our secret stuff!" He leaned forward and seemed to whistle through his teeth. "Are you *sure* you want to ask about your family?"

Don hated how the bastard titled his head, smiling as if he held the answer to an elaborate, hilarious riddle.

"Yes, I'm sure."

"Your family left you, Don. They took a ferry to Seattle and left you behind."

"Bullshit!" Don cried out. "I checked with the police. There was no footage of my family taking the ferry!"

"It was a lie, and the Chief was in on it. Helped orchestrate it, in fact. Your family was scared of you! Your wife said you'd gone off the deep end with your crazy conspiracies and endless tinfoil-hat bullshit. She wanted to get your kids away from you, Mr. Bellows. Wanted to keep them safe."

"No!" Don furiously shook his head, his entire body burning hot with rage. He yearned to break free from his restraints and punch the lying fucker in his big, fake eye.

"Oh, yeah," Kaiser continued as his smile spread wider. "In fact, the chief wasn't even going to go along with it until one of your boys, Ryan, I think, cried about how his daddy was scary and might kill him in his sleep."

"Fuck you!" Don shouted. "That's a lie!"

"No, Mr. Bellows, I don't lie. Unlike you. You've been lying to yourself, lying to others, lying to that poor Milo Anderson kid. Getting people all worked up with your crazy conspiracy theories! *You* are a threat, Don, to yourself, and everyone around you. Your wife was right to take the kids and leave. She was right to protect her family and keep them safe from you, because you and I both know you were just days from going all Roger Heller on your family."

"No!" Don cried. "I would never hurt my family! I loved them! I love them!"

Kaiser laughed. "You keep telling yourself that." He slowly approached Don, still nursing his smug and ugly smile. Three feet from his prisoner, Kaiser's phone buzzed. He pulled the cell from his shoulder pad and read the screen. "I'll be back, Mr. Bellows. I have some pressing business. When I return, you *will* tell me the truth."

He exited without another word, closing the door behind him, leaving Don with a knot in his throat and a deep pit in his soul.

Is it possible he's telling the truth?

Are Lucinda and the boys in Seattle?

Could they possibly be alive?

Don was filled with both hope and dread. Hope that they might be alive, but dread that Kaiser was telling the truth and that they were afraid of him, like *he* was some sort of monster.

If that was the truth, it threatened every other truth Don had come to accept through his last three, long years.

What if I am crazy?

Chapter 5 - Warren Conway

Warren sat in the living room, staring at the TV screen as it broadcast news coverage, both local and online already, about the dead girl found near the pier.

Melinda sat beside him. "Oh, my, do you think it's her?"

"I don't know." Warren felt like an asshole for what he'd said earlier to Jon when he called and told them Emma was missing. "Again? Really, Jon, you need to keep better track of your kids if you're going to be a father."

Jon, instead of rising to the bait, asked for some phone numbers of Paladin officers he could enlist in the search. Warren gave him the numbers, and even felt bad about his unnecessary comments, but couldn't bring himself to apologize. Now, as he watched the news and felt an overwhelming dread settle on his shoulders, he felt horrible.

No, he didn't care for the girl's family, but Emma had, in a way, reminded him of his own daughter and their relationship — which mirrored his recent and especially icy relationship with Melinda.

Warren stood. "I'm gonna go check on some stuff. I'll be in my office. Let me know if you hear anything definitive."

"Okay." Melinda's gaze was still glued to the screen, and her voice was somewhat softened.

Inside his office, Warren pulled out his phone and dialed Jon. He wanted to set things straight, in case Emma *was* dead and hadn't just run away for some white trash drama as Warren initially thought.

Jon didn't answer.

Damn it.

Warren sat at his desk and was about to put his phone away, when instead, he decided to make another call.

He dialed and waited.

"Hello?" Anastasia sounded groggy, as if still in bed. Her video screen was off, and he tried not to think that maybe she wasn't alone. He knew she'd had a few relationships, but still, she was his little girl. He didn't want to think of her as sleeping with some asshole.

"Hey, honey."

"Daddy?"

"Yeah, I just wanted to say, um … hi, and see how you are?"

"Is everything all right?" she asked.

"Yeah, yeah," Warren said. *Are my phone calls so rare that the first thing she thinks is that something's wrong? Jesus.* "I just wanted to hear your voice."

"Um … hi." She laughed. "How's it going on the island?"

Well, let's see, I'm trapped in a loveless marriage, I'm sleeping with a man, I'm plotting to kill Grandpa, and Jon came back after Sarah died, but now it seems like Sarah's daughter, and Jon's, too, by the by, Emma, is dead as well. But other than that …

"It's more or less the same," he lied. "I …" he wasn't sure what to say. He paused, gathering thoughts. What does one say when one's life is off the tracks? How does one make up for years of being an absent father? What words could undo his actions, and more importantly, his inactions?

"Dad?" Ana said. "You there?"

"Yeah." He felt stupid.

"Can I call you later?" she asked. "I was up late studying and have a test in a few hours. I'd love to catch a few more z's."

"Yeah, yeah, I'll talk to you later, honey. And ... um, good luck on the test."

"Thanks, Dad. I love you."

"I love you, too." He held the phone in his hand long after the call ended, staring at the screen, feeling like both the World's Worst Father, *and* World's Worst Son.

Warren thought of his argument with Blake and tried to imagine himself in Father's impossible-to-fill shoes. He wondered what he would have done if he were Blake, facing the same pressures the elder Conway was always facing, having the same people to answer to while attempting the impossible and, despite all odds, slowly turning it into reality — enhancing humans to their greater potential.

Would Warren have made the same call to pull the plug on Project Raven, too?

Warren knew little about Blake's Project Phoenix, despite being the company's CEO and working hand in hand with many elements of the project. He still hadn't met the enlisted scientists. Didn't even know where their offices were. He assumed they were on the island's north end, where Blake probably disappeared so often when away on "business trips."

Father had explained it was best for everyone if Warren and the upper echelons of the company maintain plausible deniability in case anyone ever found out how they managed their results. Warren knew bits, of course — how they monitored citizens and used experimental drugs and technology without informing the patients. There was no way to do his job without knowing that much. But there were many things Blake kept from him, such as the origins of much of the technology, which Warren suspected involved international corporate espionage.

You don't become a great man like Blake Conway without breaking a few laws.

As Warren considered this, he realized it was impossible to ever truly appreciate the pressures Blake was under or why he was so concerned about public scrutiny. Warren wondered again, would he, in Father's position, also shut down Project Raven.

And the answer was yes.

Just like that, Warren felt sick to his stomach, hating himself for even being able to consider killing his father. Blake was acting on logic, based on a set of criteria Warren could never fully appreciate. It didn't mean Blake was being an asshole, or had it in for him, as Warren had been weak enough to let himself believe.

How could it have come to this?

Kaiser had been on him for some time to "grow a pair" and make a move, though not necessarily killing Blake — Warren's idea even if Kaiser owned it as his own. Kaiser was always harping on about Blake's constant disrespect toward Warren. Now, it seemed perhaps the one-eyed man had practically shoved *Warren* into the decision.

But I can't do it.

He dialed Kaiser's number.

Kaiser answered, but not until the sixth ring. "Yes?"

"I want to call it off."

"What?"

"You know what I'm talking about. I don't want to do it."

"What the hell, man?" Kaiser clearly wanted to discuss it in depth, but definitely not over the phone. Even when speaking on encrypted connections, neither *ever* took a foolish chance by articulating plans which might be overheard.

"We'll talk later," Warren said.

"When?" Kaiser asked, impatient and angry.

Warren's office door exploded open, Blake knocking only after he was inside. "Got a moment?"

Warren held up his finger. "One sec."

Blake retreated back into the hall, staying in earshot. Warren said, in as casual a voice as possible, "Okay, then I'll talk to you later. Thanks again."

"You better believe —"

Warren ended the call, cutting him off.

"Yes?" Warren said from behind his desk.

Blake stepped in and closed the door behind him.

"I just wanted to let you know we have a press announcement next week. We'll both be in attendance, the two of us in front of the hospital."

"What?"

"Next week, we're announcing a new, state-of-the-art Sarah Hughes Psychiatric Hospital, in dedication to the memories of everyone who lost their lives in the recent, senseless tragedies."

"Why are we doing that?"

"Because we have reporters looking too closely at us, kicking boot tips into all this shit you stirred up, Warren. You know reporters traffic in heartache because misery clicks. Of course, they're going to start asking all the wrong questions, wondering out loud why there's a sudden excess of violence on the island, especially when Conway Industries foots the medical bills for the citizenry and pays for Hamilton's psychological welfare. It's a natural question — how shoddy *are* our services? That's a question we don't want asked, and that means we need to get in front of this and control the story, not react to it."

"But we *just* built a new psychiatric wing on the hospital."

"Yes, well, this one is bigger, and has all the right names attached. You will announce donations to families of the shooting victims *and* that we're establishing full scholarships for any child affected by the tragedy."

"Jesus!" Warren said. "You'll have people lined up to the ferry for free scoops from that gravy train!"

"Bad publicity and endless criticism will leave their claws on all of us, but the *right publicity* is worth more than anything else in the C.I. budget. I'll be there, but I want *you* in front on this thing, glad-handing all the right people. I *can* count on you, correct?"

"Yes," he reluctantly agreed. Maybe that would be enough to get Blake to leave him alone. Sometimes it was.

Unfortunately, this time, it wasn't.

"The biggest problem in your life, Warren, is your failure to be bold."

Here it comes. Warren licked his lips so he wouldn't grit his teeth. "I am bold."

"No, you're not. You just *think* you are. Bold doesn't mean wearing a bigger belt buckle then letting extra weight wobble your knees, son, which is exactly what you're prone to do. You're all bark and no bite. There's no fight in your dog. *You* should have thought of this, not waited for me to. *You* should have been out in front of this thing on Day One, making the moves to keep the press at bay, not me. You should have taken care of the Heller situation earlier, and perhaps we could've avoided more death. But you didn't, did you? You always wait for me to tell you what to do. You need to stand up and fight for this company, son, not act like every task is a burden not worthy of your time."

"I fought for the DOD contract, Father. And now you're taking that away. And *you* said not to fight you on Raven, that I'd lose. So why bother?"

"The DOD contract isn't bold, son. It's easy. Obvious. It does nothing for our cause. Our job is to do what others won't. Be bold when others are scared. Timidity is a cancer I don't allow inside me. Frankly, yours shames me. I will not apologize for my goals and am tired of making excuses for yours. I will *never* feign modesty in the face of lesser-thans. Neither should you."

"I don't," Warren said, now through gritted teeth.

"You're right, Warren. You don't. But the way you don't makes you look like an untrained dog."

Blake turned to leave. His hand was on the panel when Warren called out, "Have you heard anything more about Emma?"

"No," he said, his back to Warren. "I'm waiting for Jon to call."

"News said they found a body near the pier — a little girl."

"Wow, that's a shame," Blake said, not turning. He opened the door and left, as if the awful news of a child's death meant nothing to him — not in the face of "important business."

He couldn't care less that his granddaughter might be dead. He should be on the phone consoling Jon, or doing something, not sitting here lecturing me and manipulating good press. Kaiser's right. The man is a cold-hearted monster, and respects no one.

He wants bold?

I'll show him bold.

Warren stared at the door, left open on purpose by Father — another passive-aggressive push at his buttons. He went to the door, closed and locked it, then dialed Kaiser again.

"Yeah?" Kaiser said, answering on the eighth ring.

"Forget what I said."

"What?"

"It's on."

"You sure?"

"Dead sure," Warren said, staring at the closed door.

Chapter 6 - Stephen Anderson

Stephen killed the car's engine and sat, staring through his window's glare at the tinted façade of the Paladin offices. His heart pounded, every cell inside him uncertain, knowing he *had* to confront Kaiser, but feeling as if a march into hell to meet the Devil himself lay before him.

He got out, slammed the car door, then tromped through the parking lot, up the concrete walk, through the front door, and over to Allison — the young receptionist who had manned the Paladin desks since Stephen first started working with Conway. She'd looked twenty-five back then, and now six years later, hadn't aged a day.

"I need to see Carl Kaiser." Stephen tried to keep the upset clear from his throat.

"Mr. Kaiser is out of the office today," Allison said sweetly. She smiled, her green eyes dancing in the office's warm light. "Sorry, Mr. Anderson."

Still checking his temper, and doing a horrible job despite Allison's friendly smile and bright eyes, Stephen growled, "He's here, I know it. And he'll want to see me, I'm certain. Tell him I'm waiting."

Allison didn't look frightened, exactly — it was probably

easy to feel safe in an office outfitted like an armory — but she did look concerned. Allison offered no argument, just swiped her screen, leaned into her glass, then whispered. "Mr. Kaiser, Stephen Anderson is here to see you … yes … at the front desk … now … that's correct."

She nodded at whatever Kaiser was saying through the piece in her ear, swiped the glass again to kill the call, and turned her pretty eyes to Stephen.

"Mr. Kaiser will see you know. His office is just …"

"I know where it is." Stephen cut her off, then turned, shoved the glass door open, stormed down the hallway, and burst into Kaiser's office.

"Mr. Anderson," Kaiser said, already standing behind his side of the desk. His mechanical blue eye made a whir, dilating as it fixed on Stephen.

Light brushed Kaiser's scar and sent Stephen into a deep chill. He swallowed involuntarily, suddenly wanting to run. Instead, he pressed his feet harder into the floor, rooting himself in place. "We need to talk."

"Yes, of course, we do," Kaiser smiled. "About your boy Milo, yes?"

"Yes," Stephen said, trying not to stutter. "Wh … what you're doing is wrong."

"Of course it is, Mr. Anderson, but no more wrong than what you do to earn your handsome check, and no more wrong than what your boy did to earn his consequence."

Kaiser turned to his monitor, squinting as if in study, then shook his head and returned his eyes to Stephen. "I'm sorry, Mr. Anderson, but there's nothing I can do. Your son was caught consorting with known terrorists, that means people seeking to harm Conway Industries and bring chaos to Hamilton Island. This is unacceptable, and as you've surely seen in your decorated yet inflated position, we cannot allow chaos to reign. There are consequences for actions which stray outside those borders which keep us safe. Your son has put us in jeopardy, and lest you forget, it's my job to manage danger and curb risk on this island."

Kaiser rounded the desk and stood a foot from Stephen, his rough hand sitting hard on his shoulder.

Stephen wanted to punch him.

"I warned you, Mr. Anderson, I told you we would activate your son's chip." Kaiser's face soured, as if bearing no pleasure in duty. "But don't worry, he won't be on your watch screen. We'll be assigning Milo to another Watcher. We would hate for there to be any conflict of interest."

Stephen fumed, wanting to lash out, strike Kaiser, hating that he was forced to stand there impotent. "Where is he?"

"Safe. Getting his memories wiped. Let's hope, for both your sakes, it sticks, eh, Mr. Anderson? Or else, we'll be forced to eliminate the threat."

Stephen wanted to scream, but with hands dancing in little quivers at his side, all he could say was, "Okay."

Chapter 7 - Cassidy Hughes And Jon Conway

CASSIDY

THEY WERE STILL in The Hillside's security room when Jon got the text from Brady.

Cassidy watched as Jon took the call from Chief Brady — watched as his eyes told her more than all the words in the world.

"We'll be there soon." Then he ended the call.

She stared at him, shaking her head. "No."

"They found a girl washed up by the pier and want us to come look at her. Brady says he's pretty sure it's ..."

He broke down.

"No!" Cassidy repeated, this time in a scream.

The world around her quit its existence, blurring into an angry vortex, swirling in fury to inhale all she loved, everything she held dear.

Cassidy felt as if someone had shoved an icy blade deep into her core, twisting it and burying it deeper by the turn. Worse than killing her, worse than killing Sarah, the blade had taken Emma.

It's killing my child.

Then in the chaos, a moment of clear thought.

My child? What the hell? She's not my child. She's Sarah's.

Sarah and Jon's.

For a moment's flicker, Cassidy felt as if she had almost forgotten who she was. For a moment, which made no sense to her at all, she actually thought she was Sarah — feeling Sarah's emotions, feeling Sarah's connection to Emma as if it were her own.

As the world found its shape around her, and Cassidy found herself hugging Jon, who himself was a wreck.

And she wished like hell he hadn't flushed her pills down the toilet.

JON

THEY ARRIVED on Hamilton Island ninety minutes after getting the call, taking a cab from the docks to the hospital, where Chief Brady waited downstairs in the morgue. The medical examiner's office was sending someone over to take "the body" back to the city for an autopsy. But first, Jon and Cassidy had to identify the girl.

Outside the room, Jon stopped and met Cassidy's red eyes. "You don't have to do this. I can identify her."

"No," she said. "I need to do this."

Jon didn't ask why — if it was that she didn't trust him to identify his own daughter, or if it was some sort of needed closure. Perhaps she was hoping to see something which would rain hope that it wasn't Emma, something Jon might not recognize.

"Okay." Jon reached for her hand as they followed Brady. Cassidy kept her hands folded in front of her and her eyes set straight ahead.

They entered a door marked "11" and stepped into the basement morgue. Jon remembered learning on a movie set once that morgues didn't usually identify themselves in hospitals. They often had innocuous names, or in this case, a number, facing the public's view.

The room was small and sparse, with four drawers sunk into the left side wall and two empty gurneys against the right. A door to an office, also on the right, was open, though no one manned the desk.

Brady went to the closest drawer and pulled it out, revealing a small shape draped beneath a dark gray blanket. A cool mist rolled out from the refrigerator. He wasn't sure what he expected — the scent of death, or what — but all Jon could smell was seawater. His knees shook as he stepped forward.

Brady looked up at Jon and Cassidy, to ask if they were ready or maybe give one of them a chance to back out.

Jon nodded to his old friend, then Brady pulled back the sheet, revealing Emma's dead body.

"Oh, God," Cassidy cried out, falling beside the drawer.

Jon stared at his daughter, her pale gray flesh, her wide-open eyes staring at nothing. The same tiny eyes that just one month earlier he had seen dancing with life as Emma mischievously looked over at him while sneaking cookies into her purse at Sarah's funeral. The same eyes he'd imagined one day asking for help her with homework or to borrow the car or meet a boyfriend. The same eyes he thought he could spend an eternity looking into and never fully realize the depths of his love.

The eyes which had reminded him so much of Sarah's were now staring up at him, hollow and dead.

Jon shook his head. It was too much to take in. Too much to believe.

Cassidy stared, tears streaming her red face, hand over her wide-open mouth, screaming on mute. She fell to the ground, waving Jon away as he tried to help her up. After a moment, she stood, staring down at Emma, devastated.

"It's her," Jon said, nodding at Cassidy to see if she was also verifying, hoping she might see a blemish, some birthmark that wasn't right, anything which would say no, this is not Emma.

She nodded instead.

Jon looked down, closed his eyes, and reached out. His hand found Emma's, but when his fingers felt the coolness of death rather than the usual warmth from her hugs, he cried harder.

"How did this happen?" Cassidy asked. "And did you find the bastard who did it?"

"We don't know how yet," Brady said. "There were no visible bruises or signs of foul play, so we'll have to wait for the medical examiner to make a determination. As for Mr. Houser, we have him in custody."

"What?" Cassidy asked.

Jon's eyes shot open and caught the rage in her expression.

"Yes, we found him at your house, Jon. His rental was parked in front, and when we went inside, he was oblivious to our bursting through the front door. He was just sitting on the floor in front of the TV, PlayStation controller in hand. We approached him and he turned, looking at us with a blank expression. He's not said a word since we booked him."

"I want that motherfucker dead!" Cassidy said, spitting.

Jon wanted to defend Houser, advise that they not rush to judgment. But staring down at Emma, thinking of how she had been so fond and trusting of his friend, sent a surge of anger through Jon's body. He wanted to lash out, hit something, break something, make someone pay. Make Houser pay.

"I want to see him." Jon met Brady's gaze.

"I'll see ..."

"No," Jon said, put his hand on Brady's chest. "I want to see him. Now."

Chapter 8 - Sarah Hughes

Sarah tried sorting through her mind's conflicting images as they strobed her senses with no order or reason. She reached as far as she could, back into her memory, but her frayed band would only stretch so far. She had no idea where she was, or how long she'd been there.

She thought she was in space but couldn't be certain. There were people up here, if it was indeed "up" wherever she was, and those people wanted to keep her confused. It seemed as if half her time was spent in a numbed and narcotic state. The other half she spent bewildered.

Sarah could be dead, but she had no way of knowing.

In the time she had been held in wherever, Sarah had vacillated between several certainties, from dreaming she was in space, to seeing Blake Conway, to the assault from an endless battery of tests. It was difficult — if not impossible — for her to sift fact from fiction.

She dropped the steak into her mouth and chewed. It was delicious, like all the meat she'd had in her room. If Sarah *was* in space, the station had access to premium beef. They fed her well, but only with meat and vegetables. Both were the best she had ever had, by far.

Sarah remembered the doctors — if that's what they were — coming into her room and questioning her diet. They explained some stuff she knew and a bit she didn't. Told her proteins, carbohydrates, and fats were life's building blocks, and more specifically, blood type dictated a person's ideal diet. They asked her if she knew what dry aging was and she said, no, not really. They told her about flesh and enzymes — both human and cow — and explained molecules in food behave like molecular cooks. And they said that back home, Sarah had spent a lifetime poisoning herself.

Most modern meat, they explained, was prepared for mass consumption on an assembly line, which wasn't how humans were supposed to eat. Animals were slaughtered, separated, packaged, and distributed. Dry aging, on the other hand — like every bite of mouth-watering meat she had tasted since first arriving wherever she was — meant the carcass was set in carefully controlled conditions (cool temperatures, with relatively high humidity) for anywhere from weeks to months, allowing sufficient time for the enzymes to work.

They said that sort of aging was best for her body, though something told Sarah they were doing something sort of the same with her mind.

That was one of the reasons they were always watching.

She felt as if she was being observed, every second. And she always felt extra eyes while taking the tests, both when they showed her images on cards and when they told things she didn't understand.

Sarah was certain they were wiping memories from her mind every time they handed her one of those stupid cups filled with pills. But as much as she hated each swallow, the pills helped her feel like there were fewer eyes on her, crawling across her skin like an army of insects.

She spun toward the door, for some reason expecting it to suddenly fly open and the tall lean doctor with the white coat to come running inside. Sarah didn't know his name, even after sifting through memory, but she could clearly see his face behind her closed eyes.

The door didn't open. Instead, Sarah's head exploded— a violent eruption of needles stabbing her brain and sending flashes of bright white lightning before her eyes.

She lost her balance and fell to the floor.

When Sarah looked up, she was no longer in her room or her mind. Her world was swimming, bleeding, like sudden color swirled in creamy soup. She was so dizzy she couldn't stand, and it took her a moment to realize the world was now being seen through someone else's eyes.

She blinked, wondering who she was and what sort of madness the doctors were broadcasting into her mind. After a half-minute spent with a racing heart and pounding head, she blinked again, now realizing with a deep certainty she couldn't explain that this was real — not from the doctors — and she was looking through Cassidy's eyes.

Sarah *was* Cassidy, standing in a room with Jon.

They were in a small room, with four metal drawers in the left side wall — a morgue. The Hamilton Island Chief of Police Kevin Brady stood beside them. Brady looked at Jon, then at Sarah — or more accurately, at Cassidy — as he pulled a drawer from the wall — a lump draped under a gray blanket.

Jon nodded, and Brady tore the sheet from the lump, revealing her daughter, naked and staring straight up at the ceiling. No, not staring — dead.

"Oh, God!" Sarah screamed from behind her sister's lips, falling to the cold concrete floor. She felt the hard chill in her knees, even though the morgue was likely thousands of miles below her.

Jon reached out to Cassidy/Sarah, sobbing with her hand over her mouth, wanting to scream, though she was unable to make a sound. She waved Jon off as she found the strength to stand.

"It's her." Jon closed his eyes and reached for Emma.

Sarah screamed, suddenly back in her body, back in her room, "Someone needs to come in my room! Now!"

When no one answered, she started throwing things. Her plate, her fork, her knife. Another minute of silence sent her deeper into fury. She wanted to break something, starting with her dresser mirror.

Sarah took her chair and hurled it at the glass. She grabbed a shard, held it to her flesh, and pressed it into her skin, drawing a line of wet crimson across it.

"COME on," she screamed. "I know you're watching!"

The door opened, as Sarah knew it would. In rushed a doctor — not the tall skinny one with the bright white coat — this one didn't really look so much like a doctor at all. He wore all black and held something that looked mostly like a gun.

He took one second to aim, then pulled the trigger.

Sarah felt something horrible, followed by delirious happiness. Then she fell to the ground and saw nothing but black.

Chapter 9 - Don Bellows

Don had no idea how long it had been since Kaiser left him to marinate. It felt like hours and might have been a full day. When he finally reappeared, Don was hungry, thirsty, and not sure how much longer he could hold out. His throat was raw, and the roof of his mouth coated with the copper taste of blood.

He was ready to tell Kaiser anything and everything. They had won. He was broken, unsure if Kaiser was telling the truth — that Lucinda had taken the boys and run off — or if it was an elaborate part of the conspiracy. Everything was fuzzy, and Don no longer knew if he could trust himself to mine nuggets of fact from a river of fiction.

Kaiser came in, and Don spilled his guts, telling him everything he knew, suspected, or theorized. He admitted he had jack shit from Heller and never saw the flash drive. He admitted he and Milo were trying to retrieve it from the empty Heller house earlier, and also explained that Milo shouldn't be held accountable since the boy was merely a means to an end. He also told them about the list Milo found. Judging from Kaiser's human eye, that bit of news was a surprise.

"He's a good kid. He didn't know anything. After losing

his girlfriend, best friend, and then that *thing* with his step-mom, he was looking for answers, like me. I used him to try and figure more of the truth, but we both had shit together."

"And what about Mr. Houser?" Kaiser asked. "What did you tell him?"

"Same as I'm telling you. Hell, I figured he might be working for Conway, anyway. But yeah, I told him the same thing — the truth." Don wasn't sure what he'd had time to tell Houser, but figured Milo must've told him everything in their time together, so Don may as well cop to it and maybe spare Milo some trouble.

Kaiser looked at Don, almost sympathetically, then stood from his chair. "Thirsty, Mr. Bellows?"

"God, yes," Don said.

Kaiser left the room. Don was amazed by how quickly his resolve and anger toward Kaiser had crumbled — his hate now in pieces too tiny to gather. All he wanted was a drink of water, and, hopefully, release. Then he could piece life back together, maybe talk to the chief, see if there was a way he could see his family again, prove he wasn't nuts, or any sort of serious threat.

Kaiser came back and unscrewed the plastic cap of the bottle of water.

Don apologized, tears streaming down his face, feeling an overwhelming and sudden gratitude towards Kaiser that further proved the speed and strength of his break. But he didn't care. All he wanted was his old life back. "I would never hurt my kids. I swear."

"I know." Kaiser's voice was calm and reassuring, his smile less threatening.

Maybe Don had misinterpreted the man from the start.

He swallowed the water in small gulps, a sudden cool burning the parch in his throat.

"Take it slow," Kaiser said. "You don't want to puke it all up."

He did as instructed, drinking the water, allowing it to rehydrate his throat.

Kaiser pulled the empty bottle away and sat back on the seat across from him.

Don was afraid to push his luck but spoke his mind anyway. "I told you everything. Can I go home now?"

"You know," Kaiser said, "I almost feel sorry for you."

A shiver ran down Don's spine.

Trouble.

"Because here you are, certifiably crazy as a loon. But you're not *wrong* about everything, Mr. Bellows. In fact, you have quite a lot right."

Don swallowed, dread creeping like a cold through his body.

Kaiser held up the water bottle, swirling the small amount of liquid at the bottom before lifting the bottle closer to his eyes, putting it between his blue robotic eye and the light above. "Funny thing about nanobots, Mr. Bellows. They're naked to the human eye. But not so much to the augmented eye."

Kaiser shook the bottle, then threw it at Don's chest.

Panic swelled inside him. Don flinched, almost certain he could feel the *things* inside him, rushing through his esophagus, into his belly, even though it was probably impossible to feel something you couldn't even see. *Unless they're self-replicating!* He wanted to puke, and started coughing as if it might help, not knowing it would only burn his throat more. With his hands bound, there was nothing Don could do to vomit whatever he'd swallowed.

Kaiser leaned forward. "Right now, there are hundreds of nanobots running in a current through your body. You know what nanobots are, don't you, Mr. Bellows? You did write a bit about them on your blog. Again, you got quite a lot right. And our tiny, little robots *can* do some not-so-tiny things. I'm sure you can imagine a few of the things these self-replicating beauties can do, especially after reaching your brain."

Don screamed, "No!"

Kaiser smiled. "Now, Mr. Bellows, you're about to find out just how deep our rabbit hole goes."

Chapter 10 - Jon Conway

Brady drove Jon and Cassidy to the station after agreeing to let them sit outside the interrogation room, watching through the two-way mirror while he questioned Houser. But he refused to let them speak to the suspect.

Jon understood, at least on some level. Didn't mean he liked it, though.

As he led them into the observation room and closed the door, he turned to them, compassion for everything they'd been through. "I know this is hard as hell on both of you, and I can't possibly imagine how you feel right now, well, actually, I can, since my own daughter's been missing for six months. But I don't know if she's alive or dead, so maybe I can't truly know how you feel. I just want to say that the only way I'm getting any answers from Brock Houser is if I can reach him somehow, win him over to my side. That means I can't have you doing anything stupid, understand?"

Jon said, "Yes."

Cassidy nodded, though it looked like she was shoving a thousand pounds of effort up a hill to agreement.

"I'm only allowing you both to watch because I want, and maybe need, your input. You know him better than me. I'll come back in here at some point during the interview, and ask you a few questions, then I'll figure the best way to approach him."

"Okay," Jon said. "I understand."

He wanted to say he still couldn't believe his friend could have possibly done something so awful —there had to be some other explanation. But until he figured out what that explanation might be, he wasn't about to apologize for the man who might have murdered his daughter.

Officer Henry, the jug-eared young man Jon met during his brief incarceration last month for "trespassing" on the island's north end, entered the room. Brady said he would be there to sit with them. He instructed them to let Henry know if they needed anything.

The officer nodded, smiling sheepishly. "Good afternoon, sir, ma'am."

"Hello," Jon said. Seemed he was only able to muster one-word answers for the time being.

Cassidy nodded, her attention bolted to the other side of the glass where a second officer led Brock into the room. He wore an orange jumpsuit, and silver bracelets bound his hands in front of him.

Houser looked solemn, and in the small room, even larger than usual — somehow scarier when you considered he had kidnapped and likely killed Emma.

Cassidy froze as she glared through the glass, as if she could melt it and fire lasers from her eyes into Houser.

Jon felt rage, too, but his anger was offset by the nagging feeling that something was wrong. It might have been denial — him not wanting to think someone so close could have betrayed him, that he could be *so* wrong. Jon considered himself a stellar judge of character, and Houser was one of the most sincere men he'd ever met.

Something seemed off.

Jon remembered his friend's pure joy at finding Emma

after she disappeared the first time, but the memory was swallowed by a second thought.

How did he know where to look? Was he responsible?

No, he was in California when Emma went missing the first time. He couldn't have had anything to do with it! Stop thinking stupid shit, Jon.

The second officer left, then Brady entered the room. He wore no gun in his holster. Smart policy — never enter a cell while armed.

Brady sat and plopped a closed manila folder on the table. "Are you aware why you're here, Mr. Houser?"

"You all think I took Emma," Houser said, his face a stone.

"Yes. And did you take her?"

"I don't remember," Houser said.

"Liar!" Cassidy shouted.

Officer Henry and Jon both turned to her. For a moment Jon was certain Henry would ask her to leave.

"I'm sorry." She slapped her hand over her mouth and pressed it tight against her lips.

If Houser or Brady had heard her, Jon couldn't tell. They kept talking, their voices bleeding through the observation room speakers.

"We have video of you leaving the hotel last night with Emma wrapped in a blanket. You put her in your rental and left. Remember any of that? Or dispute it?"

"I can't remember a thing." Houser's voice was void of emotion. Sedated.

Jon had never heard the giant so quiet.

Houser wrung his hands in front of him on the table, slowly, as if washing them.

"So, you're saying that wasn't you?" Brady asked. "In the video? It was another tall, black man with a fake leg?"

"I don't know," he said slowly, nonplussed.

"What the fuck?" Cassidy said, her voice much lower than the prior shout.

"Something's not right," Jon said.

"Really?" Cassidy asked. "Dude just murdered our child and you think something's not right?"

Our child?

Jon stared at her, waiting for Cassidy to catch her slip, but she threw her attention back to the glass, either not realizing her error or too embarrassed, or maybe angry, to correct it.

Brady opened the folder and pulled out a stack of photos. He took one from the top and slid it across the table. Houser picked it up and stared at the image from the security footage of himself carrying the blanket.

He shook his head as if they'd shown him a picture of himself on the moon with a cosmonaut. If Houser had any recall at all, it was missing from his face.

"Do you remember this, then?" Brady slid another photo toward Houser.

This one was of Emma's dead, naked body lying on the shore. Cassidy gasped. Jon held his calm, studying Houser's face as it trembled, then cracked.

Emotion bled through.

"Emma?" The photo shook in his hands. "She's ... dead?"

"Yes," Brady said.

"No." Houser shook his head, slowly at first, then faster and faster until it was moving with fury. His voice turned swollen, and missing emotion poured out it in buckets. "No, no, NO!" Houser screamed, hands trembling as he tried pulling free from his cuffs.

Brady jumped up, startled, but didn't back up too far, as there seemed little chance Houser could pull an Incredible Hulk and break free from his chains.

"Mr. Houser, I need you to calm down," Brady said, his voice soothing.

"Who did this?" Houser shouted. "Who killed Emma?"

"I can't watch this bullshit." Cassidy headed toward the door.

Officer Henry stepped between her and the exit, as if he could stop her. "I'm going to the lady's room," she snapped. "Do I need permission to pee?"

"Yes, ma'am." He stepped quickly out of her way. "I mean, no, you don't need p ... p ... permission. It's just down ..."

"I know where it is." She brushed past him.

Jon watched as Houser's long howl tore through his soul. Was it the wail of a man in pain or in emotional duress stemming from guilt? As Jon stared, waiting for Houser to stop sobbing, he thought of Brady's gun, the one not in his holster.

Where is it? In his office? Is it locked up?

He thought of Cassidy, out in the hall, alone.

Shit.

"I need to use the bathroom, too." He pushed past Henry before the man could say boo.

Heart racing, Jon opened the door and was ready to run down the hall. He was surprised to find Cassidy standing right outside, leaning against the wall, crying. Without a gun.

She looked up. "I can't watch any longer."

"You don't have to," Jon said. "But I should go back."

Cassidy grabbed his hands and met his gaze, "You don't think he's innocent, do you?"

Jon didn't know how to answer. He knew what Cassidy wanted to hear, and what would make his life easiest. It was also what might provide her the most momentary solace — but it wasn't the truth.

"I don't know," he said. "Something's not right."

Cassidy looked at Jon as if he'd punched her in the gut. "How can you say that?"

"I'm not going to lie, Cassidy. I don't know. Yes, we saw the video, and yes it's damning, Houser carrying that blanket over his shoulders. Extremely damning. But shit, it just doesn't make sense with the man I know."

"Maybe you're not such a good judge of character," Cassidy said. "I mean, you didn't know I was a junkie, using again, did you?"

Jon shook his head, his eyes wet and sad. "I'm going back in. I need to hear what he's saying."

He opened the door and slipped back inside. Cassidy stayed in the hall.

Houser was still sitting at the table, again stone silent, his gaze lost to the photo of Emma's dead body.

"Did I miss anything?" Jon asked Henry.

"Nope, he hasn't said a word since you left."

Jon approached the two-way glass to get a closer look at Houser, hoping to draw something from his empty expression.

Brady resumed speaking, easing back into conversation. "Can you tell me what the last thing you *do* remember is, Mr. Houser? I'd love to help you, help us both, get to the bottom of this, but I need something to work with. Something I can follow up on. Can you give me anything?"

Houser started rocking, ever so slightly in his seat. He said something Jon couldn't quite decipher through the speakers.

Apparently, Brady couldn't either. He leaned "What was that, Mr. Houser?"

Houser kept rocking, and mumbled again, this time his voice was split by a staccato crackling of static in the speakers, followed by several seconds of high-pitched, piercing feedback, then a squawk, which caused all the men, in both rooms, to cover their ears and turn their heads from the speakers. The lights flickered, off, on, off, on, the last off stretching a full five seconds before the lights came back on.

When they did, Jon looked up to see Houser holding a small knife to his own throat, about to dig in.

"No!" Brady screamed, trying to intervene.

Houser shouted, "Stay back, or I'll do it!"

Brady halted then retreated carefully back to his seat. Calmly, he said, "You don't have to do this, Brock."

His hand shook at his neck. "Tell Jon I'm sorry."

Jon banged on the glass and screamed, "No!"

Houser turned, staring at the two-way mirror, though he couldn't possibly see his friend. Houser's eyes were wide, tears streamed his face.

"Jon?" he asked. "That you?"

Jon turned and raced past Officer Henry, who tried to stop him but was too late. Jon ran into the hall, noticed Cassidy missing, but didn't stop to wonder where she might be as he twisted the knob on the interrogation room door.

Locked.

"Let me in!" he shouted to Brady.

The door opened and Brady appeared between Jon and Houser, who was trying to look past the chief to his friend.

"Let me talk to him." Jon's voice dripped with desperation. "Please."

Brady stepped aside and let Jon into the room, obviously trying to avoid a suicide in his interrogation room.

Houser's eyes narrowed in confusion. "Jon? Is that you?"

"Yes, buddy, it's me."

"Please tell these people I didn't do it. I didn't kill her."

Houser's knife shook violently, tipped with blood. His hand seemed a second from slicing, but some part of him continued to resist, a part that seemed to be trying to connect with Jon.

"Please put the knife down," Jon said. "*Please.*"

Houser looked down at his hand as if it confused him. "Do you believe me, Jon? You know I didn't kill her, right?"

Jon stepped closer, now six feet from Houser.

Houser's expression turned angry, "Don't come any closer, Jonny. I'll do it."

"Please, don't."

Houser stared at Jon. His expression turned from angry to

confused, and then to scared. "I need to know you believe me, Jonny. I need to know."

"I ..." He took a cautious step closer, watching the man's eyes, watching the blade shaking in his hand, Houser lowering it just an inch or so ...

"... believe ... " He reached out, kept his gaze locked onto Houser's, praying his friend wouldn't suddenly jerk the knife into his throat,

"... you." He reached out and draped his hands gently over his friend's.

As their hands touched, Houser's eyes went wild. His hands shot up, eager to drive the knife into his throat.

Jon grabbed Houser's hands with both of his and used every ounce of his strength to slowly pry Houser's fingers from the blade while trying not to slice his own. "Let go!"

Houser's wild eyes locked onto his and they battled for the blade.

Brady was then at Jon's side. Between the two of them, they managed to wrest Houser's knife from his hands. It fell to the floor with a clang.

Houser's eyes met Jon's then went blank, as if he were stunned to see his friend inside the room. "Jon? Is that you?"

Brady spun around, screaming into both the mirrored wall and the camera. "Who the fuck patted him down? How the hell did he get a knife in here?!"

Jon's heart pounded as he stared at Houser, who looked either utterly confused or batshit crazy.

Or a third option — both.

Epilogue

Sarah woke with no idea how long she'd been sleeping.

Like every other time, it could have been an hour or might have been a week. And, like every other time, it was impossible to know truth.

A memory hit her, slapping Sarah hard in the face.

Emma is dead.

But was it real?

She wanted to cry but tried to control herself, tried to tell herself it was a false memory, just like so many she'd experienced since waking in this place days, weeks, months, years — who knew how long — ago.

Maybe Emma's death was a fabrication, too. They were testing her responses to stimuli. Why? She didn't know.

This was just another test. It had to be.

No, it was real. And you know it.

She ignored her pounding head and fuzzy brain, then stood from her bed and called out for help.

"Someone? Anyone? Where's Emma? Is she okay?"

As usual, and exactly as expected, Sarah's cry went unanswered. She screamed repeatedly, until her lungs numbed and fell silent.

She eventually grew hungry, and that filled her with hope. Though Sarah couldn't focus long enough to rein in a specific memory, something told her she was never hungry long, and a rumbling stomach meant company soon. As if to answer her thought, a door on the room's far side whooshed open.

None of the lab doctors entered, and there was no food. Blake Conway smiled instead. "We need to talk."

He is here! He is real!

"Oh, God!" Sarah's lump fattened in her throat. "I know it's something horrible, but I have to know. Just tell me. Is Emma really dead?"

An odd look flushed his face. Blake's eyebrows flared high then almost immediately settled. He narrowed his gaze, seeming to study her. Finally, he said, "Interesting," then paused, hesitating as if he wanted to say more. After a moment of silence, he added, "How do you know that, Sarah?"

Oh, God, it is true.

"I saw it," she said, trying not to break down. "Through Cassidy's eyes. I saw my baby, dead in the morgue, lying under a blanket. Jon was there, too. That couldn't have been real, right, Mr. Conway? It was like the birds, right? *Right?*"

It took everything inside Sarah to keep herself from sobbing. But then, quite suddenly, everything inside her wasn't enough. Sarah fell into a heaving sob, pulling a deep plea from her depths. "Is Emma dead?"

Blake smiled, his face kind and sympathetic. "I think we should speak somewhere more private." He looked around the empty room — a silent wink to the hidden cameras Sarah suspected were peeking from every corner — then held out his hand and gently linked his fingers through hers. "Come with me."

The door whooshed open. He stepped out into the hallway, pulling her behind him. Then the door whooshed back closed, and he led her down the hallway.

"Where are we going?" Her heart was racing, not just from Blake's reserved silence, and whatever answers or horrors might be only moments away, but because of her journey down the hallway, which was wrapped in majesty from both sides.

The long corridor, though edged in alloy, was mostly glass, including the floor, which made her feel as if she were space-walking, surrounded by stars. Earth's giant, blue marble hovered larger than dream's a hair to her right.

They reached the hallway's end and a solid wall disappeared. Blake stepped through the fresh aperture and gestured for Sarah to follow.

She stepped through the open door and gasped.

It was gorgeous, earning her awe despite just leaving a hallway that had her swaddled in the eternity of endless space. Vast, lush gardens spread before her, almost like a different world, with butterflies diving through the air by the hundreds. Thousands of vibrant flowers smeared the room in every shade and color. Tulips, mums, poppies, lilac, peonies, lilies, and roses were bundled in clusters, erupting in patterns that should not have been possible. Flowers that shouldn't grow together — especially at the same time of year — defied logic as if to prove beauty won at the end of the day. Fountains of orchids rained over the head of a giant alloy statue, looming high in the corner — not *quite* a man, but something else that Sarah didn't understand, though most of her felt like she should.

Blake sat on a long, stone bench, facing the wide window wrapping Earth in a circle. He patted the seat beside him.

Sarah joined him.

He continued to say nothing as he stared out at the massive garden, Sarah silent beside him. Then she noticed how steady her breathing had become.

Blake, as if reading her mind, asked, "Relaxed?"

Inexplicably, she was. She nodded.

"Then I'll be right back." He departed, leaving the opposite direction they'd come.

Sarah didn't turn to see where he was going, since she could see nothing but more garden in every direction, anyway. She wasn't worried, or alone for long. After what felt like two or three minutes, Blake returned from yet another direction.

This time he wasn't alone.

Beside him, holding his hand, was Emma.

Emma's eyes widened, and a smile spread across her face. "Mommy!" she cried, running through the garden toward Sarah.

My baby is alive!

Episode 12

Prelude - Warren Conway (Age 31)

Ten Years ago ...

Warren sat in his office, surrounded by black, his favorite room nothing but shadows but for the bottled, blue glow of his monitor bleeding from the screen as he stared at the children lining the wall, backs to the concrete and bodies bathed in the spotlights raining down from the ceiling of an otherwise dark laboratory basement.

The children were called forward one by one and asked to stand on a square. There were six, their ages ranging from seven to eleven, three boys and three girls, dressed in shorts and T-shirts, as if in gym.

But this wasn't gym, though it was an exercise — the most recent exercise in **Project Eleven**. Warren was seeing a climax from fourteen months of relentless testing.

The first child to center a square was male, Number 741, the numeral highlighted by a large, red sticker on his chest.

The boy waited, readying himself for the next part of the test, gaze flitting nervously at something in the darkness off-screen. When a second spotlight revealed his challenge, the boy's eyes widened.

The computer screen's picture split in two. The other image displayed, through a second angle, what the boy was seeing.

A girl, Number 744 on her shirt, was in a glass box, half-full of water. Above her, a large pipe poured more into the box, controlled by a large red handle on the valve — out of reach since the girl's hands and feet were bound. She cried, "Help!"

The boy looked at his instructor off-screen. "I can't do this!"

"You can and you will," a man's voice sharply insisted.

"No, I can't! I failed my last two tests. I can't!"

"Then Number 744 will die," the man said. "And it will be your fault."

Warren was mesmerized, even though he'd seen the video twice since Blake brought it to him that morning.

He watched as the water continued to spill, rising higher, up to the girl's chest. Instead of focusing his thoughts on the handle as he should have, the boy squandered his energy arguing with the instructor.

"Please, turn it off! I can't do it!"

"No," the instructor said sharply.

As the water reached the girl's chin and her screams grew increasingly panicked, the boy raced toward the box.

He was intercepted by two men in black, shoving the boy back and wrestling him to the ground.

"Not with your hands,' the man commanded. "With your mind, boy!"

The boy, struggling on the floor under the weight of the men, stared intently at the handle, attempting to twist it with thought.

His face turned crimson as sweat beaded his brow. He stared harder at the handle but the water kept rising, up and over the girl's nose, then her mouth.

She struggled, taxing her body to squirm free from her

ropes, trying not to panic but unable to stay calm. The girl thrashed, holding her breath as long as possible, still trying to break free.

"Stop it!" the boy screamed. "You're going to kill her!"

"No," the instructor said. "You're going to kill her!"

"No!" he repeated in anguish.

Then it happened — something shifted in his gaze, only slightly. When Warren paused and rewound the video, he saw it — a fire in the boy's eyes going immediately bright.

The tank exploded, sending glass and water in a rippling cascade across the concrete floor as the girl fell to her knees and gasped, violently sucking in air.

The boy broke free from the men in black, who no longer tried to force him down, and ran to the girl. "I'm so sorry, I'm so sorry," he said holding her tight. Then he glared at the instructor. "You almost killed my sister!"

"No," the instructor said, "*you* almost killed her."

Warren clicked off the video and smiled. It had worked. The experiment had finally paid its first dividend, much to his surprise.

"Wow," Warren whispered to himself.

"What the hell was that?" Warren's wife was suddenly behind him.

He turned. "Melinda!"

Her eyes were wide as she stared at him, shaking. "What was that?"

"Why are you sneaking up on me?" he asked. "I'm working!"

"It's three in the morning, Warren! I woke up and you weren't in bed, so I came to see if you were okay. What the hell *was* that?"

"I can explain," he said.

"I'm waiting," she said, arms crossed, shaking her head.

Warren's lies were molasses, unwilling to drip. Finally, he

managed a feeble line from the truth. "It's an experiment we're doing, testing telekinesis."

"On children? By drowning them?!"

"They weren't going to let the girl drown," he said, hoping to convince her with his most winning smile. "The point of the test was to put the subjects under duress to draw a reaction."

"These are children!" Melinda said. "Close to Anastasia's age! How can you do this?"

"It's not as bad as it looks. Most of the tests are super easy stuff, Melinda, trying to get the kids to move blocks, balls, and stuff like that — it's fun! I swear. This is the only thing like this we did."

Melinda shook her head. "I'm talking to your father!"

"No!" Warren yelled. "He can't know that you know about this. This is top secret, classified, like government stuff, Melinda. You aren't cleared to know this."

"Not cleared? I'm your wife, for Christ's sake!"

"You *know* how our business works."

"No. I thought I knew, Warren. I thought you were trying to help people, cure diseases, improve artificial limbs, other stuff that does good in the world. Not this crazy shit! This looks like some Cold War, mumbo jumbo, psychic warfare stuff, and you're using kids!"

Warren shook his head. "Please, don't say anything."

"Or what? Will the government come and get me?" She paused. "Does the government even know what you're doing here?"

Warren wasn't sure how to answer.

Melinda caught his hesitation. "They don't, do they? Oh, my God!"

"Stop, Melinda, you're overreacting. Let's just calm down and discuss this. I'll tell you anything you want to know."

"No, I'll wait and speak with Blake tomorrow."

"Please," Warren said. "You can't."

"No." Melinda pointed to the TV. "*He can't* do this! And if you're not man enough to stand up to him and tell him, I will!"

Melinda turned on her heel and stormed from Warren's office. She turned at the door. "And don't bother coming to bed. Just sit here and watch your snuff films!"

Warren sighed and shook his head, then collapsed in his chair and feared the worst.

Warren couldn't sleep.

He sat at his desk, ruminating through the rest of the night, wondering what in the hell he should do.

Though nails in his eyes might have been more pleasant, he *had* to call Blake — couldn't let Melinda blindside him. Warren waited until 5:15, then went to Father's bedroom door and tapped lightly, knowing he would be slipping on his jogging shoes and getting ready for his morning run.

Warren was dressed to jog, as well.

Father opened his door. "What is it, son?"

"We need to talk."

They'd been jogging through the Gardens for ten minutes by the time Warren finished his confession to Father. He waited in silence as Blake continued to quietly run.

Father wasn't usually the strong and silent type, though he wasn't above a cold shoulder to serve him.

"Well? Are you going to say anything?" Warren finally pushed the words through his heavy breathing as they ran onto the path leading through the woods.

"I can't believe you were so careless."

Warren swallowed, trying not to sound whiney. "I said I was sorry,"

"Sorry changes nothing, Warren. I'm not having this discussion with Melinda."

"Well, she thinks she's talking to you."

"You're her husband, you take care of this. This isn't, and shouldn't be, my problem."

"What do you want me to do? I already begged her not to say anything last night. I even said it was classified and she shouldn't know."

Blake stopped running. Warren stopped short beside him. Father met his gaze. "You should never have to *beg* your wife to do anything, son. She's got you whipped."

"I don't need a marital speech."

"Well, *boy*, apparently you do. Marriage means having someone who'll stand by you through all the trouble you wouldn't have had if you'd stayed single. Melinda made a mistake by walking into your office in the middle of the night, and you made a bigger one by allowing it to happen like a fool. Now you have to sweep the floor. That's life, Warren. You're born, you die, and in between you make a shit heap of mistakes. That's expected. Unfortunately for you, this is one of your stupidest and requires a rather immediate solution. You will call Dr. Nelson this morning and order a wipe for Melinda."

"What?" He barely believed he heard Father right. "You can't be serious."

"I can't — no, *we* can't — risk this getting out. And I can't trust your wife to keep her big mouth shut. Can you?"

"She won't say anything," Warren insisted, as if conviction in his voice could turn it true.

"I'm not arguing with you. Order it done."

"But the wipes aren't perfected, we've seen the side effects."

"They're minor and affect less than five percent of patients."

"No." Warren shook his head. "I won't risk turning my wife into a vegetable!"

Blake took a step closer to his son, wearing the same red eyes and twitching cheeks that usually came before he cast people from his life or employ forever.

"After all I've sacrificed for you and this family, after working my ass off every day to ensure our futures, and after trying to do something for the betterment of mankind, you're going to tell me *no* on a simple procedure?"

"It's not a simple procedure, Father. It's a brain wipe!"

"It's a minor part of the brain, for Christ's sake. You need to learn a thing or two about sacrifice, son. You don't get where I am without being willing to make the tough calls. The right decisions aren't always the easy ones."

Warren shook his head, eyes to the ground, feeling seconds from vomit. He couldn't let his nerves better him, not in front of Father.

"But there's gotta be a better way." He stood straighter, trying to shake the feeling from his body.

Blake met his gaze. "If there is, then do it. But I'm telling you now, I will *not* allow your wife, or anyone else, to ruin all I've worked for."

"What does that mean? Are you threatening her?" Warren barely resisted the urge to shove him. "Don't threaten my wife."

Blake smiled, as if the thought of a physical altercation with Warren amused him.

"It's not a threat, son. I'm confident you'll make the right choice and finally prove yourself willing to sacrifice for the greater good. Now, if you'll excuse me, I'd like to finish my jog. Alone."

Father ran down the path, leaving Warren to turn and

head home, knowing with a sickening certainty his choices were none.

~

Melinda woke in her hospital room one week later and opened her eyes to Warren.

She had been told she slipped and fell hard in the kitchen, banging her head right into a hospital stay — the same story given to everyone else.

The doctor, who had already spoken to Melinda the day before, reported she didn't remember the men coming to take her away. She also didn't remember the video she'd seen which made the mild operation a major success.

This was the first time Warren had seen Melinda since she surfaced from her medically-induced coma. She smiled when she saw him, but there was something off in the smile, just as there was something off in her eyes.

It was Melinda, but as they spoke, Warren felt something missing — the fire that burned inside her and made Melinda his wife was now dim. It was as if they'd taken molecules of her personality and spun them to nothing, alongside her memories of the video and subsequent argument.

"What's wrong?" she asked sweetly, noticing Warren's concern.

"Nothing," he lied, suddenly realizing that it hadn't been his sacrifice — it was Melinda's, and she was never given a choice.

Chapter 1 - Cassidy Hughes

Cassidy opened her eyes in the frigid, dark room, her head pounding and thoughts fuzzy, memory an amnesiac's diarrhea. She looked around the dingy studio apartment and its embarrassment of mess. Beside her, the queen-sized bed was empty. From the bathroom, rain pounded the shower floor. On the nightstand, a crooked row of empty beer bottles circled her painkillers' upturned cap, no pill bottle beside it.

She panicked.

Where are they?

Cassidy leaned over the bed, looked down at the carpet, then found the bottle on the floor. She grabbed it. *Empty!*

Cass dropped to her knees, still naked, then crawled on all fours, combing her fingers through shag, reaching under the nightstand and bed, praying to find at least one, hopefully two, to rid her pounding bitch of a headache.

She brushed over a line of junk under the bed — clothes, boxes, tissues, and God knew what else — until her fingers finally found a tiny pill. She grabbed it, careful not to lose it in the carpet, then studied it in the dim light seeping through a thin crack in the blanket draping the windows to make sure it was, in fact, the right pill. Satisfied, she popped it in her mouth. Dizzy, she looked at the bottles of beer on the night-stand, found one with a swallow at the bottom, and washed the pill down her throat with the slightly cool beer.

She was back on the floor searching for pills when Craig's voice wrinkled the air from behind her, coming from the bathroom.

"Whatcha doin'?" He stepped out of the bathroom, naked and drying his hair.

Cassidy looked up at Craig, who looked smug, smiling like Cheshire Cat.

"Nothing, just looking for pills. The bottle's empty." Then she searched for her clothes. Too much nudity in the room. What felt so right in the previous evening's momentary heat felt wrong in a new day's judgmental light. It felt like the horrible mistake it was.

Cassidy retrieved her Shipwrecked tee from the floor and slid the black fabric over her body, followed by her panties and pants.

"Relax." Craig scraped a thin towel over his long, shaggy hair as she dressed. Done drying his mop, he tossed the towel onto the bathroom floor. Then he went to his dresser, opened the top drawer, pulled out a large white plastic bottle that looked like it could help weather any storm with a thousand-pill harbor, and said, "How many you need?"

Cassidy swallowed, hating the question almost as much as the man it came from.

"I dunno." She didn't want to seem as needy as she felt, but she also didn't want to ask for too few, knowing she would only wind back up at Craig's in the middle of the night again in a couple of days, desperate. "Fifty?"

"Okay. Gimme your bottle."

She grabbed the bottle, along with the lid, and passed it to Craig, hands shaking.

He smiled. "Don't worry, no charge this time."

"Why?" she asked. "I have money."

"Consider it payment for services rendered," he said, wearing his stupid fucking grin.

Cassidy wanted to claw him. She took a step back, turned, and found her purse on the ground. She rooted through it, grabbed a wad of bills — last night's tips — then threw the wad on top of Craig's dresser, not even bothering to count.

"I'm not a whore." Then she snatched the freshly-filled bottle from his hand.

"I didn't say you were," Craig was defensive, but still wearing the smile that made her want to scratch him. "Just trying to help a friend."

Cassidy wanted to correct him, tell him they were *not* friends. They were fuck buddies at best, retired after too many wasted years spent stupidly partying. A final mistake. She should have never come over, should've gone to Jon's instead. She needed escape, a familiar face, the warm glove of an old habit — two old habits, actually — someone she could trust to shut his fucking mouth and keep it closed.

But Cassidy said none of that. Better not to piss off her dealer, one of the only people on the island she *could* trust to be discreet.

"Thank you," she said, not meaning it. Cassidy scanned the floor, searching for her shoes. She found them, brought them over to the bed, then sat at the edge to put them on.

"Are you mad at me?"

"I've got a lot on my mind."

"Your niece?" he asked, even though they'd already talked about that last night when he'd come to the bar and ordered too many drinks. Craig had consoled her, giving her comfort in words, which felt nice, even if glazed in guile — it was tough to tell with Craig. Regardless, it was exactly what her moment had needed.

Things with Jon were odd. There was a sudden gulf between them since Emma was found, widening by the hour. Saddled with stress, they found themselves arguing about everything from Houser's guilt — obvious to Cassidy — to funeral details for Emma.

Extra shit in the pie came from Vivian siding with Jon, two to one when it came to arranging the funeral. If Cassidy couldn't count on her own fucking mother to stand behind her, then the pills would do in a pinch.

Craig coming into Shipwrecked had been her best chance for escape. And the worst thing she could have done.

She'd slipped. Again.

"Or is it Jon Conway?" Craig said into her silence. "What's the deal with you two, anyway?"

Cassidy snapped, "None of your business."

"Oh! Sorry, Cassidy m'lady. Didn't mean to offend thee."

"Fuck you, Craig." She stood, eager to leave.

Craig stepped between her and the door, then set his hands on her shoulders, in a gesture likely meant for comfort. She felt like being touched by no one, longing for her apartment, a shower, and, if possible, some single-serving amnesia.

"We've known each other a while, right, Cass?" Craig asked like a concerned friend.

"Yeah."

"So, I'm gonna say it. What are you doing with that Hollywood douche bag? I mean, he might be Hamilton Island, Cass, but he's not *us*."

"You don't know him."

How much about her and Jon was public knowledge? She'd ignored the news, for too many reasons, least of all the gossip. But the island was tiny compared to the eruption of concrete and glass cramming the mainland. On Hamilton Island, everyone knew too much about everyone else. Or was at least convinced of their ability to see through walls and fill in the blanks.

But what could others know of private moments passed? Judgment blinked instants to irrelevance — confidences traded, glances in secret, tender moments between lovers alone. People lived three lives — shared, private, and *secret*. True privacy, confident behind the curtains of judgment's hollow, nursed that pause between what *is* and what could be.

Craig could think he knew what was happening between her and Jon, but he could never truly know or appreciate their private moments.

His eyes widened as he grinned through his idiot drug-dealer smile, hanging on his suntanned face with the weary weight of a long decade spent in arrested development. "Oh, shit. You're in love, aren't you?"

To hear someone speak of her blooming love for Jon, particularly someone she'd just slept with, made Cassidy's already sick stomach that much sicker. Craig had no right to speak of Jon. Or judge him.

"I wouldn't expect *you* to understand," Cassidy said.

He laughed. "Oh, right, what would I know, I'm just some Hamilton Island burnout loser ... like *you*, Cass." He laughed louder. "You think you're any different from me?"

Cassidy said nothing, wanting to push past the asshole and fly out the front door. But he blocked her way, determined to finish what he wanted to say.

"He comes around, slums it with you and shit, then what? Now you think you're Conway royalty? Ha, get real, sister. It's only a matter of time before Jonny Hollywood's walking the long, red carpet back home with the latest eighteen-year-old supermodel. You're a memory waiting to be banked, a good time and nothing more."

Cassidy smacked Craig across his face, so hard he nearly stumbled back into the wall. She wanted to hit him again, longed to unleash a string of obscenities, anything other than what she did — her shoulders collapsed, and she fell into tears.

Craig reeled, face crimson and angry, likely ready to smack her right back, but when he saw Cassidy crying, vulnerable in a way he'd never seen — she had shown that side of herself to no one but Jon — he froze.

"Sorry." He reached out to touch her.

Cassidy pulled away, then shoved past him, leaving his shit studio without another word. She got in her car, slammed the door, checked the rearview to make sure Craig hadn't followed her outside, then closed her eyes and sobbed as she pounded the wheel with her fists. She reached into her purse, grabbed the bottle, then paused, hating herself too much to continue, yet so desperate to muffle her sorrow that she craved the noose at her neck.

Not now.

Not now.

As her hand hit the bottle, Cassidy saw her cell sitting at the bottom of her bag. She grabbed it and turned it on for the first time since silencing Jon's incessant calls from the night before.

Twenty missed calls from Jon, with twenty matching messages.

She synced the phone with her car and played his voicemails, starting with the first as she pulled out of Craig's apartment complex and started for home. Each message was more of the same, Jon wanting to know where she was.

"I'm worried, I went by your work, and nobody knew where you were. I went by your mom's and your house, and nothing."

Then Jon's final message, left at 7 a.m., three hours ago. "Please, call me. Even if it's to tell me to fuck off. I just want to know you're not ... Well, to know you're okay. Please, Cassidy."

Not what? Overdosed somewhere?

Fuck you, Jon.

Cassidy was angry, but she would have been angry had he not called at all. She was irrational and knew it. A wreck, and an addict, just like her mom, with no emotional fitness.

Cassidy prayed she could get her shit together before Emma's funeral tomorrow.

Chapter 2 - Sarah Hughes

A week ago ...

EMMA RAN TO SARAH, throwing two arms around her mother and squeezing her hard.

Sarah couldn't believe it. She held Emma tight, inhaling her daughter's scent — the smell she thought she'd never inhale again, one she worried she might forget.

"Oh, God," Sarah whispered repeatedly while rocking her baby girl.

"You're alive!" Tears streamed down her little face. "We thought you were dead. We had a funeral and everything. Aunt Cassidy and my dad were there."

"Your dad?" Sarah pushed Emma far enough from her body to clearly see her face.

"Yeah, I met my dad, Jon Conway! Why didn't you tell me he was my daddy? Or that Blake was my grandpa!"

Sarah turned to Blake, who stood in the garden watching their reunion with a smile. She wanted to know everything there was to know but didn't dare to cut a sliver from Emma's moment.

Sarah tried thinking of answers for Emma regarding her father. Her daughter certainly deserved them. Though Sarah had scripted responses over the years, she couldn't remember any of them at the moment. Her memories were hit and miss with all the stuff the doctors were putting her through.

"I don't know," Sarah said. "It's complicated. We'll talk about it another time, I promise. How are they? How's Cassidy? Grandma? How is your father?"

"They're good, but everyone misses you so, so much," Emma said. "We cried a lot. Why didn't you tell us you were alive?"

"I wish I could have," Sarah said. Did her daughter even knew they were in a space station? How had Blake brought her up? And, more importantly, why was she here? Was she "dead" too, like Sarah? She had so many questions but didn't want to ask Emma. She had to ask Blake instead. He was the one with the answers. Sarah's job was to be a mother. to act normal and harbor Emma's illusions that things were fine for as long as she could.

"The important thing is," Sarah said, closing her eyes and hugging her daughter, slowly rocking her back and forth, "we're together now, and everything will be okay." She opened her eyes to find Blake still watching.

Then, as if finally realizing he was eavesdropping on their moment, he turned and walked down a path between a cluster of bushes, and out of sight.

Sarah guided them to a bench. "How did you get here?"

"I don't remember. I was staying with Houser — that's Daddy's friend — while Daddy and Aunt Cassidy were having a date night. Then I woke up in a white room, like a hospital, and Grandpa was there. He said someone wanted to see me, and then he brought me in here to see you."

"Date night? Jon and Cassidy are dating?" Sarah asked, trying not to laugh or appear as if the news upset her — which she was surprised to find, it did, and quite a lot.

So, the dreams are true.

She'd been having dreams that she was with Jon, and that they were in love. But at times, it felt like she was her sister rather than herself. The dreams were odd, and vivid. They felt too real, like dreams rarely did, with memories following her in the morning and thickening through the day.

"Yeah," Emma said, only just realizing the news might hurt her mom. "I'm sorry."

"It's okay." Sarah brushed her fingers through Emma's soft hair. "I haven't seen your daddy in a while."

"Why not?" Emma asked, either forgetting or ignoring that Sarah said they would discuss it later. "And why didn't *you* tell *him* he had a daughter?"

Emma's hurt was still fresh, and clear on her face. She looked as if she had been waiting forever to ask.

"Your daddy moved to California before you were born, honey. There were a lot of things happening for him there, and I didn't want to mess it up by telling him how much his life had suddenly changed. I didn't want to ruin things for him."

Emma stared at her mom with tear-misted eyes. "I would have ruined things for him?"

"No, no, honey." Sarah searched for words without stingers. "Jon and I were different people. The last thing in the world I wanted for me, or for you, was Hollywood and all the stuff that comes with it. It's hard raising a child in this world with a normal life. Once you hit Hollywood, it's …"

Sarah trailed off. She couldn't think of the right arrangement of words, an assembly that would stay close to the truth but not reveal Jon as the alcoholic, womanizing actor who had slept with maybe half of Hollywood's starlets and would clearly have been a horrible father. Or that she hadn't wanted to raise a child with *that* Jon. Whomever Emma had spent time with wasn't quite the Jon she knew.

Emma waited for more, her eyes still welling with tears,

but she didn't break down. The girl was strong, stronger than Sarah thought.

"I don't know if I can ever make sense of things in a way that you'll understand. I was young. We both were, and I didn't know what to do. I did what I thought was right, for you, and us. But," she admitted through a swallow, "that doesn't mean I would do it the same way again."

Emma stared at her mom, and for a moment, Sarah thought she might explode in anger.

"How dare you make my decisions!"

"How can you keep me from knowing my father?"

"Why would you lie to me?"

But Emma said nothing of the sort. Instead, she said, "It's okay, Mommy. I think I understand. You did your best."

Sarah held her tears and hugged Emma again. "You're such a sweetheart — I'm so, so sorry."

"It's okay, Mommy. I promise." Emma pulled away and smiled as she looked around at the garden. "This place is so pretty. Where are we?"

"Where did Mr. Conway tell you we are?" Sarah asked, assuming Emma had already asked him.

"He said we're in a special place, and he would tell me more later, after I saw the person who wanted to see me. That was you, Mommy!" Emma pushed her pointer finger into her mom's tickle spot, the one Emma used most, right under her right ribcage. "So where are we, Mom? And when can we go home?"

"I don't know," she said, hating to admit it.

Emma asked. "You don't know where we are, or you don't know when we can go home?"

Before she could answer, Blake's voice came from behind them. "Ah, glad to see you girls are catching up."

Sarah turned to find him standing with his hands folded across his chest, smiling like a kindly benefactor rather than their warden. She buried her contempt — it wasn't just herself she had to worry about, not with Emma now in her arms.

A red-haired woman who seemed to be in her early forties appeared behind him. She was wearing all white, much like the others Sarah had seen.

Blake turned to the red-haired woman, then to Sarah and Emma. "Ladies, this is Bernice. She's going to show Emma around our school."

"School?" mom and daughter said together, surprised.

"Yes, we have a few children here with us." He stood beside them and smiled. "I believe you'll love the campus."

"Where are we?" Emma tugged on her grandfather's suit jacket. "And when can we go home?"

"You, my girl, are in a very special place. I call it The Source. You'll know more soon, a lot more, and I promise to let you know as soon as you can go back home. But first, I need to talk to your mother while Bernice shows you around. Is that okay?"

Emma looked at her mom.

Sarah nodded, disguising her unease. She had to stay calm, trust that if Blake brought Emma to her, he wasn't likely to hurt her. Not now. Whatever was happening, it probably didn't involve hurting her daughter. She had to play nice, hold it together, and give Emma no reason to fear.

"It's fine, honey. I'll see you in just a bit, all right?" She was asking Blake though her eyes were on Emma.

"Of course." He continued to smile. "We can share lunch in the observatory."

"Observatory?" Emma repeated. Even confused and clearly nervous, she held excitement in her smile.

"Yes, the observatory," Blake said. "You'll love it."

Sarah wasn't so sure, especially if the observatory showed Emma they were in space with Earth turning in the distance.

Bernice draped her arm around Emma, then Sarah said

goodbye, and Bernice led her from the gardens to show her the school.

Once alone, Blake waved to the empty spot beside Sarah. "May I?"

"Yes." She scooted to her left as Blake sat on her right.

"I'm sure you have questions." He leaned forward, elbows on his knees, staring not at Sarah, but at the far end of the garden where a squirrel scampered across the grass. Sarah followed his gaze and stared at the squirrel.

"Is that real?" she asked, surprised since she had seen no trace of wildlife or pets of any kind on the space station, unless you counted butterflies. At least, none she believed to be real.

"Yes, we're trying to introduce new life up here, as much as we can, experimenting with different blends of creatures, insects, and such. This is but one of our many ecosystems. But Sarah, is that *really* what you wanted to ask?"

"No," Sarah said. "I want to know happened to Emma. Why is she here?"

"I had to bring her," Blake said. "She was starting to remember too much, displaying recall she shouldn't have."

"Remembering what?" A brick of ice pressed on Sarah's chest.

"Memories from times we've brought her here before."

"You've brought Emma up *here*? When? Why?"

"Several times since she was an infant, Sarah. Same as you. I said you were important to our cause and meant it. Same with Emma."

"What the hell is happening here?" She grew angrier by the second, loathing the monster beside her, and hating she couldn't make a scene without endangering Emma. "What gives you the right to interfere in other people's lives?"

"We're not interfering." Blake continued looking at the squirrel rather than Sarah.

The rodent lowered on its haunches and chewed a nut, freshly fallen from one of the garden's many trees.

"We're working to save humanity. It's part of a program started under my father, a program that will usher humanity into our next evolutionary leap, as I've told you already. But it's also a program which will allow us — you, me, your daughter — to live *forever.*"

Sarah stared at him. "Forever?"

"Yes, forever. We're quite close."

"But what if I don't want to live forever, especially on some station up in space?" Sarah scooted a few more inches from Blake. "I'd rather live a short life with people I love than stay here forever with you and your crew or cult, or whatever this is, Mr. Conway. Did you ever think about *asking* people if they *want* to be part of your experiments? Nobody asked me. Or Emma."

"No, we didn't ask." All traces of Blake's smile and warmth melted away. "We *saved you*, Sarah. Without our intervention, you would be dead. Would you prefer death, and never seeing your daughter again?"

Sarah didn't know if Blake was threatening her or not, but she didn't want to chance ticking him off.

"What about Emma? You didn't *save her*, did you? I deserve to know why you've been bringing us here, why you've been bringing Emma — she's a child, for Christ's sake, what can she possibly do for you?"

"Come." Blake stood and offered Sarah his hand. "I'll show you."

Sarah rose but refused Blake's hand. Then she followed him out of the garden.

Chapter 3 - Warren Conway

Warren was starting to dread his meetings with Kaiser, though the same rendezvous used to excite him. Forbidden. Illicit. Taboo. Wrong used to feel right. Their dalliances would thicken his cock and make him feel like a man.

Now he felt like a child, forced to explain himself, as if he wasn't Kaiser's superior. He had a hard enough time with one father. He sure as hell didn't need two.

Warren climbed inside the black Paladin van and fell harshly back against the vinyl seat as Kaiser pulled from the curb before Warren had even finished closing the door. He turned to Kaiser. "What gives? We going somewhere?"

"I just think it's best to keep moving," Kaiser said.

Warren was nervous. He wanted to call off the plot to get rid of Blake but didn't know how to broach the subject without Kaiser giving him shit, questioning his masculinity and such.

The rage Warren had nursed for a week was starting to flee his body. Only the weak stayed slaves to their anger, and though Warren might occasionally lose a battle with himself in a moment's heat, he would never lose the war. Releasing his anger didn't make Warren careless. It was the simple acceptance that the only thing a person could truly master was himself.

Father was an appropriate target for Warren's anger, but he had to focus his rage in the proper degree and with appropriate purpose. Warren had to intimately know his most desired result if he expected to get it. Blake Conway could be a heartless bastard, but he was also a helluva leader and a better head for Conway Industries than Warren.

"I can't do it," Warren spit out as Kaiser stopped the van at a red.

He turned to Warren, raising his eyebrows. The synthetic brow above his bright blue eye arched slightly higher. "What?"

"I can't do it. It's a mistake." Warren's right palm bounced against his knee. "I'm sure of it."

Kaiser laughed, then accelerated through the green light. "You've gotta be kidding me? Christ, you're worse than a waffling politician. Pick a fucking platform, Warren, and stand on it like a man." He drummed his fingers on the steering wheel. "And just so you know, you're on the wrong one."

"This isn't right," Warren said, "and not because I don't want to. I don't think it's what's best for Conway Industries. And if it isn't best for Conway, it isn't best for me. Or you."

"Bullshit," Kaiser said. "That's just you being a pussy, again. The old man is exactly that — an old man. What's best for Conway Industries, *and* for you, is to clear the way for a man who can clearly see the company's future. Someone who prides himself on strong vision and the health of Conway's broader business, instead of governing growth according to some grandiose manifesto. *Now* is the time, Warren. Time to stop being a pussy and go for the only play that makes any sense. This is *your* life, and your future. It's what you've given your heart to. You *deserve* to run Conway, and once you do, you can pick any damn project you want to fund. You *know* what that means."

Kaiser was right, at least about one thing — with Warren at the head of Conway Industries, he could greenlight whatever project he wanted.

But Kaiser being right made Warren at least a little wrong.

Blake might make a better leader for Conway Industries than Warren, but Warren was best at running Project Raven, and that project had more potential — for both Conway Industries and the world — than any of Father's pipe-dream, transhumanist bullshit. People would never evolve, not enough to make up for the fact that they're all animals, subject to the same weaknesses.

"It's up to you," Kaiser said from the driver's side. "You call the shots, but I'm telling you man, your father's lost it, and we both know you're the future of this company."

Warren sighed. He had to trust his tomorrow and surrender his yesterday. Murder was liquidation, unclogging a stuck drain.

"Okay," he said. "Let's do it."

Chapter 4 - Jon Conway

Jon sat on the couch, waiting, staring up at the blank wall monitor while sorting through the same half-dozen agitated thoughts he'd been wrestling through a night of not sleeping.

Making excuses was exhausting, mostly because Jon had such a low tolerance for the exercise. As Father often said, to the delight of reporters and quote harvesters everywhere, "Get good enough at making excuses, and you'll make yourself sorry at pretty much everything else."

Jon had made plenty of excuses for Cassidy but kept circling back to the fact that she should have answered her goddamned phone.

Sure, she didn't always have her cell, and might not have heard it the first dozen times it rang, especially when working in a noise-polluted place like Shipwrecked. Her battery could've been dead, or Cassidy could have fallen asleep watching the second season of *The Dark Tower* — she had been bingeing since Jon told her she *had* to start watching. She wasn't obsessive about being reachable, and Jon didn't think she should be. He understood since he was the same. More so, though for different reasons, Jon longed for a time he'd never known but had often dreamed of, when cells weren't in every pocket.

Jon made the excuses, but they all felt wrong. He felt like a dick for doubting her, since he knew what she needed most was for people to believe in her. But Jon wasn't stupid, and Cassidy wasn't known for staying sober.

The doorbell's sharp ring was immediately followed by the rat-a-tat-tat of knuckles on wood. Jon's front door swung open, and Cassidy said, "Hey Popcorn, you home?"

He stood and crossed the living room, homing in on her.

She held his gaze through her approach, swallowed hard as she stopped, a foot from him, still staring. Her hair was wet, like she'd just gotten out of the shower, and she wore a blue tee and jeans, which meant she'd at least been home since leaving work.

Her eyes looked like they had something to prove. Cassidy seemed tentative, guilty, only half there. She had fallen off the wagon — again.

Shit.

"What happened to you last night? I waited all night." Jon held her stare, digging for truth in her eyes. "I was worried."

"I'm sorry," Cassidy said. "You know how late Shipwreck closes, I didn't know I was supposed to check in with you when I got off."

"I didn't say you had to check in with me, Cassidy. But that *is* what we've done every night we've not seen one another for the last month. We call each other, we say good-night. Expecting a call isn't unreasonable."

"Oh, Jon, I never took you for the needy type." Defensiveness turned her smile mean.

She walked past Jon, giving him no kiss or hug. At the fridge, she flung open the door, grabbed a tall bottle of water from the back, then slammed it shut. After taking a long pull of the beverage, she leaned against the kitchen counter and stared at him.

He tried telling himself this wasn't Cassidy. She was defensive — likely fucked up, and probably wrestling guilt. He knew the cycle well, having spun through it more than a few times himself — raising ire from his life's important players through his sudden, erratic behavior.

His next words mattered.

The situation was volatile, with both Cassidy and Jon on edge. Tomorrow they buried Emma — his daughter and her niece — as each of them ran from the twin demons of guilt and regret.

Jon managed to stay sober. Cassidy, however, needed her pills. That weakness, if she allowed it, could overwhelm her and kick her life back into an abyss. He had to be there for her, without being judgmental. Tough love was often effective with addicts, at least in his experience. But how could you give tough love when unconditional love was needed most?

"I was worried about you," Jon said. "That's all."

"I'm a big girl, Jon Conway. I don't need to be rescued, and this isn't the end of *Pretty Fucking Woman*."

"Where's this all coming from?" Jon flinched, no longer caring if his mounting frustration showed.

"Where's *what* coming from?" Cassidy sipped her water, ready to self-sabotage her way through a fight.

"This," he said waving his hands between them, "this way you're acting, like I did something wrong. I don't get the hostility."

"Maybe I'm pissed because when the man who killed our daughter tried to kill himself, you stopped him!"

Our daughter?

Cassidy seemed to notice her slip of the tongue. She turned from him and set her water on the counter. Then she crossed her arms and lay her head down, chin to chest.

Jon couldn't tell if her shuddering breaths were heaving through anger, tears, or both. Everything was happening too fast to pull sense from the sudden insanity. This was the third or fourth time he could remember Cassidy slipping with something like that, calling Emma *her* daughter. He wanted to say something, but every thought in his head felt like one that might break her to pieces.

Obviously, she realized her error. And clearly, she's embarrassed.

But he couldn't help it. "Why do you keep doing that?"

"Doing what?" Cassidy asked, her head down and still avoiding his eyes.

"Saying 'our daughter.' And you said 'your daughter' another time. What's going on?"

"No, I didn't." Cassidy slowly lifted her head, shaking it.

Jon studied her face, sorting lie from delusion.

Did she really not notice?

"I get that Emma's your family," he said, his voice as careful as it was gentle. "You've known her for nine years. She was closer to you than me. But she was *my* daughter, and if you think I don't miss her, or that I'm not angry, you're wrong."

Cassidy wasn't crying, but her eyes were crimson, a shade darker than her face. "Then why did you stop him?"

"Because I know Houser didn't do it."

"How can you say that?" Cassidy screamed, fists balled at her side. "You saw the fucking video! You saw him carrying her out of the room! Even if you didn't, Houser was the last person with her! We trusted him, and he took her from us." She trembled, on the verge of tears.

Seeing her so close to the edge brought Jon closer himself. His chin quivered, but he staved off the tears, just as he would if cameras were rolling. He had to hold his shit together, for both their sakes.

"I can't explain it," Jon said. "Other than I trust my gut. And Houser. You spend enough time with someone, you learn what they're capable of. And I know he's not capable of killing a child."

Cassidy glared at him, "People spend their lives with

monsters they never see, Jon. Evil children, monstrous husbands, perverted people living in shadow. Blind love makes it easy to believe those truths that are convenient to weave. What makes *you* think you know how to spot a monster?"

Jon couldn't help but feel as if Cassidy was flogging herself. She wasn't evil, but she did occasionally bubble with self-loathing. For what, he wasn't sure.

Then it hit him — Cassidy blamed herself for Sarah's fate, and now for Emma's.

If she'd not gotten into trouble ten years ago, if she wasn't a *worthless fucking addict*, as she often said, the Conways would never have managed to coax Sarah into hiding her pregnancy from Jon. He probably would have returned to Hamilton and taken them both to Hollywood.

The past month would never have happened.

Sarah and Emma would both still be breathing.

Something in Jon's expression must have surrendered his thoughts. She met his gaze, then Cassidy collapsed into his chest, sobbing.

"It should've been me," she wailed into his soon to be soaked shirt. "It should've been me dead. Not Sarah, not Emma."

Jon held her, trying to be strong, chewing his lip and willing himself not to cry. But cameras weren't rolling, and with only Cassidy in his living room, Jon could do nothing to stop it.

～

JON WOKE from his nap just as the sun was dipping behind the horizon.

He looked over to see Cassidy, still in her pajamas, put on after her earlier shower. She was sleeping, eyes moving rapidly under her lids.

They spoke for hours after their fight, until they eventually made up, not with sex, but by lying beside one another on the bed, falling deeper into thoughts birthed on their tongues and sent to the air. They spoke of their previous weeks together, about the next day's funeral, and of the many things they thought might happen. Cassidy questioned the dress she had picked out for Emma to be buried in — light pink with tiny clusters of lilacs and daffodils, the one Emma had worn to church only twice. Did she actually like it, or did she only tell Sarah she did to make her happy? Jon said either way, it was perfect. They touched only safe topics, not even dancing around anything else — no mention of Houser or drugs or a future together.

It was time to heal. And grieve. They could worry about the future once tomorrow lay behind them.

Chapter 5 - Chief Kevin Brady

Brady couldn't sleep.

It was two in the morning, and he'd been tossing and turning for two straight hours, his mind an unsettled storm. Tomorrow was the funeral for Emma Hughes, and he couldn't push Brock Houser out of his mind — the man behind bars for her murder.

No matter how many times Brady stared at the evidence, and there was plenty tied to her disappearance, something seemed off. For one, Houser had no clear motive. By all accounts, he was a decorated cop and an excellent PI. He was also close friends with Jon Conway and had found the girl the first time she vanished, a month or so back.

The autopsy, which came in earlier, reported the girl's cause of death as blunt force trauma to the head. No signs of sexual abuse or any other signs of violence. The medical examiner said it looked like a single blow with a blunt object, likely a metal rod of some sort.

It was the kind of case that had accidental death written all over it. But Houser wasn't a young parent panicking in the aftermath of manslaughter accidentally killing his child then having no idea what to do. He was a former cop. If it was an accident, he had to know he could make that case. Hell, if it *wasn't* an accident, he could have easily set it up to look like one. That was the hill Brady couldn't see past. If Houser had it in his heart to murder the girl, he wouldn't have run off with her. Not when he could have easily set up any number of scenarios to shift blame from him to another.

But that hadn't happened. Houser took off with Emma, wrapped in a blanket, no less, and was captured by security cameras as he put her in his trunk, then drove onto the ferry. He had to know he'd been seen by cameras, tracked by the GPS in the rental car.

Why would he allow himself to be seen?

Then again, despite the lapses in logic, Brady could think of nothing that might clear Houser. He was the last person with the girl and was clearly carrying her from the room in his arms.

Unless she wasn't in the blanket?

Brady's eyes shot open.

He thought of the blanket, found in the car's trunk and now still in the evidence room at the station. Had hair or fiber tests had been run yet? The tests may have been set aside for the time being, since they clearly had the guy on video.

Houser was carrying *something* in the blanket. If not Emma, then who? Or what?

Brady thought about the room and crime scene photos. Was there anything missing, something large? He needed photos from a similar suite so he could run side-by-side comparisons and see if he could find something missing from Houser's room. He needed to call the hotel and see if they reported anything gone from the room. He had to call Jon in the morning and see if he could think of something that might be missing that he'd not thought of earlier.

Why wrap something else in a blanket and take it?

Why make it look like you're kidnapping the girl?

And if Houser didn't take her, how the hell did she leave the hotel? Or get to the island?

Brady slipped out of bed and grabbed his uniform. If he couldn't sleep, he may as well go into the office and look over the evidence again. He wasn't sure what he could do without lab techs for processing, but perhaps he'd find something which only required good old fashioned police work and not high-tech sleuthing.

He scribbled a note for Molly and left it on the kitchen counter, hoping to return before she woke. He opened the back door, slipped quietly outside, then headed to the station guided by a hunch more than anything else. But sometimes, hunches could

BRADY DROVE IN SILENCE, startled as a pair of black vans sped by about a quarter-mile from the station.

What the hell are they doing out so late?

Paladin usually ran cars at night, saving the vans for day duty, or if they were bringing in SWAT units for something big. It was rare to see one van out at such an hour, let alone two in tandem. Were they responding to a call he'd not heard on his radio? Maybe something he missed while in bed.

Brady called into dispatch using a private channel.

"Dispatch," a woman's voice said over the radio.

"Hey, Lori, it's the chief. Heard any big calls tonight?"

"No, Chief, it's been quiet. Not a peep from Officer Willis in over an hour. What are you doing up so early, or late?"

Brady said, "Unlike Officer Willis, who's probably snoring in some parking lot, I couldn't sleep. I figured I'd go for a ride. I was just wondering, you heard anything on Paladin's radio?"

"Not a peep there, either. Though they use their back channels more often than their normal ones, I'm guessing."

"Yeah," Brady said, "that's what I figured. Thanks."

He killed the exchange. A moment later, Lori returned to the radio. "Hey, Chief, in case you're wondering, Willis' car is at the station. I'm looking at it outside the window now."

"Okay," Brady said. "If you see him, don't tell him I'm up. I'm making a surprise swing by the station."

"Okay, Chief." Lori laughed. "Mum's the word if he happens to come over to my side."

"Thanks, Lori," Brady said.

Lori had been working dispatch for fourteen years and knew which of the officers were lazy and which pulled their weight. Willis belonged firmly in the former category, with a laziness nearing legendary status. Unfortunately, he was also one of the only officers who loved working the night shift. He was an excellent cop when not slacking, with more than twenty years' experience in South Florida before moving cross-country to the Pacific Northwest. He was an older officer, but still in great shape and probably second toughest on the force. He wasn't great, but was as good as Brady could get.

They followed the same routine every few months. Brady, fed up with looking the other way, would bust the officer's balls. Willis would apologize, promise not to sleep on the job, then stick to his oath for a few months before slipping.

It was their dance, but Brady wasn't much in the mood to tango. Not tonight. He wanted the comfort of his bed and the sleep that teased him. If the chief couldn't close his eyes, then he'd be damned if Willis would be catching z's on duty.

Brady pulled into the station, then swung to a stop beside Willis' cruiser. He got out of his car, casting his eyes at Willis'. The window and hood were both frosted, with no one inside. The bastard hadn't left the station in hours.

Night-shift officers were responsible for certain patrols each night. On slow nights, like tonight, with just one officer on duty, it was important to be out of the station, not sitting on your ass. A single night clerk at reception handled the rare citizen who entered the station in need.

Brady approached the front doors, touched his palm to the pad, and listened for the lock's release. He opened the door then entered the lobby. No one at the reception desk, either.

Elmer was the scheduled clerk, a sixty-year-old retiree out of New York, chummy with Willis. Brady half expected to find the pair playing poker and would be livid if he did.

He didn't much care if Elmer and Willis were shooting shit in the lobby, as they'd been known to do, but Brady had also heard a few stray whispers of impromptu card games. If he caught them tonight, he would fire one or both officers on the spot. That was more than crossing the line, it was taking advantage of Brady's good nature, and fuck if he was in the mood for molestation.

Brady waved his hand over the panel, then quietly stepped through the doorway leading into the office area, not wanting to give Elmer or Willis a heads-up.

He passed every office door. All were open but his, and all were dark.

Are they in the lounge?

Brady stepped inside the lounge and saw the TV broadcasting one of the twenty-four-hour news channels. No one was inside.

They can't both be in the bathroom.

Brady opened the bathroom door — no one in there either.

Were they in the holding cell area? They could have arrested someone last night and brought them in. Or maybe Houser had given them trouble, even though the big man was shackled to his bed following his little outburst and had been quiet since the psych exam.

What the hell?

Brady went to the back, waved his palm on the panel beside the holding cell door, then stepped inside.

Episode 12

His hand reached for his gun the second he saw the bodies — Willis and Elmer, both lying in a pile, dead on the ground with gunshot wounds to the head.

"Jesus!"

Brock Houser's holding cell was open. And empty.

Chapter 6 - Jon Conway

Jon hoped to God this was the last funeral service he'd ever have to attend until he was the one in a long box.

He didn't think he could stand to see another body lowered into the ground. The sequence of misery that started when he buried Sarah had now ended, four bodies later (including Mrs. Heller and her son), with the burial of Emma, the daughter they shared in DNA but never in practice.

The thought of Emma's name conjured images of her peaceful, angelic face, a sweet smile now frozen in an open casket at the front of the church, then underground in a few more hours. Emma would be buried, six feet under, in a plot beside her mother's. How long until her skin started to rot? How long until the bugs came to chew through her carcass?

Jon tried not to think such horrible thoughts, but a rising panic forced him to consider those and more. What if Emma wasn't dead? He had read stories of people's brains still being alive days after their bodies had passed. He wasn't sure how long, or if it was theory, wives' tales, or scientific fact, but he couldn't help imagine that some part of Emma might be alive and conscious of her funeral.

Soon, they would lower her into the ground as she screamed for her daddy, "No, please don't bury me! I'm not dead!"

Jon shuddered, closing his eyes as he tried to bleach his mind of awful thoughts.

To his right, beside him on the pew, Cassidy reached out and slipped her hand into his.

From Cassidy's far side, Jon heard Vivian crying, along with her neighbor, Mrs. Lindley, who bawled as if it were *her* daughter being buried. Had she known Emma well, or was she crying for attention?

As he held Cassidy's hand, Jon could feel Father, sitting to his left, glancing down. He didn't dare meet his judgmental gaze. Not here, or now.

Blake, Warren, and Melinda sat side by side to Jon's left. While he was glad they showed up for support, a part of him wished they hadn't. Their presence made Cassidy *extremely* uncomfortable, as did the hundreds of others in the church. Jon wondered how many people knew Sarah and Emma versus how many had swooped in like vultures, eager to feast on the spectacle — a funeral for Jon Conway's daughter.

He tried not to think like that — tried not to make the day about him. Tried telling himself these people were here because they loved Sarah. Clearly, he and Sarah had run in separate circles. Her circles were where people meant what they said and cared for one another. He admired Sarah for her ability to see the good in so many people. That quality was what made her so popular on the island. When tragedy struck Emma, it struck them all, it seemed.

Jon listened as Pastor Avery spoke of Emma, God's will, and all the other bullshit pastors spouted when parishioners lost a loved one. Did anyone ever feel true comfort through such well-worn clichés and platitudes?

Jon certainly didn't.

Though he heard the words, they rang hollow, and their dull thud added to the pain of knowing his daughter was lying dead and waxen in front of the room. Jon wept as the pastor spoke of Sarah and Emma, telling stories of them at church. Listening to Avery's details reminded Jon of how much he had missed in nine years without them. Hearing the pastor speak of things as mundane as a drawing Emma made for a child with cancer, made him wish he could travel back in time and live through those moments beside them, holding tight to Sarah and Emma then never letting go.

"Would anybody care to say a few words?" Avery asked.

Jon swallowed. If he didn't force himself into motion, the missing moments would crush him later.

He stood, then quickly approached the front of the church, stopping beside the casket and peering down at his daughter. The last time he'd seen her, she was gray and lifeless. Now, her death was glossed with make-up, painted to look like a sleeping child who might wake at any moment. A horrible lie, teasing a future that would never be.

"Two months ago," Jon said, staring out at the crowd, "I didn't know I had a daughter. I won't bore you with details — I'm sure the gossip apps have done that plenty already. Until last month, I had no idea Emma Marie Hughes was my daughter. I came here when her mother Sarah was senselessly taken from her.

"I'm not sure how well you can truly know someone in a month, but it does seem that Emma and I managed the remarkable by fitting many years of nothing into a month of wonderful somethings. I've spent the last weeks watching my daughter with wonder, from trying to memorize all the presidents and first ladies so she could recite them in order — for no other reason than to say she did — to making up new recipes to tickle or torture my tummy, with no way of knowing which it would be until the fork was in my mouth.

"In all my life, I've never seen a creature so sweet. Until a month ago, I was living, and thought I was alive. Then Emma entered my world, and I finally saw what it meant to truly love someone with those parts of your heart so rarely used that the brain fooled you into forgetting they were there.

"To love someone so much that you would surrender all that made you *you*, just to make them happy, and gladly fall on any sword that might threaten them. That you would do anything …"

Jon paused, found his breath, then finished.

"Thank you, Emma, for allowing me into your world. For not hating me. For reminding me what it is like to be a child, and more importantly, what it means to live and love.

"Thank you, Emma. We will all miss you more than you can ever know. And though I've never been much of a believer, I hope and pray to see you in Heaven.

"I love you, Emma."

Jon closed his eyes, fighting tears. He walked without stumbling — against the odds — back to his seat, where Cassidy was waiting with open arms. He fell inside them as Vivian leaned over and dabbed her eyes with a kerchief.

"That was beautiful, Jon."

"Thank you," he said to Vivian, still fighting tears. "I hope she thought so, too."

~

FOLLOWING THE SERVICE, churchgoers were led outside into the hall so family members could say their final goodbyes in private before driving to the cemetery for Emma's burial.

Jon, Cassidy, and Vivian stayed behind, as did Mrs. Lindley, clueless that she wasn't wanted. As Vivian and Mrs. Lindley traded stories about Emma, Blake leaned over toward Jon and Cassidy and offered his hand to Cassidy.

She took it, muffling her certain revulsion.

"I'm sorry for your loss, Cassidy. Emma was a beautiful, thoroughly happy child who will be missed."

Cassidy's eye twitched. "Thank you." She cleared her throat. "I think I'd like to pay my last respects." Then she went to the front of the church.

Jon watched as Cassidy leaned down to kiss Emma, then collapsed into tears. He thought about going up to the casket and giving her comfort, then thought better, knowing she would want both space and privacy.

"I'm sorry, son," Blake said.

"Yeah." Jon suddenly craved the fight he had put off a week before, desperate to rip into Father, blame him for everything. Yet, as Jon saw Cassidy crying over Emma's body, he felt a stronger desire to safeguard the moment's sanctity and not embarrass Emma's memory with a stupid and unnecessary fight.

He itched to set things straight once and for all with his father, but surely it could wait.

Melinda said, "How are you holding up?"

"We're doing the best we can." Jon hated funeral small talk even more than celebrity party gossip. He would probably have to hear another hundred "I'm sorries" and bullshit about how "She's in a better place" from people outside wishing him comfort but offering nothing but sorrow instead.

Warren had given Jon a nearly silent "I'm sorry" when he and Melinda first arrived. Now he said, "Jon, we're doing a press conference tomorrow afternoon. Conway Medical Center is building a new psychiatric ward in memory of the people who recently lost their lives."

"Okay," Jon said, wondering why in the hell Warren was bringing up business, other than the obvious reason that he was a clueless tool without any class.

"We're offering donations to the victims' families. We'd like to offer something to Vivian and Cassidy Hughes. Do you think they would show up for the conference? We are naming the building in Sarah's honor."

Jon's jaw dropped.

Don't they need permission to do something like that? Did they go talk to Vivian? They sure as hell didn't approach me or Cassidy!

Blake turned to Warren. "Don't be so daft, son. Jesus." Then he turned to his younger son. "I'm sorry, Jon. They don't need to come. We can, and should, discuss this some other time."

Jon rubbed his jaw, staring at Warren. "Are you really trying to pay off the Hughes family with guilt money and naming a fucking building after Sarah?"

"What?" Warren said, eyes wide and face twisted into a mockery of shock.

"Don't think for a moment that I don't know what you're doing," Jon whispered, eyeing the front of the church to make sure Cassidy was still saying goodbyes to Emma. "You're using victims to buy publicity at a discount."

"Now, now," Blake said, "forget Warren said anything. It was insensitive."

Jon wasn't ready for a leash. He met his father's gaze.

"Tell me, Father, is this about trying to make Conway Industries look good, or are you feeling guilty?"

"What?" He wore the same thin sweater of feigned shock as his eldest son, though time and practice made it neater on his face.

Jon didn't want to fight.

Not here.

Not now.

He knew he shouldn't, but his mouth kept going anyway.

"Don't think I'm oblivious. I *know* what you and Boy Warren have been doing to the Hughes family. How you blackmailed Sarah, using Cassidy for leverage. How you prevented me from learning about my daughter. And now you

351

bastardize Sarah's memory by naming a fucking psych hospital after her? Really?"

Warren looked away, but Blake's stare grew in intensity until it bore through Jon.

"Now is not the time for this, Son. Nor the place."

"You're right." Jon's voice rose several decibels louder than he wanted. His leg twitched with nervous inertia, wanting to burst. He couldn't believe he was finally about to lay into his father. "Now isn't the time or place. This is a funeral, for a child you tried to keep from me — a funeral that wouldn't be happening if you hadn't fucking interfered!"

Jon pointed his finger at both Blake and Warren.

"You two walk around Hamilton like you own everything and everyone on the island, as if people are your personal puppets. It's about damned time someone called you out."

Blake stood, expression placid, though his face was a volcanic red.

Jon sensed he'd attracted everyone's attention, but he wasn't willing to turn to look and risk his resolve.

"I want you gone," Jon said. "Take your money and choke on it, Father. Choke until you die."

"I know you don't mean this, son," Blake said, reaching out to place a hand on Jon's shoulder, trying to guide the moment toward a better memory as he was so famous for doing.

But Jon wouldn't be controlled. Not anymore.

"Get out!" he roared.

Warren stared at Jon as if seeking a rematch of their fight at The Gardens.

Blake glared at Jon, then dusted the front of his suit with his long, strong fingers as if his son's words held no meaning. He turned and left the church with Warren and Melinda walking behind him.

She turned at the door, sending one last sheepish look back at Jon and mouthing the words, "I'm sorry."

Jon stared at the trio, watching until they disappeared through the doors. He felt Vivian's gaze, along with Mrs. Lindley's, then turned to face them.

Vivian clapped, stood, and threw her arms around Jon. "Goddammit, I love you, Jonny!"

Cassidy staring at him from the front of the church. She nodded a silent *thank you* as she rubbed tears from her eyes.

Jon joined her at the front of the church.

"Wow," she said.

"Yeah, wow."

"I bet you're not getting a Christmas card this year, though you guys probably send each other endangered species or some shit."

She laughed and so did Jon, pulling her closer to him. He looked at his daughter lying in the casket and wondered if she, too, heard his outburst. And if so, he wondered if it had given her comfort, wherever she was. He remembered how happy Emma had been when he decked Warren, how she looked at him like her hero.

To think, I'll never see that look again.

"Can I have a few minutes?" Jon asked. "I want to say goodbye to Emma."

Cassidy nodded, kissing Jon on the cheek before returning to her mom and their neighbor, who was a few threads short of a sweater.

Jon looked down at Emma, so still, so innocent. So dead.

He reached out to touch her, running his fingers through Emma's hair, remembering again the first time he'd seen her in this church. He remembered her shoving cookies into her purse and couldn't help but laugh through the tears now streaming his cheeks.

"I'm so sorry," he whispered, leaning down and kissing her on the head. Then he stayed beside her, whispering secrets only she could hear.

"I wish I'd met you sooner. I'm so proud of you for being

such an amazing little girl. So many people here love you so, so much. As do I."

Jon went on, telling Emma all the things he'd wanted to say — how he would miss the many adventures they'd never get to have and that he hoped to see her soon.

Jon kissed her one last time, on the cheek, and offered one last secret. "Tell your mother I love you both."

Chapter 7 - Sarah Conway

Blake led Sarah through several long and winding hallways, cavernous and dark, corridors that illuminated only as they entered then fading once they left.

They kept walking until they reached a doorway with an odd, blue insignia, scrawled in a style Sarah had never seen. She wondered if the symbol was a logo or perhaps written in an unfamiliar foreign language. The character seemed vaguely Asian.

Blake stopped in front of the door and turned to her. "I'm about to show you something that will shock you. I need your promise that you will control yourself. Can you do that?"

"Yes." Sarah stared at the door, eager to see what was waiting behind. She ignored her bristled hair and chills and nodded as if to punctuate her *yes*.

Blake waved his hand over the insignia. The door parted, and he stepped into the pitch-black room. Sarah hedged, wondering if Blake planned to kill her on the other side.

"Come, now," he said, kindly enough.

Sarah entered the room, and the door slid shut behind her.

"Lights," Blake said.

A giant ball of blue hummed to life above them, hovering a few hundred feet in the air. It was stunning, like a blue sun in their artificial sky, with arcs of powdered azure flames dancing in swirling circles around it.

The light revealed the room — a giant dome, about the size of an indoor arena.

Sarah gasped at the chamber's enormity. "How big is this station? I've never seen anything like this on TV."

"You know," Blake said, "I'm not quite sure. It isn't mine."

"What do you mean? I thought you said it was your space station, your lab in the sky, or whatever you called it." She couldn't be certain if that was a real conversation they had shared, or one of her false memories.

"Well, it is, I just don't own it. But, Sarah, that isn't what we're here to discuss. I think, *this* is what you wish to see."

Blake pointed toward the ceiling, and the light grew brighter.

Sarah then saw them, though she couldn't believe it when she did — hundreds, maybe thousands of glass doors, like coolers in a supermarket, stacked in rows ten high and God only knew how many across, lining the walls on either side. Behind the doors, people.

She gasped, grabbing Blake's arm as if the doors were seconds from opening and spilling forth with zombies attacking.

"Relax," Blake said. "They're in a state of induced stasis."

"What? And who are they?"

"Stasis is like hibernation, or at least that's the best way to say it. They are sleeping, and will stay that way in these chambers, awakened only when needed. As for who, come with me."

Sarah followed Blake, not really watching where she was going as she stared at the army of frozen faces buried behind the glass, though she couldn't draw many details from the still-dark coffins.

They stopped walking after reaching the far-left wall, a few feet from a lowered row of chambers. "Chamber lights on, 1114 through 1120."

Light spilled into the boxes.

Sarah whimpered, screamed, then fell a long, involuntary step back. "What the hell?" She turned to Blake, then back to the six illuminated doors, five with nude girls who looked exactly like Emma.

"What the hell is this? What have you done?"

"They're clones," he said. "Clones of several of Hamilton Island's inhabitants."

"Why?"

"Part of our project," Blake said, as if offering the Rosetta Stone of answers.

As Sarah stared through the glass at the girls in the boxes who looked so much like her daughter that she couldn't sift reality from sham, she felt herself swelling with a sickening realization. She turned from the empty box to Blake. "Wait! Is the girl you brought to me one of these ... clones?"

Blake smiled. "No, no. Emma is the real deal."

Sarah shook her head, not sure she believed him. "How do I know you're not lying?"

"Well, you can't ever truly know, I suppose," Blake said. "I mean, you could ask your daughter questions and see if she passes some test of your design, but anything she knows, the clones know, as well."

"How?"

"They're all ... connected. Whatever one feels, sees, does, the others experience. In fact, we've sent clones down while some of the islanders have been up here for extended evaluations."

"You're saying there have been times when my daughter

wasn't really my daughter? That I've had one of these — *these things* — in my house without even knowing it?"

"No, we never send children down because they're more likely to notice when things aren't quite right. Or get the feeling that they don't belong. We tried it early on but had a few of our subjects lose their minds."

"How do you get these? How do ... wait, the body Jon and Cassidy buried? Was that one of *these?*"

Blake nodded, "Yes."

"You killed one of these children?"

"Well, *I* didn't, but yes. However, Sarah, you really shouldn't consider them children. They're clones, medical subjects. Bred for our needs. It's best not to get attached."

Sarah couldn't believe her ears. "But they're people, right? People you somehow grew, by taking our DNA and eggs or whatever, and growing them in a dish or something, but they're still people — flesh and blood and hearts and souls, aren't they?"

Blake nodded.

"You have your daughter now. That's what matters, right? Emma was receiving too many of the clones' memories up here and treating that recall as her own. I had to do something, because I've no idea how much her clones know and can't afford to take any chances. Would you prefer we had killed her for what she knew, Sarah?"

"You would kill your own grandchild? What kind of monster are you?"

Sarah also wanted to ask what memories Emma had picked up on, thinking the clones were asleep.

Blake grabbed her wrist, hards. "I *didn't* kill her, did I? I brought her here to be with you. You would be well served to show some appreciation!"

"You killed a child! And what? Dumped her on the island so people would stop looking?"

"We're through here," Blake said, his voice icy. "Chamber lights, off, all."

The coffins went dark. Blake turned, and started walking back the way they'd come.

Sarah stared after him, unsure what to do, but not wanting to follow.

He called out, not bothering to look back. "I suggest you come along, or I'll leave you here, alone in the dark."

The thought of being trapped in the blackness with who knew how many clones scared the living hell out of her. She quickly followed the man she now hated.

Blake said nothing as he led her back to the garden where Emma and Bernice were still sitting on the same bench. Blake turned to Sarah. "I've arranged for you and Emma to share a new suite, something larger, more like home."

Sarah wished she'd kept her mouth shut in the clone room. There were so many things she wanted to ask, chief among them, when could they go home? Had Blake been lying to Emma when he said they'd discuss it later? Or were they stuck among the stars, maybe *forever?*

"I hope you'll excuse me, ladies. I have a meeting. Bernice will show you to your new quarters. Please let her know if you need anything. I promise she will take excellent care of you."

"Wait, Grandpa," Emma said.

The word "Grandpa" was a blade in Sarah's gut. She wanted to wrap her arms around her daughter, protect her from the monster who had made many in her likeness.

Blake turned, a warm smile on his face as he looked down at Emma with something that looked close to actual love. "Yes?"

"I thought you said we could see the observatory?"

"Another time, dear, okay?"

"Okay," Emma said, disappointment dulling her voice.

Blake turned and left the garden.

Sarah met Emma's gaze but couldn't help thinking of her

daughter's manufactured twin, murdered to bury a secret. Anyone willing to kill a clone, Sarah was certain, wouldn't flinch at killing his own flesh and blood.

She wrapped her arm around Emma and followed Bernice from the garden toward their suite. She had to figure a way to get back home — *but how?*

Chapter 8 - Warren Conway

Though it was four in the afternoon, the sun tucking itself behind wide swaths of dark, billowing clouds made it seem closer to twilight.

The press event was held outside the hospital in an oversized tent at the building's north end. Hundreds of people gathered inside, networking, glad-handing, and taking advantage of the elaborate spread laid out across a long table draped with fine linens. A DJ played soft jazz tunes, the horrible kind. The sort Warren hated. Miles Davis, John Coltrane, Wes Montgomery, that was the real stuff. He preferred a hot band with great improvisations, a tight rhythm section with the horns in tune. Jazz fusion was awful, something Warren was convinced no one truly enjoyed, though people never had the balls to pipe up and demand the shit get muffled. Jazz should never be fused with anything.

Karrie Penderson, the long-legged blonde who headed communications for the hospital, paced between Blake, Warren, and the journalists in attendance, ensuring everyone was well taken care of.

Warren stood beside Blake as he spoke to Kenneth Everly, a member of the hospital's board of directors. Warren did his job by kissing Father's ass and spouting bullshit about what a terrific idea it was, adding the psychiatric wing to Conway Medical.

He could hardly concentrate as his gaze constantly traveled from one side of the crowd to the other, weaving through the swarm, forever settling on Carl Kaiser, working security with a half dozen other Paladin officers.

Kaiser nodded once, which Warren assumed meant that everything was proceeding as planned. He wanted to get things over with. Until they were, he feigned enjoyment, making small talk and counterfeiting affections.

The music dimmed at fifteen past the hour. The crowd settled, turning its attention toward the rear of the tent where Warren and Blake stood side by side, behind Ms. Penderson, fronting the podium as she delivered introductions.

As the conference started, Warren pressed his palm to his stomach, as if it might mute the acidic sloshing inside it. He had decided to slaughter his father, but because every cell inside him knew it was wrong, his brain kept making new excuses, manufacturing fresh justifications for why it was okay.

He had convinced himself that Father had committed the original atrocity by destroying the person Warren was meant to be — a more subtle, but no less evil, sort of slaying.

Then he tried convincing himself there was nothing wrong with murder. History, after all, had smiled on some of the worst. The issue was scale. Stop a single man from breathing, and you were a fiend, but killing in large enough numbers could earn your parade. Perhaps murdering Blake would prevent other deaths set in motion because of Project Phoenix.

Sweat beaded Warren's forehead and covered his palms. He would never get away with it. Even as everything inside him said he *couldn't*, they also agreed that he *shouldn't*. He'd certainly be caught. Most murders were committed by someone close to the victim, whoever had most to gain. Even billions in the bank and a personal police force might not keep the courts from uncovering the truth.

He had to pull the plug.

Blake took the podium, waited for the light applause to die, then started speaking. Warren tuned him out, in no mood to hear another rousing speech that would see quotes pinned all over the Web by morning.

Warren tried drawing Kaiser's attention, but the man wouldn't turn. He stood at the tent's entrance, searching the crowd for nothing in particular.

Look over here. Look over here.

Warren wanted to give Kaiser some sign, a red light of sorts, to stop the shooting.

But Kaiser wasn't looking.

Was Kaiser intentionally ignoring him? Not affording him a line to change his mind so he could force their plans into reality?

Come on.

Warren palmed his cell, then thumbed his text to Kaiser. He was taking a chance sending a message which could be used as evidence later, but as Blake continued to speak, Warren felt minutes spilling like blood from a cut.

"Cancel," he wrote.

Warren watched as Kaiser looked down and pulled the cell from his pocket. He was too far for Warren to accurately gauge his expression, but Warren imagined him rolling his eye, disgusted by his conspirator's impotence.

Kaiser looked up from the cell, then turned to Warren, shaking his head.

What?

Warren palmed his cell again.

"I said cancel!" he wrote.

Kaiser looked down at his cell again, still shaking his head.

How dare he ignore me?

Warren grabbed his phone and texted, "Do not shoot Blake Conway."

Warren smiled as Kaiser read his message. If he refused to abort the shooting, their texts would be traced, and evidence of their involvement would damn them both.

Kaiser met his gaze and shook his head again.

Blake turned to Warren. "And now, my son, Warren Conway, is eager to tell you all about our plans to give back to a community so shaken by these senseless acts."

Shit, shit.

Warren turned to Ms. Penderson, waiting beside a scattering of beneficiaries standing by for their oversized checks. He smiled then took the podium, glanced at his cell, and read his speech from the screen.

Two paragraphs in, Warren saw Don Bellows brush past Kaiser, heading straight toward the front of the tent, walking with purpose, hand in his jacket.

Oh, God!

"Murderers!" Don screamed as he aimed his pistol at Blake.

The crowd erupted in terror as Don pulled the trigger.

Warren turned to Blake, to warn him to duck. Sharp pain split his back like a lightning bolt.

He spun, shocked to see Don firing not at Blake, but at him.

Bellows fired a second time, hitting Warren twice. Once in the chest and again in the gut.

Warren fell to the ground, confused, scared, crying out.

As he fell, gunshots echoed throughout the tent while Paladin officers unloaded their weapons into the *crazy* gunman.

Warren stared up at the tent's canvas, his world blurring at the edges.

Why did he shoot me?

He struggled to turn his neck but could barely move. He felt suddenly desperate to make sure his father was safe.

Blake walked over, dropped to Warren's side, and met his son's gaze.

Warren cried, "Am I dying?"

Blake looked down at Warren's injuries, then turned and yelled, "Someone help my son! He's been shot."

His father set a comforting hand on Warren's chest, leaned forward, and brought his mouth to Warren's ear. "There, there," he said in a soothing voice. "It'll all be over soon enough."

"What?" Blake said, or tried to say, but instead coughed up blood.

Blake whispered again, "You didn't really think you could outsmart your father, did you?"

Warren looked up into Father's eyes and saw the betrayal inside them.

Kaiser!

Blake leaned in closer. "I'm sorry, son. I really didn't want it to end this way, but you left me no choice. You've always had such a problem with sacrifice."

Warren looked into his father's eyes wanting to ask *why?* or *how?*

But Warren could only die.

Chapter 9 - Cassidy Hughes And Jon Conway

CASSIDY

"MY NAME IS CASSIDY, and I'm an addict."

Cassidy made eye-contact with each member of the assembly, even though it was painful to see anyone and killed her to hold their gazes. But that was the true point of a Narcotics Anonymous meeting — to learn who you were as your soul stood naked in front of others not too different from yourself. Everyone in the library wished to forget, and not one of them could. They could admit the truth and soften the edges, but only a day at a time. Anything more was chasing clouds through the sky.

"It's been seven days since I last used."

A dozen people in hard plastic chairs sang as one.

"Hi, Cassidy."

"I've not shared in a while. Usually, I come to these meetings and listen, knowing I'm a fraud and feeling like I don't belong. I'm always so nervous, thinking everyone is watching, which is silly, I know, since everyone else in here probably feels the same way. I sit, usually at the back with my stomach in knots, hating myself and the Addict who owns me."

FUCK, she hated this.

"Addictions all share their roots. From weed and liquor to rocks, needles, and pills — they're all the same. Addictions numb our pain, give us a glimmer of hope when we're otherwise failing, hold our fear at arm's length so it can't swallow us whole. But that relief is fleeting, and once faded, we know in our hearts the next time won't last quite as long. Though we long to stop, desperately craving an end to the madness, we don't know how, or secretly believe it will be too hard and that we'll never be able to do it. We believe we'll eventually slip, and because we know we will one day fail, we refuse to postpone the inevitable, surrendering to the slip, letting go, and falling down that same spiral where we've tumbled until bruised so many times before."

Cassidy blinked to keep from crying, managed her voice to keep it from cracking, then continued.

"I'm tired of not trusting, exhausted from not believing in myself or others, and terrified I'm going to be an addict for the rest of my life, sabotaging the good days I know I could have." Cassidy looked out at the crowd. "I need you, all of you, and know I can't do this alone."

She managed to make it through her share without losing a tear, then she dipped her head, stepped from the front, and returned to her row at the back. She listened to three more people traffic their stories, then stood as the room scattered to leftover donuts and awkward crumbs of conversation.

Cassidy had been going to NA meetings at the back of the Hamilton Library on and off for years. Themes varied from book study to newcomers, Q&A, participation, single speaker, and topic discussion. Meetings stretched from an hour, but often ran to an hour and a half. There was never any surveillance, an extra blessing in a place like Hamilton. Community was easier to build when members felt safe, and community meant everything to recovery. Because Jon didn't want to distract the meeting with his appearance, and Roberta couldn't make the meeting, Cassidy's community was waiting outside.

She muscled her way through several exchanges, dropped a half-eaten donut in the trash, then went outside to Jon.

"How was it?" he asked as she slammed the Blacklander's passenger side door.

"Okay, I guess," Cassidy said. "My sponsor couldn't make it, but I survived. First time I spoke in a while. I really hate that shit. Always feels like I'm saying a slightly different version of the same crap, not just bullshit I've already said, but bullshit I'm tired of hearing from everyone else."

"It's helping you get in character," Jon said.

"What?" Cassidy spun on Jon, unsure whether she should be offended.

"Character," Jon repeated, then, probably because he sensed her defensiveness, added, "It's like practicing lines. I'm not a lawyer and could *never* be a lawyer even if I wanted to — no way I could sit still long enough to make it through law school. But people believed me in *Hung Jury*. That's because I believed it myself. And the only reason *I* believed it was because I repeated Murdock's lines out loud until they finally felt like they were born inside me."

He put his hand on Cassidy's knee. "You're human, Cass. With human responses. If you think about it, we're like organic robots — machines with skin around us. We only change our behavior through reprogramming. Think of your NA meetings — standing up in front of the group like you did — as writing yourself some new code."

Cassidy wondered who wrote Jon's newest code as she found herself loving him more than she already did.

She held up her chip. "Made it one week." She smiled. "So, what is this, then? An update to my app?"

Jon laughed. He took the chip from Cassidy, studied it, flipped it in the air, then caught it and passed it back to her.

"Yup, this definitely looks like a software upgrade. Congratulations." Then he pulled her into a tight hug across the console. "I'm proud of you."

Cassidy left her head against his chest, drawing his scent for several silent moments until Jon broke the quiet. "Ready to go home?"

She loved that *home* meant his place, *their place*, together. "I was ready before we got to the library."

Jon started the Blacklander, pulled from the lot, then turned into the street, heading toward Chateau Popcorn, as Cassidy had taken to calling it.

The drive was silent, but never uncomfortable. One of the things Cassidy loved most about Jon was that he never felt a need to swap words for comfort. It wasn't his millions or fame that made him special. It was knowing he could shut the fuck up and be happy.

They pulled into the garage. Cassidy knew it felt as empty for Jon as it did for her, without Houser and Emma. Worse, it seemed bloated with so much horrible shit stuffed inside vacant memories and so much crap they couldn't say.

They were quiet as Jon followed Cassidy into the house. The front door shut behind them on the way upstairs. Cassidy walked down the hall and into Jon's room, peeling the sweater from her body at the threshold and dropping it on Jon's carpet a foot from the doorway's opposite side. She collapsed on his mattress and stared at the ceiling.

Jon joined her a moment later, holding his silence along with her hand, staring up at the ceiling beside her and nursing the harmony of their quiet together.

Her breath fell into a calming rhythm, the sort that made it as easy to count as to dream, her head slightly blurry as lines between thoughts started to crumble.

The promise of sleep was seconds away.

Jon's breathing matched hers as he, too, slowly fell asleep beside her. A soft "I love you," slipped from his lips — the first he'd said it since the night Emma was taken from their lives.

Cassidy felt high, but different from the kind that came in a pill.

She stared at the ceiling, wondering what would happen next. Would they leave the island now that there was no Emma to consider? Was Jon's *I love you* temporary, and would he strip it from her as he had eventually stripped it from Sarah?

Cassidy wrestled with those, and a hundred other thoughts, all threatening to bar sleep from her body. She finally ordered herself to relax and returned to counting and dreaming, ignoring her Addict and agreeing with her better half that it was best to take things a day at a time — Jon and sobriety alike.

She turned from the ceiling to Jon, and stared at his handsome face and the happy smile crashing into his pillow. She curled into his lean body and fell asleep, feeling for the first time in a long while that she was truly where she belonged.

JON

JON OPENED his eyes in a garden.

He thought he might be dreaming but couldn't be certain. The world looked like a dream, though it felt nothing of the sort. It had the woolly atmosphere of reality, and the unmistakable scent of truth, sweeter for the abundant blooms that flowered his surroundings and made him believe that perhaps he was wrong and the dream real.

The garden was filled with pinks and purples, lavenders and whites, greens and reds and blues. The room erupted in fountains of color, though it was empty of people, which made the vacant stone bench surrounded by lilacs and roses seem especially lonely.

When Jon went to sit, Emma raced toward him. She jumped up, leaping into her father's arms. "I'm so happy to see you," she yelled, her voice giddy.

Their embrace was so powerful, it might have been magic. Emma *had* died, which made this a dream, though it wore the weight of reality and carried its scent.

Despite the impossibility, Jon wanted the dream to be real.

And if it wasn't, he didn't want to wake. Not ever. Not for Cassidy or anyone else. Not if he had Emma.

"I thought you were dead," Jon said.

"No, I'm up here, on the space station, with Grandpa and Great Grandpa. And Mommy."

"What?"

"Yeah, I'm with Mommy," Emma said, her voice filled with glee. "And we miss you so, so, SO much! Grandpa said you could come, but only if you want to."

Jon woke.

Epilogue

Blake Conway stepped into the dome where the old man waited.

"Well?" Billy Conway shouted, standing far back in the room, in front of the last row of stasis chambers. "Did you do it?"

He was one hundred seventy-four years old, yet Blake's father still looked like, and had the booming voice of, a healthy sixty-year-old.

"Yes," Blake said. "I can't believe his nerve. How damned ungrateful!"

"And were you able to get him to the hospital?"

"Yes," Blake said. "For all anyone knows, he's in a coma."

"Good," Billy Conway said. "Perhaps this one will be a bit more loyal. Chamber 1198 open."

The chamber hissed open, and Blake looked at the last of Warren's clones.

"Yes, this one had *better* work."

What to know what happens next? The adventure continues in *WhiteSpace Season 3*.

GET WHITESPACE SEASON 3

A Note from the Author

Thanks for reading *WhiteSpace Season 2*.

If you liked this book, please leave a review on your favorite bookselling site so others can enjoy it too. Just a couple of sentences would be great.

Thanks!

Sean & Dave

About the Authors

Sean Platt is an entrepreneur and founder of Sterling & Stone, where he makes stories with his partners, Johnny B. Truant, and David W. Wright, and a family of storytellers.

Sean is the bestselling author of over 10 million words' worth of books, including the Yesterday's Gone and Invasion series. Sean is also co-author of the indie publishing cornerstone, Write. Publish. Repeat. and co-host of the Story Studio Podcast.

Originally from Long Beach, California, Sean now lives in Austin, Texas with his wife and two children. He has more than his share of nose.

David W. Wright is the co-author of edge-of-your seat thrillers including the best-selling post-apocalyptic series *Yesterday's Gone*, the paranoid sci-fi *WhiteSpace* series, and the vigilante series, *No Justice*, as well as standalone thrillers *12*, and *Crash* which was recently optioned for a movie.

David is an accomplished, though intermittent, cartoonist who lives in [LOCATION REDACTED] with his wife and son [NAMES REDACTED.]

He is not at all paranoid.

He is "the grumpy one" on the *The Story Studio Podcast* with fellow Sterling and Stone founders, Sean Platt and Johnny B. Truant.

You can email him at david@sterlingandstone.net

We swear, he almost never bites. Unless you feed him after midnight.

Also By Sean Platt

The Dead World Series

Dead Zero

Dead City

Dead Nation

Dead Planet

Empty Nest

The Beam Series

The Beam Season One

The Beam Season Two

The Beam Season Three

Robot Proletariat Series

En3my

Robot Proletariat

The Infinite Loop

The Hard Reset

Cascade Failure

Reboot

The Tomorrow Gene Series

Null Identity

The Tomorrow Gene

The Tomorrow Clone

The Eden Experiment

Karma Police Series

Jumper

Karma Police

The Collectors

Deviant

The Fall

Homecoming

Yesterday's Gone

October's Gone

Yesterday's Gone Season One

Yesterday's Gone Season Two

Yesterday's Gone Season Three

Yesterday's Gone Season Four

Yesterday's Gone Season Five

Yesterday's Gone Season Six

Tomorrow's Gone

Tomorrow's Gone Season One

Tomorrow's Gone Season Two

Tomorrow's Gone Season Three

Available Darkness

Darkness Itself

Available Darkness Book One

Available Darkness Book Two

Available Darkness Book Three

WhiteSpace

WhiteSpace Season One

WhiteSpace Season Two

WhiteSpace Season Three

Stand Alone Novels

Burnout

The Island

Crash

Emily's List

Pattern Black

Devil May Care

The Secret Within

Also By David W. Wright

Yesterday's Gone

October's Gone

Yesterday's Gone Season One

Yesterday's Gone Season Two

Yesterday's Gone Season Three

Yesterday's Gone Season Four

Yesterday's Gone Season Five

Yesterday's Gone Season Six

Tomorrow's Gone

Tomorrow's Gone Season One

Tomorrow's Gone Season Two

Tomorrow's Gone Season Three

Available Darkness

Darkness Itself

Available Darkness Book One

Available Darkness Book Two

Available Darkness Book Three

WhiteSpace

WhiteSpace Season One

WhiteSpace Season Two

WhiteSpace Season Three

Stand Alone Novels

12

Crash

Emily's List

Threshold
The Secret Within

www.ingramcontent.com/pod-product-compliance
Lightning Source LLC
Chambersburg PA
CBHW010522100726
47903CB00011B/2865